P9-DZA-930

THE DEVIL'S TRIANGLE

"*The Devil's Triangle* is an imaginative, fast-paced thrill that I could not put down."

"Evil twins, family drama, world domination, conspiracies, some science fiction, a little religion, even a little romance—*The Devil's Triangle* was a fun concoction and a whirlwind of a ride."

"Warning to anyone who is starting it—you won't be able to put it down. This book is absolutely a winner."

"I loved it! The same kind of high as watching an Indiana Jones movie. I don't know how you do it but please don't stop!"

"What a page-turner! You and J.T. have managed to weave together another great story."

"*The Devil's Triangle* is the best of that series so far. The plot was amazing. Talk about a page-turner."

THE FBI THRILLERS

A BRIT IN THE FBI THRILLERS (WITH J.T. ELLISON)

CATHERINE COULTER

AND J.T. ELLISON

THE
SIXTH
DAY

POCKET BOOKS

NEW YORK LONDON TORONTO SYDNEY NEW DELHI

Pocket Books
An Imprint of Simon & Schuster, Inc.
1230 Avenue of the Americas
New York, NY 10020

This book is a work of fiction. Any references to historical events, real people, or real places are used fictitiously. Other names, characters, places, and events are products of the authors' imagination, and any resemblance to actual events or places or persons, living or dead, is entirely coincidental.

First Pocket Books paperback edition April 2019

POCKET and colophon are registered trademarks of Simon & Schuster, Inc.

For information about special discounts for bulk purchases, please contact Simon & Schuster Special Sales at 1-866-506-1949 or business@simonandschuster.com

The Simon & Schuster Speakers Bureau can bring authors to your live event. For more information or to book an event contact the Simon & Schuster Speakers Bureau at 1-866-248-3049 or visit our website at www.simonspeakers.com.

Manufactured in the United States of America

10 9 8 7 6 5 4 3 2 1

ISBN 978-1-5011-3820-1
ISBN 978-1-9257-5055-3 (ebook)

Thank you to everyone in my Home World who protected me from holiday chaos in the final stretch of *The Sixth Day*—Karen, Yngrid, Lesley, Catherine.
You are the stars in my firmament.
—Catherine

For my parents: The ultimate first readers.
—J.T.

ACKNOWLEDGMENTS

Beautiful brilliant J.T.—may you continue to soar. Our fifth thriller, amazing.

—Catherine

I'm surrounded by incredible friends who are also authors and share in the triumph of every finished manuscript: Laura Benedict, Ariel Lawhon, Paige Crutcher, Jeff Abbott—thank you for the support, always.

Jen Bergstrom, Louise Burke, Lauren McKenna, and the whole Gallery team for the care and love of our words.

Amy Kerr, my right hand, right brain, and sister-in-arms.

Sherrie Saint, who always puts up with weird emails that start with "So if I wanted to kill someone . . ."

Helen Macdonald, whose brilliant *H Is for Hawk* brought the cabal alive.

Scott Miller, for all the reasons, and then some.

Mom and Daddy, for all the idea-bouncing and griping and celebrating.

Randy Ellison, the rock all my waves crash against, for never-ending support and plot whispering.

And to Catherine, for always allowing my imagination to soar.

—J.T.

De chiens, d'oyseaulx, d'armes, d'amous,
Chascun le dit a la vollee,
Pour une joye cent doulours.

In riding to the hounds, in falconry,
In love or war, as anyone will tell you,
For one brief joy a hundred woes.
—FRANÇOIS VILLON

PROLOGUE

Vlad Dracul III knew the battle was lost. The ramparts were burning, orange flames leaping into the night sky, licking at the windowsills, closer and closer. Choking smoke billowed in like black death. His soldiers' screams were nearly drowned out by the cries from within the castle, where the walls to the kitchens had been breached.

Behind him, his twin half brothers huddled together on the cold stone floor, Alexandru watching and listening to the growing mayhem, his thin face white with fear, not for himself, Dracul saw, but for his brother, Andrei, a sickly lad, his brain weak as his body; one scratch, and he bled and bled. Dracul watched Alexandru clutch the dirty manuscript to his chest, his other arm around his brother, who was rocking back and forth, keening and wailing.

Dracul saw Alexandru draw Andrei close and speak in words Dracul actually understood, "Shh. All will be well. I will protect you. I will always protect you."

But Andrei, who didn't understand what was happening, rocked and cried, the horrific screams and the hellish flames too much for his mind to grasp.

Dracul's other brothers, his legitimate brothers, were warriors and had proved their worth countless times. But these two, beget of a maid in a darkened corridor by his father's indifferent seed, had never shown any worth until yesterday, when a sword had sliced a grave cut through Dracul's hand. The burning pain was nothing, but knowing his hand might be cut from his body to save his life terrified him. Alexandru, the strong twin, the one who communicated for both of them, had smeared on a strange yellowish salve he and his brother had made. Almost immediately, the pain was gone, the deep cut closed, and Dracul could continue fighting. And this morning, the hand was unmarked, as if there'd never been a wound. Whatever they were—the devil's evil spawn, or spawn from a magic realm he didn't understand, their alembics and herbals all recorded in that tome that never left their sight—they had saved his hand, possibly his life. They weren't warriors, but they had value and, he thought again, mayhap magic.

Dracul's guards nearby heard the brothers mumbling their unholy garbled sounds and prayed to God to protect them from the devils. Like his soldiers, Dracul knew the villagers were afraid of these cursed twins, as they were called, who belonged to the visiting Romanian Orthodox monks. There were dark rumors surrounding the boys. It was whispered they drank blood, spoke in a language none could understand, drew strange pictures, and wrote strange words. Their evil had brought the enemy down on the villagers, which, Dracul knew, was nonsense.

He was the one with the power, he was the one people really feared, not these two scraps of humanity. Dracul reveled in the fact he was known to all as more monster than man. It was whispered he was merciless, without conscience, a creature who wallowed in death, butchering those who displeased him with joyous abandon. Impaling them. Ah, what a sight it was, the screams, the smells, the devastation of a human body, all done according to his whim. Even the twins couldn't save a man he'd selected for death. He hadn't killed his worthless half brothers. No, he'd sold them to the monks, but now the monks were back, bringing the boys with their strange book and ill tidings—his cousin Vladislav's army was on their heels.

When the monks came for a visit a year earlier, they had tried to give the boys back, but Dracul refused, reasoning they would be better off cloistered

and protected behind the abbey walls. For he'd
known then how everyone despised them as much
as feared them, so different, so strange. If he was
called a monster, the twins were called ungodly—
their garbled talk no one understood proving they
were spawns of the devil. Their very existence was
blasphemy.

Now six Romanian monks had returned
only days before, bringing the boys back yet
again. The twins were evil, Father Stephan said,
unholy, mad, a portent of death. In his fear,
Stephan had screamed at Dracul only an hour
earlier, "Look behind us—the hills burn, people
are spitted on bloody pikes! Those mad twins,
they've brought this horror upon you, upon your
people. Kill them!"

Of course it wasn't true. The monks had led
Vladislav's troops to him, not that it mattered now.
Perhaps he should have killed the boys and been
done with it. But he couldn't. No matter their
blood was tainted with commonness, probably
with madness, they were still of his blood. Instead,
Dracul had run Stephan through and left his
twitching body on the flagstones, the other monks
cowering back against the wall.

The flames drew closer, and he turned to his
half brothers, wretched, dirty, their clothes rags,
rail thin—obviously the monks had starved them.
He saw hate in their eyes, for the monks and for
him, and fear, gut-wrenching fear. And oddly, he

saw a reflection of himself. Not as he was at this moment, his black clothing drenched in soot and gore, the blade of his sword red with blood, but himself in an ancient past. And he knew that the warrior blood coursing through his ancestors down through the years, he shared with them.

Now he knew he couldn't help them, not anymore. He couldn't help any of them. The castle was falling, and Vladislav's army was ready to take the battlements. Everyone left inside his ramparts, choking on the bitter black smoke, would die if he didn't allow himself to be taken.

Dracul strode to the window and stared down at the chaos, the slaughter of his brave warriors. Only he could stop it. He, Vlad Dracul, the Walachian prince, had to become a hostage again, and these two miserable scraps who were his half brothers would be killed or tortured, or both, by their enemies, by the villagers, by his own soldiers.

Behind him, he could hear the smaller twin still howling like a wolf to the sky, and the other, Alexandru, muttering his nonsense words meant to calm and soothe. Dracul turned away from them, readying himself for what was to come—a hostage, death, who knew?

Taking their master's turned back as a signal the boys were no longer under his protection, the guards moved on them, a fitting sacrifice to stop the evil at their gates. Alexandru backed away, standing in front of Andrei, holding the book close, but a guard ripped it away. Alexandru sprang at him, fighting tooth and claw to retrieve it. In the fight, the small bindings broke, and pages floated free. Andrei was huddled, crying on the floor, but seeing the pages torn away, he scrambled up to save them. A guard kicked the pages into the air, laughing to see the vile whelp cry out as he tried to catch them.

Dracul whirled about, snapped his fingers at his men, shouted for them to stop. They didn't want to, but they didn't want to die with a pike thrust through their bellies, either. Dracul looked at the boys frantically trying to gather the torn-out pages. He held out his hand, and a guard gave him the book. Before, whenever he'd been forced to confront their existence, he'd seen them only as objects of scorn, to be hidden away. But looking at them now, looking at the filthy book that held what surely had to be magic, he simply did not know. He flexed his healed hand, felt fear skitter deep inside, and he hated that, as well.

It was Alexandru who handed him the loose pages. Dracul shoved them back inside the book. He looked beyond to Andrei, pathetic, small, wizened like an old man, who bled at a simple scratch.

He looked down into Alexandru's eyes as he gave him the book. "Take it and go." He lightly laid his once-wounded hand on the boy's thin shoulder. "The book—guard it well. It is beyond what a man can understand."

Alexandru had expected to die, not this. He

drew Andrei up to stand beside him, and he whispered to the brutal man who was his half brother, "But where will we go, my lord?"

Dracul pulled three gold pieces from his tunic. "It does not matter where you go, anywhere but here. Take these and leave now, before you face the flames, or the enemy. Take the back tunnel, go to the village."

"They will kill us in the village. Fear of you is the only way for us to live. The monks were afraid of you, so they didn't kill us, though they wanted to. If you aren't here—"

Dracul saw something in the boy's dark eyes that gave him a start, like a curtain that covered something not of this world, and the curtain could lift at any moment. What would he see? What would happen? The curtain didn't hide the sort of violence he knew. It wasn't anything he understood. Yet again, he felt a stab of fear.

"Why would you not come with us? You can be saved. If we can escape, so can you."

"I will not abandon my troops." Dracul heard the shouts, the screams, too close, too close. "Go now, this is your final chance." He rose to his full height. "I am giving you your lives." He looked a moment at their book, covered in writing he couldn't read and strange green drawings, some looking vaguely human, but most strange shapes alien to him. "You have your book. Protect it. I command you to survive."

Dracul turned and snapped his fingers again at the guards, who followed him from the room, one staring over his shoulder at the two ragged boys now running down the stone stairs, to the tunnel in the dungeons. Did he hear them speaking in the language only they understood? Surely they would be caught, killed.

Alexandru and Andrei snuck away from the castle under cover of darkness and flame, screams fading in the distance.

No one ever saw them again. They lived on for a while in stories and legends that spoke of the mad twin brothers who drank the blood of innocents. Eventually the brothers disappeared into the fabric of time, but the idea of them lived on. When the precious book was finally shown to the modern world, it was still missing the ripped-out pages. And no one knew the pages, like the book, had fluttered through history.

Their half brother Vlad Dracul, the Impaler, emerged from the shadows of history to be immortalized on the page and the screen. He became Dracula, the archangel of evil. They said he made others like him. That he and his kind walked the earth, draining the lifeblood in their pursuit of immortality.

But as all things are lost, they are also found. And with them come the plagues of hell.

CHAPTER ONE

Be motivated like the falcon, hunt gloriously.
—Rumi

The Nubian Desert
Sudan
Seven Months Ago

The desert tent was sumptuous and meant to impress, but it was not wasteful. Spiked into the shifting sands, its billowing fabric roof dipped and swayed in the desert breeze. Inside the tent, a long table was centered on a wooden platform covered with a red-and-orange oriental rug. Five falcons with leather cords on their legs and suits of black armor across their bodies perched on the backs of chairs, silent and watchful.

The air was scented with cardamom and grapes from the festive lunch the four men and two women had just enjoyed, mixing agreeably with the seared desert air around them; the quiet strains of Pink Floyd played in the background.

Champagne cooled in silver buckets, awaiting the revelations to come.

They spoke among themselves, occasionally laughing as they finished the sweet cream custard mixed with dates and almonds in small golden bowls. They laid their linen napkins beside their plates and drank the last superb bottle of 2010 Chateau L'Evangile French Bordeaux.

Conversation turned to the falcons and how very well-behaved the five were, all their attention on their master, who sat at the head of the table.

Their master, the host of the party, was Roman Ardelean, an Englishman of Romanian descent, in his prime, tall, broad-shouldered, a beak of a nose, dark hair, and eyes like smudges of coal. He pushed back his chair. "It is time, ladies, gentlemen. Come with me, and you will see the capabilities of our new army."

Each of the six knew this was to be a demonstration and a celebration of what they were financing—a drone army—yet none knew exactly what to expect. It would be a lovely surprise for all of them, Roman knew. The investors—the Money, as he thought of them—followed him out into the desert, blinking in the blazing sun and immediately sweating. Behind the tent, twenty yards away, was a line of folding chairs. On each chair was a set of ear guards and large eye shields.

Roman watched the Money take their seats, then turned his back and slipped a tiny stamp on his tongue, felt it melt, tasted the fleeting metallic hit. The microdose of LSD, a special version made for him by his twin, Radu, would help keep him calm and focused. It would also make the colors of the coming display more dramatic and the acrid desert air soften against his face, but no one needed to know that. He slipped the small box where he kept his tabs back into the pocket of his cargo pants and looked again at the Money. All were dressed as befitted a desert spa jaunt—crisp new earth tones and neck scarves, all provided by Roman's company, Radulov Industries. The Money blended into the desert, looked like they were meant to be there, which Roman found amusing. But camouflage was important right now, for all of them.

Once they were settled, Roman stood in front of them, hands behind his back. He was a clever man, a charming man, a leader who knew exactly what he was doing. He cleared his throat, met each set of eyes, and began to speak. His clear, commanding voice was exactly what the Money needed to hear, just as his tall, fit body was what they needed to see.

"Ladies and gentlemen, I applaud all of you. You are patriots and visionaries. You all know what will become of us if the spread of radical Islam isn't halted. You have envisioned this future, so you were ready to place your resources in my hands to build a drone army. I gladly took on this challenge.

"What you're about to witness is the result of my efforts. The drones are the latest in personal defense stealth technology. They are my design, technologically so advanced not even our military has this capability yet. Despite these advancements, they are easily manned by even the most inexperienced operator. You don't need pilots with thousands of sorties behind them to navigate these babies.

"They also have internal gyroscopes allowing them to maintain a constant horizon, which means they cannot be accidentally crashed. You can hand the controls to ten-year-olds, and they'll be able to fly them with ease. Of course, most of the ten-year-olds we know are so advanced with their computer games that this might seem boring to them." Pause, laughter all around.

"But not the children where we're sending these beauties. No, they have nothing to help defend themselves against the constant encroachment of the terrorists. Nothing but leftover weapons from failed wars, guns that barely work, if at all. Thanks to all of you, we're about to change that.

"It is our goal to stop the incessant march of radical Islam across Africa, across these small disadvantaged countries with no hope of fighting it. We are going to arm the people so they can defend themselves. What Britain and the United States refuse to do, we will do for them. Covertly, quietly, and most importantly, cost-effectively. I will have no overruns on project costs, no excuses, no delays. When you decided to go with Radulov, I *guaranteed* the massive drone army *would* be built. And this is my promise, my investment in this amazing venture.

"This is what all of you wanted, what all of you agreed to, and why you hired me to make it a reality.

"And yes, everything you're about to see here is beyond classified. I am going to pass out nondisclosure agreements for you to sign. This will assure me that even if you want to talk about these weapons, you cannot without disclosing your involvement in their development. None of your own investors would regard this with a favorable eye, to say the least, nor would the government. Call it an insurance policy."

Whispers and outright hostility swept through the group.

Roman's partner, Corinthian Jones, Lord Barstow, late of Her Majesty's Security Services and now a consultant for the Crown, was shaking his head. "Roman, do you think it is necessary? As you said, I brought these six patriots to you to build this drone army in the first place. Of course they will keep silent about their involvement."

Be quiet, you old fool, I know what I'm doing. "My lord, I'm sure you'll understand when I say this is for my protection, as well as all of yours. We all know what happened when the Americans tried to arm the Contras. It turned into the scandal of the century, and a patriot had to fall on his sword. I have no desire to be that man. As such, I'd hardly fail to protect my interests on such a large investment, and neither would you. And as you know, this is a very large investment, for all of us.

"Now, we need to get started before the sun

sets. Please sign the nondisclosure agreements, pass them back to me, put on your ear guards and goggles, and let's get this show started."

There was still grumbling, particularly from Paulina Vittorini, the Madonna bitch, as he thought of her, but finally even she signed the agreement. He wondered idly if he was the richest among the six of them. His firm, Radulov Industries, manufactured cybersecurity software that resided on almost every modern computer in the world. Apple and Microsoft now shipped with Radulov's flagship program MATRIX already installed as part of their most recent operating systems. In many ways, he'd saved the computer age from hackers and terrorists.

Not that he wasn't humble about it all, at least in public.

It was fitting he'd made his money in cybersecurity, because cyber warfare was the next—the only—logical step. The terrorists had their own weaponry, their own drones and IEDs—improvised explosive devices—and, in some extreme cases, planes. They moved through the dark web unseen, unstoppable, buying and selling drugs and weapons, accumulating wealth and influence, recruiting more and more lost souls to their cause.

Roman's entire life had been built on preventing the flow of negative information, stopping black hat hackers in their tracks, protecting the vulnerable, the ignorant, the gullible. His values had made him rich; his brilliance and charm had made him popular. In the last piece *Forbes* did on Roman and Radulov Industries, they'd called him Cyber Superman—he was Bill Gates, Steve Jobs, and Elon Musk rolled into a single brain, with a touch of Tony Stark's humorous arrogance. He'd liked that.

When Barstow had approached Roman about an off-book black-ops program he'd pictured in his mind—specifically, putting together a private drone army to help the smaller countries the United Kingdom wasn't able to legally protect—Roman was impressed. He'd jumped at the chance to stop the evil that was spreading unchecked across Africa.

Barstow had quietly assembled the Money—the six people here for the demonstration who would fund the operation, if, that is, they were impressed enough to transfer half the total funds required to a special account Barstow had set up. When the drone army was ready to ship, the other half of its total cost, two billion pounds, would be paid. Barstow had also assured him the Money had the resources to move the drones into place. As for Lord Barstow, he referred to himself as Roman's partner, a small conceit Roman allowed him. He would remain the financial bridge between the Money and Roman. He himself wasn't rich, merely comfortable, but through his title, lineage, and government contacts, he knew everyone who counted. Roman was amazed Barstow had the brains and guts to set this plan into motion and equally amazed he'd managed to convince six wealthy people to pay for it.

It was the make-or-break moment for Roman, but he wasn't worried. It was the perfect time—the sun was beginning to set, the sky turning lovely shades of pink and orange, signaling the ending of a very good day. It was time to show Barstow and the Money what they were going to get for their incredible investment of two billion pounds.

In the distance, there was a small village crafted by Roman's people, no living souls inside, of course, with everything a small desert village would have—huts, cardboard people and goats, even a rooster, several large outbuildings for livestock. They'd spent three weeks here in the bloody-hot desert putting it all together.

Roman grinned to himself.

Now came the fun part.

He nodded to Cyrus Wendell, his right hand for nearly ten years now. Cyrus had worked with him on the development of the drones. He was the only one of Roman's people he trusted to be there for the demonstration. Cyrus pressed a button on the laptop. Roman lifted his arm, now encased in leather. His wrist held what looked like a small computer keyboard and screen.

"All of the weapons are remotely operated through a computer program I've written, controlled by this small device on my forearm. As you can see, this weapons system is portable, discreet—you could even take it on a commercial airline flight. It's rechargeable and runs on a proprietary lithium-ion battery for long life. It has the latest in Radulov's biometric security—iris coding and facial recognition, with a DNA backup, as well. Should your device be stolen, or, heaven forbid, you're forced to unlock it against your will, the system is built to recognize distress in your facial features and take an immediate DNA sample to make sure no one else is trying to control it. If it's not you, it will shut down."

Paulina Vittorini, who ran a wealthy shipyard for her family and was considering a run for MP, said, "Impressive, Mr. Ardelean. These measures concern me, though. Are you expecting people to try to steal the technology off our wrists?"

Roman smiled, a hint of flirt on his face. "Wouldn't you? I take nothing for granted in this world, Ms. Vittorini. Protecting my people and their technology is paramount.

"Now, let me show you what you'll be getting for your buy-ins."

Roman pressed the button on his wrist, said nothing, waited three seconds.

It sounded like a swarm of bees, coming closer, closer. The murmurs stopped. The five falcons went on alert, but with a muted command from their master, sat back, yellow eyes watchful.

Seemingly out of nowhere, the drones flew directly over the tent and the presentation space, then stopped and hovered overhead. Roman had included six different breeds—he saw the drones like he saw his five falcons: each had a strength, a pedigree, a purpose. From his tiny hovering dragonfly-like Night Hawk to the fifteen-foot-long flagship, the Geode, each rose up in unison and got in line, ready for his command.

"Off you go," Roman said quietly, pressed a button, and they were over the makeshift village in a few moments.

The drones circled their targets, shooting off their specifics weapons—one dropping IEDs on the village, another landing and placing a bomb on the ground before soaring back into the air. Gunfire spurted out of another, loud and deadly, then was almost drowned out by the whistle of a missile launching from the Geode. To the delight of the Money, the small fabricated city and all its cardboard props were destroyed within a minute. Roman swiped a finger on the screen, and the strikes stopped. The drones came back toward them, hovering serenely twenty feet in the air.

Roman handed off the biometric glove to Barstow, who pulled it on and flew the Geode through the skies, trying hard to crash it, marveling at the auto-stabilization, then, as Roman watched, Barstow smiled slyly and dropped a hellfire missile on the city's smoking ruins.

As flames shot into the quickening night, the Money burst into applause, talking over one another, surprise, awe. It pleased Roman inordinately.

Chapman Donovan said in his gravelly smoker's voice, "Ardelean, this is brilliant—well done. Well done, indeed. Ah, together, we will halt radical Islam in its tracks! All of you, do we give Mr. Ardelean the go-ahead?"

Applause and enthusiastic nods all around.

Vittorini asked, "What does the little drone do?"

"The Night Hawk is a personal-protection drone capable of delivering a needle-size weapon into the neck of a target from twenty-five yards away. So if you need to assassinate someone, you'll want to order a few of them."

Barstow laughed, almost too heartily, gave Roman an avuncular smile, and slapped him on the shoulder. "And whom among us knows when such a need might arise? You've thought of everything."

"Thank you, my lord. I'm glad you're pleased. Now, I have one last display for you before we get down to business."

Roman gestured with his hand and gave a short whistle. With a piercing shriek, the falcons took off as one, as if they, too, were programmed by Roman's computers. The Money gasped in surprise when the falcons attacked the drones, swooping down, grabbing them by their bellies and whipping them to the ground. Within a few minutes, Roman's small drone army was destroyed.

He loved the looks of shock on their faces and said, in his charming leader's voice, an eyebrow arched, "You were not expecting a counteroffensive? We must have a proper defense to protect us from the future of unmanned warfare. If the terrorists attack us with their drones, there is nothing we can do but try to shoot them out of the sky, which rarely works. Properly trained falcons and eagles, on the other hand, can watch for incoming drones and eliminate them before they get anywhere near their targets."

He was pleased Vittorini looked properly impressed. "But how do they not get hurt by the propellers?"

"Their legs and breasts are wrapped in impenetrable specialty Kevlar."

From the looks on their faces—Barstow had been right—they were all in, as eager as children on Christmas morning. It was a victory for Barstow, whose plan it was, and a victory for Roman, who'd set his own genius to the drone development and succeeded beyond all expectations.

He smiled, nodded. "Please feel free to join me back in the tent, and I will review our production steps with you." And he bowed. "Your private army awaits. I will be there in a moment—I need to give my falcons their reward."

Cyrus wheeled up a cart of five dead rabbits. The Money stuck around to see the falcons tear them apart, one rabbit to each falcon, and marveled at their perfect conduct.

And then they followed Roman to the tent, their steps light, each face glowing with enthusiasm and hope.

THE FIRST DAY

TUESDAY

Peregrine falcons have been clocked at reaching speeds of 242 miles per hour while diving for prey, making them the fastest recorded animal *ever*. To allow them to reach such mind-blowing speeds, these birds boast aerodynamic torsos and specially pointed wings, as well as adapted cardiovascular and respiratory systems that allow them to beat their wings up to four times per second without fatiguing.

—*SMITHSONIAN* MAGAZINE

CHAPTER TWO

10 Downing Street
London

The trip from the Savoy Hotel to the prime minister's residence at 10 Downing Street normally took eight minutes, but the diplomatic run—the police escort clearing the streets before his black SUV—was faster. Heinrich Hemmler had only five minutes of silence to pull on the mask of the diplomat to give a good show to the PM, and that meant, of course, he had to hide his own excitement at what was going to happen. For three years, he'd kowtowed to the chancellor, the silly cow, and worked tirelessly behind the scenes, making contacts on the sly with those who had the power and the money. And now, all his plans were coming to fruition. The chancellor had sent him here to convince the PM to allow more refugees per year into the United Kingdom. Oh yes, he would give his spiel to the PM and then he would leave. No one knew what Hemmler was really doing in London, except his two personal security guards, who were paid handsomely to keep their mouths shut. There were five more guards in the car front and back, and he was as safe, probably safer, than England's PM, always.

After his meeting with the PM he would meet with a radical imam in absolute privacy, to discuss another agreement to add to his wealth. Soon, he would drape his wife, Marta, in jewels, send his children to the best private schools in the world, pay off his jewel-of-an-estate snuggled in the midst of the Schwarzwald, and have more than enough euros left over to send his young mistress, Krista, to visit her bed-ridden mother in Geneva.

The deal he'd made with ISIS was excellent, for him, of course, but not such a good deal for those who might die in the process. But that was life, wasn't it? You never knew when your own might come to an abrupt end. And anyway, who cared about those people he didn't know, had never seen? They were of no consequence—they didn't matter.

The agreement he'd made with the splinter Irish group was excellent, as well, but since his contact, Chapman Donovan, had died yesterday—dropped dead of a heart attack right outside his home, the British news had reported—Hemmler would need to find a new partner. He'd liked Chappy Donovan, always up for a Cuban cigar and a little cheat on his wife.

He needed the weapons to hand over to his friend the imam, but he wasn't worried. In this world, weapons were easy to come by. Weapons brokers were a dime a dozen.

No matter, he'd positioned himself perfectly in the government so when the chancellor's policies of open borders backfired as a result of multiple deadly terrorist attacks, she would be blamed and the country's confidence in her would plummet. And he, Vice Chancellor Heinrich Hemmler, would have no choice but to call for a special election to replace her. He would, of course, be elected in her place. And then he would discreetly settle his ISIS brethren in a small town in Bavaria as their foothold in Europe. They'd paid him a lot of money and given him their word there would be no further acts of violence in Germany once the chancellor was gone.

It was a pity no one would ever know how he'd pulled off secret negotiations with terrorist leaders. No one would ever know it was he who had protected Germany—only a small number of sacrifices to be made along the way. That he was making himself rich in the process was only fitting. He was his country's savior. The deal he'd made was brilliant.

A gentlemen's agreement, if one could call those rapacious deathmongering murderers *gentlemen*, but he trusted them to keep their word. Money had already been deposited in one of his private bank accounts. After the bombings in Frankfurt, Berlin, and Munich, the tide would turn irrevocably against the chancellor, and no one else would have to die, at least no more Germans. He slid a hand down his yellow silk tie and hummed, low in his throat. Nothing but silk and Savile Row for him from now on.

The car pulled onto Downing Street and stopped. Heinrich waited for a beat, as his security team built a protective wedge for him to step into.

Let's go, let's go, let's get this ridiculous business over with.

"All clear," one of his guards said as he opened the door and allowed Hemmler to step into the wedge onto the street. He moved fast, as always.

There were only five steps to the entrance. He took the first step into a very un-English warm and clear day.

Second step.

Third.

Something bit his neck, almost a lover's bite, as Krista liked to do. He slapped his hand to the spot, but nothing was there. White-hot pain, everywhere, he staggered. His eyes bulged as he dropped to his knees, clawing at himself as a burst of hellish fire coursed through him, burning him up from the inside.

He heard shouts, felt hands lifting him, dragging him to the doors, his knees scraping the cement, as he was manhandled inside Downing

Street. He heard the grand doors slam shut behind him. He clearly heard shouts for help, but he couldn't talk, couldn't move. Or breathe. They laid him on the carpet in the foyer. It felt so soft under his cheek, but only for an instant, because the flames were consuming him, making him want to scream, only he couldn't.

Heinrich knew he was dying. He had no chance to pray for forgiveness, nor did his life flash before his eyes. He only had a brief thought of his wife and his mistress before he actually felt his heart slowing and the softness of the rug beneath his cheek, and then he was gone.

CHAPTER THREE

Old Farrow Hall
Farrow-on-Gray, England

Nicholas Drummond looked through the wide breakfast room windows that gave onto the beautifully groomed back gardens, in full midsummer bloom. He saw the labyrinth, made up of thick yew bushes, vivid green, stretching up as tall as a man, and beyond, a slice of a trail that led into the home wood. He turned when his grandfather came into the room. Eldridge Augustus Nyles Drummond, eighth Baron de Vesci, was still going strong at eighty-four, still the head of the multibillion pound enterprise Delphi Cosmetics, but now he appeared upset. He sat at the table and stared down a moment at his lumpy porridge, automatically poured milk and a fistful of brown sugar on top, and took a quick bite.

"Bollocks," the baron said and shoveled in another bite.

"What's wrong, Grandfather? Are the Saracens nearly at the wall?"

The baron smacked his fist on the table, making his teacup bounce. "It's crazy, boy, that's what it is. My IT man, Giles Fourtnoy, just called, said it's ransomware, said these miscreants are demanding a million pounds in—bitcoins? What the devil is a bitcoin anyway? And a million of them? Would they fit in a teacup or an armored van? Giles said our sites are down until we pay up, and he can't fix them. But I knew you could, Nicholas, and so I told Giles. First tell me, what is a blasted bitcoin?"

This was not good. Ransomware had hit England, a main target the National Health Service—whose security was laughable—but not Delphi Cosmetics, with its top-notch security, which meant these buggers were good. He figured how he was going to fix things, which had to include Covert Eyes's cyber expert, Adam Pearce. He remembered everyone celebrating when Adam had turned twenty. He said, "A bitcoin is a form of monetary recompense used primarily online to pay for services rendered. They don't exist in the material world, unfortunately. They're virtual. Most of the services unsavory, as you've just learned. I'll try to save your systems from the ransomware attack without your having to pay anything."

Nicholas's grandfather looked relieved. "Well, that's why you came for a visit, isn't it, only neither of us realized it when you and Michaela drove up on Sunday. Well, get to it, my boy, we stand to lose millions every single day the direct delivery systems and websites are down. And you know Giles, he'll pull out all his hair if there's any delay, and he doesn't have much to begin with."

Nicholas said more to himself than to his grandfather, "They must have a back door to stop the attack once they're paid. I'll find it, disable the lockdown on Delphi's systems, push some nasty code their way to disrupt the attack, which will not only release your systems but also should stop the attacks elsewhere, as well."

His grandfather said, "Good, get to it. Oh yes, Nicholas—I want to see one of these demmed bitcoins. Bitcoins sound as silly as the name you and Michaela gave your FBI team—Covert Eyes. What is a covert eye, I ask you? You skulk about without anyone seeing you? Now, that's a laugh. The earth shakes when you're in town."

"Ah well, we're supposed to be discreet, really, we do try. There are seven of us, each with a different area of expertise, I guess you could say. We were tasked to travel anywhere in the world in order to solve problems." He snorted. "Now that certainly sounds high and mighty. First thing I'll do is call Adam. Here's Mike now—we'll get on it right away."

The baron snorted. "She's been out running again?"

"She's trying to keep up with a member of our Covert Eyes group—Louisa Barry's her name—

and she runs marathons. Mike says she still has a long way to go to get anywhere near Louisa."

The baron shoveled in another spoonful of oatmeal, smacked his lips. "Imagine, girls running around like men, even racing. But I'll say the girl keeps herself in good shape, just like your mother, always walking here and there, bending herself into strange postures, *poses*, she calls them. Your mother says it keeps her limber and strong, keeps your father on his toes. He agrees, says he never knows when she'll chase him down. Downward dog is one of her poses—that sounds as crazy as bitcoins." He paused a moment. "The girl has a brain, Nicholas, also like your mother. I say, I do appreciate a good brain in a female."

Nicholas said, "I think Mike knows a downward dog or two herself, Grandfather." He saw Mike break out of the home wood and run toward the side of the house, her long-legged stride smooth and steady. He knew she'd already done two laps around the lake. Next time, he'd join her, show her some of the places he'd played as a boy. But first he had to take care of the ransomware.

He said, as he looked down at the news flash on his mobile, "As you said, it's not only Delphi. Hundreds of companies were hit in this latest ransomware attack. You have the finest security in place, which means the hacker is very good."

"Tell me you and this Adam are better."

"We are. If my interruption works the way

I hope, my program will install a patch on your servers so no one will be able to get in again." He paused, frowned. "I'm surprised Radulov's software could be circumvented like this, but then again, even the best computer programs aren't immune to a skilled hacker with malfeasance on his mind."

Ah, that serious look, so like his father's, but with Nicholas, there was always another level to his smiles, like some mad adventure brewing with the devil lurking about. And trust Nicholas to find the devil and kick him in the hindquarters.

The baron was pleased to see the Drummond spark living on in his grandson, ah, so like himself when he was younger. Well, much younger. Odd how it had skipped Harry and bloomed wildly in Harry's only son. And yet Nicholas knew how to make a computer sing and dance according to his whim. He'd heard his IT man, Giles, say Nicholas's skills were beyond any he'd ever seen. The baron liked that, didn't think Giles was bootlicking.

So many years, and where had they all gone? The baron said to Nicholas, "Excellent. I'll phone Giles as soon as I finish breakfast—he'll probably pop off firecrackers he'll be so relieved. These bastards need to be taken down a notch. I'm glad you'll be the one to do it. Eat your porridge, then you can get on the ransomware attack."

Nicholas scooped up a spoonful of Cook Crumbe's bland porridge, filled with lumps, just the way his grandfather had consumed and loved it for thirty years. He swallowed down a bit, chased it with orange juice. He needed to get Mike some pancakes and bacon, something substantial, to recharge her after the run. Her recovery was going well, but he felt she was pushing herself too hard. It still made his blood run cold to remember her near drowning in Lake Trasimeno.

Nicholas was about to ring the bell, to order the eggs and bacon, when Lenny Kravitz's "American Woman" burst out of his pants pocket. His grandfather, who normally hated mobiles at the table, said, "Is it about the ransomware attacks?"

"I don't know yet. It's the FBI in Washington. I'll take it outside." He was already walking out of the breakfast room, his mobile to his ear.

"Drummond here. Sherlock? Is everything all right?"

"It's Savich. I borrowed Sherlock's phone. Sean dropped mine in the toilet. No, don't go there."

Sherlock called from the background, "Sean fished it out and brought it to me. I'm giving it a quick bath. Sean wants to know when you're coming over so he can beat you at his current video game. Sorry, the name of this one escapes me."

"Tell him maybe next week and no matter what sort of wild aliens he has in store, I'll bury him. Now, what's happening?"

Savich said, "I take it you don't have the television on?"

"No, I was breakfasting with my grandfather.

We have ransomware attacks going on over here, one against his company. I'm going to try to reach Adam. What's happened?"

"The vice chancellor of Germany was assassinated minutes ago on the steps of 10 Downing Street."

CHAPTER FOUR

B loody hell."

Nicholas strode across the foyer to the kitchen, the closest television. The staff was watching the BBC, even Cook Crumbe, her eyes narrowed, her apron clutched in her strong hands. They started to leave when they saw him, but Nicholas waved them back. All gathered again around the television, with Nigel, Nicholas's butler, and Nigel's father, Horne, the Drummond butler since the flood, the baron was fond of saying, and Nicholas standing behind them.

Nigel turned up the volume and said in his clipped voice, "Another bloody terrorist attack, and that's what it was. I know it."

"Our continuing coverage of what might be yet another assassination of a leading political figure on our soil. First was Chapman Donovan's sudden collapse and death outside his home in Chelsea yesterday. Now the vice chancellor's death outside 10 Downing Street. We are awaiting a press update from New Scotland Yard. To recap what we know so far, the vice chancellor of Germany, Heinrich Hemmler, has died after collapsing outside of 10 Downing Street—"

Nicholas stepped away from the group and said to Savich, "This is worrisome. I'll call Penderley at Scotland Yard, see what I can learn. Two high-profile deaths in two days? I know the folk in Northern Ireland have to be up in arms over Chapman's death, and now the German vice chancellor is dead, as well? Both supposedly natural deaths? It doesn't feel right, does it?"

"No, and we must know as soon as possible if the deaths are assassinations, and related. As you might know, President Bradley is scheduled to meet with the PM in London on Sunday to discuss how the U.S. can assist in dealing with possible consequences of Brexit."

"Not much time," Nicholas said, "but I'll get right on it. It's time to talk to the Security Services. I'll be discreet. I'll call you when I have something."

"Thank you. I hate to cut your vacation short, Nicholas, but Vice President Sloan agrees with me. She knew you and Mike were in England, knew you could get information for the Secret Service so they could determine if the trip is still advisable. I'd like to be able to tell her we have this situation well in hand. Let me know if I need to jump on a call with you when you speak to Security Services. Your dad is involved with them, isn't he?"

"Yes, he's back with them as a consultant. I imagine he's up to his neck, what with these two deaths."

Sherlock said, "We'll let Zachery know you'll be looking into this for us. You and Mike be careful—no more near drownings for Mike, and no more nearly falling into volcano craters for you."

Nicholas swallowed. "No more deep water, no more volcanoes, I promise."

Nicholas punched off and immediately dialed his old boss at New Scotland Yard, Hamish Penderley, the big gun with a title to match: chief superintendent of the Operational Command Unit.

"Drummond? I'm not surprised. I suppose you already know we're rather busy this morning."

"Sir, this is about the death of the vice chancellor at 10 Downing Street a few minutes ago."

"And you want to know because . . . ? You, I understand, are here with your partner to relax and to soak up the rays, as the Yanks say, if there ever are any rays to be found in England. How did you get involved in this mess?"

"Agent Dillon Savich called me, asked me to lend a hand because the president is due to arrive on Sunday to meet with the PM And that's why

I'm calling you, sir. I must know what's happening, or my hands are tied."

Penderley sighed. "Honestly, we don't know anything for sure about the vice chancellor. They have to do a postmortem first. For the time being, the public will be told Hemmler had a heart attack, just as we've done with Donovan.

"Don't get me wrong, Drummond, I do not miss you, but there are times I could use your brain. And now is one of them."

Nicholas frowned. He heard stress and fatigue in Penderley's voice, a sure sign of how serious the situation was. "I'm happy to help, sir. We'll put the full strength of Covert Eyes at your disposal. Have you completed the autopsy on Donovan? How did he die?"

"We don't know yet, but as soon as I find out, I will call you. As you know, Donovan collapsed outside his house and was dead nearly instantly. Here's the truth: no one saw anything, no one touched him, nothing. And now Heinrich Hemmler collapses right outside 10 Downing Street? Yesterday and today, we've had two major political figures drop dead on our soil with no good reason."

Nicholas said, "If these two men were assassinated, we must catch whomever is behind the deaths as quickly as possible, or President Bradley's trip will most likely be canceled. So tell me, sir, what do you think is happening?"

"I haven't the faintest yet, but there is one thing different in today's attack on Hemmler. Several people have reported seeing a small drone in the area, like a toy, almost. One witness even took a picture of it."

Nicholas's blood stirred. "Ah. Have you enhanced it?"

"Yes. Am I correct to assume you would like to have a crack at it?"

"I would, yes."

"I'll send it along, in addition to everything else we have. Report back to me the moment you discover anything, would you, Drummond? I'd like us to be on the same page before the media storm hits." A pause, then the familiar no-nonsense order from his old boss: "Get it sorted, Drummond."

He couldn't help himself, he grinned into his mobile. "Yes, sir. I'll be in touch."

Nicholas hung up the phone as Agent Michaela Caine walked into the kitchen, a towel around her neck, her face glistening with sweat, her blond ponytail at half-mast. Despite the vigorous run, she still smelled faintly of jasmine. He took the towel from around her neck and patted her face. "There, perfect again." Knowing a lot of eyes were watching, he took a step back, studied her face for a moment. "Not too tired, are you?"

"No, I'm good. You're vibrating, Nicholas. What's going on?"

How could she know? "Nothing, well, not exactly nothing. I know it's our vacation, but we have a case, a very high-profile case. Fact is, two big-time politicos, one of them the vice chancellor of Germany, are both dead within twenty-four hours of each other. Both simply collapsed, dead very quickly." He saw her blue eyes light up and grinned. "You in the mood to work a couple of deaths that are very probably murders?"

CHAPTER FIVE

Mike loved Old Farrow Hall, particularly its multitude of fireplaces, all of them with a provenance, it seemed, that kept the huge house warm even on a chilly day in July. Nicholas's office was no exception, with its nineteenth-century Venetian green-veined marble fireplace, glowing embers occasionally sparking off flames. His mother had decorated his office and made it both inviting and efficient. And not at all shabby. The fireplace was framed by dark wood paneling. Bookshelves lined the walls, filled haphazardly with paperbacks and hardcovers. A small desk and chair sat in a corner. But what made the room really welcoming were the burgundy leather sofa and two comfortable chairs, complemented by colorful dhurrie rugs. Her mind flew off to his visit to her suite of rooms in the opposite wing the previous night and—

"First things first," Nicholas said, pulling out his cell phone.

"What? Oh, right, you want to take care of the ransomware problem first."

He stared at her a moment. "Wool gathering, Agent Caine?"

"Maybe. A little bit, maybe about last night. You're going to call Adam about the attack?"

"Yes, I want to get him working on both the drone and the malware. What about last night?"

She gave him a mad grin. "Oh, just a little of this, a little of that, nothing much of importance. First, tell me, does Penderley have any idea why the vice chancellor was murdered? Did Hemmler do anything to make himself a target, like someone who hates Germany for their dominating role in the E.U.? And what about this Chapman Donovan?"

Nicholas sat on the sofa and booted up his laptop, saying as he typed, "No, evidently no one has the foggiest idea. Hemmler was meeting with the PM to discuss England's stand on open borders, maybe to try twisting the PM's arm, but that's not earthshaking. Nor does Penderley know why someone would target Chapman Donovan, a wealthy Irish landowner. Family's been in horse racing for two hundred years, very rich, and an MP from Belfast West."

"What about the drone someone spotted near where Hemmler died?"

"Penderley is sending a photo along with all his files any minute now. With luck, we'll be able to identify the drone's maker and put a stop to this straightaway. I'll call Adam now. He'll be able to enhance the photo faster than I can. And I'll wager he knows all about the malware attacks and will be able to help with that."

"It's the middle of the night in New York."

"You know Adam does his best work at two in the morning." Nicholas grinned at her when Adam's face popped up on the screen immediately. He didn't seem tired or sleepy, had his earbuds in, a bright blue *Star Trek Voyager* T-shirt on, and a can of Red Bull in front of him, as always.

Adam said, "Hey, you guys are supposed to be on vacation. Did you get called in on the vice chancellor's murder or the malware attack?"

Had he ever doubted Adam wouldn't already know about both? No, he hadn't. He said, "Both. First, how are your photo-enhancement skills?"

"You wouldn't ask if you didn't know I'm about the best on the planet. Sending me a file?"

"Any minute, as soon as Penderley sends it to me."

Mike said, "Hi, Adam. Would you believe I'm getting a suntan in jolly old England? No? Stop laughing. Is everything okay there?"

"Absolutely. I'm bored to tears, and you know what happens when I get bored."

Nicholas said, "No, and neither Mike nor

I want to know. Tell me you've been solving the malware problem."

"I will say I'm looking into it, but I haven't solved it yet. I can tell you the initial hack appears to have come out of western Russia, and I've been purchasing website domain names, thinking I'll hit on one that might be able to halt it. On the other hand, the attack could be from Tahiti, with someone really bright at the helm, disguising its point of origin. You want me to keep working on it?"

"Not to play favorites, but my grandfather's firm has been hit, as well. Feel free to use his site to halt the attack. Giles Fourtnoy is his IT man. I'll send him a text, tell him to expect your call. I am also sending a wee bit of code you might enjoy deploying when you find the back door."

He hit send, and a few moments later, Adam's eyes lit up, and he whistled. "Dude. Where does your brain come up with this nasty stuff?"

"It's a gift. I have the photo from Penderley, sending it now." And again, Nicholas pressed send.

Mike could see Adam frowning as he looked at the screen.

"This resolution sucks. Was this shot with a cell phone?"

Nicholas said, "As far as we know, yes."

"It almost looks like a toy helicopter, doesn't it? If I have the scale right, based on that window on the right side of the photo, it looks like it could fit in the palm of your hand."

Nicholas waited, and, sure enough, after only a short pause, Adam said, "If I were a betting man, I'd say it was a military-grade micro UAV—unmanned air vehicle." Adam clicked a few keys, and the specs came up on the screen. "The small ones like this are almost always either toys or military-grade. This photo matches dimensions with a British military Black Hornet drone. They call it a nanodrone. Four port cameras, battery-powered, it can stay aloft over twenty-five minutes. It can fly pretty quick, too, if someone needed it to make a getaway. Not something you can buy at Radio Shack, even if you can find one nowadays. Who does this belong to?"

Nicholas said, "That's what we have to find out. It was hovering over the crime scene today. A person in the crowd forwarded the photo to Scotland Yard. I suppose the drone could belong to a member of Downing Street security and it's all a coincidence—"

"Or someone wanting to do bad things, more likely," Adam said.

Mike was leaning over Nicholas's shoulder. "Like murder the vice chancellor."

"Yes," Nicholas said. "If it is murder, then this drone could have the capability to deliver some sort of weapon."

"What kind of weapon? I mean, it's a super small drone, so the weight of any larger ordinance, a gun or a missile, wouldn't be sustainable. Drones like this are mainly used for surveillance. What are you thinking?"

"Let's see." Nicholas clicked a few times, and Mike watched the screen break into segments—Adam, the drone, the specification blueprints of the official Black Hornet devices, and a close-up shot of the undercarriage of their mystery drone.

Nicholas said, "If this was not a surveillance drone, it must have a delivery mechanism for a weapon that can kill. Hold on, Penderley's sent us a message. Several attachments."

Nicholas scanned the contents of the email.

"I'm reading from the files Penderley sent over. This is the first I've seen of this, so bear with me—interesting, Chapman Donovan's death was heart failure brought on by poison. He had something called epibatidine in his system, a neurotoxin derived from a small South American tree frog. According to the report, epibatidine was once explored as a substitute for morphine but was deemed too toxic, too unpredictable."

Mike asked, "They get this neurotoxin off frigging frogs?"

Adam said, "Epibatidine was originally derived from the Ecuadorian poison-dart frog. Which means whoever's using it bought it online, because when these particular frogs are bred in captivity they're almost always nontoxic. Their alkaline levels aren't the same when they don't feed on insects in the wild. Whoever killed Donovan either went to

Ecuador and harvested the poison from the frogs, or he or she bought or stole it from somewhere. You know you can purchase anything online now, legally or otherwise."

They both looked at him, eyebrows raised.

"What? I watch the National Geographic channel."

Mike laughed, then said, "Logic says we have a small drone capable of delivering a neurotoxin. So the delivery mechanism must be a small tube of some sort filled with the frog neurotoxin?"

"Yes," Nicholas said. "More important, why were these two men targeted?"

CHAPTER SIX

Falconry: **The art of training a raptor to hunt in cooperation with a person and to return to the falconer on signal.**

**—Wingmasters.net,
"The Language of Falconry"**

Over Northern England

The G650 blew north, a quick hop from London to Roman Ardelean's headquarters near North Berwick in Scotland. He'd been asked why he'd elected to set his headquarters in Scotland. And not where? he'd wondered. Romania? A stupid question. Just because he was of Romanian ancestry, he was an Englishman and a businessman who understood the tax structure was better here, not to mention he wanted his headquarters near to home so Radu could run things more easily. He checked his email and the news reports, smiled, and made a brief, encrypted phone call.

The voice on the other end was furious, just as Roman knew he'd be, and it pleased him.

"What do you think you're up to, Ardelean? Murdering Hemmler in front of 10 Downing Street was insane, and less than twenty-four hours after Donovan died, and in exactly the same way? Are you trying to ruin all of us?"

"Why so upset, my lord? Hemmler was dirty to his bones, and you knew it. MI6 was gathering evidence on him. He was communicating with ISIS, was planning to give them land, legitimacy, and weapons to stake their claim in Europe. I did you a favor eliminating him—no, I've done the whole world a favor."

"Yes, yes, he was a traitor to his country. I'm glad he's dead, but you didn't need to draw so much attention to yourself. And what about Donovan? I know he was balking at the amount of money he was still expected to pay for his share of the drone army, but I would have talked him around. Why did you kill him?"

"Because he wasn't innocent. When I was looking into Hemmler, I saw a string of private messages that seemed odd. When I explored further, I realized they were between Donovan and Hemmler. I took a quick peek inside Donovan's computer to make sure, saw even more correspondence on a private chat. Well, it wasn't private to me. He broke our nondisclosure agreement, talked to Hemmler about supplying him with weapons.

He knew Hemmler was in bed with ISIS, and yet he still wanted to deal with him. He was a threat to Project Cabal, and I eliminate threats." He paused a moment, then added, "I guess you didn't know he moved most of his assets to five separate Swiss banks? Why? I think he was brokering some major deal with Hemmler, one not to our benefit, and wanted cover. Donovan was playing fast and loose with his loyalties, and of no use at all to us. In fact, if I hadn't eliminated him, he would have told everyone about our drone army. Good riddance."

Barstow sputtered, then said, "I always thought Chappy Donovan was a good man, not to mention he was as rich as Croesus. And he always wanted to go along with my ideas, like Project Cabal. You're certain? I've heard nothing like this."

"Believe me, Barstow, since he was one of the six Money, you can count on the fact I'd be certain. Perhaps as their hotshot consultant, you can get MI6 up to speed."

There was dead silence, then Roman said, "Now let's get to what's important. Today is the day, Barstow. I'm officially notifying you the drone army is assembled and ready to ship out. It's payday. Nearly one billion pounds, minus Donovan's share which we never were going to get in the first place."

"All right, here's the truth. The rest of the Money are balking, don't get me wrong, not for the same reason as Donovan. No, they want the drones immediately, before they pay their final installment."

"That wasn't our deal, Barstow. No money, no drones."

"I know, and so I told them. I'll speak to them all again, try to talk them around. I'll get back to you tomorrow."

Roman felt a tidal wave of rage, quickly thumbed a tab onto his tongue. What was going on here?

Barstow's voice grew conspiratorial. "Roman, you know why we're doing this. You know how vital our project is. Think about delivering those drones today. Think about how the army you created—your great army of death to the terrorists, all the Islamic radicals who want to subjugate the world. You can begin your war to destroy them. But only if you ship them immediately."

"You are the conduit, Barstow. Convince them, remind them this was the agreement they signed."

"Yes, yes, I will remind them."

"Don't take that tone with me. You forget, Barstow, you approached me with your vision. Not only did you want me to build you a private drone army, you now want me to deliver before the accounts are settled. What sort of businessman would I be to allow such a thing? The Money will pay up, and I will turn over the drones, happily."

He paused. "Or there will be consequences. Remind them what happened to Donovan."

"The rest of the investors aren't stupid. They already realize you killed one of them. They're mad and scared."

"Feel free to tell them why, Barstow."

"They won't believe Chappy Donovan was a traitor."

Roman laughed. "Do you want me to send them the proof?"

"No!"

Roman heard Barstow's labored breathing. He hoped he didn't stroke out.

Barstow said, "There's something else. Terry Alexander notified me, said he'd been told by a reliable source this was all a scam, that there wasn't a drone army, that you planned to keep the money. He said he was out of the project, but he assured me he wouldn't say anything to anyone."

A punch to the gut. Who would have told Alexander that?

Roman said, "Of course you assured him the rumor was false."

"Yes, yes, of course I did, but look, I'm sorry, but I think he might be lost to us."

"My billion pounds is shrinking rapidly, Barstow." Roman added quietly, "Did you trace the source of this rumor?"

"I can't, and believe me, I've tried. Sorry, Roman."

Rage bubbled and roiled. Alexander would pay, he would see to it. Still, when he spoke, his voice was calm. "You will call me tomorrow with good news, namely, the others have paid up and no more of our flock have slipped out of the fold." He tossed the phone onto the leather seat across from him, leaned his head back, and closed his eyes.

Roman would give him a day to talk the Money around. If Barstow failed, then Roman would take action. He knew Barstow was ruthless: he would kill his own mother if it would get him what he wanted. He wanted the drones very badly, so perhaps he would twist arms like he'd said. Why had the Money gone against the agreement—final payment, then drone delivery? And Alexander, who had been told there were no drones? That Roman was a crook?

He picked up his tablet, scrolled through the list of names. Six Money were involved in Project Cabal, four men, two women, representing four different countries. Well, now four since Donovan's face-plant yesterday and Alexander's defection. So he'd lose a hundred-fifty-million pounds. Donovan's death already improved the world. Had he really not paid Barstow? Had Barstow lied, deciding he could keep the money rather than giving it to Roman?

But Alexander. A shock, that one. Roman had liked Terry Alexander, worked with him on occasion, found him committed to keeping England safe from terrorism. Who had told him Roman had lied about the army?

Roman slipped a stamp onto his tongue, leaned his head back against the leather seat, and closed his eyes again. He thought back to the day, nearly two years before, when Barstow involved him in what was then an incredible dream. Barstow had proposed bringing together several wealthy individuals to fund the building of a drone army. Naturally, the governments of democratic nuclear nations couldn't be seen supporting upstart democratic wars in Africa, not anymore. Even when the enemy was so clear—the nightly news was full of terrorist bombings, cars driving into crowds, innocents' blood spilled on the streets— the select six were eager to finance the project but insisted they had to work behind the scenes so, whatever happened, they wouldn't be held accountable, wouldn't be targeted by ISIS. They knew to take the terrorists on openly meant they'd likely be handed their heads.

Very few people knew Roman was already trafficking in arms for the smaller nations fighting ISIS. He'd be lauded as a hero if he was found out, of that he had no doubt. Of course, ISIS would probably come after him. It was worth the risk.

But there was more—there was always more— and he accepted his hatred of ISIS was more personal, more deep and abiding.

He wanted a weapon of his own manufacture

to take out his greatest protégé and now his greatest enemy, Caleb Temora.

Temora was one of the reasons he'd agreed to
work this drone army black op with Barstow in the
first place. The chance to destroy Temora the way
Temora was trying to destroy him was too good to
pass up.

Roman had hired Temora right out of high
school, with no formal training. He was a natural, a
brilliant coder. He had a way of seeing through one
code to the next in a ballet of unexpected and elegant ways that produced remarkable results. Roman
knew of only two others as brilliant with code—
himself and his twin brother, Radu. If he were
honest with himself, Roman saw Temora almost as
a surrogate younger brother. He'd mentored him,
taught him, groomed him. Roman was Temora's
mentor, Temora was his acolyte. He'd trusted him.

Yet Roman never realized how volatile and
unpredictable Temora was. When he'd had no
choice but to cancel one of Temora's pet projects
because he knew it simply wouldn't pay off for
them, he'd watched Temora change. He grew more
formal with Roman, then skipped work, or when
he showed up, he was drunk or stoned, and then
one fine Friday, he'd finally disappeared entirely.

Roman did everything he could to find him.

Word soon leaked out that a girl called Aisha
had recruited him after Roman had pulled his
project. When Roman took apart Temora's com-

puter after he'd disappeared, he realized quickly Aisha was a black widow. But before Roman could find Temora, Radu discovered Temora had traveled to Syria and joined the caliphate.

To lose a computer genius of his caliber to ISIS, to know his former protégé was enabling their communications on the dark web, using private messaging services he'd developed for them, plummeted Roman into a well of hate.

Now, five years later, Roman and Radu had still failed to find him. He knew Temora was at the forefront, he recognized his work in the terror organization's technology. And at Temora's back, protecting him, stood the world's most feared terrorists.

Yes, destroying ISIS was paramount, but Roman wanted more. He wanted to find Temora and stick a knife in his heart, let his twin, Radu, look on and applaud as Roman danced in Temora's blood.

Roman knew in his gut Temora was behind the spectacular malware hack of Radulov's flagship product MATRIX, Roman's combined operating system and antivirus cybersecurity program. He'd pushed a worm through MATRIX, in essence taking every computer running the program hostage. It had his fingerprints all over it. No one else could have pulled it off, certainly no hacker he'd heard of could have managed to burrow into the first three layers of security on MATRIX. Only Temora, who knew the system as well as Roman himself.

And now he was demanding money from each business in the form of bitcoin to release it.

What to do about the errant worm that had dismantled hundreds of businesses, even the National Health Service, losing them millions of pounds if they didn't pay up? How was Roman to secure MATRIX once and for all? No mystery there, he had to find Temora and kill him.

Roman simply had to focus his magnificent brain on what needed to be done. Roman knew his twin, Radu, could possibly secure MATRIX from any more Temora hacks, knew he'd work as hard and fast as he could, because Radu hated Temora with all the soul-deep hate Roman did, maybe more. Temora had befriended Radu, had shown him respect, given him endless praise and affection. He'd made Radu his god, and it was all a lie.

The pilot announced they would be landing in five minutes. Roman took a deep breath, fingered another microdose tab into his mouth. He now had to focus on how to deal with Raphael Marquez, his manager at the Scottish facility, the heart of Radulov. His people had failed to protect MATRIX, they'd let Temora in. What should he do?

He thought of Alexander again, and knew what he would do.

Corinthian "Corry" Jones, Lord Barstow, stared at his silent mobile. He'd known he was playing with fire when he'd allied himself with Roman Ardelean, but he prayed all the risk would be worth it. He thought about the first Corinthian Jones, who'd ridden on the field of Blenheim at John Churchill's side in 1704, a hero to England, as much as Churchill, and Queen Anne had made him the first Viscount Barstow. All the men in his illustrious family through the succeeding centuries had schemed for England, had fought for England—all of them had accomplished great deeds.

And now, at last, he would follow in their footsteps. He would make his own mark. He would be known throughout history as a patriot and a hero. His name would be immortal. He smiled. He was smarter than those before him, because along with his fame, he would be wealthy beyond imagining.

Ah, but there were so many chess pieces on the board, so many moves to consider, all to bring down Roman Ardelean, the Black King, and secure the drone army. Today the game had started, the game that held his own life in the balance. And Ardelean had given him a brilliant idea.

CHAPTER SEVEN

Old Farrow Hall
Farrow-on-Gray, England

Hold on . . . wait a sec . . ." Mike saw Adam stare into space for a brief moment, then he started typing furiously. She heard a *whoosh*, and an email appeared. Adam looked excited.

"Click the link. I'm going to run you through an idea I just had."

Nicholas ran the mouse over the link. The photo was a tight close-up of the bottom of the tiny drone. They could see four small rails running the length of the undercarriage.

Adam circled four spots on the bottom of the drone with his finger. "This drone doesn't come with rails normally, which means they're retrofitted. As you can see on the specs, they're not part of the original unit. And I checked: this drone is a couple of centimeters bigger than the military-grade Black Hornet. Look here. It seems to have a trigger in the center. Do you see that?"

Mike said, "Yes, we do. Could it be a remote trigger? Maybe a trigger on a timer?"

Nicholas said, "Could be, but it would take a lot of coordination." He sat back, drummed his fingers on his laptop. "No, my bet is whoever sent up the drone was watching from afar and, when the opportunity presented itself, pulled the trigger."

Mike said slowly, "Like a sniper attack, only miniaturized, and controllable from, say, twenty, twenty-five feet."

Nicholas touched the screen, using his fingers to swivel the angle. "This rail . . . when you turn the photo at this angle, you can see the channel. It's hollow, probably carried a tiny needle or spike coated with the neurotoxin."

Mike said, "If you look at the photo of the drone, it looks maybe fifteen feet away, so say the killer using the drone was another ten feet away."

Nicholas said, "Okay, does the needle embed itself in the skin or prick the skin, then fall off onto the ground? If that's the case, it could still be at the scene, possibly still coated with the neurotoxin, and still dangerous. We'll have to find it."

Mike said, "We can forget the Donovan crime scene. It's most likely already too contaminated since it's a well-trafficked area. We might have a shot at Downing Street, though—it's a more controlled environment."

Nicholas typed a quick text.

> Can the Downing Street crime scene be swept for a piece of a small, hollow metal tube or a needle?

Penderley texted back almost immediately.

> A metal tube? A needle? You just heard my groan, yes, Drummond? Will do.

Mike said, "This seems to be an entirely new weapons system. Has there been any talk of this, Adam?"

"There's always talk, Mike, but about a drone firing frog spit? I'll start looking in the dark web, but as far as I know, this is something new. There are lots of warnings about weaponized drones, but this is beyond anything I've seen. Like I said, the drone's undercarriage looks like the base of a Black Hornet, but the military Black Hornets are mainly for reconnaissance and close personal use for soldiers in the field. This is something different. This one has been custom-made to kill."

"Tear it apart, Adam, and let us know what else you find."

"It would help if you could FedEx one to me. Just kidding. I'll see what I can do."

Adam's portion of the screen went black.

Nicholas saw Mike staring at the marked-up photo of the undercarriage of the drone.

"What is it?"

She touched the screen, enlarged a small section behind the back rail. "It's fuzzy, but I can make out something, right here."

Nicholas circled the spot and clicked a button, and the spot grew larger.

Mike took off her glasses and bent down, nose nearly to the screen. "Nicholas, could that be a serial number? I think I see a letter *R* and the number seven."

Nicholas bent close as well. "Good eyes. It might be." He clicked on the screen, sent the shot to Adam with a brief note:

Check this out, too, please. Possible serial number.

Mike sat back down, cupped her chin in her hand. "A weaponized drone this size? It boggles the mind. We have a serious problem on our hands, Nicholas."

"At the very least. I need to work on the malware hack with Adam, then we'll tackle this. And speak of the devil—" Nicholas pulled up his video chat with Adam, who was grinning.

"I'm a genius, you're a genius, all is well in the universe."

"Okay, talk to me."

"Giles Fourtnoy, your grandfather's IT head, gave me access to the mainframe at Delphi Cosmetics. I created a shell that allowed me to look at the entire system, from orders to emails, and I found the malware's entry point. Not exactly a sophisticated ruse, done with a DDoS—distributed denial of service—attached to an email that looked like it was internal, but the email address had been spoofed. When the email was read, and the employee clicked on the attachment, he opened the doors, and the worm swept in. From there, it took little to no effort to hijack the system."

"So the attack is over?"

"Of course. That code you sent me? It worked perfectly. I piggybacked on the open door, uploaded it to the server, and it went on the attack. I looked through the servers and made sure nothing was left behind. They're back online as we speak."

Mike leaned into the screen, kissed Adam's face. "Well done."

"I'm not going to kiss your screen face," Nicholas said. "But Mike's right, you did very well, Adam, and you were fast. Now, please tell Fourtnoy to make sure he keeps the software updated. MATRIX is designed to prevent these kinds of incursions, but if the patches Radulov releases aren't in place, the software is vulnerable."

Nicholas punched off, sat back, and beamed. "One down."

"Now onto the next," she said. "Give me

the files Penderley sent. I'll start looking for ties between Hemmler and Donovan, see if anything stands out." She patted his face. "I wonder how I would have punished you, Mr. Superhero, if you hadn't managed to arrest the malware attack in what, an hour?"

Nicholas smoothed her eyebrows, kissed the top of her nose. "If I hadn't, I'd have given you permission to deep-six my keyboards."

"Hmm. How would I have done it? I know: it's the middle of the night, you're sprawled on your back, a silly smile on your face, trying to get your breath back. I'd snatch your keyboards, sneak out to the lake and in they'd go."

"Really? A silly smile?"

"Be quiet. Now, I'm going to clean myself up, then get to work." She paused at the doorway. "I must admit, I'm impressed, Nicholas. You've saved Delphi Cosmetics and countless other businesses millions of dollars. Hey, while I'm gone, maybe you could figure out who sent those drones, maybe even save the world while you're at it."

"I will certainly try to save my small part of it, Agent Caine."

CHAPTER EIGHT

A hood is a more sophisticated version of a simple blindfold. Hoods . . . make hawks sit quietly, . . . during traveling and whilst being carried, particularly if another hawk is being flown at the time.

—Emma Ford, *Falconry: Art and Practice*

Radulov Industries Lead Server Facility
North Berwick, Scotland

Raphael Marquez's hands were sweating. He knew the time of reckoning was close. There, out the window of his office, he saw his boss's plane drop from the overcast sky and land smoothly on the tarmac with a whispered squeal, the sound only a customized Gulfstream G650ER could make. He was on his feet in an instant, heart pounding with dread and fear, running to the large auditorium in the center of their massive, pentagonal structure to meet Mr. Ardelean. Raphael knew the boss hated the pomp and circumstance of the "arrival" ceremonies so many other CEOs craved, and he admired him for it, but not now, not this time.

The boss was, in Raphael's opinion, one of the best coders in the world. Along with his coding genius was his ability to lead, to draw others to whatever he suggested. He had, single-handedly, made Radulov Industries the most respected cybersecurity firm in the whole bloody world. They were renowned not only for their extensive security protocols but also for their software programs, the guts of every computer mainframe, laptop, phone, and tablet in the world. Both Apple and Microsoft had done deals with Radulov. His security settings were the new industry standard.

Raphael kept walking, his brain squirreling around with the various scenarios awaiting him. He'd screwed up badly enough that the Head of the World, as he thought of Roman, had come in person to what? Fire him? Kill him? But it wasn't entirely his fault—it was the other's. He hated to say his name, even think it, for fear it would mushroom in the air itself and choke him. A hated name, the betrayer's name. Temora.

What was the worst that could happen? He'll fire your ass, and you'll be publicly humiliated. You'll be out the door with nothing to show for your past fifteen years of innovative work at Radulov but finger calluses and a permanent computer-screen squint. Your reputation, accolades, salary, all gone. Please, God, please, God, don't let him fire me, let me stay, let me try to fix it.

Raphael hurried faster. It wouldn't do for the Head of the World to beat him to the auditorium, where all the employees were gathered. It would mean the boot for sure, maybe worse.

He wanted more than anything to remain in charge of this spectacular installation, Radulov's lead server farm in the world. It resembled the American Pentagon, only not as large, with one external and four internal layers of offices. It was a buzzing honey-comb of digital activity. But unlike the Pentagon, the server installation was underground, for protection against a possible electromagnetic pulse—an EMP—strike, or worse. In short, if their servers went down, the computer systems all over the world would, too. Every Radulov server farm had redundancies, and they resided in similar but much smaller facilities in more than thirty countries, the only way to keep up with the load. But the heart of Radulov was right here in Scotland. Put a dagger through the heart, and everything would be lost. And that was what Raphael had allowed the hated other to do. He'd known Temora was a genius, known he was capable of anything, and they'd taken every precaution, but still, somehow, he'd found a way in.

The auditorium was inside the final layer, deep down, with filtered air and ventilation systems, kitchens, food stores, and massive vertical support beams like metal ribs. It had been designed to convert into a dormitory for all the employees of Radulov Industries housed in the facility, two hundred at any given time. Roman was always prepared for the worst.

Faces looked up when Raphael burst through the door. He called down from the catwalk high above, "He's here. Shape up, everyone."

The room synchronized, everyone finding their place, ready for this impromptu meeting called by the head of the company. The Head of their World.

Everyone knew why Ardelean was there. Everyone knew Raphael had failed. And as such, it meant they had all failed. What would happen? The air was thick with anxiety.

Raphael waited on the catwalk, tapping his forefinger against the railing, trying his best to look calm, relaxed, in control. He was the manager of this amazing facility, the leader of all those workers below. He wondered if anyone could see him sweating. He certainly knew every one of them expected him to take the fall. All knew Roman Ardelean did not suffer mistakes, and this was a doozy.

Raphael felt ill, but pushed it down. He refused to humiliate himself when Roman was here to do it for him. Maybe a public flogging before his imminent dismissal, something to frighten the rest into performing better? After all, Raphael knew someone had to fall on his sword after the magnitude of the malware attack had been discovered.

The buck had to stop with him. Thankfully he had good news that would lessen the boss's anger.

He looked up to see the floor-to-ceiling screen at the front of the auditorium spinning the twelve-foot-high Radulov logo, a highly stylized falcon made of black and gray triangles on a deep bloodred background, wings outstretched to form the *V* of the Radulov name. The effect made the falcon look as if it were flying across the space, lazily swooping back and forth. It was a clever bit of coding, not sophisticated, but effective.

Raphael could pretend all he wanted, do the stiff upper lip, but he knew he was about to be the goat. If he had a brain, he'd do a runner, quit, leave, because he didn't think what was coming was going to be pretty. He knew he wasn't kidding anyone. He gave up pretending nonchalance and started chewing on his thumbnail.

The doors to the catwalk flew open, and Roman stepped through. Raphael found himself staring at him. He was beautifully dressed in a soft gray Savile Row suit perfectly tailored to his tall, lean body. His long black hair was swept back from his face, tied with a black cord at the base of his neck. His nose was too hawkish to allow for handsome, but it didn't matter. He was imposing, his mere presence impressive, even without his opening his mouth. Business reporters loved him—his candor, his genius, his humility, feigned, naturally. He could charm the feathers off a lark if he was in the right mood.

He could also intimidate, scare a man to his bones if he wasn't happy.

Roman spied Raphael standing next to the railing, his face as white as the snow that occasionally fell in North Berwick. Contrary to expectation, he smiled when he grabbed Raphael's hand and pumped it, hard.

"Raphael, my old friend, how are you?"

"F-fine, sir. Ah, how was your flight?"

"I came up from London, so it was short. Walk with me." They started down the catwalk, toward the main stairs and into the auditorium, where there was a stage and microphone. Raphael ignored the hundreds of workers below, even though he felt their stares, heard their murmurs.

Roman clapped Raphael on the shoulder. "I suppose you know why I'm here, don't you?"

Here it comes. "Yes, sir, I do, and, sir, if I could just explain, tell you what's happened—"

They were still on the catwalk, high above the auditorium, Roman's hand square on Raphael's back. He leaned down, whispered, "It would be so simple, Raphael, to push you over the edge. It's a long way down. You'd have time to think about your massive failure on the way. But death would be too easy a punishment, wouldn't it? No, you're going to fix this mess internally, and remember my benevolence toward your egregious mistake. Aren't you?"

"Yes, sir. A moment. I have good news."

Roman stared down at his manager, an eyebrow up. "You have found some good news in this mess?"

"Someone put a hack into the hack, and now the malware itself is infected. It stopped the attack in its tracks. No one will have to pay ransomware. It happened only an hour ago. Sir, the threat has been eliminated."

This was a surprise. "Someone was better than Temora? You're telling me this person made Temora pull out completely?"

"Yes, sir. I don't know who did it, but I will have a name within the hour. I've tracked it through fifteen servers with our new tracking software. I know it came from a server north of London."

"Yes, yes, every time someone activates a Radulov VPN, we can trace every step they make. So, besides Temora, you're telling me we now have more people inside our servers?"

"Ah, yes, sir. It seems so, sir."

Roman took a breath through his nose and shut his eyes. Another as talented as Temora.

"As I said, sir, I'll have a name within the hour."

"Give it to me the moment you have it." Roman gestured to the stairs, a fresh grin on his swarthy face. "After you."

Raphael scrambled down, his boots ringing on the metal. Roman enjoyed watching Raphael squirm, watching him wonder what was going to happen to him. It gave him no small pleasure to have the power of life and death in his hands. That's what good computer code was at its heart, anyway, the lifeblood of the machine, the brains, the heart. Without it, the screens wouldn't light up, and humanity would be lost again.

Roman walked onto the stage, the flying Radulov falcon looming above him. He didn't say a word, simply stood, waiting. The entire room became silent as death, the only sound the quiet whirring of the air pumps, feeding in fresh oxygen.

When, at last, he spoke, his soft words carried throughout the vast auditorium. "I am very disappointed."

Dead silence.

The soft voice grew meditative. "A wolf entered our henhouse and created havoc. The name of the wolf is Caleb Temora, a name already known to many of you. He is a brilliant coder and worked extensively with me on MATRIX. You have also doubtless heard he was lost to us five years ago, to ISIS. I have no doubt this attack on MATRIX is his doing—there is no other who could do this amount of damage. His malware attack could have cost our clients billions of pounds, but Mr. Marquez has told me another hacker attacked Temora's hack and put a stop to it. Who this other person is, we will find out very soon. Regardless, even though he stopped Temora's hack and demands for ransomware, he could be as great an enemy.

"I had believed MATRIX invulnerable, but someone left a door open and allowed Temora in. Now every client, every computer, every software package in the world is vulnerable. We must do the right thing for our clients, and if that means we're working twenty-four/seven for the foreseeable future, so be it. There is no overtime"—there were several muffled groans, bold of the buggers, he thought, wished he knew who they were—"no, don't even think about complaining. We are going to take MATRIX apart. We are going to work relentlessly to find every last bit of malware in our systems. We are going to examine not only Temora's hack but also the other's hack as well. Then we are going to reengineer MATRIX to make it perfect, impervious to anyone who wishes us and our clients harm. I want sheer brilliance, and I will accept nothing less. No more ransomware attacks."

He paused a moment to build drama. "The one among you to find the problem source will receive a year's salary as a bonus."

Now the whole room was sitting on the edge of their seats.

"And the person who designs me a code that is truly impenetrable gets ten years' salary, equal to my salary. Are we clear?"

Audible gasps now. Raphael did some math,

felt his heart take off at a gallop. That was some-where near forty million pounds.

"Temora's hack of MATRIX makes us look bad. We need to make it clear to our customers that Radulov is stronger and more secure than ever, that MATRIX continues to be indispensable to their livelihoods. Now, get to work."

Roman gestured toward Raphael, and together they walked from the stage. Roman ignored the buzz of excitement coming from the floor. The of-fered bonus would get his people working harder than ever, gave them the hope of unimagined riches.

In the elevator, Roman fixed his dark eyes on Raphael. "I am increasing my efforts to find Temora. Even so, he should not have been able to get into MATRIX. This was done on your watch, Raphael. Should I fire you?"

"I would prefer to offer my resignation, sir."

Roman contemplated his manager. Fifteen years, and he'd done a spectacular job, no denying that fact. And this short, bespectacled little man was too good to lose, especially now. And Roman had to hand it to him: at least the man was looking him in the eye, even though Roman could smell his fear.

"No, I don't think so. That would be too easy. You will personally oversee this project, Raphael. You will repair and patch and fix MATRIX, and make sure every single client is up to date. You will ensure that MATRIX is made impenetrable. And you will give me the name of the one who stopped Temora's attack.

"I will track down Temora and shove code into his terrorist systems that will disable him and his compatriots forever."

Roman looked pensive, then said in his terrifying soft voice, "Do you understand what I will do to you if you fail?"

Raphael straightened, and Roman was struck again by the show of courage. Beaten but not broken. Good.

"Yes, sir. I won't disappoint you again. I swear it."

"See that you don't. Give me the name as soon as you find it. Now, I need updates on Project Cabal. Where do we stand?"

Raphael realized that was why he wasn't dead or ignominiously fired. *He needs me to keep track of the shipments.*

"Follow me, sir. The hanger is almost full. The shipments have been coming in regularly from your six building sites, and I've been handling the deliveries myself, no one else, like you said."

The hangar was ten minutes away. Raphael gave him updates as they walked. "The boats come in after dark, as you wanted, and the crates are unloaded by the boat's foreman himself. Then I move them here. I've been very careful."

The hangar doors opened. Inside was a small Cessna, retrofit for battle, with missiles and guns, stripped down so as not to over-weigh the plane, customizations Roman had designed himself. And behind the plane were endless stacks of crates, floor to ceiling. Only Roman knew what was inside. And of course, his supplier knew, but Raphael had no idea, no idea at all, unless—

His soft voice. "Have you ever opened one of these crates, Raphael?"

Raphael looked shocked. "Absolutely not, sir, I would never—"

"I believe you, Raphael. Now, I'm going to share a little secret with you. I'm sure you've wondered what's been coming in from my six building sites, so I'm going to tell you what's inside the crates. And you will understand the necessity for privacy and discretion."

Raphael's eyes bugged out of his head at Roman's next words.

CHAPTER NINE

Old Farrow Hall
Farrow-on-Gray, England

Mike had been gone only moments when Adam was back on Nicholas's screen again. "I spoke to Fourtnoy, and all is good. Nicholas, I ran a few quiet inquiries about the murdered men. What do you know about Heinrich Hemmler's background?"

"Very little. He wasn't on my radar until he was killed this morning. I was told he was supposed to talk to the prime minister this morning about loosening the numbers of refugees the U.K. will let in yearly. Not unexpected, and no reason for murder I can see."

"Hemmler's been a rather vocal opponent of Brexit, and, like the chancellor, believes shutting down the borders of the U.K. is going to hurt Germany. I also heard talk about streamlining an 'allies' program, where British and German citizens could pass through security without visas."

"Interesting. But again, hardly worth killing over. What about Chapman Donovan? He's a councilman from Northern Ireland, specifically Belfast West. Did you find a connection between the two men?"

"No, but I did turn up that Hemmler traveled to Northern Ireland last week and happened to see Chapman Donovan in a local meeting. Could be something to it. There was some talk about Donovan's loyalties, but nothing specific. Maybe I could get some inside information on both men that would shed some light."

"You mean the kind of information only the government would have?"

"Sensitive info, yes."

"Adam, no hacking into the Brit databases, you hear me? Anything else is fair game, but my father would have my head if I let you have a go at their servers. I can ask directly, politely, instead."

"You're no fun."

Nicholas said, "Mike thinks I'm a barrel of fun."

"Yeah, but she doesn't count."

Nicholas wasn't about to ask him why he thought she didn't count.

"Nicholas, moving right along to the really important discovery. My Spidey senses were tingling. No, not about the murders. No one's claiming responsibility for the ransomware attack, and that's weird. Even chatter in the dark web has been off. It feels bigger than an attempt to rake in the bitcoin to me, Nicholas." Adam swigged the last of his Red Bull. "It could very well be North Korea. You know they're convinced the U.S. is working with Britain to attack them, so they would want to know everything they could find out. Yeah, a bundle of bitcoins is good for their empty coffers if the ransomware attack had worked, but that wouldn't be their main objective. But this is: Nicholas, hang on to your hat. This is the biggie— I found evidence of keystroke analysis, and you know MATRIX is designed to kill intrusions like this. You and I stopped the ransomware attack easily, but with the keystroke analysis, it could mean all government servers could be compromised."

Nicholas stroked his chin. He needed a shave. "So this nation state, like North Korea, or a powerful private citizen, wants to spy inside these computers, wants to know what these computers are saying to each other."

"Yes, and with keystroke analysis, as you know, the hackers are able to read emails, files, transactions, data, everything."

Nicholas said, "If this is the case, it means every computer running MATRIX is at risk, whether there's been a ransomware hack or not. Good discovery, Adam. You just might have saved the world."

Adam said, "A warning should be sent out. This needs to be made public."

"No announcement yet, Adam. Let's find out what we're dealing with first."

Adam, not even drinking age, was cynical to the bone. "Not that Radulov would want this to go public in our lifetime, like Yahoo! not saying a word when they'd been hacked."

Nicholas scrubbed a hand across his face. "I'll speak with my father right away, then head to London to examine the servers myself. You get on the plane—I'll call Clancy and Trident, get them geared up. I want you on the ground with me at MI5. If MATRIX itself is compromised, well, we'll see."

Adam brightened. "Only me? I get to fly in the plane alone?"

"Since Agent Houston is already here in London on vacation, doubtless squiring about my long-time family friend Melinda St. Germaine, yes, you'll have the airplane to yourself."

"Hey, she's the woman Ben got to know when he was there researching her mother's papers about the Koaths, right?"

"Yes." Nicholas grinned. "Don't drink all the champagne in the plane's fridge."

But Adam was already gone.

CHAPTER TEN

The knowledge of the falconer must . . .
extend to the countryside and to the game he
wishes his hawk to catch.
—Emma Ford, *Falconry: Art and Practice*

The Old Garden
Twickenham
Richmond upon Thames, London

Back home, Roman threw open the doors to the mews. His cast of five falcons turned in unison toward their master, beaks clacking in welcome. Nothing made him happier than this ritual—feeding his birds, checking their wings, their talons, making sure they were in perfect condition, ready to hunt at a moment's notice. He missed them when he had to leave; his travel was hard on them all. Falcons needed attending. Soon it would be time for them to molt, and it would be quiet and lonely in the mews.

"Hello, my lovelies. My beautiful cabal. Daddy's home. Do you want your blood this morning? Are you ready for another glorious day?"

His two eagles, Victoria and James, sat in the loft, away from his falcons, silent, ever watching, bored and haughty, above the petting and cooing the falcons thrived on. The falcons were of varying ages and breeds, from the tiny female saker who kept to herself in the corner to the larger blue-gray peregrines, and the lone gyrfalcon, huge, beautiful, imposing as an emperor.

His falcons were Clifford, Arlington, Buckingham, Ashley, and Lauderdale, named after King Charles II's group of advisers back in the seventeenth century, ruthless schemers all, thus the name *cabal* was coined. He thought it was funny, since his cabal did his dirty work just as the king's advisers had done so long ago.

Normally, the birds would never be able to stay together, in a single, huge mews, and unhooded, not without grave consequences, but Roman's cast was special. He had a connection with them that went deeper than the usual falcon-falconer relationship, and that connection extended throughout the cast. They were working birds; they had jobs to do and took their work seriously. It couldn't be said they were friends, but Roman knew they had a professional respect for one another.

He pulled on the gauntlet, whistled to Arlington, who was on his fist in a flash and flurry, accepting his offering of a grouse neck. He only fed them blooded meat three times a week, to keep them all at the perfect flying weight.

He repeated this process through the whole cast—they had manners, waited for their turns—until everyone was fed, and while he did, he told them of the day's news.

"Soon I will have the name of the person who stopped Temora's ransomware attack. Yes, he could be as big an enemy. When I find out his name and know what he wants, I will develop a plan." He sighed, stroked Arlington's feathers. "Only Temora would know how to find a weakness in MATRIX and break in." He fluffed her wing, and she nipped his hand in affection.

Roman accepted bird after bird on the gauntlet, cooing, loving, and they loved him back. They would do anything for him, and he knew it.

"Ah, the kill this morning was perfect. Radu could not have done a better job. Hemmler, that miserable terrorist shite, died with his lips pulled back from his teeth and terror in the whites of his eyes. Only a single trail of blood went down his fat neck, so red, so fresh, almost too small to notice, but I saw it, and I thought of you, lovelies, how you would cause the same sort of wound with a well-placed talon.

"Soon, my lovelies, soon, it will be time for you to fly free over the city and report back to me.

But not today. Today, we will hunt and you will again dine on precious blood."

He worked on their furniture, cut jesses—the supple leather growing warm in his hands— unpacked a new shipment of hoods, American made, the leather ultra-light, perfect for travel. The mews was a cozy place, his favorite in the world. His cabal not only stayed together, they also hunted together, shared the meat from a kill. They were family—predators, all.

As he worked, Joshua Bell played softly in the background. "Nocturne no. 20," a perfect accompaniment to the light rain pattering against the windowpanes. When the rain stopped, they would hunt. The birds sat on their cadges, enjoying his company, heads cocked as if listening to the music.

A low male voice called quietly, "Sir."

Roman stilled. Iago knew never to interrupt when he was tending to the cabal. The falcons turned at Iago's voice, sudden tension filling the room, as if they, too, knew this was forbidden, and would willingly take a bite of still living, breathing flesh.

Roman didn't turn, kept smoothing down Buckingham's feathers. "What?"

Iago, the keeper of secrets for the Ardelean family for more than thirty years, knew the penalties for interrupting, but there was no choice. "It is Radu, sir. He requires your attention."

"Can you not see I am taking care of the cast?"

"Sir, Radu expressed a level of urgency with his request."

At this, Roman turned from Buckingham, eyes narrowed. "What's wrong?"

"He's upset—pacing, moaning, pulling at his hair. He only calmed when I told him I would fetch you immediately."

"Very well." He said softly to his cabal, "Stay calm, I will be back shortly. Iago, you will remain with them. Take care, I hope you will not become another course in their dinner."

Iago swallowed and nodded. He looked at the birds, knew he couldn't show fear. They would smell it on him, like sweat from a pore, and attack. Would they like the taste of him as well as the grouse necks? Probably so. He imagined his master had trained them to like the taste of human blood. He held perfectly still and began telling them stories of ancient times in Romania, in a calm soothing voice, their own Scheherazade.

Roman walked quickly through the long hallways toward his brother's rooms. He'd chosen this setting with both his twin brother and the cabal in mind. It was Radu's refuge and a southern command post for the cast. It sat on the River Thames, with sweeping grounds and gardens to allow the falcons to fly free as often as possible, and private enough for Radu to occasionally sit in the sun in his small garden.

It was a palatial home and built to Roman's

exact specifications, in the Palladian style. Radu had named it the Old Garden, surely an odd name, but Roman hadn't cared. This wasn't Roman's only home, but it was his favorite. It also provided him a bolt-hole near London, should the need ever arise.

His estate in Northampton, on the River Nene, in Billing, was sprawling and old, magnificent really, but Roman preferred London to the country, unless he wished to make a spectacular hunt—the cabal, the dogs, the drones whipping through the skies over the rabbit-laden hedges, it was a reward for them all.

He turned toward Radu's wing of the house. Unlike Roman's private quarters done up in his favorite bloodred, Radu's were plain and simply furnished with very little color, all neutral grays and light blues. Anything to keep Radu calm, to keep him comfortable. Radu's happiness was more important to Roman than anything, and anyone, even his cabal.

His ex-wife could attest to that. He shoved the brief thought of Leanne away and ignored the other image that came to mind, the bundled infant he hadn't seen in four years. They made him question himself and his choices in the dark of the night, when his mind relaxed in the moments before sleep. But such questions made him weak, and weakness was not acceptable.

Nothing, no one, was more important than Radu.

Radu's second-floor suite was designed as a large flat, with a separate kitchen and dining room, a marble bath and two bedrooms—though Radu rarely slept—a sitting area—though he rarely used it—and his computers. The western wall of the main living space was a liquid crystal screen, curved inward slightly, so high-end the technology wasn't available outside of military installations. Few countries had the money to afford even a small screen of the material. Radu's computer took up a ten-foot-by-twenty-foot area on the wall. It was a living, breathing, networked connection to the great world beyond, the mediator to the world Radu couldn't face himself.

The floor above was Radu's lab, a quiet place of white and metal, whirring machines, and antiseptic smells. His specialty was genetics. If he'd bothered with formal schooling, he'd be recognized as a leading expert in the field.

Radu was special, in so many ways. Early on, various doctors had diagnosed him with an uncommon derivative autism or an unusual sort of Asperger's, or even a form of partial seizure disorder, none of which meant anything to Roman or Radu. But everything had changed when one psychiatrist had placed his brother in front of a computer for the first time. In the virtual world, Radu flew like Roman's falcons. He was skilled, his genius clear. He was omnipotent, he was a god.

Radu didn't like to speak in English or Romanian. He usually communicated with Roman in their twin talk, the brothers' special language the two had been speaking since they were babies, probably in the womb. Even Iago had no idea what they were saying, and he had been with the family for decades and with the twins for the better part of their lives. In their twin talk, Radu was fluent, verbal, well-spoken.

When Roman arrived at his twin's suite of rooms, he saw Radu pacing along the edge of the great room, clearly upset, slapping his palms to his head and keening, a frightening, lost sound.

Roman was at his brother's side in an instant, his hand on his shoulder to stop his pacing. "Radu, look at me. What is wrong?"

Radu felt his brother's strong hand on his arm and was reassured. He looked at his brother, saw his worry, his limitless love for him, and wished again Roman could stay with him all the time, though he understood that wasn't at all possible. Roman was the face of their company, he was seen as the genius of Radulov Industries, the world's premier cybersecurity firm. Roman was the one who sat down with heads of state, heads of governments, CEOs of companies and explained Radulov's incredible operating system MATRIX, which not only connected them to the world but also protected them.

Until Temora's attack this morning.

Roman would laugh as he talked about these meetings and tell him over and over that it was he, Radu, who was Radulov's heart, its blood, its very life force. He and he alone was the center of Radulov, the creator of MATRIX. It was Radu who wrote the code his brother designed.

Radu felt calm flow through him, and he turned and pointed to the computer screen. "Look, Roman."

It was then Roman saw a small flashing white skull and bones. It was Radu's danger signal.

It meant more trouble ahead.

CHAPTER ELEVEN

Ancient artworks illustrating falconry date back at least 3,500 years to ancient Mesopotamia and Mongolia. While historically falconry was an elite and male-dominated activity, we have records of several notable women enjoying the hobby, including Queen Elizabeth I, Catherine the Great of Russia, and Mary, Queen of Scots.

—*Smithsonian* Magazine

Roman kept his voice low and calm. "What is it, brother? What's happened?"

"They know," Radu whispered in their twin tongue. "They know about the drone that killed Hemmler. It was spotted."

Roman blew out a relieved breath. He'd feared Radu would tell him Temora had managed to do more damage. "Don't worry, Radu, it's easily managed. They can't trace it back to us."

"You do not understand. I monitored a call to the Metropolitan Police after the attack. One of the policemen there—Penderley is his name—he discussed the case with that Brit FBI agent, Drummond, you know, the one whose father—"

"Drummond? That prick?" Roman felt a punch of anger, then brushed it away like lint from his suit coat. "Be calm. Listen to me: Drummond will not find us. We are safe. You are safe, Radu. I will always keep you safe."

"I have a very bad feeling, Roman. Send Arlington to follow Drummond. She needs to watch him, see what he does—"

"No, no, there is no need to panic simply because some overgrown schoolboy who thinks he knows how to use a computer is aware of the drone. You know how to shield us from him. There is no reason for Arlington to leave the mews."

But despite his calm, his reassurance, Radu again began wringing his hands, pulling on his dirty hair, pacing, pacing. Then he whirled around. "Word came to you from Scotland. Raphael pinpointed the location of the attack that stopped the malware hack. It came from Farrow-on-Gray, from Drummond's house. He is much more than a prick, Roman—he has our scent, he knows about the drone killing Hemmler."

Roman was shaking his head, but Radu grabbed his arm. "We must eliminate Drummond immediately. He's going to London today, meeting with his father. If we stop him now, we can stay safe. Promise me, Roman, promise me you'll deal with him. Now."

Roman eyed his twin. Dark hair oily, too long, his skin practically translucent from being indoors so much. Was he wearing the same Police *Synchronicity* tour T-shirt and jeans he'd been wearing for the past several days? Roman would speak with Iago. This wouldn't do. Iago was indulgent with Radu, too indulgent.

Kill Nicholas Drummond?

It was a good thought. Without Drummond at its head, that ridiculous private team the FBI allowed him to put together would fall apart. But even Roman had to admit having him operating on European soil again was dangerous. And now he'd stopped the malware attack in its tracks, put his own code into the mix, and he was also aware of the drone—Roman leaned on the edge of a cabinet, crossed his arms. "Suppose you're right," he said slowly, "how would we do it? Send a Night Hawk?"

Radu's smile bloomed bright as a child's. "Wouldn't you want to do it yourself?"

He hated to dim his brother's smile, but—"I might draw too much attention, though a few drops of the special medicine in his drink would save us a lot of headaches. No, I'm sorry, Radu, I believe a strike would be easier."

Radu nodded. "He will not expect an attack. Eliminate him before he reaches London. It is something I feel strongly about."

Still Roman was undecided.

"Roman, they are closing in. I can feel it here." He smacked the side of his head. "And there is more. The latest dispatches from the Security Services show all their passwords are being changed hourly. They are putting new firewalls into place because of the ransomware attack this morning."

Roman shrugged. "It's not a problem. If I, the head of Radulov, go personally to Security Services and tell them I've come to them to install a new patch on their servers because of the malware attack, I will ensure we continue to receive all needful information."

He took his twin's hands between his. "Trust me, Radu, MI5 and MI6 have no idea who they're dealing with. Once we close off all paths into MATRIX, no one else, including Temora, will ever be able to compromise us again. I promise. Please don't worry."

Radu stubbornly shook his head. "Kill Drummond."

"I will consider it. Now, I want you to shower and allow Iago to cut your hair and make you presentable. You've entombed yourself in these rooms far too long. Tomorrow, after lunch, you and I shall go for a walk. We'll watch the cabal fly. Would you like that?"

"Don't speak to me as if I'm five years old, Roman. I don't want to cut my hair, and I don't care to see your vermin fly. We have more important tasks ahead. Speaking of Temora, you know he is as dangerous as Drummond. We must find him and cut off his head."

"I plan to."

Radu gave him a sly look that surprised Roman. "Kill Drummond and I swear I will find Temora for you."

Roman didn't immediately answer, and Radu stalked out of the room, to his kitchen. Roman followed, nodded toward the cooler he saw sitting on the granite countertop. "Have you run the Romanian's blood?"

"Not yet. How much more have I to do?" Radu turned away from his brother and busied himself with a glass, ran water through the HEPA filter, drank it down, slowly. Roman didn't like being ignored. He fought the urge to yell at his brother, but yelling would send Radu back into his silent shell, for who knew how long. As Radu had grown older, as they both had grown more dedicated, the littlest things sometimes set him off. They must remain united. They must. As if there weren't enough on their plates, he knew they both had to focus on curing Radu's illness. It was the most critical goal of Roman's life. He wanted this precious being, this genius with death always lurking in the shadows near him, to be healthy again. He no longer wanted him to fear that a simple cut could cause him to bleed to death. If only he responded to medical treatments, but he never had.

He said, "Very well, Radu. Send Drummond's tracking information to my mobile. And send this morning's video feed while you're at it. I want to see that treacherous German die all over again. He received his just desserts, like Donovan. I told Barstow I did him a favor, which he well knows. Today was supposed to be my payday, a billion pounds, but Barstow said the Money want their drones first. He'll get them in line, or all of them will regret it. He swears he'll talk them around. He told me tomorrow. Do I believe him? We'll see." He shook his head. "If only we could find Temora, drop a bomb on his cursed head."

Radu drank more water, wiped his hand over his mouth. "Temora's off-grid entirely. There's been no sign of him anywhere for the past month. But I'll find him, Roman."

"Then he's moved out of Aleppo and is working elsewhere. As soon as I've made my special upgrades on the servers, we'll know again everything MI5 and MI6 know."

As Roman walked back to the mews, he realized Radu was right. He hadn't been sure about killing Drummond, but now he knew it was the best move. He hated to admit it, but Drummond was too smart. He was relentless. He and his partner, Caine, could cause him headaches he didn't need right now. Very well.

He turned back to Radu's suite. Radu was still

in the kitchen, staring down at the Romanian's blood on the countertop.

"Caine is going with Drummond this morning, yes? To London?"

"Yes."

"Prepare a drone. But not a Night Hawk, we need to make this hit less subtle. We will take both him and Caine out on the A14, once he's past Newmarket. Use an Aire Drone. We need a final test run of the technology anyway."

Radu smiled and nodded. "Yes, Brother."

"Be sure you follow with a distraction to draw attention well away from us. When they're gone, I want there to be no question who was behind their deaths."

"Who shall we blame?"

"I'm feeling very uncharitable toward the North Koreans, as is the rest of the world. But the Irish are a better choice. Drummond took out an entire cell of the IRA a few months back. It stands to reason they'd hold a grudge. After Donovan's death, I'm sure they're on alert."

"Yes, that is good. I will take care of it."

"Be careful, Radu. We can't have this coming back to us."

"I understand, Brother."

CHAPTER TWELVE

Old Farrow Hall
Farrow-on-Gray, England

Mike showered, dressed, put her hair in a clip, and got lost only once finding her way from the east side of Old Farrow Hall to Nicholas's study on the west side. She walked in to hear Nicholas speaking on his cell. Who was he talking to?

"Yes, I've released Grandfather's servers from the ransomware attack, and, in so doing, we believe we've discovered a bigger problem. Father, I hate to tell you this, but I believe the servers at both the Home and Foreign Office have been compromised. I need Adam here to do a full sweep of the Security Services' servers. Yes, both MI5 and MI6."

Harry Drummond had been called back to London the day before, some sort of important Brexit meeting with the home secretary. Nicholas saw Mike and put his cell on speaker. She heard his father say clearly, "Nicholas, you know those servers are carefully monitored. In fact, after the malware attack this morning, we immediately set the servers to change passwords every hour. We're taking every precaution."

Nicholas said, "If MATRIX is compromised on one machine, it could be compromised on all of them. As I said, Adam is flying over, and we'd like to take a look personally at the servers. I'm glad to hear you took such measures so quickly. It's smart, but it's still not enough. There's more, Father. We're looking for possible ties between Hemmler and Donovan. Is there anything you can tell me, off the record?"

Mike heard silence, then, "This isn't an appropriate conversation for us to be having."

"So you're already pursuing this angle."

"Those were not my words."

Nicholas looked at Mike, said slowly, "Do you know if they were involved in some sort of plot, or were they targeted separately? Is there something in your files that ties the two together?"

Harry's voice became more clipped. "We have no reason to believe the vice chancellor of Germany was doing anything illegal, or immoral. Nor Donovan. Again, this isn't an appropriate conversation."

"Except they're both dead. Murdered, Hemmler, moments before a meeting with the prime minister, Donovan taken out in front of his home.

What were these men doing? If you'd let me look at their files, examine the servers—"

His father said with finality, "You do not have the clearance to see any of this information, nor are you part of our investigative services any longer."

"Mike and I are heading to London shortly, surely we can talk—"

"No, we most certainly cannot. I will pass along your concerns. Now, I will see you at the weekend."

And then Mike understood. She held up a hand, called out, "Hello, Mr. Drummond. Mike here. It would be lovely to have dinner with you this evening at Drummond House."

Mike heard silence from his father, then, "Very well. Half six and don't be late." And he rang off.

Nicholas smiled at her. "Well done."

"I realized he simply couldn't talk to you. The phones aren't secure, and there were probably people around."

"Yes. And you know as well as I do he'll let us know what's up at dinner. I wonder if there is a link between the two." He stood. "I'm sorry about cutting our holiday short, but we'll come back as soon as this is resolved."

Mike wrapped her arms around his waist, looked up at him, eyes alight with excitement. "Sorry? Nicholas, the game's afoot. I'll race you to the car."

"The game is always afoot for us. Let me tell

my mother and talk her out of coming with us. Oh, and I'm going to update Savich. Let him know what's going on. Get packed, and I'll meet you at the drive in twenty minutes."

"Tell S and S I said hello."

Nicholas watched her nearly dance out of his office. She was an excitement junkie, just like him. He was a lucky, lucky man.

He dialed Savich. "Sorry to bother you, but I need to run something by you."

"Let me get Sherlock on the phone, too—all right, here she is."

He filled them in, and they listened without interruptions, until Sherlock said, "Wait. Let me get this straight. Your theory is the victims were already being investigated by Security Services, and you think someone may have hacked the Security Services' databases and gained this knowledge? Nicholas, the Security Services' servers are the most secure in the world, as secure as ours."

Savich laughed. "Sweetheart, both Nicholas and I—and don't forget Adam Pearce—all of us could hack their databases."

"Yeah, yeah, you're all geek gods."

Nicholas laughed. "That's good, Sherlock, I'll have to tell Adam."

She continued, "But the real question is, how would someone outside know to hack the databases to find these specific names in the first place? Or are classified documents being leaked? Either way, if someone is murdering people Security Services are investigating, you do have a serious problem."

"Yes," Nicholas said. "We need to find out why these two were being investigated. You know about the massive malware attack Adam and I stopped this morning. And remember, Parliament was attacked head-on back in June." He paused a moment. "I'm thinking perhaps this goes deeper than we think."

"Deeper, what do you mean?"

"It's all coordinated with another purpose at the core of it—what, I don't know. Yet. But I'll keep you updated with what Mike and I discover."

Savich said, "Please do. I'll pass this along to the president's team. Keep us posted."

CHAPTER THIRTEEN

Nicholas cruised his Beemer down the long lime-tree-covered drive to the country road. Mike turned in her seat to look back at Old Farrow Hall glistening under the sun, the wildly blooming front gardens, and off to the side, the tall, thick bushes that formed the labyrinth. Could there be a more perfect place on this earth?

"That was fast-talking to get your mom to stay here and not jump in the car."

"Anytime I can outtalk her, I deserve a medal. She's too smart."

"I don't know how, but she said she knew we could be up to something dangerous. And the look she gave me, Nicholas, like I'd better step in front of a bullet if it came your way. Hopefully she was reassured I am your personal dragon slayer."

His personal dragon slayer? He liked the sound of that. He thought again of Lake Trasimeno, her near drowning, and swallowed.

Mike fastened her seat belt. "Your mom could give my mom a run for her money. Did I tell you the Gorgeous Rebecca acted at university?" She paused. "Wow, I said it like a Brit. Okay, she once played Petruchio's Kate. I don't know if it was her talent that made her so amazing or the fact that one look at her and every man in the vicinity fell to his knees. I told you my dad's been in love with your mom since her TV show? Well, turns out the Gorgeous Rebecca loves her, too, says she wants to have high tea with her at Browns in London."

He laughed. Nicholas had yet to meet the Gorgeous Rebecca, but he'd seen photos of her. She was a heart-stopper, no question about that. His own mother's beauty was different, more whimsical, perhaps, he wasn't certain.

Nicholas navigated the Beemer through the small town of Farrow-on-Gray and turned south onto the highway.

Once they were on the A14, Mike said, "I like to watch you drive, especially on the wrong side of the car and the wrong side of the road."

He shot her a grin. "Do you now?"

"Yes. Very capable, very steady at the helm." She gave him a wicked grin. "All in all, you handle most things quite well."

A black brow went up. "Only 'quite well,' not, say, perfectly?"

"Well, there does seem to be a small tendency to get us nearly killed. But hey, usually not more than once a week. I can deal with once a week."

"Ah. Well, Agent Caine, I will do my best not to get us dead on the drive to Westminster."

"Hey, be super careful. It's been longer than a week." And oddly, she suddenly felt a chill and fiddled with the air conditioner, turned it down a notch. "Nicholas, do you really think MI5 and MI6 were hacked? And if they were, the idea someone might be using that information to find targets, even to assassinate them, feels out of control to me."

"I agree. I do think they've been compromised, yes. Whether from inside or out, someone is accessing information they shouldn't have. But don't worry, we'll—"

There was a heavy thud against the side of the car, and Mike's window exploded, spraying glass all over her.

CHAPTER FOURTEEN

Nicholas could see there was an exit ahead in a few hundred feet. He floored the car, whipped off onto a tree-lined country road, shouting, "Get down, get down! Don't you dare get shot!"

Mike had already flattened herself against the seat. "I'm okay, lots of glass shards, but only pricks, nothing major, no blood, no pain, no bullet wounds."

The road was thankfully empty of traffic. Mike came back up on the seat and looked back. All she saw was country road.

"Did you see the shooter?"

"No, they must have been on the A14, and there's no one behind us."

Nicholas checked in the rearview mirror. Nothing. "We must have kicked the hornet's nest.

Mike, there's a gun in the glove box. Wherever the shooter is, you know he's coming back. When he does, take him out."

They were hit with another barrage of bullets.

"More bloody hornets! Hold on, Mike." He wrenched the wheel to the right, and the car started to spin. He looked grim, hard, but there was no panic. More bullets, but none struck the car, it was weaving around too fast.

Mike grabbed the Glock out of the glove box and twisted in her seat, aiming out the shattered window with her right hand, her left holding her steady. She looked behind them, to the sides, didn't see anything. "I don't understand. Nicholas, there's no one here," and then she looked up and saw it—a drone flying above them.

"Crap, it's a drone. Hold the car steady, hold it steady."

He slowly brought the car around until they were once again straight on the road.

Immediately, more shots. Nicholas gunned the gas again, and the Beemer leaped forward. The shots kept on coming, ripping into the side panels.

There was a moment's pause in the gunfire. Mike ignored the shards of glass and pushed herself up on the edge of the window, leaned out. She sighted the Glock, and her father's words came clear in her mind. *Trace the path, pull the trigger, once, twice.* It was tough to site, the drone was only about two feet in length, but she did it. She missed.

There was a flash of gunfire from the drone, and she ducked back into the car, a bullet pinging not two inches from her head. Nicholas yanked the wheel to the right, and she tumbled, hit her shoulder hard against the gearshift, and yipped. "I'm okay, I'm okay." The moment the bullets stopped, she was hanging out the window again, tracing the path, tracing the path, shooting upward. This time, with the third bullet, she hit the drone. She saw a trail of black smoke and watched the drone swallowtail out of the sky.

She pumped her fist. "Yes! Nicholas, I got it!"

Nicholas slowed. They heard the drone slam into the ground some twenty feet off to their left.

When Nicholas had backed up and they were out of the car, Mike said, "I was expecting a small fireball, maybe some burning bushes or grass, but there's nothing."

"No," he said, "nothing, only a dead death machine. Great shooting, my girl." He cursed. "You're bleeding." His fingers wiped away a trickle of blood making its way down her neck, seeping onto her white shirt.

Mike felt the base of her skull. Her fingers came away wet. "No, don't worry, not much blood. I think it's a cut from the window glass when it exploded." She grabbed his hand. "I'm all right, Nicholas. Now, how about you? That was some driving, by the way." And she whispered a prayer.

"What?"

"I'm thanking my dad. He taught me how to hit a moving target. Now, answer me, are you okay?"

"I'm mad as hell, is what I am, but my body's intact."

She saw the rage in his eyes, a killing rage. *Calm down, calm down.* She said, her voice matter-of-fact, "Let's go get a look at that drone."

Several cars were pulling over now, a few people getting out to see what was going on, but Nicholas waved them off. He shouted, "Thanks, we're fine. I've called the police."

Once alone, they walked through the tall grass until they found the crash site.

Nicholas put a hand on her arm. "Stay here. I want to make sure the thing isn't still capable of shooting or blowing up on us."

"Nicholas, forget it. I'm the one with the Glock, although how a gun would save us might be in question."

He wanted to argue but gave it up. They slowly circled the drone. The twin engines were still smoking from Mike's bullets. The drone was slightly tipped, and they saw a bullet hole through the small camera mounted inside the base of the fuselage.

Nicholas said, "Whoever was driving the drone can't see anything now, not with a bullet in the camera. Great shot, Mike."

"Great piece of luck. Think maybe it has a self-destruct mechanism?"

"It could, and wouldn't that be diabolical?" He poked about a bit, then straightened. "Okay, it looks pretty dead to me. We need to take this thing apart."

"I hope it'll lead us to whoever tried to kill us." Saying the words aloud spiked his rage. She saw it, grabbed him around his neck and squeezed him tight. He buried his face in her hair, felt a small shard of glass and felt more rage pound through him. Then her voice, light, nearly laughing, "Now, Nicholas, don't forget, it's been more than a week since our last adventure, so don't go all mushy on me."

He drew a deep, calming breath and pressed his forehead to hers. "Yes, you're right. Now, I have no intention of putting this thing in the boot and driving it down to London. I'm calling Penderley. He can handle it."

Mike listened with half an ear as he explained what had happened to Penderley. She knew the fallow field they stood in would soon be overrun by a Scotland Yard forensic team, or a drone team. Was there any such thing yet?

Who was trying to kill them? How did they know where they'd be? How did they even know she and Nicholas had poked the hornet's nest?

We're being watched.

She pulled out her phone. Her last call was two days ago; she'd spoken to her parents, telling them she and Nicholas had arrived at Old Farrow Hall. That was it.

Nicholas punched off. "Penderley is sending a special group to deal with the drone." He stared off into space a moment and said slowly, as if reading her mind, something he did entirely too often, "Whoever sent this drone has access to us, our phones, the computers. How else would they know to send something after us when we were only assigned the case this morning?"

"I haven't made any calls since we arrived. But you have, Nicholas, to Savich, then to your dad, an hour ago."

"Bloody hell, you're right. Someone could have tapped the phones at the Home Office, no other way to find us."

He took the battery out of his mobile, tossed it toward the car. Mike followed suit. They walked a good distance from the smoking drone. Twenty steps later, he said quietly, "Mike, we have to assume whoever is behind these attacks can only hear when we're directly communicating, so we'll accept everything electronic is compromised. Not only keystrokes, they might very well have audio, as well."

"We're talking someone with a lot of money, probably a lot of power, as well, Nicholas. That drone—how much do you think it cost to build?" She felt her neck again, no more blood. She pulled another small shard of glass from her hair.

He raised his hand, worked another piece out of her ponytail. "We're going to make sure we can't be overheard discussing this from now on."

She leaned up, whispered, "Let's have meetings in the park like spies."

He pictured Hyde Park, the two of them huddled on a bench on the banks of the Serpentine. "Good idea. Now, as I see it, the problem is, if they've penetrated the Security Services' firewalls, they can certainly access the CCTV and watch where we go. Your glasses are crooked."

"But why are they so scared of us? I mean, they came after us within two hours." She took off her glasses, blew on the lenses, wiped them off on her shirt, straightened each temple, set them back on her nose. "Okay, good?"

He cupped her chin in his palm, studied her face, her ratty ponytail. "Yes, glasses straight, perfect. Do you think our reputation has preceded us?"

She snorted, then frowned. "Well, you did save the president's life—that was pretty big news—and we know it leaked out that you saved Washington, D.C., from a Godzilla-size tsunami. You think maybe someone's trying to get even, for whatever reason?"

That didn't sound right, but Nicholas didn't say anything. The people involved in orchestrating those two affairs were all dead.

Nicholas walked around the drone, studying

it, while Mike studied the sky. Nothing, only rolling white clouds.

"Nicholas, why? What could we possibly know this soon? You know this could happen again."

He whispered in her ear, "Because whoever is behind this doesn't even want us nibbling around the edges. We know now for certain my father's been hacked, which means all the Security Services have been, as well. How deep does it go?"

Mike whispered back, "Their operating system is MATRIX, installed worldwide. Are you assuming MATRIX has been completely compromised? Okay, go with me on this. If yes, then it's possible, isn't it, that our FBI servers have been hacked?"

He nodded, continued in a near whisper, "Which means when I spoke to Savich and Sherlock this morning, I could have compromised them, as well. I'm going to have to find a secure method of communication with them, with the team."

She stared down at the still-smoking drone. "Nicholas, we haven't been hacked, more like we've been infiltrated. Who can breach the phones and computers of the most secretive organizations in the world?"

"Like you said, someone with a lot of money, someone powerful, someone who can infiltrate MATRIX." He took her right hand in his, ran a finger over the callus between her thumb and fore-finger, built up spending years on the range. "Remind me to thank your dad when I meet him. You shoot brilliantly."

"That's what I tell my dad. When I was a kid, we'd trek off into the wilderness to this remote range and shoot for hours until I was so tired I could barely hold my shotgun. Then he started me on rifles. Finally, I graduated to handguns. I got pretty good. He loved to show me off to his friends. And don't change the subject."

Before he could answer her, a distant siren grew louder.

CHAPTER FIFTEEN

The Voynich manuscript: **A mysterious, undeciphered manuscript dating to the 15th or 16th century.**
> —Beinecke Rare Book and Manuscript
> Library, Yale University

British Museum
Great Russell Street
Bloomsbury, London

The cab pulled to the curb with a screech, throwing Roger Bannen forward. He looked at his watch. He was late. He quickly paid the driver and bounded out of the cab without a receipt. He'd deal with the expense report later.

He ran into the building and took the grand stairs into the foyer at a dead run. He hit his shoulder on the door as he entered, dropped his notebook, and tripped over his brolly trying to pick it up. He ignored the amused looks from the people nearby.

Would this day ever go right? He'd woken late—not his fault, his alarm clock was on the fritz—his coffeemaker had spit grounds into the carafe instead of coffee, and he'd stepped on the cat's tail to get at the pot before it boiled over onto the floor. He felt like a fool, he, one of the *Sun's* best reporters. Well, he could be if he didn't screw up. Maybe.

He gathered his things, looked up, and cursed once. The hall was full of reporters, some talking on their mobiles, others fiddling with the cameras and lights. What were they all doing here? This was his chance to get the boss's notice. He had no idea what the topic of the press briefing was, only what Molly the stringer, a former girlfriend, had told him when she'd called his desk. "British Museum, rare discovery, special briefing, Rog, get yourself there at noon, could be a big story."

Bless Molly's heart. But how was he going to get an exclusive, with everyone else already here? And then it hit him. Everyone else had received the same call. From Molly? His Molly? Bollocks.

Roger pushed his way toward the middle of the reporters so he could see the head of the antiquities department, Dr. Persepolis Wynn-Jones, Persy, Roger had heard his friends called him. He was at the top of the stairs talking to a pretty young woman beside him, holding a laptop to her chest. *Intern*, he thought, dismissing her. So where were the big guns? Still, whatever this was all about, Dr. Wynn-Jones was a friend of Roger's mother, so maybe he'd be willing to share a special tidbit with Roger after the briefing.

He fell in beside a few reporters he knew. "What's this all about, you lot?"

Three heads turned, a few grins, a few frowns. Todd Benedict, who believed himself to be blindingly brilliant, shook his head. "No one knows anything, Rog. How's, ah, tricks at the *Sun*?"

"All's well, all's well." *You toffee-nosed ass.* "You still a stand out at the *Guardian*? Hey, maybe we could grab a pint after." If he still had a bleeding job at the end of this day of disasters. "Oh, here we go."

Dr. Wynn-Jones made his way to the landing, tapped the microphone three times to gather attention, then smiled at the gathered crowd.

"Thank you for coming on such short notice. We have a very exciting announcement, and we will be passing out supplemental papers to give you the full background on our newest find. Trust me when I say it's capital." Roger watched Persy's eyes land on him, and Persy broke into a grin and nodded to him. Roger smiled back at the crazy old corker. Crazy like a fox, but still.

Dr. Wynn-Jones studied the hungry faces a moment, knowing they'd heard fantastical things about this briefing but had no idea. He wasn't going to disappoint today. The library often made discoveries, but this one was going to change the world, he could feel it in his bones.

"It's very exciting, very exciting indeed. As many of you know, we are sometimes very lucky in our discoveries, and today's news is no different. I am talking about an inestimable treasure, one we will be spending a significant amount of time and energy on going forward. And so, I present to you Dr. Isabella Marin, our very own Oxford doctor of cryptology and our foremost expert in the Voynich manuscript. She will present our most exciting discovery. Dr. Marin? The floor is yours." And he gave her a royal bow.

The Voynich? Roger couldn't believe it. He stared at the young woman he'd believed of no importance. Well, she was as beautiful as a bloody foreign princess, dark sloe eyes, gold complexion. She had something to do with the Voynich? What had she found? Roger couldn't believe his luck.

Dr. Isabella Marin squared her shoulders, took a deep breath, and told her heaving stomach to calm down, it wouldn't do to honk all over the mass of reporters staring up at her. She knew her boss was having the time of his life—put him in front of a microphone and an audience, and he positively bloomed. It was said, not within his hearing, of course, that he'd never met a microphone he didn't like. But now he was giving her a chance to make her name in both the cryptology and antique manuscript world. Granted, she was presenting the find, but his presence beside her showed substance and gravitas to the world.

Still, there were so many cameras. Had any of these reporters ever even heard of the Voynich?

I hope this works, mixing truth and lies.

Her boss waved her to the mic. She walked out onto the stage, her laptop still clutched as tight as a newborn to her chest, and wondered for the twentieth time if she should have worn panty hose as a sign of respect. But then the mic was in her hand and the people in the front row were staring at her and she started to talk.

"Good morning. As many of you know, last year, the Voynich manuscript was stolen from the Beinecke Rare Book and Manuscript Library at Yale University in the United States. Despite worldwide efforts, the Voynich is still lost. Not its contents, of course. Yale published the manuscript in its entirety online. But losing the precious original pages is a tragedy.

"All is not lost, though." She leaned close in to the microphone, ready to share a secret. "Last month I found a quire of papers stuffed inside a manuscript in the upstairs library loft of the British Museum. This is not an unusual occurrence. It is a library, after all, and old paper is our business."

Laughs, chuckles, and she relaxed a fraction. It was her boss's phrasing—old paper is our business—something he was fond of saying all the time. He beamed at her, and she knew she'd pleased him, using his joke in her press-conference debut. She cleared her throat, continued in the same confiding voice.

"The quire, like the rest of the Voynich, is written in a language or a code that hasn't yet been translated, even by experts in the cryptology field. Alas, that includes me."

A few laughs, and she was tempted to tell the truth, but no, she had to keep to her script, mix the lies and truth.

She said, "When I found the pages, I immediately set out to determine if they were real."

The reporters leaned forward as one. But one, a dark-haired gent in the middle, was staring at her as if she was about to announce the secrets of creation.

Isabella placed her laptop on a chair, hit a button, and the lights dimmed a bit. The huge screen behind her lit up with a series of photographs of the discovered pages.

"After extensive testing using radiocarbon dating, we have determined the papers I found are indeed a part of Beinecke manuscript 408—known colloquially as the Voynich manuscript, because of its rediscovery in 1912 at the Jesuit college of Frascati near Rome, by Wilfred Voynich. The quire in question is labeled as pages fifty-nine to sixty-four of the manuscript. These pages have been lost for centuries. And that, my friends, is not all."

The reporters knew immediately Dr. Isabella Marin was about to drop a bomb on them. Roger sat forward now along with the rest of them, never taking his eyes off her.

CHAPTER SIXTEEN

Isabella paused another moment for effect, then said, "Being able to study these pages in-depth for the past few weeks has reinforced my belief that the indecipherable language in which the Voynich is written is not unbreakable, as scholars before me believe.

"It is now my opinion the Voynich is written in an idioglossic language, that is, a language common to areas where only a few people live, where, in isolation, they develop their own language and words. But I believe the Voynich's idioglossic language is even more specific. It is cryptophasic, that is, a language developed between twins, commonly known as twin talk. This is why, so far, no one has been able to read the Voynich. Over the years, it has been approached as a code, when in fact, it is a unique language.

"Are we to believe the person or persons who wrote the Voynich were twins who communicated in twin talk? That they wrote and shared the Voynich between themselves, their own private book? Very possible. And I wonder, can any set of twins read the Voynich? The answer is obviously no, or the manuscript would, over time, have been seen by twins and read. But this hasn't happened. So very special twins only.

"Which twins? From a specific place? From a unique line? I don't know. In any case, this is my working theory.

"It's been speculated in the past that the book is some sort of herbal. If this is the case, perhaps these twins wrote experiments in it. Why did they write in a language no one but they themselves could understand? An excellent question to which we have no answers. Yet.

"More important, is there a key to help decipher it?" She nodded, waited, waited. "I have found the key."

There was a buzzing of voices.

"The key turns out to be a single page that was with the missing quire." She held up one finger. "Only a single page. Here it is." She pressed a button, and the slide on the screen switched. To the audience, it was more of the same nonsensical writing. But Isabella smiled and pointed to lines of text. "There is a repeating pattern here, which lines up perfectly with the lettering in the book. This page is labeled seventy-four, and, it is the only page of the Voynich manuscript physically cut from the book. Page seventy-four is from the astrological section and has a few new drawings never seen before. I've verified the quire and page seventy-four is a match to the original Voynich. Why was page seventy-four cut out?

"I believe it was cut out because it provides the clues needed for non-twins to translate the Voynich. It is still not completely clear to me, but I am working hard to figure it out." She paused again and looked out over the fascinated faces, her heartbeat picking up. She leaned forward—*sell it, sell it*—and deepened her voice.

"Today begins my hunt to find the special twins able to read the Voynich. With our current communications technology, I believe I will succeed. And when I have, I will introduce these twins to the world, and they will stand before you and read the Voynich."

She paused, drew a deep breath. "I do understand from the pages that they must be reunited with the original manuscript, the one stolen last year from the Beinecke." *Did that sound too crazy? I hope not. I couldn't very well say the pages told me so.*

"I am begging those who stole the Voynich to return it. Here, to me, at the British Museum. Please."

She looked out over the faces, many of them talking low on their cell phones, many others simply writing. *Did I convince you? Did you believe me? Or do you believe I'm a fake?*

"Now, I'm going to turn this over to Dr. Webster Hoag, distinguished professor of chemistry at Princeton and a leading expert on manuscript radiocarbon dating. We have worked closely with Dr. Hoag, and he will now explain how we verified the provenance of the quire we discovered. Dr. Hoag?"

A cadaverous man came from the wings of the landing, a massive grin on his thin face. He was a tall man with wispy hair, a paunch, the exact opposite, Roger thought, of the beautiful, dark—and young—Dr. Marin. But he had to say, he liked the man's small red-and-white polka-dot bow tie.

Dr. Hoag took the mic from Isabella. She smiled once more at the group and left the stage. Her heart was kettle-drumming. She'd done her best. If her performance hadn't convinced—well, she'd tried. This announcement was the only way she could think of to draw out the thief who'd stolen the manuscript from the Beinecke. The thief would surely want the newly discovered missing pages and the key, page 74.

Persy patted her shoulder when she stepped off the stage. "Well done, my dear, well done. Look at them, they're practically salivating, and that's saying something for a group of hardened vultures." He stopped and eyed her. "You're on the green side. Doubtless due to overwrought nerves, but thankfully you didn't show it. It's very interesting what you said, and rather mystical about the pages having to be reunited to the stolen manuscript. We'll see what happens, now won't we?

"Let's get you a nice cup of tea, and you can put your feet up. I'm very proud of you. One day you'll be able to do this without a thought."

Little do you know. What she couldn't tell him was that she would tell the world the truth once she had the Voynich in her hands.

"Sir, don't you need to stay for the rest?"

"Oh, no. Webster will talk himself blue in the face and won't stop until the reporters walk out. You know how much he loves the Voynich. He'll give them the entire history of it, from start to finish, take at least an hour. Oh yes, he whispered to me he didn't believe for a minute the quire and page seventy-four you found will enable you to read it, not that you claimed they did, exactly. He's jealous, poor fellow."

She didn't say anything as they walked to the cafeteria, only ran the announcement about her twin search over and over in her head. While she waited for her boss to bring her tea, she tried to calm herself with deep breaths. She knew she'd put herself in danger—she could feel it creeping up on her. Nearer, nearer, but she'd had no choice, the pages had told her to reunite them with the manuscript.

Roger Bannen had followed Dr. Isabella Marin and Dr. Wynn-Jones to the cafeteria and stood watching her while she waited at a small table for Wynn-Jones to bring her tea. Should he try to get her alone, ask her more questions, get more clarification on exactly what was in the quire pages and page 74? He took a step toward her, then stopped. No, Wynn-Jones was coming back with her tea. He didn't want to deal with the old buzzard.

He turned into an empty corridor and pulled out his mobile, his heart beginning to pound in his chest. Roger wasn't worried about a story anymore, or keeping his job at the bloody *Sun*. A couple of reporters came into the corridor.

Roger hurried outside. It was raining, but he didn't notice. He punched in a number, drew a deep breath. The phone rang once, twice. Finally, a sharp voice, "What."

"It's been found."

"What? What's been found? What did you say?"

"The missing quire and page seventy-four, the only page cut out of the manuscript. A cryptologist unearthed the pages at the British Museum, in the archives. What are your instructions?"

"Who knows this?"

"The free world. A Dr. Isabella Marin found the pages. She claims the language is idioglossic, more specifically, cryptophasic, twin talk. Claims she's going on a search to find the special twins who can read the Voynich, said she made this out on page seventy-four, said it was the key. She said something about how the loose pages had to be reunited with the stolen manuscript, begged the person who stole the Voynich to bring it to her at the British Museum."

A sharp hiss of air. "Get the pages. All of them. Now."

"There will be no way for me to get them. They'll be under lock and key."

"Since you appear incapable of performing this task for me, get me every bit of information you can on this Isabella Marin. I will acquire the pages myself."

Incapable? Roger knew he'd only sound defensive if he argued. He said, "Certainly, sir. I will have a dossier for you this evening. Now, about my fee—"

"If the free world is aware of the lost pages, Mr. Bannen, why should you be paid a fee?"

Oh no you don't, you blighter. "Is anyone else in the free world calling you right now?"

The cold-blooded laugh made Roger's heart stutter. "Good point. Your bank account will receive a finder's fee tonight. Now go."

Roger went. He felt a punch of guilt. He hoped he hadn't signed Dr. Isabella Marin's death warrant.

The Voynich, twin talk? Was it true?

Roman Ardelean hung up the phone and closed his eyes at the galloping of his heart.

Finally. Finally.

CHAPTER SEVENTEEN

Quire (n): Four sheets of paper or parchment folded to form eight leaves, as in medieval manuscripts.

—*Oxford Dictionary*

FBI Special Agent Ben Houston listened with half an ear to the older chemist, Dr. Hoag, from Princeton, run through the various methods his team had used to date the quire. Ben was familiar with their methods, being the former head of the art crimes unit for the New York Field Office, and now the art (and other things) expert for Covert Eyes. Whereas Dr. Marin had made her dramatic announcement short and sweet, Hoag was droning on and on. Few remained to listen.

He and Melinda were sitting at the back of the room. He leaned close. "This is amazing, imagine the Voynich written in twin talk. But only certain twins, and now Dr. Marin is on the search. Gleaned from this page seventy-four? I wonder if she will find the right twins who communicate cryptophasically—is that a word?"

He was nearly bouncing with excitement.

Melinda said, "I don't know, do you believe her?"

"Why not? I know Dr. Marin is a renowned expert, spent her career so far with the Voynich. Do you doubt her?"

Melinda was frowning. "I'm not sure. I just felt she was holding something back."

"Well, that makes sense. Why throw all your surprises out at one time? Melinda, thank you so much for bringing me here today." He eyed her. "Did you know I worked the case of the stolen Voynich manuscript from Yale? That I became an amateur expert on the Voynich?"

She gave him a quick kiss on the cheek. "Didn't I tell you? As a member of Her Majesty's Parliament, I'm required to know all specialized information about my lover."

Her lover. Melinda's lover. He loved the sound of that.

"I thought it was particularly good timing the announcement came while you were here in London. And yes, a little birdie whispered it in my ear. You'll meet him later. Imagine, Ben, the lost pages from the Voynich. I wonder when they'll go on display? If it's true, it's amazing."

Ben said, "Dr. Marin believes only specific twins can read the Voynich, which means, I guess, twins in Africa do not speak the same twin talk as twins in Norway."

Melinda took his hand. She loved to touch

him. "Yes, according to Dr. Marin, only special twins. If and when she finds the special twins, she'll inform the world."

"Ben, if she doesn't find answers before you leave, you can come back to London. Maybe you could even time it to a break when Parliament isn't in session. Just think, we can share the joy of spending our days staring at a bunch of moldering old paper."

Ben laughed, and she laughed with him. He couldn't believe how lucky he was to be here, in London, on his first real vacation in years. He still couldn't get over this incredible woman, a member of Parliament, or MP as the locals said, who had awoken next to him this morning, seduced him again, then offered him tea, which made him shudder to remember. He looked at her mouth, the pink lipstick a bit smeared after the quick kiss he'd given her in the taxi. They were both redheads, and wasn't that something? And she fit so nicely against him.

He said, "I suppose I know as much as the next fellow about the Voynich."

She brought his hand to her lap. "Tell me about it. Oh yes, use little words, since it's old art."

He cleared his throat. "Simple words then. Short version: the book itself dates back to the early 1400s. The parchment paper is said to be indigenous to that time and is prepared in the northern European style.

"A while back some said Sir Francis Bacon wrote it, as a joke, perhaps. Then it fell into the hands of John Dee, an alchemist and adviser to Queen Elizabeth I. Dee tried to translate it, but he couldn't, said his best guess was the manuscript was medical in nature. Which makes sense, because it's broken into several parts: herbal, astrological, balneological, pharmacological."

"*Balneological*? I thought you were using small words."

"Of or related to bathing. There are a lot of drawings of women bathing in unidentifiable green liquids."

A dark red eyebrow went up. "I seem to recall some green figures. Naked women bathing? Sounds more like medieval porn."

"Could be, who's to say? Anyway, John Dee sold it, and it became the property of Emperor Rudolf II, who also had no luck decoding it. Lots more hands got ahold of it over the years—I can't remember all the names—but it finally ended up with the Jesuits outside Rome for a few hundred years.

"In 1912, a rare book dealer named Wilfred Voynich discovered it with the Jesuits at Frascati. He'd been a pharmacist in Russia, so he knew his chemistry and had a natural interest in alchemy. He'd traveled to Italy looking for books to stock in his store. He brought it back to London, where he was setting up shop, and eventually tried to sell it to his friend Richard Garnett, at the British Museum. Garnett declined. After Voynich died, his wife tried to sell it—no takers. They could never find a buyer, and finally, it was bequeathed to Yale in the late sixties. Once the Beinecke got their hands on it, they did the radiocarbon dating and proved it antedated Bacon by a couple of centuries, so there's no way he wrote it. They made it a big deal and awakened worldwide interest. And even with worldwide attention, no one could translate or decode it."

"So bottom line," Melinda said, "this weird indecipherable collection of pages, some of them porn with naked women bathing, discovered at a Jesuit yard sale outside of Rome, is still a mystery—until today, with Dr. Marin's announcement. So maybe she'll find out which twins wrote it, and which twins can read it. I'm sure hoping for a cool set of twins, maybe from Siberia or deepest Africa. This is fairly exciting, Ben. I bet you'll stay up very late tonight reading all about it. Once I go to sleep, that is." And she gave him a sweet smile.

"I'll try to be a gentleman. Do you know all my quirks?"

"Not all, but I'll learn them, won't I? Ask Nicholas, he'll tell you I enjoy doing my own research about someone who's important to me, which you are. Very. And that, Agent Houston, is of course why I brought you here today. Now, who stole the manuscript from Yale?"

He shrugged. "We don't know. Someone drilled out the locks and walked right into the room where it was kept. A security guard interrupted the robber, but he or she managed to escape, with the

Voynich. We never caught the thief, and the case is still open. Melinda, I really should get in touch with the office and let them know about this incredible find and what it could mean, even though I'm no longer on the case, since I was assigned to Covert Eyes. The FBI will want to send an agent to talk to the museum and Dr. Marin about the found quire."

She said, "Yes, you should call the FBI. Where have these lost pages been all these centuries, I wonder? And how did they end up in the library upstairs?"

A dark-haired man pushed past them, making his way toward the door, nearly knocking Melinda in the shoulder. Ben said, "Hey!" But Melinda shook her head. "Ignore him. That's Roger Bannen, a reporter. He once covered Parliament for the *Guardian*, but he had a spot of bother with a young girl a few years ago, the idiot. I haven't seen him in quite some time. He's with the *Sun* now, I hear. I wonder why he's in such a hurry. Why are you staring at me?"

"I love to listen to you talk, a female version of Nicholas, all cool and proper upper-class Brit. After I make this call, would you like to go to a pub, get a pint?"

"Don't you sound British? Sounds lovely. First, though—" Melinda looked at her watch, then stood. "Come on, Agent Houston, I promised you a meeting."

She led him up the stairs into the museum itself and took a right toward the antiquities department. A thick red rope blocked a stairwell heading up the next flight of stairs.

Ben automatically stopped. "Are we supposed to be doing this?"

She looked down her nose at him, impressive, since he topped her by nearly a foot. "Agent Houston, I'm in Parliament. Do you think a rope is going to stop me?"

"Where are we going?"

"To see an old friend."

He pulled her around, kissed her, smoothed his finger over her eyebrows. "A last kiss before we get arrested."

She laughed and grabbed his hand. "Into the breach." Ben followed her up, then down a long, blue-walled hallway. Three doors down, Melinda stopped and knocked.

The door opened. It was Dr. Wynn-Jones, the chair of the antiquities department himself, who'd introduced Dr. Marin at the press conference. And behind him stood Dr. Isabella Marin.

"My dear Melinda, come in, come in. And who is this very intelligent-looking chap, who, interestingly, was holding your hand?"

Melinda received a bear hug, then stood back, and introduced them. "This is my good friend, FBI Special Agent Houston, from the New York FBI. No, no, despite your reputation he's not here to arrest you."

The two men shook hands. Dr. Wynn-Jones

said, "And this is Dr. Isabella Marin. She's my wunderkind. Isabella, this is Melinda St. Germaine and Agent Houston. I've known her family for years, smart as whips, all of them. I was crushed when she decided to go into politics, since she has one of the best eyes for art this side of the Thames. It's been too long, my dear girl."

Best eyes for art? So you planned this whole thing for me, did you? And then you asked me to give you a history of the Voynich? She probably knows all the names I've long forgotten.

Melinda said, "Sir, Agent Houston is a fan of the Voynich. He worked the case last year when it was stolen from Yale. I wondered, do you think it would be possible—?"

Dr. Wynn-Jones beamed at her. "Ah! You want to see the pages? Of course, of course. Isabella, shall we all go down together and take a look?"

Ben was staggered. He shook Dr. Wynn-Jones's hand. "That would be wonderful, sir, thank you."

"Call me Persy, although Melinda here refuses to. From the looks of you two, I'd say you're very good friends indeed." He looked from one to the other and chortled.

Two hours later, Ben felt shell-shocked. The missing pages were so very old he'd been afraid to touch them. He kept shaking his head, staring at them. When he and Melinda were back on the street, waiting for a taxi, Ben looked at his watch. "I'm glad Nicholas waited to text me until we were leaving Dr. Wynn-Jones and Dr. Marin. He and Mike are coming to London, asked me to come by. How far is it to Westminster from here?"

"Twenty, thirty minutes, depending on traffic. I wish we had my car. We'd get to Westminster faster than in a taxi."

Ben knew that was fact. She drove her black Range Rover like a bat out of hell, which made his heart occasionally freeze, but he liked it. He'd asked, and no, she'd never had an accident.

As they waited for the taxi, Ben chanced to look up. He saw a small drone flying overhead, then it veered off, toward the east. "Did you see that, Melinda?"

"See what? There's our taxi." She threw out her arm and caught him just as he started to step off the curb. "Whoops, you look left, right, left, here, not right, left, right. You're in London, remember? I don't want you to get run over by a bus."

"Thank you. There was a drone overhead. It took off to the east. I wonder what that's about."

"A drone? Now that's odd. I thought the only folk allowed to fly drones in the city are Scotland Yard. Maybe they were testing a new one."

It took them fifty-seven minutes to get to Westminster.

"Next time," Melinda said, "it's the Ranger Rover for us, Agent Houston."

CHAPTER EIGHTEEN

For almost 100 years, experts and amateur
researchers have tried to solve the riddle
of a handwritten book, referred to as the
"Voynich manuscript," composed in an unknown script. The numerous theories about
this remarkable document are contradictory
and range from plausible to adventurous.
—Klaus Schmeh, *Skeptical Inquirer*
Volume 35.1

Roman punched off his mobile, stared blankly
down at his hands. The lost quire found, by a
nobody, at the British Museum? How could this
be? How could it be possible?

And she knew it was twin talk? She was
going on a hunt for the twins who could read the
Voynich?

He remembered the gut fear he'd felt when the
Voynich had been stolen last year from Beinecke
at Yale. Even though the manuscript had been
digitized and released into the world, someone had
wanted the original badly enough to break into the

Beinecke and steal it. And that meant someone believed there was something in the original pages no one had seen? No, that was ridiculous. Then why was it stolen? Why hadn't it appeared on the black market? He was always listening, but he'd never heard even a whisper something could be hidden in the original Voynich pages. If he had, he'd have stolen the bloody manuscript himself. She'd said the pages had to be reunited? He felt a frisson of alarm, of uncertainty.

First things first. Roman sat down at his desk, a massive slab of driftwood, and pressed a button. An LED-crystal computer screen slid upward out of a hidden, built-in frame. He pulled the keyboard and mouse from his center drawer and went to the British Museum's website. He saw they'd wasted no time. He pressed the link and watched the press conference twice, the second time pausing every few minutes. She was a Voynich expert, she admitted she couldn't read it all, but she believed it was written in twin talk.

How could she have possibly figured her way to that? And only certain, unique twins could read it? And she was going to find the twins who could? Isabella Marin was lying, not everything she said, but enough. Why?

"I have found the key." It was this missing page 74? It was written so a reader could figure it out? That was nonsense; she was absolutely lying. She finished with her plea to return the stolen manuscript so the pages would be re-united.

Reuniting the pages, that shook him to his core. How could she possibly know that? Had she truly found the missing pages by accident, or had that been a lie, too? Had she had them all along?

He'd been looking for the missing pages for years.

What game was she playing?

He read her bio on the British Museum website. She was from Florida, her B.S. in computer science from Yale, M.S. in science of information security from Yale, a Rhodes Scholar, she'd achieved her doctorate in cryptography at Oxford, and was now doing a supplemental year of research on ancient coded manuscripts at the British Museum, developing a new methodology to translate the texts. She'd been awarded several prestigious internships before this new position—translating runes on newly discovered sarsens in Sweden, interesting, but who cared? She loved to travel, blah, blah, blah. So she was smart, knew computers, and an American—the bio gave him nothing more.

He scrolled further and stopped cold at a photo, dated last year, of Isabella Marin accepting the Best Paper Award from the International Association for Cryptologic Research.

She was accepting the very award Roman himself had been awarded several years before, and that meant she was indeed an expert in cryptology.

But it wasn't the award that stunned him, it was something in her face. Yes, she was dark, beautiful, exotic—like the women from his homeland—but there was something more to her. What was going on here?

Roman walked to the large window in his office that looked over the Thames to the London Eye making its slow circle, and Parliament, shadowed in the darkening afternoon clouds. He thumbed an LSD tablet onto his tongue, waited a moment, then unboxed a disposable cell phone, added his encryption software, and made a call to the British Museum, a number he knew by heart. A pleasant female voice answered on the second ring. Never the first, always the second. Roman envisioned her there, long legs tucked under the desk, crossed at the ankle, her clear plastic umbrella sitting in the stand to her right and a cooling cup of tea on the desk in front of her.

"Dr. Wynn-Jones's office, how may I help you?"

He slid seamlessly into his alter ego, his voice changed, became slightly higher, his speech more pedantic. "Hello, Phyllis. It's Dr. Laurence Bruce. I need to speak to Persy, please."

"Oh, hello, Dr. Bruce," she said, her voice now infinitely warmer. "I—we've missed seeing you. How have you been? Both Dr. Wynn-Jones and I loved your piece in *Anthropology Today* last month—what a discovery. Hold for a moment, I'll get him."

Seconds later, Persy came on with a hearty, "Laurence! It's been too long. How are you, my boy? Still ticking along on those John Dee diaries you discovered? Read your piece in *AT*, by the way. Phyllis couldn't stop talking about it."

"Thank you for the kind words. I am quite well. I hear you've had a bit of excitement today. Why didn't you share with the rest of the class?"

"Oh-ho, you know how it goes. Close to the vest, make a big splash, get some extra funding. A real coup for the museum to have discovered a piece of the Voynich, especially after the original manuscript went missing last year. But you know all that already. The truth is, I wanted my brilliant young colleague to have a chance to shine. Tough to believe anyone could find those missing Voynich pages, but she did. Yes, yes, I'll admit she tossed a bit of mysticism in there, what with the loose pages needing to be reunited with the manuscript, but it made for good drama.

"And yes, before you ask, they've been fully authenticated, by Hoag, that windbag, or we wouldn't have announced otherwise. You need to watch the video of the announcement, you'll find out everything. You're actually the tenth call I've fielded in the past hour. My goodness, we even had a member of Parliament—I'm sure you've heard of her, Melinda St. Germaine, a former student of mine at Oxford—she and an FBI agent came in to see the pages this afternoon."

Roman's pulse jumped. An FBI agent? Could it be Drummond? No, that posturing nob was dead somewhere on A14, his partner with him. But why hadn't he heard yet from Radu? Not important at the moment—he kept his voice cool, disinterested.

"The FBI? It didn't take them long to show up. I suppose after they bungled the case last year, when the Voynich was stolen, they need to make a good show of it. I wonder how they found out about the discovery beforehand."

"Oh, this was nothing official. He and Melinda happened to be in the lobby when we called the press conference. Capital fellow, art history buff, here on vacation, ah, might be some interest there between him and Melinda. He was quite excited, quite excited indeed."

"What was his name?"

"I'll tell you, Laurence, I've heard so many names today I can't keep them all straight. I do remember his name was the same as one of those sprawling big oil cities in Texas, but the day's gotten away from me, so many things, so many calls. Exciting times, Laurence, exciting times."

Roman stored this information away for later. He dropped his voice, made it low, conspiratorial. "I'd love to see the pages, Persy."

"Of course, of course, and we'd love to have you. I'm sorry we weren't able to arrange a private exhibit before the announcement, Laurence, truly I am. As I said, I wanted to give Dr. Marin a big splash, let her shine. And did she ever—shine, that is. All the reporters were eating out of her hand. When would you like to come by?"

"I'm already in London. I can't spend all my time working. Came up to see the retrospective on"—he tapped the keyboard of his tablet and picked an exhibit at random—"Giacometti. At the Tate."

"Oh, I had no idea you had an attraction to that modern trash I find so appalling and depressing. Ah, well, it's something I'm sure I'll never understand nor appreciate."

This startled a real laugh out of Roman. "Man can't sustain himself on antiquities alone, Persy. We must look ahead, as well as behind. I can be by in an hour."

Persy said with a small laugh, "You know Phyllis will be ready for you."

CHAPTER NINETEEN

To the military, they are UAVs (Unmanned Aerial Vehicles) or RPAS (Remotely Piloted Aerial System). However, they are more commonly known as drones. Drones are used in situations where manned flight is considered too risky or difficult.

—BBC.com

Drummond House
Barton Street
Westminster, London

Nicholas and Mike were questioned by Penderley at Scotland Yard until the drone attack began to feel surreal to Mike, like it had happened to someone else, someone in a training film, perhaps. But after two hours of questions from Penderley and his minions, all she wanted was a glass of wine, maybe a hot shower to wash the rest of the glass out of her hair, maybe even change the Band-Aid on her neck, but she knew she had to hold it together a while longer.

It was another eon before Penderley released them, saying, "You two have really poked the gorilla this time. Shall I assign some men to stick close, Drummond?"

Nicholas turned this down, and they shook Penderley's hand and those of his two inspectors. Ten minutes later, they climbed into his banged-up, well-photographed, debulleted Beemer and made good time to Nicholas's house in Westminster. Mike spent the drive absently picking more glass out of her hair and straightening the temples of her glasses again, even though they didn't need it. He reached over, patted her hand. "You feeling all right, Agent Caine?"

"Right as rain. Hmm, I never understood that saying." She looked out the window. "Speaking of rain, any minute now."

Nigel met them at the door to Drummond House, tall, shoulders straight, immaculately dressed, and he wasn't happy. He looked out to the BMW—the sides and roof littered with bullet holes, the windshield cracked, the side window shattered. Mike saw a muscle twitch in his jaw. He turned back to them, ushered them into the house, and gave them both one long look.

"Hi, Nigel," Mike said. "We're in one piece, don't worry. Superintendent Penderley and his people have examined our heads for the last two hours."

Nigel didn't crack a smile. He said slowly, never looking away from her, "Master Nicholas said you'd been shot at. He did not say, however, that you were covered in blood and glass, looking like you'd been dropped into a war zone."

"I'm fine, Nigel, really. It's all on the surface, not like Nicholas's poor Beemer."

"No, Mike, you are anything but fine, and Master Harry will be here in an hour. You will go with Daisy. She'll draw you a hot bath and help you get cleaned up. I will handle Master Nicholas." To her surprise, Nigel took her hand, held it tightly for a moment. "I am so relieved you are both all right. I understand you shot down the drone that attacked you."

"She did indeed, Nigel, and a brilliant job she did of it. When Daisy is through with her, I would appreciate your looking at her. She has a cut on the back of her head. No stitches necessary, but it does need cleaning."

"Unnecessary. Daisy will tend to her nicely. Do as she tells you, Mike, and all will be well. Ah, yes, drinks will be served promptly at half six, dinner at seven."

Once Mike and Daisy had disappeared down the second-floor hallway, Nicholas said to Nigel, "We will talk while you get me ready for my father." He lowered his voice. "We don't know what's going on yet, but it isn't good. I believe there are ears everywhere. We all have to take care now."

Mike didn't mind a bit being in Daisy's very kind, competent hands. She was a woman about the age of the Gorgeous Rebecca, but there all comparisons ended. She was stout, her hair in crimped curls around her face, but like Mike's mother, Daisy had a brilliant smile and lovely white teeth.

By six fifteen, Mike was dressed in her favorite little black dress, pressed by Daisy, her hair shiny and clean and free of glass. "No need for Mr. Nigel," Daisy had said as she'd lightly touched an antibiotic on the cut and covered it with a Band-Aid, luckily hidden beneath her hair.

Daisy handed her the heels she'd packed with the dress and stood back. "Goodness, you're a tall one. But it's perfect you are, Ms. Mike."

Perfect? Like that would ever happen, but still it sounded nice. Daisy left her sitting on a chaise longue, researching drones on her iPad. A ton of information, none of it particularly helpful. Ah, she found something else that was fascinating. She looked up at a soft knock on the door, then Nicholas stepped in. His hair was damp from his shower. As usual, he looked James Bond picture-perfect, tall, dark, garbed in an incredible black Armani jacket and pants that fit him to perfection. She wanted to kick him and jump him.

"Don't tell me these came out of your carry-all?"

"Well, no, Nigel picked them up yesterday, he told me."

"On sale, I suppose?"

"He didn't say." He stepped back as she rose, looked her up and down. "You look as sharp as you did on our memorable night in Venice. But I do miss the boots with your black dress, not that the black heels don't make your legs look a mile long—and give me ideas."

She didn't want to kick him now, only jump him.

He walked to her, lifted her hair. "Nice Band-Aid. No more shards in your hair?"

"All good. Daisy checked me out thoroughly."

He leaned down, breathed in her hair. "Jasmine. You smell like my mother." He grinned, tapped her chin. "You look lovely."

She shook her head, cupped his face in her hand. "Nicholas, do we have to whisper when we meet your father downstairs?"

"No. I've taken care of things, at least for tonight. Don't worry. My father is due in ten minutes. What are you reading?"

She shrugged. "A bit about drones, until this caught my eye. Interpol has an orange notice out for a killer operating in Europe. He's a serial, Nicholas. They don't normally get serial killers moving across the borders. They're calling him Dracula, and that's what caught my eye. Whoever it is, he is preying on Eastern Europeans mostly, lots of

Romanians, in several countries. He has a rather horrific MO to match his nickname. He kills them with blunt-force trauma to the head, then exsanguinates them. There are even bite marks on their necks. The whole Dracula deal. Creepy."

"Very creepy."

She studied his face. "You already knew about this, didn't you?"

"I believe I saw something from Interpol, yes."

"When? You didn't have time. You never sleep. I know, you're the vampire they're searching for."

Nicholas said, "Not me, I never had a taste for blood. I can see this fascinates you, so why don't you give Menard a call? I'm sure he'll have all the inside scoop."

"Yes, perhaps I will. It's not every day you run into Dracula roaming free with his fangs out and bloodied. It's nice having a friend in Interpol. Pierre's like you, he never sleeps. Hey, maybe he's the vampire."

Nicholas laughed, then grew serious. "I spoke to Adam. He hasn't had any luck identifying the drone from the assassination this morning. Penderley called to say he has nothing on the one you shot down, either. They're taking it apart, piece by piece, but it's not one of theirs, nor ours. A phantom drone."

"Then it stands to reason someone has their own private arsenal."

"Add that to the list of who's selling—and

buying—drones on the black market. And I'm still trying to figure out exactly how they knew where to find us, but I know someone's listening to us. I scrambled the call with Adam, not to mention our plane has incredible defenses. Nigel swept the house for listening devices and found nothing. With any luck we can get an idea of what's going on from my father at dinner. I think that's why he agreed to dinner so quickly. He wanted privacy to talk."

He found himself once again touching her shiny hair. She'd scared him today, again. He could still see her leaning out the shattered window, firing up at the drone. "I'm tired of seeing you bloody, Agent Caine."

She laughed. "Me, too. I promise not to jump in front of a bullet unless I have to protect you. It's what I promised your mother."

CHAPTER TWENTY

Harry Drummond arrived promptly at half six and immediately went to Mike, wrapped her in a tight bear hug, then turned to his son. "I'm so glad you're both all right. We will get to the bottom of this, I swear it." He studied Nicholas a moment, patted him on the back, then nodded. After his un-English show of affection, he accepted a Scotch from Nigel and toasted them.

Mike grinned at him and raised her glass of wine. She knew Nicholas would look very much like his father in thirty years, tall and straight, dark eyes burning with intelligence. And endless curiosity, like his son.

Harry looked around the long, narrow living room and slowly nodded. "I haven't stayed here for a while, not since I signed Drummond House to you when you turned twenty-five. When I'm up, I stay at Clapton House. I like what you've done, Nicholas. Updated it to the new century, but not quite." He pointed to the heavy golden draperies and the exquisite Regency marquetry table Nicholas's mother had picked out years before. He nodded to the three Turner paintings on the opposite wall. "Old friends."

He turned back to his son. "Do you have any idea who tried to kill you today?"

Directly to the point. Nicholas loved that about his father. "No, sir, we don't. Nor do we know why or how they knew where to hit us. Which is almost as important as the attack itself. Drones are easily summoned, but I'm hard-pressed to think someone has been sitting outside Farrow-on-Gray simply waiting for us to leave. The attack felt much too coordinated. So we're hoping you can tell us what's happening, Father. I know there's more to this than we've been told."

"I'm glad I had people in my office earlier and couldn't talk, because if you're correct, and there is an infiltration, I might have given too much away. We acted upon the intelligence you provided me this morning. Your computer genius, Adam, sent us some information as well. Sit down, and I'll tell you what we know."

Once settled, Harry said, "First, the drone you shot down, Michaela. I had it removed from Superintendent Penderley at Scotland Yard and brought to our forensic experts. They verified it isn't registered to any legitimate company we've been able to trace. They believe it's a prototype. Custom-made. Drones with these capabilities, and by that I mean weaponized drones, are a multimillion-dollar investment. Even if there's only one, whoever's behind these attacks is well funded."

Mike said, "Nicholas and I believe there's more than one drone."

"I fear you are correct. Now, let me digress a moment. ISIS has more or less stopped recruiting young spies because of the time and cost to groom them. They now focus on the people with decision-making power in a government. They offer promises of money, freedom, power, honor, whatever they believe will work with a particular individual. They strike deals with them to allow their soldiers to cross borders. Italy, Austria, Sweden, Germany. It's actually counterespionage at its finest.

"They are well funded, some believe by the Russians, others say leftovers from the failed overthrow of Assad. Either way, they've been successful, in my opinion, twice that we know of. First, Heinrich Hemmler. I've done some digging, found out Hemmler had a private meeting with an ISIS leader in Aleppo. Said leader is no longer with us, thanks to a U.S. drone strike. Obviously, Hemmler can't confirm, but his secretary has admitted he set up the trip. Hemmler's bank account was suddenly quite flush, as well.

"I suspect he was trying to stage a quiet coup in the German government. With the chancellor gone, he could easily call for an election, install himself in her place. To what end? If he's been meeting with ISIS leaders, I think we can agree he was giving them something in return for his new position. No idea what, we'll need to look closer.

"As for Chapman Donovan, he helped broker the cease-fire in '98. He was a good man, aboveboard, as far as we know, and so rich I can't imagine he'd want more. No idea why he would be targeted."

He looked at each of them. "Worse, we have no idea who killed these two people."

Harry took a sip of his drink, eyed his son and Michaela. Such a beauty she was and completely unaware of it, not unlike his incredible wife. And, as his father said, she was a right sharp little whip. He couldn't call her Mike, couldn't even think of her as Mike, the name of a bullyboy at school who'd once made his life a misery until his father had told him to kick the little blighter's arse, which he had. He looked to his son. "Nicholas, one more thing. Since someone managed to overhear your conversation this morning, it seems clear we've been compromised."

"Yes, we believe so, sir. And whoever's infiltrated your systems can read your emails, your notes, listen to your phone calls. The question is, has the intrusion happened from outside, or inside MI5?"

Harry nodded. "Look at all the people around us, those with the money and ability to pull off such a massive intrusion, those with a motive. A drone carrying a poison, shooting it into the victim's neck, and I wonder, why kill in such a flamboyant manner?"

Everyone thought about this, then Nicholas said, "Would you be willing to let Adam and me have a crack at it?"

Harry said simply, "Yes."

And there it was, Nicholas realized. His father had complete faith in him and his skills. He prayed neither he nor Adam would fail him.

Nigel came into the room. "Master Nicholas, Master Harry, I'm sorry to interrupt, but you have guests."

Nicholas said, "Guests? Who? We aren't expecting anyone. Father?"

"I'm not, no."

Nigel merely smiled and left. He returned moments later with Agent Ben Houston and Melinda St. Germaine.

He looked at Nicholas. "Shall I have two more places set for dinner?"

CHAPTER TWENTY-ONE

Nicholas grinned at Ben. "I was wondering when you and Melinda would cross our path. You will stay to dinner, of course. Melinda, you know my father, and this is my partner, Agent Mike Caine, New York FBI."

Harry hugged Melinda, kissed her cheek. "I am so very sorry about your mother, Melinda. Her death hit us all very hard."

"Thank you. I—it's difficult."

"How ever did you meet an FBI agent from New York?"

"A very long story, sir."

Harry turned to the young man whose hair was nearly the exact shade of red as Melinda's. He looked bright, fit, all in all, a nice-looking young man. "I recognized your name. You're part of my son's and Michaela's Covert Eyes, aren't you?"

Ben nodded. "Yes, but this trip wasn't business. I'm here on vacation."

"I hope Melinda is showing you all the tourist sites."

Ben considered saying he hadn't come to London to see the Tower of London but to hook up with a member of Parliament, but he thought better of it. "Well, sir, there hasn't been that much time as of yet and . . ." He stalled.

Melinda grinned, curse her, and said, "Ben is Covert Eyes' resident art historian, isn't that right, Ben?"

"Ah, yes, that's perfectly correct."

"I've been taking him to all the museums this week. This morning we were at the British Museum." A lie here, the truth there, a little of each.

Ben lit up. "Melinda set it up, without telling me, a big surprise. It was a press conference, given by a cryptologist at the museum who'd happened to find missing pages from the Voynich manuscript buried in among the archives. She said quite a lot—" He looked over at Melinda. "I don't think my MP here believed she was on the up-and-up entirely."

"No, I didn't, but that's neither here nor there."

Ben squeezed her shoulder, couldn't help himself. "Well, Melinda knows the director of the antiquities department, Dr. Wynn-Jones, so we were able to see the discovered quire and the long-lost page seventy-four. It was remarkable."

Melinda added, "Dr. Wynn-Jones was a teacher

of mine. Believe me, he was thrilled to show off this astonishing discovery to Ben, a big honcho FBI agent from New York. Nicholas, why are you frowning?"

"Well, there's something odd about this. Ben, you were in on the investigation when the Voynich was stolen from the Beinecke last year, right?"

"Yes, I was. We were unable to discover the thief—well, actually, we didn't find out anything useful. The case, of course, remains open. At the press conference today, the professor who found the missing quire and page seventy-four begged the thief to come forward, to reunite the pages to the manuscript." Ben added, "Now I think about it, maybe you're right, Melinda. It is very odd this young cryptologist just happened upon these missing pages. I think I should see where Dr. Isabella Marin was last year when the Voynich was stolen."

Mike said, "You have a beautifully devious mind, Ben, I've always thought so, and to see it in action—"

"Yes," Melinda said, her voice complacent, "he does have quite an astounding brain, doesn't he?"

Nicholas said, "Yes, absolutely astounding and I'd like to put it to good use, if you can find the time, Ben. And if you're willing to do some work on your vacation."

"We need your help, Ben," Mike said.

Melinda said, "We come over to say hello, and

now you want to work him to the bone on his first vacation in too long a time?"

Ben, whose eyes had already begun to shine, smiled down at her. "Not quite to the bone. Sure, Nicholas, Mike, what's going on?"

Melinda held up a hand, her mother's ruby ring on her index finger. "If you want Ben, you have to include me, as well. We are both on vacation, and we are a matched set. No, don't you dare shake your head, Nicholas. I helped you solve two serious crimes only weeks ago."

Nicholas's head was still shaking. "No, Melinda, not this time."

Mike said, "Nicholas, can I speak to you privately for a moment?" He followed her into the hall. "What's the matter?"

"Listen, I think Melinda could be of serious use. She has connections, she knows people, she has influence, she operates in a different sphere than we do, than your father does. More brains on the problem, Nicholas. Let's bring her in, have her help us from a different angle."

"My father will never allow it."

"I disagree. She's outside of MI5 but still a part of the government. Plus, she's in all the major intelligence briefings anyway, isn't she?"

"Yes, but—"

"Nicholas, if England's highest communications are compromised, we need someone on the outside whose aren't."

She'd hit him with a brilliant stroke of logic. He folded his tent. "All right, I'll ask, but I think it's a moot point. My father is a spy at heart. He's going to want to keep this as close to the vest as possible."

"Let's go ask him and see."

When they went back into the living room, Ben, Melinda, and Harry were speaking, their heads together. Harry looked up and said, "I've been telling them what's going on, from the assassinations to the drone attack on you two this morning to MI5 and MI6 being compromised. I believe Melinda is uniquely positioned to be of service to us. She's agreed to help, and I've accepted."

Who knew your father could surprise you?

Melinda said, "This is incredible. I'll do whatever I can to help end this situation."

Mike asked, "Infiltration or leak, Melinda?"

"Infiltration, without a doubt." She shuddered. "And it makes it all the more dangerous."

Harry said, "But we are the British government and have much higher security standards than average. Plus, as far as I know, we've avoided being hit with any malware attacks. When the WannaCry attack happened, we doubled our security, layered in new programs to assure our firewalls would hold."

"New programs from where, Father?"

"Radulov Industries, of course. Roman Ardelean himself was in the office last week setting it up. I'm confident no one else can get in and get any information."

Mike whistled. "There's no doubt Radulov is the best cyber-security firm in the world. I doubt there is a computer in the world that doesn't have some form of Radulov software on it, primarily MATRIX. Even so, the hackers behind WannaCry managed to get through. What did Mr. Ardelean have to say about his systems being hacked?"

"Roman suspected the entire ransomware attack was based in human error," Harry said. "He claims his software systems and security firewalls are impenetrable from hackers—if used properly. There's the caveat—he can't control what happens once the end user has his MATRIX operating system on their machines. He pointed out the industries and companies who were affected by this latest attack hadn't updated to the current version of the MATRIX operating system, leaving themselves open to attack."

Mike said, "I know MATRIX releases weekly updates to stay on top of any and all threats. But here's the question: Even if someone inside opened something they shouldn't have, the anti-virus programs should have kicked in. Yet they didn't."

Harry said, "But after a thorough check, Roman couldn't find any evidence of an intrusion. And of course, we are religious about our updates."

Mike watched Nicholas drum his fingers on the coffee table, knew he was writing some code in his head. For his visit to MI5 tomorrow?

Melinda asked, "If MI5 and MI6 were infiltrated, wouldn't it stand to reason other branches of Her Majesty's government have been compromised, as well? And Parliament?"

Nicholas stopped his phantom typing, rubbed his thumb in the dent of his chin. "Possible, yes. Father, when Adam and I come to your offices to do a full break-in assessment, we'll make certain you're now as safe as possible. I think it would be helpful to have the great man himself there again to run us through the setup. Perhaps Adam and I will see something he's missed."

Harry looked up to see Nigel at the door. "I can arrange for it, certainly." He rose. "Now, let's have dinner, and, Ben, you can tell us more about the Voynich manuscript."

Over Cook Lattimer's braised beef tips, prepared in the French way, with asparagus and crunchy rolls, Ben said, "All this talk of the drone attacks made me remember when Melinda and I left the museum today, I spotted a drone overhead. Melinda thought it was Scotland Yard's, but now, I'm not so sure."

Nicholas and Mike snapped to attention. Nicholas leaned forward. "Describe it, please, Ben—big, small? Was it marked? All of Scotland Yard's drones are clearly marked."

"No markings. It was tiny. Like a mini helicopter. Or maybe the size of a mutant Jurassic Park dragonfly. Small enough I wouldn't have noticed it if it didn't fly right over my head. I heard the whirring and looked up."

Nicholas hated this, but he had to consider someone was watching Ben, as well. Perhaps Melinda? He said slowly, "Mike, we need to identify who owns these drones, right now."

CHAPTER TWENTY-TWO

The Voynich manuscript: Described as a magical or scientific text, nearly every page contains botanical, figurative, and scientific drawings of a provincial but lively character, drawn in ink with vibrant washes in various shades of green, brown, yellow, blue, and red.
—Beinecke Rare Book and Manuscript Library, Yale University

British Museum
Great Russell Street
Bloomsbury, London

Roman Ardelean presented his credentials—Dr. Laurence Bruce's credentials—to the security desk at the British Museum.

Dr. Bruce looked the part of the scholar—glasses, longish brown hair, a thick beard and mustache, and a rather ugly brown tweed suit. Radu had created a perfect legend, a full identity, education, history. They'd even gone so far as to publish papers on the various "manuscripts" Dr. Laurence Bruce studied.

Dr. Bruce's published papers were computer-generated by a sophisticated AI program created by Radu. His program used modern language skills built into a hand-coded system designed specifically to do contextual analyses of rare manuscripts, cryptography, and history, then used the information to generate scholarly papers. The papers and their theories were as fake as a green sunset but real enough to fool the various places they'd successfully published. Bogus research was a well-known problem in the academic field, but Roman wasn't worried. Radu would stay ahead of it. He was that brilliant.

Dr. Laurence Bruce had a moderately respected reputation, one built entirely online by Radu. He and Radu had been nothing if not thorough. They had contacts all over the world in antiquities departments in museums, universities, and private endeavors. Dr. Bruce was known for being a bit different but harmless, and smart enough. And no one doubted he was completely dedicated to the Voynich—indeed, he was passionate about it. When it was necessary to move in the open, Roman pulled on Dr. Bruce's ugly tweed suit, pasted on a beard, and topped his head with a wig, letting it settle in until it fit him like a second skin.

And, of course, Dr. Laurence Bruce had made friends with Dr. Persy Wynn-Jones, as well as supposed experts on the Voynich, knowing one day those relationships would come in handy. And today, it had paid off.

He would soon see the lost quire and page 74, touch them, read them. He was vibrating with excitement and thumbed a tablet onto his tongue to calm himself down as he was escorted to the elevator. He had himself well in hand when he reached Persy's office. He'd visited three other times and saw Phyllis the moment he entered. Always with a large blond bun on the top of her head and a chain attached to her glasses around her neck. She was standing beside a filing cabinet, but Roman knew it was her immediately. Her beauty always surprised him, made him wonder how she'd ended up as the secretary to a crusty old man. Perhaps if he met her as Roman, he'd ask her, but Dr. Laurence Bruce was a man of few words, his brain always focused on some esoteric topic, unaware of those around him, particularly underlings. He knew she liked him, quite a surprise given how unprepossessing Dr. Laurence Bruce was. No matter, Dr. Bruce wasn't one to think romantic thoughts about secretaries. Still, she might one day be useful, so he gave her a special hello and smile when she showed him into Persy's office.

There stood Persy's newest prodigy. Dr. Isabella Marin, young, dark hair, lean and fit, taller than average, and leaning over his ancient mahogany desk. Persy was always plucking the best students from the various universities to come work for him. And Persy did so love having handsome young people around.

He said, "Hello, I'm Dr. Laurence Bruce. Where is Dr. Wynn-Jones?"

She gave him a pleasant smile. "He's been detained in a budget meeting, I'm afraid. I'm Dr. Isabella Marin." She came around the desk and stuck out her hand. "And you are Dr. Bruce. It's a pleasure to meet you, sir."

He took her hand, found it soft and dry. "It's lovely to meet you. Persy's said great things about you."

"He is very kind."

He couldn't help but stare at her. It wasn't that she didn't look like her photo or the video—she did—but in person she looked younger, no more than twenty-five years old. Again, he was struck by her dark skin and the eyes of the women from his family's homeland. And her name, Marin, and so he said, "Are you Romanian?"

She cocked her head to one side. "I am. How did you know?"

"You have the look of a very good friend's family. They are from Bucharest. Where were you born?"

"In Florida, but my mother is from Oradea. As I'm sure you know, Oradea used to belong to Hungary."

He nodded and came closer, the handshake not enough. She smelled exotic, like spices, cloves and nutmeg, and up close, he could see her dark eyes had a ring of gold around the iris, very unique.

She was Romanian, and there was something

about her that called to him on the most visceral level—and in that moment, Roman knew he had to have her blood, had to have it for Radu. Did it smell of cloves and nutmeg as well? Could she be the one? Would the coppery tang carry the special taint, the rare compound he'd been searching for?

He realized Isabella was still speaking about Oradea, a town he knew well.

He was pleased his voice didn't shake. "Please tell me more, Dr. Marin."

She cocked her head to the side, studying him. "My story isn't all that unusual, Dr. Bruce. My mother immigrated to the United States from Romania before I was born. She met my father while she competed there. She was a gymnast, you see, Olympic level.

"When her career was over, she wanted to be an artist. But the government wanted her to train young gymnasts. She applied for asylum and got it.

"Sadly, I'm not coordinated like she was, nor do I have the necessary talent. To top it off, I'm much too tall for gymnastics. That's my father's fault. He was six foot four, and my mother was barely five feet. They always looked mismatched in photos, but they adored each other. I've lost them both. My father to a heart attack and my mother to cancer. I miss them." Why had she said so much? It wasn't like her.

"Now, enough about me. You're here to see

the Voynich pages I found. I have them laid out for you. Look, but please don't touch. I'll turn the pages as you need me to."

No, no, he wanted more, he wanted to hear every memory she had of her mother and Romania, where she'd traveled—and more, had she lied at her press conference? Was she a twin? Could she read the Voynich? If so, why hadn't she come forward years before? He wanted to grab her and haul her out of there despite Phyllis in the outer office, despite— No, no, not yet, but soon, very soon. *Calm, calm.* After all, it was his lucky day. The papers and a new bloodline. If only Drummond had died, he'd have won the trifecta.

"Oh, yes. The papers. Let me see."

"We'll start with the full quire, pages fifty-nine to sixty-four of the manuscript. I know you're an expert on the Voynich, so I don't have to explain the importance of this section."

Was she lying?

"With page seventy-four, I believe I'm very close."

And what did that mean? Maddening, she was maddening, and he knew she was hiding something, but what? Her spicy scent wafted to his nose as she bent and carefully, gently, turned a page. "These are from the astrological section, and as you can see, they are crowned with constellations."

"These match no constellation I've ever seen."

"I believe it's Taurus." She laid down the page on the desk, picked up another. "The long-lost page seventy-four. Someone cut it out, folded it into thirds, put it inside the quire, and stuck it in an original Marcus Aurelius, *Meditations*. Yes, the handwritten version." Her lies came so easily now, after so much repetition. "A collector named Sweig had it. His collection was donated to us two months ago, and I found all of this while I was cataloging the collection. It was an incredible moment. I mean, you can still see the bast fiber threads on the linen support. That alone shouted at me. But when I saw the Voynichese, I knew what I had."

Page 74. He couldn't believe, yet he was standing there, actually looking at it. Words were difficult. "It—it's incredible."

"I know, right? We have the provenance of the Aurelius manuscript intact and verified. It originally came from the library of an Italian estate outside of Venice, Gradara Castle." A bit of truth: she'd placed the pages there, a tribute, really, to Gradara, to whomever had drawn the picture of the castle. How many centuries ago?

"Gradara? Many a Voynich scholar have speculated the castle on page eighty-six might be Gradara. You know, the one with—"

She grinned. "Right, the one with the curved merlons. Yes. No one has ever known for certain which castle the drawing represented, but I'm certain it's Gradara. It must have been added to the manuscript at least a century, maybe more, after the Voynich was originally penned. I like to picture a young prince looking through the manuscript, drawing the view outside his window. And I wonder if he was punished." She laughed. "I know, I have a strange imagination."

"More likely an imprisoned monk drew what he could see from his cell."

"I like my imagining better—yours is much too dark."

You have no idea how dark, or how true, my dear.

"Well, Dr. Marin, since you have all the insights, do you know who wrote the blasted thing?"

She leaned back against the desk, arms crossed over her chest. "No. Your guess is as good as mine. The castle drawing, though, has always looked like a doodle to me. Like someone was drawing a view, not putting it in the manuscript on purpose. Or maybe we're all wrong, and it's the signature of the writer." She shrugged. "Another mystery surrounding the manuscript."

Roman stared at page 74. He had only a moment before she turned it over and gathered the loose pages very carefully together and slid them into a soft folder. He couldn't wait to tell Radu, couldn't wait to have the pages in his keeping.

"Make me a copy of these pages. I need to study them."

Something in Dr. Bruce's voice made gooseflesh rise on Isabella's arms. His voice was too harsh, too intense, and he was standing too close, staring at her as if he was going to—what? She didn't know, but she suddenly felt a bolt of fear and knew she didn't want to be alone with him for another minute. Even if he was an expert and a friend of Persy's, only an odd man, she still wanted to get away from him. Time to get him out of here. She straightened and closed the folder, took a step back.

Roman cursed to himself. He'd alarmed her, been too preemptory, sounded peculiar, obsessive. But he knew these pages were exactly what he needed—he knew it to his soul. He wanted desperately to touch them, to remove the protective casing and feel the gall ink under his fingers. There was blood in the ink, he was sure of it, mixed in with the berries. The blood of his ancestors, and their blood was calling, calling to him over endless expanse of time. He could almost hear their voices.

Roman could see her edging away, her beautiful face now set and pale. Had he said it aloud? His breath was coming faster. *Her scent, her blood, the pages—get a hold of yourself!*

He straightened, tried to look benign and a bit befuddled. "Forgive me, Dr. Marin. I'm overexcited by this incredible find. I would greatly like to study these pages. Perhaps I could lend my expertise, and together we could—"

Isabella shook her head. "I'm sorry, Dr. Bruce, but we're not ready to free them into the wild just yet. No one is allowed to remove even the most simple facsimile of these papers from the museum. Not even me."

"When will you go on your twin search?"

"I begin in earnest tomorrow." Why had he asked? Again, she felt that tingling fear. Could he have stolen the manuscript? Could her plan have worked so quickly? No, surely not. He was simply an overeager scholar. Still, she hugged the folder to her chest. "Dr. Wynn-Jones asked me to show you the pages, Dr. Bruce, as a courtesy, but now I'm afraid I have to get back to work. Thank you for your interest. Good day."

Roman pulled on his Dr. Laurence Bruce self again, all deprecating smiles, as unthreatening as a puppy. "It was wonderful for you to take the time, Dr. Marin, thank you. I'll be keeping close tabs on you so I can share in your achievement when you publish. Congratulations."

And he left the room.

Isabella stood frozen a moment, then calmed herself. She'd overreacted. She was walking a dangerous line and was going to see thieves and crooks in every face until the true criminal came for her. Still, she put the folder with the facsimile of the quires back into Persy's safe, then grabbed her things. She wanted to leave, to clear her head.

"Phyllis, I'm going to head home early. I've overdone it today, I think, and I have a headache. Tell Persy I'll see him bright and early tomorrow morning, will you?"

Phyllis wasn't stupid. She saw something was wrong. Had Dr. Bruce said something? No, no, not possible. Dr. Bruce was a sweetheart, the pro- totypical absentminded scholar. She patted Isabel- la's hand. "It's been indeed a wild day for you. You deserve a nice dinner, maybe some champagne, too. Celebrate, Dr. Marin. You're going to be even busier from here on out."

"I hope so, Phyllis. See you later"—and she was out the door and racing up the stairs to her own office one floor above. She closed and locked her office door, opened her safe, much smaller and less grand than her boss's, and from it, she lifted out the real pages wrapped in soft linen and put them carefully into her backpack. She hadn't lied to Dr. Bruce. No one was supposed to take the quire from the museum. And as far as anyone knew, the originals were in Dr. Wynn-Jones's safe. She couldn't be separated from the pages.

She realized she did now have a headache. Too much stress and, yes, fear, all catching up with her. Still, she felt the remembered excitement of her very first press conference, remembered every fluent lie she'd told. It was probably online for all the world to see, and she was at center stage. And wasn't that something? She thought of her mother, her small, delicate mother, who'd died only last year, the cancer taking her so very quickly. In her will, she'd requested Isabella to sell or donate everything she'd owned.

Except for the pages. And that's where the pre- cious quire and page 74 had really been hidden, not in the ridiculous British Museum but buried in her mother's garden. She knew her mother hadn't wanted her near the pages, but still, she'd obviously felt compelled to tell her daughter where she'd buried them. Why? So she could make up her own mind what to do with them.

Of course, after she'd dug up the pages, she understood everything. She was too late to steal the Voynich herself and reunite the pages—it had been stolen only one month before her mother had died. But she knew, deep where knowledge resided, that whoever had stolen the Voynich from the Beinecke would come for the rest of the pages. Eagerly. And so she'd set her plan into motion.

And when the thief came for the pages, as she knew he would, she would kill him. The pages were sacred, the Voynich was sacred. She would reunite the pages as she was meant to.

Now it was done. Surely the thief knew about the pages after the grand announcement today. All knew who she was.

But none knew she'd managed to buy a gun, no easy manner in England. She would be ready when he came.

She looked around carefully as she pedaled her bike out of the garage, but she didn't see the man in glasses watching her from the shadows.

CHAPTER TWENTY-THREE

Drummond House
Barton Street
Westminster, London

It was late. Nicholas and Mike sat alone in the living room, pleasantly buzzed on excellent cabernet and the warmth of the fire.

Nicholas rose to stir the fire, making sparks fly upward. He said over his shoulder, "I refused to put a gas fireplace in. I love the smell of woodsmoke."

Mike yawned, stretched. She'd kicked off her high heels and tucked her legs under her. "It's easier to burn documents in a real fire, too. By the way, I saw a DHL office down the street—how late is it open?"

He glanced at the massive grandfather clock in the corner, there since the middle of the eighteenth century. "Another hour, why?"

"Let's overnight letters to Zachery and Savich,

warn them we don't know how deep the infiltration has gone. They can decide whether they feel they can keep the president safe when he arrives here. It's Tuesday night and he's scheduled to arrive Sunday. Not much time for us to nail the bad guys."

He arched a dark brow. "When do we ever have the luxury of time? Happily, we know more about this suspect than he, or she, realizes. First, whoever is behind this is independently wealthy. To build your own drones to this level of capability takes huge financial backing. Like my father said, the one you shot down cost millions. And the tiny ones aren't much cheaper, especially retrofit to carry a poison payload like it was."

"So where do we get a list of filthy-rich billionaires currently living in England?"

"My father," Nicholas said, and he wasn't smiling.

Mike shook her head, pushed her glasses back up her nose. "Let's get those letters to Zachery and Savich written." She rose, smoothed down her dress, slipped her shoes back on. "I doubt they'll cancel the trip, but who knows? The CIA and FBI will sure be scrambling to see if they've been infiltrated."

They drafted the letters, laying out the situation, giving them suggested protocols for communication.

Mike said, "We're so used to instant communication. It feels strange to be out of touch until this is finished."

Nicholas yawned, checked his watch. "We've got to hurry. A quick walk to post these letters at DHL, then perhaps we can find a way to pass the time until morning."

Mike was surprised when she stepped outside and felt the crisp, cool air and shivered. "It's the bloody middle of July, for heaven's sake."

He didn't answer, and she turned to see him staring up at the sky. Her heart ticked up a notch as she looked upward, and her hand automatically went for her Glock. But of course it wasn't there. Penderley's men had confiscated Nicholas's Glock she'd used to shoot down the drone. Her own Glock 27 was in her purse, upstairs. "What? What is it?"

He pointed. "It's a falcon, in the birch tree across the street. Move slowly, don't startle it."

Mike didn't move. She couldn't see the bird, but she did see a red dot emanating from the branches.

"I don't see the falcon. What's that red light?"

The falcon flew into the air, hovered overhead for a moment, then shot away into the darkness.

Nicholas said in a whisper, "The red light, it was a camera. That bleeding bird was spying on us."

CHAPTER TWENTY-FOUR

> To see a hawk in flight is to be privileged to watch a master of the air. . . . It is a unique hunting partnership—you tame her, tend her, train her, and work her to the peak of physical condition, then release her to the elements whilst you become no more than a mere spectator.
>
> —Emma Ford, *Falconry: Art and Practice*

Arlington resumed her journey, wings stretched, soaring over the city. She hadn't been allowed to fly free like this for some time and was tempted to simply keep flying and never go back, but she loved her master and so followed his instructions to the letter.

She flew south, the Thames a smoky ribbon below her, over bridges, adjusting here and there for the GPS coordinates programmed into her special collar. The pulses gave her a path to follow, small pings that focused her flight. If she deviated more than ten yards off course, it gave a tiny shock, nothing so great as to drop her from the sky, only a reminder to adjust back to the proper heading.

She'd trained with the rest of the cabal for months and was the best of them all at following the signals. When she returned, she knew she would be given the choicest morsels to eat and the best cadge.

The camera on her head was an annoyance, nothing more. She was accustomed to wearing a hood; it was part of her daily uniform. The small sliver of leather fit perfectly, designed and cut specifically for her. Each falcon and eagle in the mews had its own hood and special leggings made of Kevlar to cover talons and legs. It was a part of their job to learn how to soar over the rooftops with the tiny cameras recording all they saw.

Although Arlington was trained to hunt drones, to take them from the sky, tonight her mission was one of surveillance only.

The collar pinged, and she pulled up, soaring to her right, toward the final coordinates. She saw pigeons in a nearby tree scatter when they saw her, but she ignored them, flying to the third floor, descending to land gracefully on the brick windowsill. She tensed. She wanted to follow the pigeons, bring them down, talons flexed, tear into them.

A small pulse at her neck.

She looked away from the scattered flock back through the window, to her target. The camera transmitting back to her other master—the quiet one—whirred gently. She trusted him, but she didn't feel the same affection for him. Still, she would do as she was told. It was what she'd been trained to do.

For ten minutes, Arlington perched calmly, beak forward. A pulse, her head to the left. Another pulse, her head to the right. The camera whirred.

Back at the Old Garden, Radu looked into the flat. He watched the woman undress, though it didn't excite him. She showered, made a cup of tea, then sat down at her computer. The computer, now that made him feel something. It was twenty-eight inches diagonally, a perfect size for viewing from across the room. He zoomed the camera onto the screen and started capturing the shots, one after another, as she flicked through the pages.

The quality of the camera on Arlington's head was professional-grade, which meant he could see every detail, every scratch in the ink, every crease in the paper. The room was well decorated, the computer screen top-notch. He wondered idly how a young woman fresh out of college interning at a museum could afford such a computer, then forgot it, it didn't matter. They were lucky she had made the investment, because it was making his job easier. Radu loved the spying. Roman was the one who enjoyed the hands-on work.

The woman flipped through the pages, her chin resting on her palm, oblivious to the falcon outside her window watching everything she did. It was a pity, he thought again, that Drummond had not been so oblivious. Radu had a premonition about this Brit, and it scared him. But he knew Roman wouldn't listen to him if he tried to warn him away, and so he would keep it to himself. Yes, their drone had missed Drummond this morning. Radu would not miss again.

Ten minutes of watching, reveling in reading the words that could cure him of the uncontrolled hemophilia. He'd been told his disease was unique, that unlike most hemophiliacs, a small cut could drain his blood and he'd be dead. Modern medications had no effect. It terrified him. Ah, but these pages—Radu felt they had all they needed. He sent a pulse, and Arlington flew away. His brother said from behind him in their own private language, "Wait, stop her. Look at the desk."

Radu hadn't realized Roman was in the room, he'd been lost in the words in the lost pages, seeing them, reading and understanding them.

Radu sent another pulse to Arlington, and she flew back and crouched again on the sill. Again, her head moved to the right, then to the left, the camera whirred.

Radu said, "The camera is hitting its limit. We will lose everything if I don't shut it down soon."

Roman sounded amazed, disbelieving. "Soon, but not yet. Imagine, Radu, that woman has the pages, the actual physical pages. There, in her flat. It is all so prosaic, so common."

Radu said, "Those aren't the real pages, surely they're facsimiles."

"No, I don't think so. I believe she made copies, and those are the ones locked in a safe at the museum. Radu, look at the corner of her desk. More pages. I don't believe they're part of the quire she announced finding today."

Radu looked closely. His eyes weren't as good as his brother's, and even with the exceptionally high-resolution camera, the angle was too much for him. "But why wouldn't she release them with the others?"

"I don't know, but I do believe she has them all. Radu, trust me. I have a feeling about this."

"Then we need to see those pages."

"Yes. She is Romanian, you know. I could smell it on her even before she told me, gypsy blood calling to mine. Never has that happened before, even when I sought other blood for you. No, this was unique. And I don't believe she found the pages in some old book at the museum. I think she had them already, brought them into the museum, planted them there so she could 'discover' them at the proper time."

"But how did she get the originals?"

"Are you not listening? She's Romanian. I knew

when she announced she'd found the pages in that Marcus Aurelius, it wasn't possible, that she'd made it up. Like you, though, I don't know how she came to have the pages and why she picked now to announce it. She made a huge point of asking the person who stole the Voynich from the Beinecke to return it so the pages could be reunited. Yes, she said those exact words. Reunited. She knows something, Radu. And then there is her blood—"

Radu remained silent, watching his twin pace, back and forth, back and forth. Roman stopped, whirled around, and out it all came. "Is it possible the lost pages were somehow found by her family long ago and passed down through the generations as the book was written by ours? We will research her, see if she has a twin. Maybe that is why she can decode the language. Her blood, Radu, I know it's our blood. I felt it calling to me today when I met her. Can she read the Voynich? Why not? We can."

Roman struck his fist to his palm. "But why is getting the Voynich together so important to her? You saw the press conference online. She begged for the thief to bring back the Voynich, to reunite the pages. Why? And if it's so important to her, then why didn't she steal the Voynich herself?"

He flipped his hand toward the computer. "Turn off the camera, bring Arlington back. Research Isabella Marin, Radu. And I will get those pages."

Radu said, "I wish we could find out who stole the book from Yale."

"Perhaps Isabella Marin will help us find the answer. Does the thief also want the pages? We'll see, won't we?"

Radu turned to the falcon, pulsed her collar, and away she flew, coming back to them. The screen shook with the powerful thrusts of her wings. Radu looked away. It made him ill, motion sick, to watch the falcons fly like this.

Roman dropped to his knees next to his brother. He took his twin's shoulders in his hands. "I swear to you we will cure you of this disease, I swear it." He paused. "I love you, Radu. I want you to be able to experience the world as I do, without death hanging over your head."

Radu clasped his brother's hand. "I love you, too, Roman. The world as you have it—it is something I would like to try. Will you be bringing me the woman tonight?"

"You must research her thoroughly first. I want to know everything I can about her before I act." He rose, and his eyes lit up.

Radu was sure Roman would make something happen, very soon.

"She will tell us all she knows about the Voynich and how she came by the pages," Roman said, and kissed his brother's cheek. "In the meantime, I have a command performance at the Home Office tomorrow. Is there anything new about Drummond I need to know?"

"Nothing after they left the house. Drummond spotted Arlington. I don't know how, the man must have cat eyes. Did he see the camera light? I don't know. But the latest from inside MI5 says Drummond will be there in the morning, and he and one of his Covert Eyes team will be with him. To speak with you."

Radu sighed heavily. "They've caught on, Roman. They aren't conducting any conversations by phone or email. Only in person. And whatever Drummond held in his hand as he left the house tonight—envelopes, I think—it's very possible they've decided to communicate by good old-fashioned mail."

Roman said, "Oh yes, a number of people were at the house tonight. Harry Drummond, now a full-time consultant to MI5. Nicholas Drummond and his FBI partner, Mike Caine. What's worrisome is, of all people, that Tory bitch, Melinda St. Germaine, showed up with another FBI agent—his name's Ben Houston, and he's one of the Covert Eyes team."

"Yes, very worrisome. It's a good thing you'll be there to talk to them. You can find out exactly how much they know and what they suspect. What are you planning, Roman?"

"I will get Marin. You'll have her by this time tomorrow, I promise. It's all coming together, at last. Soon, Brother, soon, you will be free."

CHAPTER TWENTY-FIVE

Say, will the falcon, stooping from above,
Smit with her varying plumage, spare the dove?
Admires the jay the insect's gilded wings?
Or hears the hawk when Philomela sings?
—Alexander Pope

Hungary
1493

The battle was won, and Giovanni Sforza d'Aragona was on his way home to Italy, away from this blood-soaked land and the vicious war, back to Rimini and the warm glow of his castle and his young sons. He had ten ponies taken from the razed stables carrying jewels and trunks of gold and weapons, all recovered from the field.

He would give a small portion of his spoils to his priests, to thank them for their intercessions, a greater portion to the pope, Alexander VI, thus currying favor with the blessed father, and the largest portion to his cousin, Cardinal Ascanio Sforza, to expedite the marriage agreements with the Borgias. Giovanni's first wife had died a couple of years ago, and he wanted Lucrezia to be his second.

It would be an excellent alliance. She was the daughter of the pope, albeit from the wrong side of the bed, and well educated. He'd been told she was interested in many things, and her greatest love: falcons and the hunt.

Giovanni had seen many things, but he'd never forgotten the man he'd met in Hungary, a man who carried the falcon on his fist. His name was Zoltan Szabo, and he'd allied himself with Giovanni, provided him soldiers. He was a pale-skinned man with long black hair. He'd spoken Italian, but with a thick accent, and ate his meat raw and bloody, like his bird. The two men had hunted together, nothing unusual there, but the relationship Zoltan had with the bird had given Giovanni pause. It was an eerie sort of communication, had made Giovanni wonder exactly what the two shared. He'd never spoken of it to Zoltan. He supposed he'd been afraid to. At the memory, Giovanni crossed himself. He hoped Lucrezia's love of falconry wouldn't lead her to the unnatural. Or to eating raw meat.

He prayed she would give him many children and hoped the circumstance of her own birth would allow her more easily to accept his sons, born of his mistress, not his wife. The twins would be old enough to ride now. He looked forward to seeing them.

The ride was hard, the days long, and at night, the soldiers would sit around the fire and tell stories. Giovanni was especially fascinated about a tale of a powerful Hungarian prince who drank blood. It was sacrilege to listen to such things, but he couldn't help himself. He listened long into the night, and when he slept, his dreams were nightmares of men in armor with fangs the size of wolves, who could not be slain, no matter how many times he struck them with his sword. They carried falcons on their fists and spoke with heavy accents.

The next day, unsettled and eager to be gone, Giovanni hurried his groom to saddle his horse. The groom, a lad named Franco, nervous, trying to please his master, left the cinch too loose, and as Giovanni mounted, the saddle pulled to the side, dropping both Giovanni and the saddlebags to the ground. Giovanni was cursing his groom when he saw a book of papers wrapped in a white cloth slide out of the saddlebag.

"Careful, Franco. I'm planning to give it to my new bride when we wed."

Franco whispered, "I looked at it, sire. It is a fine book. Will she be able to read it?"

"Of course she will. She speaks many languages."

Franco scuffed his shoes in the dirt, then he leaned close. "Sire, I must tell you, I've heard the pages. They speak, at night, from your saddlebags, to me. They tell me to do things."

Giovanni clouted Franco's head. "You've been drinking the ale again, haven't you? Do not say such ridiculous things."

"Sire, forgive me, but truly, the words they speak are not ridiculous."

What was this all about? Giovanni said, "Don't say such things to the rest of the men. They might not understand, may decide to drop you off a cliff."

And Franco bowed his head, nodded.

But that night, when the fire was low, Franco heard the words again, whispers in his head, growing louder and more insistent. He went to the saddlebag, put his ear against the worn leather, and the pages spoke.

He couldn't understand the words, exactly, but the whispers told him many things, including listing the names of the men who were planning to murder his master and steal the treasure for themselves.

Franco took up a sword and went to where three of the men still sat beside the fire. The nearest man was almost too easy to kill, the sword slid through his neck like butter. The second and the third were also easy. The fourth, though, alerted by the crack of a branch under Franco's foot, jumped to his feet. His death was loud and roused the rest of the camp. The fifth ran from Franco, screaming. The rest of the soldiers wrestled the sword away from Franco. Giovanni, asleep farthest away from the fire, was awakened by the fighting.

Franco was on his knees by the fire, hands bound behind him.

Giovanni looked at the four dead soldiers, then back at Franco. "What have you done?"

Franco raised his eyes to Giovanni's face. He whispered, "I did as the pages instructed. I killed four of the men who planned to kill you. I was protecting you. The fifth escaped me." And Franco nodded toward the soldier.

"But my men wouldn't kill me." He looked to the fifth, and the man fell to his knees, crying, "They were forcing me, sire. They wanted me to poison your food, but I refused, I would never—"

His words were cut off along with his head, which rolled into the fire.

The soldiers looked on, wondering what magic had come to the groom.

Giovanni raised Franco to his feet and embraced him.

"Thank you for my life. Now, explain to me how you knew about this plot."

"It was the pages, sire."

Gradara Castle
Near Venice, Italy
Three Months Later

"Tell me the story again, Papa. The one in the book you brought home about twin brothers who drank blood."

"One more time, Marco, and then it's off to sleep with you. Once upon a time, there were two brothers." Giovanni would never admit to his sons he couldn't read the book, that it had been Franco, his groom, who'd told him the story of the twin brothers from long ago.

"Like Luciano and me?"

"*Sì*, like you and Luciano. They shared a womb and were born within minutes of each other. It was soon apparent that one of the brothers was stronger than the other, even though they should have been exactly alike. When the weaker began to sicken and waste, his brother, devastated, searched high and low for a cure."

Marco whispered, "Like Luciano and me." But his father didn't hear him.

"He rode east, to the farthest corner of the earth, and collected strange herbs and the blood of young beasts. He then rode north, as far as he could, where it was light all day, and stayed a summer with a shaman who taught him how to use the herbs and the blood to live forever. He rode west, then, where the women were pale and staring, and collected books that would help expand his brother's mind. And then he rode south, to his brother's side, and, together, they experimented.

"They boiled the herbs, and they tasted the flesh of the young animals, and they drank the blood of the women in their village. And they grew strong, together, and the weaker brother wrote everything down in a book so they would never forget."

The fire crackled, and sparks flew in the air. Giovanni looked pensively into the flames for a moment, then turned back to his sons. "Everywhere they went, blood followed. And the brothers saw the villagers they'd spared die after growing old and sick, leaving behind another generation, who grew to maturity, married, created children, and still, the brothers preyed among them, and still, there was no gray in their whiskers. They remained tall and straight and vigorous.

"All of their tales they recorded, how they drank of the necks of virgins under the full moon, how the howls of wolves and bears never struck fear in their hearts. They moved unseen, unknown, until they set upon other young women and girls."

"The book you brought home, Papa, it is the story of the brothers?"

"It is, young Marco."

"I want to drink the blood of virgins," the child whispered, and his father slapped him across the mouth, hard.

His father stood over them, his face suffused with blood and anger.

"I am sorry, Papa," Marco whispered, wiping the blood from his mouth. "I was only thinking of Luciano, of ways he could be strong again."

"It is a story, Marco," Giovanni repeated, praying it was so. "It is not real, only a tale like the ones the bards tell us when they visit. You must swear to me you will never believe this tale or any like it. You must swear you will never act upon anything in this story. Swear to me!"

He shook both Luciano and Marco. Marco, terrified for his brother, yelled, "We swear, Papa, we swear. Let him go, please, let him go. We won't ask to hear the tale again. Please tell us about the campaign. Tell us about the men you killed in battle."

Luciano said, "Yes, Papa. Tell us about the campaign. Tell us."

Marco watched his father draw a deep breath. Still, he kept himself between Luciano and their father, holding his brother's hand so it wouldn't shake, and pretended to listen to his father tell of fighting and death and pillage, all those deaths ordained and commended by the priests.

When their father left them and they were alone in their soft feather bed, Marco and Luciano spoke of the tale, of the long-ago brothers, twins, just like them, who lived for generations, and how they were able to do so.

Marco held his brother tight, afraid to say the word aloud, but he did. "Perhaps the blood of a virgin will help give you strength, Luciano, like the brother in the book."

Luciano, a thoughtful boy, said, "It is possible the blood of another has healing properties. This must be why the physicians bleed us. Perhaps they give our blood to those weaker than us. I agree this may work. Are you going to steal Papa's book?"

"I need the instructions. Perhaps there are ways to make the blood taste better."

"You know he keeps the book on the shelf in his outer chambers. He plans to give it to our new mother as a gift for their wedding."

"Then I must go tonight. I pray he will not catch me."

"He isn't in his chambers. He is bedding a chambermaid."

"How do you know, Luciano?"

His brother's gray eyes darkened. "I watch, I listen. I feel this strange book may be my savior. Even with it here in the castle, I feel stronger."

Marco slipped into his father's rooms, comfortable in the knowledge his father was busy with a chambermaid.

It was easy to find. The book sang out to him. It felt warm in his hands. He opened it and studied the drawings, but he didn't recognize what they were. And the words on the page were in a strange language he'd never seen—yet somehow they seemed familiar. Several pieces of paper were loose inside the binding. He could see the numbers were out of order.

But the sense of them—Marco didn't need to read the words to know what they were saying.

They needed blood. The pages needed blood.

He hurried back to his brother, and, by candlelight, they sat with their hands linked, each touching the book. The loose pages held instructions, Marco knew it. He pulled them out. Other pages were bound, so he left them intact. Luciano had to draw on one of the pages, he had to mark it, he said, and it had to be in blood. Marco pricked his arm and Luciano drew a picture in his blood on the page. Luciano had to have the page, had to. One page had a drawing that called to him. He used the edge of his knife to slice out the page. He slid it inside his pillow along with the pages that held the recipes. Marco prepared to return the book to his father's rooms.

The roar of their father's voice was nearly enough to blow out the candle. It guttered and flickered, then strengthened again. "What are you doing?"

Giovanni grabbed Marco's small arm, dragged him upright, and pulled him from the bed. "I know you stole my book! This is a gift for your new mother. How dare you?"

"I'm sorry, Papa, I'm sorry. I thought it called to me, but I was wrong. It is blasphemous. I was bringing it back to you. We don't want it."

Giovanni's heart pounded hard. He said between gritted teeth, "It is merely a book, of no importance at all. Only a book. Go to bed." And he grabbed the book and left their bedchamber.

Giovanni was frightened. He remembered his young groom Franco was called to kill his compatriots, remembered how he'd told Giovanni about the two brothers, the twins. All along he'd believed the groom was lying, making it up. Ridiculous, but now—Marco had said the pages called to him? Just as his groom had said?

He sat up with the book all night, but he couldn't understand anything in it. The next morning, he summoned the visiting Jesuit, here to officiate his marriage. He wrapped the book in a white cloth and put it in a box. He called the Jesuit aside. "Father, please take this book away with you. Back to Rome. I no longer want it in my home."

The Jesuit took the book without a word. "As you wish, my lord. However, I am not to see Rome for quite some time. I travel to England at week's end. With your blessing, I will take it there, far away from your lands."

The book left soon after.

Marco and Luciano stood on the ramparts of the castle, watching the priest ride away. They thought they heard the book crying, crying for the parts of it left behind.

Soon, from one of the pages, Luciano found how to get the blood he craved. And how to make it palatable.

THE SECOND DAY

WEDNESDAY

According to a published list in [the] 15th century, a different species of raptor was assigned to different ranks in society. How strictly this was adhered to, no one is very sure.

From *The Boke of St. Albans*, published 1486:

Emperor—eagle or vulture
King—gyrfalcon
Prince—peregrine falcon
Duke—Falcon of the Rock (another name for peregrine)
Knight—saker or sakeret
Squire—lanner or lanneret
Lady—merlin
Young man—hobby
Yeoman—goshawk
Priest—sparrow hawk
Holy water clerk—musket
Knave/servant—kestrel

—THE FALCONRY CENTRE

CHAPTER TWENTY-SIX

MI5 Headquarters, Home Office
Thames House
12 Millbank
Westminster, London

Identification, please."

Mike handed over her FBI creds to a security officer who looked bored to her, but then she saw his eyes roving between her and Nicholas and decided no, maybe not so bored after all. She had to admit, going into the vaunted Home Office was a bit of a thrill. The security was similar to theirs at home—tight, biometric, and impenetrable—but to an American ear, there was something special about hearing the British accents.

She discovered she liked London quite a bit, almost as much as New York. No, that was going too far.

They were issued badges, and a young man with glasses similar to Mike's stepped from behind a column.

Nicholas saw him, smiled, and stuck out his hand. "Ian. Good to see you. Mike, this is Ian Sansom, my father's right hand. He plays cricket, but don't hold it against him."

"You're mad I beat you the last time we faced off. You still owe me a pint. Mike, it's good to meet you. Harry has said nothing but good things about you. Did I hear correctly, you shot down a drone with a Glock?"

"Lucky shot."

"Bollocks," Nicholas said, and punched her arm.

"I agree," Ian said. "I hardly think that's the case. Now, please follow me. Harry is waiting."

Harry Drummond's office was on the fifth floor. When they got out of the elevator, Mike stopped. She saw beautiful dark woods and marble-topped tables in the hallway, all heavy, imposing, and older than the White House.

People were everywhere, many of them agents, she supposed, but it was strangely silent. The air was charged. Everyone knew something was up, but with typical British restraint, no one was talking openly. It was eerie, seeing a whole floor of agents go silent like that.

She wasn't surprised to see Harry's office was as elegant and understated as the man himself. A massive mahogany Victorian desk, the surface clean except for a leather desk pad and laptop and a discreet banker's lamp dominated the room. A heavy mahogany credenza behind the desk held photos of Nicholas as a boy, Mitzie as a young woman, and a current shot of the whole Drummond family. And, inexplicably, on the wall, beside the flag of the United Kingdom, a large stuffed trout. She wanted to laugh, but everyone was speaking in low, worried voices. She planned to ask Nicholas later if the stuffed trout was a humorous homage to the castle ghost of Old Farrow Hall, a gentleman she had yet to encounter—the infamous Captain Flounder.

Harry immediately rose and came forward. "Good morning to you. Do come in, make yourselves at home. You haven't been in my office for years, have you, Nicholas? Ian, can you bring a tea and two coffees, please?"

Ian nodded and slipped quietly away, closing the door behind him. When they were alone, Harry slid a note across the desk to Nicholas and Mike. The words made her heart kick up like a mule.

> *Found two listening devices in the office. Have swept for more but not sure we've found them all. Very sophisticated, very well-placed. Have informed the home secretary. Authorized to use whatever means necessary to rout the suspect.*

When they nodded, Harry put a lighter to it and dropped it in a large brass ashtray. As the acrid smoke curled into the room, he said, voice jovial, "I'd love to show you around the place, Mike. Let's take a tour."

Five minutes later, the three of them were walking up Page Street to St. John's Gardens. No rain this morning; sun streaked through the green trees onto the paths filled with people bustling about.

Harry led them to a quiet bench under a birch tree, and they settled themselves. Nicholas saw his father looked haggard in the strong morning sunlight. He looked older. It scared him. His father had always been a rock, impervious to upset or stress, full of strength. This morning, he looked every one of his sixty-two years.

Nicholas said quietly, "What else have you found?"

"Outside of the listening devices? Sophisticated buggers, those. They aren't putting off the normal signatures. I only found them because I started taking apart my office the moment I arrived this morning. We sweep for bugs daily anyway, and they passed a standard sweep, which isn't very standard. The whole building's being swept now, and your Adam is set up inside our server mainframes, looking for anomalies. Without a doubt, someone inside has infiltrated us, and now we must discover who it is."

Mike asked, "What do you think his end goal is?"

Harry looked off across the park. "I have no earthly idea. But they want something."

He glanced at his watch. "Roman Ardelean is due shortly. Let's talk to him, see what he can tell us. Radulov Industries has moved quickly to issue patches to the software affected by all the security breaches this past week. Getting past a Radulov firewall takes some talent. To me, this feels like a well-funded, state-sponsored assault. It's the cyber-attack I've been fearing, the real deal, not a couple of Russian hackers in a basement in Moscow.

"Now, we've taken apart Chapman Donovan's life, and I'm sad to say, he was talking to Heinrich Hemmler about a transfer of money. We don't yet know what it was for, but it certainly reinforces the notion he was up to no good, and someone needed to get both men out of the way. Are the two situations tied together? I don't know yet, but I'm willing to bet they are."

Nicholas said, "So the two were working together and double-crossed a partner, so he had them killed?"

Harry shrugged, then sat forward, his hand on Nicholas's arm. "All possible. What really scares me is that you've been targeted as well, Nicholas, both you and Michaela. I know you don't have any ties to Hemmler or Donovan. So why you?"

Nicholas said, "We hit on something, clearly."

"Still nothing useful on the drone, outside of the weapons used. The consensus is you and

Michaela are very lucky to be alive." He rose. "We're going in circles. Let's get back. I want to see what Ardelean has to say."

The sirens were sudden and close. Mike looked at Nicholas, who had shielded his eyes and was looking back toward the Thames.

She saw Harry's assistant running toward them, his jacket flapping.

Nicholas said, "This doesn't look good."

Ian skidded to a halt, panting. "Sir, please come at once. There's been another attack."

CHAPTER TWENTY-SEVEN

FBI Headquarters
26 Federal Plaza
22nd Floor, Home of Covert Eyes
New York City

New York SAC Milo Zachery was in the office nearly, enjoying the relative quiet after supervising a "knock," FBI talk for serving a predawn search warrant on a suspect. The knock had gone well, and he wasn't needed, so he poured a cup of coffee and was reading the morning briefs when his secretary, Gladys, knocked on the door. "Special delivery for you, sir. From Agent Drummond and Agent Caine."

"What's this all about?" He took the envelope. "An overnight from London? He better not invoice this, do you have any idea how much it cost?"

The overnight envelope was thin. Zachery ripped it open. Out fell a thick, creamy envelope with Zachery's name on the front in elegant script. Inside was a three-page handwritten letter.

Sir,

*We apologize for the subterfuge, but
we had no other way to warn you. Our
communications have been compromised.
Agent Caine and I were attacked
yesterday on the way to London to look
into the drone murders. Ironically, we
were attacked by a drone, which Agent
Caine shot down. With a Glock.*

*There was no way for anyone to know
we were working the drone murders
unless they were listening to or watching
our communication with Agent Savich.
We believe the Home Office has also been
compromised.*

*We can only assume your communications
are compromised, too. I put Adam on a
plane to London last night. Tomorow, he
and I will try to discover the depth of the
breach at MI5 and who is responsible.
On your end, I suggest Gray do a full
intrusion protocol on every system we
utilize. And yes, I know how much
overtime that will cost.*

*Agent Caine asks me to remind you
that Savich is probably in the same boat.
We leave it to you as to how you wish
to communicate with the CAU going
forward—a similar letter has been sent*

*to him as well. You must assume all
phones and servers are being monitored.
If listening devices are in place, I'd
be surprised, but right now, we aren't
ruling out anything. I'd suggest taking a
walk—without your phone—with Gray
to initiate the protocols necessary to keep
us all safe. Any software updates from
the past six months need to be checked
thoroughly. Anything that resembles the
code for the WannaCry malware attack is
suspect.*

*I'm afraid we're going to have to
communicate the old-fashioned way for
the time being until we get a handle on
how we've been infiltrated, and how deep
the breach goes. NO COMPUTERS.
We will report in daily by cable or
letter, and you can send your replies to
Drummond House in Westminster. Oh,
yes, Ben is working with us. I trust you
can assemble the rest of Covert Eyes and
fill them in on the situation. And yes, we
will do our best to stay alive and out of
trouble.*

Drummond & Caine

Zachery read the letter once more, then hurried to Gray Wharton's cubicle one floor below.

Zachery wasn't surprised to see Gray rumpled,

his suit coat hanging half off the back of his chair, a granola power bar in his hand. Coffee cups littered his desk, and four computer screens were lined up in a curved array, each with a different program running.

"The breakfast of champions doesn't come in a wrapping, you know. If you don't start eating real food, I'll be forced to hire you a chef. Now, Gray, according to Drummond, we have a problem." He handed Gray the letter. He read it quickly, whistled.

"Seems the problem isn't only with Drummond." He stood up and grabbed his jacket. "Shall we take a walk, sir?"

Five minutes later, Zachery and Gray were out the front doors and onto Worth Street. Zachery saw a line forty people deep already winding around the side of the building, most waiting to get into the passport office or apply for citizenship. It might look like a security nightmare, but, in truth, this building was probably the safest place in all of New York City.

Still unspeaking, they took a right on Lafayette and then veered into Thomas Paine Park. Zachery could see the morning traffic was nose to tail, heard honking and swearing, a typical New York rush hour under way. It made him smile. He loved this city, loved it to his bones.

They took a bench that faced back toward Federal Plaza, and Zachery found himself wondering if Drummond and Mike, like he and Gray, were utilizing parks for their conversations.

Gray asked, "What have Nicholas and Mike gotten into? Someone tried to kill them with a drone attack?"

"Apparently so. I would have liked to see Agent Caine shoot a drone out of the sky. But first things first. We have to take them at their word we're compromised, too. How can we get secure communications with Washington, and with Drummond?"

"Letters, cables, dedicated encrypted sat phones. It's a six-hour flight between here and London— Clancy and Trident can make it in five, so if we're desperate, we can use them, too."

"Flying messages across the Atlantic? I'd love to hear the director's thoughts on that manner of transmission."

"Only until we figure out what's happening. Don't look at me like I'm crazy. It's the safest, most secure method. You know the terrorists move all their high-level information by hand. They aren't crazy enough to do it electronically anymore. And now we're in the same boat."

"I know that, Gray."

"Sir, how anyone could have gotten into our systems is a mystery to me. We are fortified on all levels, and I would think an intrusion would have already shown up in the code. Does Nicholas have any idea who's behind it?"

"You read the letter—he says he doesn't, but you know Drummond, he probably already has four suspects in mind. And he's hours ahead of us. He's known this since last night. I would like to touch base with him immediately if you can figure out a way to do so securely."

"We should coordinate with Savich and the CAU in D.C. right away. Though I'm not sure the best way to do it. We can simply buy disposable phones on our end, but how will they know to do it themselves?"

"Burner phones—" He broke off, looked across the park. "Is that Agent Scott?"

Sure enough, Agent Lia Scott was running across the street with a package in her hand, obviously looking for them. When she saw them, she put on a burst of speed. Gray couldn't help but admire her latest outfit—conservative blue pantsuit, black low-heeled boots, and, underneath the tailored blue jacket, a Def Leppard concert T-shirt from their *Pyromania* tour. She never wore a nose ring at work, but her left ear glinted with hardware.

Even before she stopped, she said, "Sir, a package came a few minutes ago from Agent Savich in D.C. It says *emergency* on it. I saw you and Gray leave together, so I decided to try to catch you."

Zachery took the envelope. "Thank you, Lia. Stay put, we need to get you up to speed." As he ripped opened the envelope, he said, "In short, we have a comms breach."

He laughed when he looked inside. It was a burner cell phone and a note with a phone number on it.

He dialed the number.

CHAPTER TWENTY-EIGHT

Criminal Apprehension Unit, CAU
Hoover Building
Washington, D.C.

Special Agent Dillon Savich drummed his fingers on the desk, looking out into the empty bullpen. It was early, and only Ruth, yawning, was at her desk, coffee and briefcase in hand.

He'd come into the office to clear out some paperwork. And there had been Nicholas's letter waiting for him at the front desk. He'd ripped it open in the elevator, read it, and then turned right back around, went to the nearest 7-Eleven, grabbed a set of burner phones, and walked straight to the courier office on 14th Street. It was 5:00 a.m., and the courier could be in New York by seven thirty, for a price, of course. They were used to doing cross-city runs, but the kid who was there was more than willing to go to New York for the morning. He was at the train station fifteen minutes later, Amtrak chugging him up to the city.

Savich checked his Mickey Mouse watch again. Almost 8:00 a.m. "Come on, come on."

The burner cell phone on his desk buzzed. He snatched it up.

"Took you long enough."

Zachery said, "Are you inside? If so, get outside and call me back."

"Give me a minute." Savich punched off, ran down the stairs and onto the street. He ran south and stopped two blocks from the National Mall, probably the safest place to talk, considering all the joggers and tourists. It would confuse the signals if anyone had already figured them out.

He found a quiet bench and called back the previous number.

Zachery sounded almost cheerful. "Glad you anticipated we'd need to have a chat this morning. Made our lives much easier. You're outside, on the off chance the communications breach includes an audio component?"

"Yes, even though Nicholas thinks it's a stretch, but who knows?"

Zachery said, "Anything's possible, but burners, outside? We should be okay. The offices, not so much, and email, certainly not."

"Are you going to send Covert Eyes to London?"

"Drummond already has Mike, Ben, and Adam, more than enough boots on the ground, I think, especially if we don't want them to know we know we're onto them. Whoever *them* is."

Savich said, "Hopefully, he'll know more after a meeting at the Home Office this morning with the head of Radulov, Roman Ardelean himself. They'll be checking MATRIX together. Let's speak again at ten a.m. Drummond's meeting should be done by then, so he'll have some new information for us."

"Copy that. Gray and Lia are going to start running diagnostics here, see what we can find. If anything. Hopefully this is a false alarm on our end and it's only the Brits who are compromised."

"I'll begin a sweep on my end as well. I trust there's serious discussion at the White House about the wisdom of the president traveling to England at the end of the week, given the assassination of the vice chancellor of Germany."

"You know he'll dismiss it, claim he won't be cowed by terrorists."

Savich sighed. "You're probably right. We'll speak again at ten." Savich punched off, went back to the office, and opened MAX. He didn't know exactly what to look for, so he plugged in every parameter he could think of so MAX could search through all the communication systems for the Bureau and pick out anomalies.

An internal warning banner came across MAX's screen.

"Are you right, Nicholas?" Savich switched to

the BBC website just in time to see the panicked face of the anchor wrapping the segment. He turned up the volume.

"We will certainly have more on this shocking attack soon, but for those just joining us, the BBC is reporting that Defense Secretary Sir Terry Alexander has been pronounced dead at the scene."

CHAPTER TWENTY-NINE

The Ministry of Defence (MoD or MOD) is the British government department responsible for implementing the defence policy set by Her Majesty's government and is the headquarters of the British Armed Forces.

—Wikipedia

MI5 Headquarters, Home Office
Thames House
12 Millbank
Westminster, London

Ian filled them in as they rushed back to the Home Office. "Sir Terry Alexander was heading into an early lunch at *Marianne* in Notting Hill. The car dropped him off, and according to witnesses, he stopped to take a call, then stumbled, went down on the curb."

Nicholas asked, "Was there a drone?"

"We don't know. My God, sir, three in three

days. We were told by the associate he was meeting Alexander for lunch, then Alexander was leaving for Paris."

"I think Mike and I should head to Notting Hill, see the scene firsthand. It has to be a drone, and we have to find someone who saw it."

Harry nodded. "All right. I'll reschedule Ardelean. I'll call ahead, let them know to expect you, so you won't have a problem getting past the police blockade. Adam can continue searching the servers."

Nicholas tossed out an arm, and a taxi stopped with a screech. He and Mike bundled into the back seat, and Nicholas said, "Take us to *Marianne*, in Notting Hill."

"Won't be able to do it, sir, the area's been cordoned off. Some sort of attack."

Nicholas said, "We're coppers, they'll let us through, trust me. And while you're at it, could I trouble you for your mobile?"

The driver gave Nicholas a quick stare, then tossed his phone over the seat. Nicholas dialed Penderley's mobile. No answer. Nicholas left a brief message, saying they were headed his way.

The driver had them there in twenty minutes flat. He was forced to drop them at the corner of Shrewsbury and Westbourne Park Roads, as close as he could get. Mike passed over several pounds, and they were running down the street. They saw the flashing lights a block away. "There. Let's go."

Media vans were parked along the way, their satellite dishes turned toward the sky, and Mike could see at least fifteen officers in black uniforms wearing black baseball caps with a black-and-white checkerboard pattern around the brim and fluorescent lime-yellow reflective vests. POLICE was stamped on the back of the vests, and long truncheons lay at their sides.

There were a few heavily armed officers as well, with ear defenders on, heads turning, looking for threats.

Several silver Metropolitan Police BMWs blocked the road, their blue and lime-yellow paint screaming a warning. Mike saw a K9 officer leading a large German shepherd along the street, letting the dog sniff chairs and postboxes and car wheels, looking for explosives. White-and-red PO-LICE LINE crime-scene tape was stretched across the side streets, keeping people from entering the area.

Mike and Nicholas showed their credentials at the roadblock that gave onto Chepstow Road. The officer said, "Superintendent Penderley told me you were coming, Agents." He pointed. "He's down there, on the right side of the road. Penderley said specifically you are to avoid the media, no interviews, no chatter, nothing even off the record."

Nicholas said, "Understood," and wrote their names on the list of people attending the scene. They both ducked under the tape and headed down the street. They found Penderley standing under an awning talking with a woman Nicholas vaguely recognized from his time at New Scotland Yard.

Penderley was wearing a bulletproof flak jacket over a white button-down shirt and gray slacks and was gesturing around the scene. He was obviously the top brass. He spied them and called them over, shook both their hands, and introduced them to the woman by his side. "Drummond, Caine, meet DI Clare Griffith, she's one of our best and brightest, and she's running this scene. I have to get back to Scotland Yard and start the damage control. We're going to have every eye in the free world on us within the hour, so figure out what the bloody hell's happening, would you? Oh, yes, and we checked the other two crime scenes, and nothing like a needle was found, though there was plenty of metal trash. It's all been taken into evidence."

"Thank you for trying, sir. Good to see you."

"You, too, Drummond"—and after a nod to Mike, he added to Nicholas, "I thought I asked you to get it sorted." And he was gone.

DI Griffith looked sharp, tall, black hair twisted up in a roll at the back of her head. She was wearing a blue suit with a bulletproof vest under her blouse. She looked once at Nicholas, looked again, something Mike was used to from nearly every woman who spotted him. To her credit, Griffith got her cop brain turned back on and said, her voice official, "Agent Drummond, I was actually in uniform when you were Penderley's go-to. You're a hard act to follow, but I'll get there." She looked him up and down, all cop now, shook her head. "Imagine, you left us to become the first Brit in the American FBI."

Nicholas smiled, said immediately, "Can you tell us exactly what's happened?"

Griffith waved across the street, where Mike could see the gray wainscoted front of the restaurant; its name, MARIANNE, on a sign hanging over the door. People were huddled along the old red-brick walls, numb and gawking. There were faces staring out of the restaurant windows at the chaos outside.

And Mike saw the shape of a body under a white tarp.

Griffith said, "Mr. Alexander is lying where he fell. Too soon to know exactly what happened, but witnesses say he stopped on the sidewalk right outside the restaurant, to make a call. He slapped a hand to his neck and went down. He was dead before the first emergency calls went out. If we hadn't had two other influential people die in two days, I don't think we'd be looking at this as anything other than a heart attack or stroke, but clearly, it's much more."

Nicholas asked, "May we see the body, please?"

"Certainly." Griffith smiled at him, but it was professional this time, cop to cop.

Mike asked, "Were there any drones reported in the area?"

"We haven't heard of any, and believe me, I've told all our officers to ask, given how Mr. Donovan and Mr. Hemmler were murdered." She led them across the street, where two officers were guarding the body.

Nicholas went down on his haunches and pulled back the sheet.

They looked down at the congested face of the former secretary of defense. His bulging eyes stared back at them.

"Not a peaceful death," Griffith said.

Nicholas shook his head. "No." Using his forefinger, he gently moved the head from left to right. "Nothing on his neck I can see. May we roll him over?"

Mike said, "No, wait, Nicholas. Look there, right under his ear. There's a red spot."

"Good eyes, Agent Caine. You're right, there is." He began scanning the ground. So much dirt, rocks, little bits of litter, detritus on the street.

He grinned up at Mike. "You know what we need, don't you?"

"Yep. DI Griffith, any chance you have a magnet around?"

"A magnet? I don't—wait, I do, sort of. The cover of my iPad is magnetized. It's constantly picking up loose paper clips from my desk. Why?"

Nicholas grinned. "That will work. Can you fetch it, please?"

"Thank goodness Scotland Yard froze the scene," Mike said, "or we wouldn't have had a chance of finding it."

Griffith returned, handed over her red-cased tablet. "Here you go. I also put a call in for someone to bring us a magnet a bit more powerful, just in case."

He opened the cover. First, he slowly ran it over the body. "I don't think it's here."

"It?"

Mike said to Griffith, "We believe there is a very small needle, or something similar, somewhere nearby."

Nicholas whooped, stood up. "And here it is, not three feet from the body." The edge of the case now had a small, thin piece of metal stuck to its edge.

Mike examined it. "Say hello to our murder weapon."

CHAPTER THIRTY

Drones have been around for more than two decades, but their roots date back to World War I when both the U.S. and France worked on developing automatic, unmanned airplanes. But the last few years have been significant in terms of drone adoption, usage expansion across industries, and global awareness.

—*Business Insider*

The Old Garden
Twickenham
Richmond upon Thames, London

Roman smiled when he saw the name on the caller ID. He said to Radu, "He's right on time." He said into his mobile, "Hello, Barstow. I trust you have my money?"

Barstow shouted in his ear, "Are you barking mad? This has to stop! Do you understand me?

Once again you've acted stupidly, thoughtlessly!" A pause, Barstow sucked in a breath, and he sounded calmer. "All right, tell me why you killed Alexander."

Roman said, "You told me yourself he wanted out. He cost me another one hundred and fifty million pounds. I trust the others have paid?"

There was a moment of silence.

Roman asked softly, "Who else wants out of our project?"

"No, no one, at least not yet. I'm working on her, she'll come through."

"We have two women. Which her?"

"All right, it's Paulina Vittorini—but, Roman, I can talk her around, but you need to let her see the drone army first. All right?"

"You talk her around, Barstow, and no viewing the army before I'm paid. So how much money do you have for me?"

"They're still balking. I told you, they want the drone army, then they'll pay. Think about it, Roman. It doesn't really matter, does it? I mean, you'll be paid, and we'll begin our fight against radical Islam in Africa. Have a little faith, man."

Roman was silent. Barstow rushed forward. "Listen, you're going to get yourself caught at this rate, and then where will we be? Too many people are paying attention, and we can't afford for you to be exposed.

"Roman, I understand your . . . frustration,

but I've promised our investors the drones will be in their hands as soon as you're paid. I will convince them to trust me, to trust you."

"I expect to be paid in full. I also suggest you find two more investors. Do it quickly, Barstow. Do you understand?"

"Yes, yes, I'll find two more investors to pay the back-end costs. I'll get as much as I can possibly manage for you tomorrow. You know I must be careful about any large transfers, especially since you've brought the Drummonds to breathe down our necks. Why in the name of all that's holy did you try to take out Harry Drummond's son?"

Roman smiled into the phone, said softly, "I don't know what you're talking about."

"Oh, you don't, do you? Didn't you know? The Home Office has possession of your drone."

His heart froze. "What?"

"Ah," Barstow said, his voice malicious. "You didn't know? And here I thought you knew everything."

"But that isn't possible, the drone has a self-destruct mechanism. We activated it—"

"And it didn't work. Your little game must end now, Roman. We can't afford to have any more attention that might lead to the discovery of our project, a discovery that would destroy both of us. If you stop murdering people, I'll find a way to make sure no one links the drone to you. But, Roman, don't think I can protect you forever. If you continue to behave in such a reckless manner, I will be forced to intercede in ways you will not like. The prime minister would be most interested in the real reason his defense minister was killed, don't you think?"

Now this was laughable. "Do you truly think you're in a position to threaten me, Barstow? Even if the drone failed to self-destruct, no one can trace it back to me. I've made sure of that. I'm not as careless as you evidently think. Now, the money, tomorrow, or you really won't like my next step. As for your telling the prime minister anything at all, think about your own illustrious neck. Now, wouldn't your ancestors turn over in their graves if the eighth Viscount Barstow was hung for treason?"

He cut Barstow off, turned on Radu.

"What does he mean the self-destruct didn't activate?"

"Stop yelling, Roman! I don't know, I don't know. I did activate it—of course I did. Here, look." Radu's fingers moved on the computer's keyboard, elegant, fast, graceful as a concert pianist. "See? It shows the self-destruct was entered three minutes after the magazine was emptied." Radu pointed to the schematic. "The system shows it detonated. I don't understand, the drone should be in a thousand pieces."

"Well, it's whole, isn't it, and it's your fault." He felt rage building, building, realized his brother was cowering, obviously frightened. Of him. He took three deep breaths, fingered a microdose into his mouth. He shut his eyes and felt the LSD begin to smooth him out.

His rage fell away. He lightly touched his palm to his brother's cheek, felt him flinch. "I'm sorry, Radu. I would never hurt you. I shouldn't have lost my temper like that. The failure of the self-destruct, these things happen. You will find out why the drone didn't self-destruct as it should have and we will correct the problem. Obviously, the prototype isn't ready. We'll have to make more adjustments.

"I told you my meeting at MI5 with Drummond was moved back. It's time for reconnaissance. We must make certain I am not suspected. Or that fool, Barstow. If he thought he could get away with it, he would bring me down in an instant. I can't believe he threatened me with the PM, the jabbering old fool." His hand continued to lightly pat Radu's face. "He claims he will add two more investors. If he manages that, they'll get a good deal, given both Donovan and Alexander already paid in half.

"I believe Drummond is the biggest threat. Arlington is already stationed at the Home Office. Have her follow him, and if it's possible, send a drone to kill him, the others, as well." He leaned down, kissed his brother's forehead. "As always, I am counting on you, Radu."

Roman was relieved when Radu smiled up at him. "Yes, I will do that."

"Let me know as soon as it's done. Tomorrow, at last, Barstow will pay us, and we can deliver his bloody drone army. I want to be rid of that blighter forever."

Roman began to pace. He placed another microdose on his tongue, felt it working almost immediately. "I must take the woman tonight, and the missing Voynich pages. Healing you is my greatest priority now."

Radu rose, placed his hand on his brother's arm. "Roman, you are stretching yourself too thin. Too many operations, too many projects. The pages, the woman, aren't going anywhere. Do you really think it necessary to act tonight?"

Roman hugged his brother to him, felt his heart pounding against his. "I want you to be cured, and that means we have to have the pages." He set his brother away from him, placed his hands on Radu's shoulders. "I want you well, a whole man. I want the world to see your brilliance, your incredible skill. I want you by my side, and that means I must deal with the woman as soon as possible. Tonight." He paused, looked back at the schematic of the drone. "You will eliminate the threat, and I will take care of everything else."

Radu had seen him take a third microdose in a matter of minutes. He knew Roman was becoming more and more attached to his LSD, and he was afraid that instead of helping him channel the brilliance, tether it, so it didn't fly away like his cabal, the microdoses were making his behavior more and more erratic, affecting his moods, his reasoning, making him more unpredictable. Radu understood the benefits to the microdoses, but now, what Roman was becoming scared him.

He thought of all the drugs he'd been given since birth, for both his Asperger's and autism, or whatever it was, and his rare form of hemophilia and how none had helped him. He knew that too much of any drug was dangerous, and too much of the LSD? Even with the modifications he'd made? Would it eventually tip Roman over the edge? Make him mad?

Soothe him, soothe him. "Don't worry, Roman, I will take care of Drummond. Please, trust me."

I trusted you before to self-destruct the bloody drone! Rage flashed, then sank back below the surface. "I know you will, Radu. You need to trust me, as well. Once we have the woman and the pages, we will work to cure you. You will kill Drummond, Barstow will give us the money, and I have an idea how to crush Temora once and for all. Never again will that traitor infiltrate MATRIX. I will personally kill him, perhaps strangle him as he stares up at me. Yes, all will work." And he rubbed his hands together, frowned a moment, thumbed another microdose onto his tongue, then strode from the room. Radu watched his strong, brilliant brother, so robust, so full of life and purpose and love for him. What would happen now? Radu slowly walked to the control panel and cooed softly into the microphone that fed directly into the falcons' mews. His voice woke the remainder of the cast, who were sleeping. It was too dangerous for him to handle the birds himself—even with Roman's protective gear, a small nick from a talon or beak would cause a bleed that couldn't be controlled—so all his directions had to come from afar. Like his directions to the drones. Like everything Radu was forced to do. Never touching. Never connecting. Except with his brother. His heart quickened. He didn't want to believe it, but maybe, maybe, the woman and the pages would lead to a cure for him. And he would walk free in the world. Perhaps he would learn to play cricket.

He sent Ashley and Lauderdale the coordinates in their collars, then sat carefully in his specially made chair, putting his hands on the controls for the drone, but he worried. So much chaos swirling about, so many problems, so many irons in the fire, a phrase he'd heard Iago once say. And Roman, the other half of him, becoming so volatile. What would happen?

CHAPTER THIRTY-ONE

Notting Hill, London

Nicholas and Mike watched Detective Inspector Griffith gently place the needle into an evidence bag.

Nicholas said, "We need it tested straightaway, but I imagine it's the same poison—epibatidine."

"Yes, I agree. I'll oversee it myself. Our lab will analyze it immediately, and I'll be in touch with you the moment we know for sure."

"Could you also have someone take a look at Alexander's computers? Actually, if you don't mind, I'd like to look at his computer, and we need the hard drives for Hemmler and Donovan as well. Even a copied hard drive will work. But send it to me by courier, and do it quietly. We're all still compromised, as far as we know, and we certainly don't want whoever is behind this to catch wind of what we're doing."

Griffith nodded. "I'll make sure this is handled discreetly."

"We need to head out now. Oh, Griffith? You do good work. Thank you for all your help."

Again, DI Griffith bloomed under that smile. "Ah, happy to help, Nicholas, Mike."

Mike grinned, but it fell off her face in an instant. She saw a flash of brown—there one moment, gone the next.

She grabbed his arm. "Nicholas, did you see that?"

"See what?"

"Remember the bird you thought was watching us last night? I think I've seen another."

A small brown feather floated down in front of them.

"Nicholas, I—"

"Wait. Listen. Do you hear that?"

All Mike could hear was the city—moving, breathing, cars flowing along the nearby streets, the murmurs and calls of the crime-scene crew. She shook her head.

"A high-pitched whir."

Mike's adrenaline spiked. She looked up. "A drone? I can't see it. Where, where?"

"There," Nicholas shouted, pointing to the eastern edge of *Marianne*'s roof.

They saw the drone rise gracefully into the sky. Mike ducked behind the crime-scene van, and Nicholas took up point at the hood.

He pulled his Glock, thankfully returned by Penderley.

She heard the barrage of bullets, too close, and drew the small Glock 27 from her ankle holster. The drone was darting left, then right, through the sky overhead, firing.

"It's shooting at us, Nicholas, get down!"

People were screaming, running, the cops firing up at it, but it was so fast no one could get a bead on it.

Nicholas didn't get down. He stood tall and squeezed three shots. The drone zipped away, then stopped, hovering over the buildings, as if mocking them.

Nicholas ran after it. Whoever was flying the drone was an expert, and he dodged between buildings as he ran, ducking behind a van, scooting around honking cars, his eyes never leaving the drone. Mike was on his heels, yelling, "Left at the corner, it's stopped. Wait, now right!"

They juked and jived, ducking bullets, another two blocks before the drone seemed to be slowing down. Nicholas realized it was running out of juice.

Mike ran up to his left. "Is the sucker out of battery power?"

"Yes. Adam said it would only have twenty-five minutes or so. If we can keep up with it, we should see it drop out of the sky. Unless your sharpshooting skeet skills are honed—"

Mike grinned as she raised her small Glock, aimed at the drone, stopped dead. "Look, there's a bird, it's heading right for the drone."

"Doesn't matter. Fire, Mike, bring it down." But before she could get off the shot, the bird dove at the drone. At the last second, it pulled up. It flared its wings to slow, legs underneath it, talons out, and snatched the drone from the air with its feet. Its wings flapped once, hard, and soared away with the drone held tight.

Mike pulled up short. "Holy crap, did you see that? That bird saved that frigging drone."

Nicholas pulled up beside her, watching the falcon wing away. "The question is, if it was one of ours, why didn't it destroy the drone. Why did it fly away with it?"

The bird and the drone were out of sight.

Mike said, "Because it's not ours. Bird and machine belong to the same people."

CHAPTER THIRTY-TWO

A typical unmanned aircraft is made of light composite materials to reduce weight and increase maneuverability. This composite material strength allows military drones to cruise at extremely high altitudes. Drones are equipped with different state-of-the-art technology such as infra-red cameras (military UAV), GPS, and laser[s] (military UAV). Drones can be controlled by remote control system or a ground cockpit.

—Dronezon.com

MI5 Headquarters, Home Office
Thames House
12 Millbank
Westminster, London

Nicholas said, as they rode the elevator up, "MI5 is manic. I don't think I've ever seen so many agents running around. At least we got an elevator for just the two of us. I can't wait to get my hands on a keyboard and find out exactly what, and how, this hack was performed. I plan to write a new encryption for our phones that will keep us safe." He tapped his temple. "Wait—I do believe a possible solution has presented itself to my brain."

She poked his arm. "I knew it, modern technology is no match for you. Maybe you should go into business like Ardelean did with Radulov. Make millions off your code. Mama needs a new pair of shoes, or you could buy me a BMW, like yours."

"Not new shoes for you, new boots. I don't want to take Ardelean's path—sorry, Mike, not enough excitement in the business world, no knockout arguments with you, no hand-to-hand fights with bad guys. I wonder how long Griffith will take to copy the hard drives?"

"Okay, new boots, and yeah, I'd give it up, too, for knockdown drag-out arguments with you. Griffith won't take long, not since she has a crush on you."

"Agent Caine, are you jealous?"

She rolled her eyes. "Come on, focus. I'm still wondering about that falcon yanking the drone out of the air and disappearing with it."

"There you go, just like a woman, always changing the subject. You're definitely jealous. Want to get revved up? Want to fight about it? Those new boots, maybe for Christmas?"

She laughed, and he couldn't help himself, he gave her a quick kiss as the elevator doors opened to three interested faces.

Adam was waiting for them when they arrived on the fifth floor, in Harry Drummond's outer office. "Hey, it's good to see you guys. I'm all up and running, and, man, do we have a problem. I need another hour at least, but I'm close to finding the hole. I'm trying to establish a clear and safe channel that we can use to talk to Gray in New York. Oh, by the way, he and Zachery and Lia and Savich are all on board. They know what's happening and they've started taking measures on their end to secure comms. I think there is an errant piece of code in both FBI-N.Y. and FBI-D.C. servers, but I don't see it's been activated, yet, which is a nice favor. We can do an end around the software, establish a clear channel, and wait to see if it's opened.

"But here, in MI5, it's activated, and everything's wide-open. Information that's supposed to be internal is feeding out through a pipeline to whoever built this hack. I gotta say, it's pretty cool." He looked at Mike. "Well, um, no, not cool at all."

"Can you secure the British Security Services?"

"I'm working on it, Nicholas. Once I have the channel between New York and us secured, then I can turn to the MI5 and MI6 systems. This is going to be huge, like Duqu, and Duqu 2.0 that unraveled Kaspersky, though I think this breach of Radulov is going to be even worse."

Mike asked, "What's Duqu? What's Kaspersky?"

Adam said, "Sorry, Duqu is the code name in the hacker community for a quiet and powerful threat hack that attacked the NSA, as well as some other organizations last year. Major cyberwarfare. Who needs nukes when you can simply open the door and steal all the secrets without anyone realizing it until years later?"

"And we're on the front lines of our own Duqu?"

"We are. Kaspersky is a Radulov competitor. They had something similar happen last year. And this looks like another big one. Hey, what happened to the defense secretary? Was it another drone attack? More frog poison? I thought I heard there might have been another attack, but I've been focused on all of this. Everything okay? Look at this code, Nicholas."

Mike touched Adam on the arm. "Adam, you didn't take a single breath, didn't have a single comma. How much caffeine have you had today?"

"I don't know, about a case of Red Bull and a few pots of coffee."

"Well, take a breath."

He pulled in a deep breath, shut his eyes, and blew it out, putting his hands together in prayer. "Ommmmmm. Happy, Mom?"

She rubbed her knuckles against his head. "You amaze me."

Adam gave her a huge smile. "I'm okay, I promise. I always tank up when I have a big project. Seriously, was there another attack on you guys?"

His eyes were red and glassy from lack of sleep and too much caffeine, but he looked as excited as she'd ever seen him. The crash would come, she knew. She'd seen Nicholas jazzed up the same way, seen him crash.

Nicholas raised his head from an examination of the code Adam had handed him. "Yes, but they missed, and then a falcon came out of nowhere and flew off with the drone."

"Wicked."

Nicholas laughed. "That's what I thought, too. Adam, you go back to the secure comms issue with Gray, then work on the breach. We have a meeting with Roman Ardelean soon. I'm going to brief my father on what we saw at Alexander's crime scene. Work fast, okay? If you find something, come get me right away."

"You got it. Tell your dad someone's been taking a look through the files here, okay? It's a big hole."

"I will. Thanks, Adam."

They watched him go, then Nicholas knocked on his father's inner office door. "I want my father to know where we stand on everything before Ardelean arrives."

CHAPTER THIRTY-THREE

Nicholas was briefing his father, Mike listening with half an ear, when a cryptic text came to her phone from DI Griffith.

> Confirmation on what you found, coated with E. HDs on their way.

The drone needle was coated with epibatidine. The victim's computer hard drives were coming.

Three in three days confirmed. And Nicholas could have easily been the fourth. Whoever they were dealing with wasn't messing around. So who was next? Or would they try for Nicholas again?

Surely, the White House would cancel the president's trip once they relayed this information to Savich and Zachery.

She was about to tell Nicholas when Ian appeared in the door.

"Sir? Mr. Ardelean is here to see you."

Harry stood, nodded to both Nicholas and Mike. "We will finish this when you're through meeting with Ardelean. Ian, please show Mr. Ardelean in."

Nicholas looked down and read the text on her mobile from Griffith.

"Want me to go call her?"

"No, wait, Mike. This is more important. Stay for this meeting."

He watched Roman Ardelean come into the room. His first impression was *this man is smart and clever.* He looked shrewd, as arrogant as an ancient warrior prince who gave no quarter, who reveled in his own strength, his own power. He was as tall as Nicholas, with dark, wavy hair and a hawk nose. He looked like the Romanian hacker he was, from his Chuck Taylors to his dark, heavy eyebrows. Nicholas hadn't even seen the man in anything but a black turtleneck and dark jeans—à la Steve Jobs, a personal hero. Did Ardelean believe imitation was the sincerest form of flattery?

Ardelean was smiling, his hand outstretched, all bonhomie. "Mr. Drummond, what a pleasure." He shook hands with Harry, then turned to Nicholas and Mike. "Roman Ardelean."

"Nicholas Drummond, and this is my partner,

Agent Michaela Caine. It's good to meet you. I'm a fan."

A dark brow went up. "You're a fan of mine? You're the ones getting all the headlines these days. Saving the American president and vice president, and I heard about that nifty piece of code you pushed into the Air Force One mainframe, Drummond. Rather amazing stuff. Not to mention the work you did helping the Israelis with Stuxnet. Rumor has it the code was of your own design."

Nicholas stiffened. How in the world did Ardelean know that? Or was he fishing?

But Ardelean waved a hand. "I know what you're thinking, but never fear, your secrets are safe with me. You know what I do. A number of people were quietly contracted on that job. I couldn't help but notice your signatures in the code. A beautiful piece of work, that. And if you ever need a job—"

Harry laughed, but Nicholas and Mike merely smiled politely. Then Harry said, "Mr. Ardelean, may I get you anything or shall we begin?"

"No, no. I'm fine. Let's begin. I'm sorry to be meeting under these circumstances. I know you have a lot to do today, after the horrific news about Alexander. I rather liked the old codger. I can't imagine why anyone would want him dead."

Mike said, "Did you know Heinrich Hemmler and Chapman Donovan, the other two murder victims?"

"I knew of them, only. Terry was always a

friend to Radulov. Had me in to do security for the Ministry. Something like we're about to do here. You're having problems, I take it, with this ransomware attack?"

Harry said over his shoulder as he closed the door, "You could say that. All of you, please sit down."

Mike and Nicholas took a seat on the couch, Ardelean sat opposite.

Harry pulled up a chair. He looked at them all, steepled his fingers, and waited. "This situation is perturbing and unexpected." He said nothing more. It was one of his father's favorite tactics, one he'd used on Nicholas as a boy when he'd committed a sin. Sure enough, he'd always jumped into the silence and confessed.

Right on cue, Ardelean splayed his hands and started talking. "I know this breach has been a disappointment to you, but I will remind you that MATRIX is still recognized as the best cybersecurity system on the market. It's Radulov's flagship, and I'll stake my life on it.

"You'll be relieved to hear we've located the issue internally, and it's been addressed. I have a press briefing this afternoon to explain how we've answered the breach.

"In the meantime, we've pushed a new software update to our servers. I'm happy to put the update into your system myself, so you can be assured everything is safe and working properly again. Collectively, we apologize for any issues you may be having, and we would like the chance to make this right."

"All well and good, Mr. Ardelean, and we appreciate your willingness to hurry a patch." Harry sat forward. "However, I'm sorry to say a simple update won't do the job. We believe someone has gotten inside your software and is spying on the Home Office. After the incidents of the past few days, we must conclude this is much larger than a ransomware attack. We've had three assassinations on our soil, the attempted murder of my son here just today, and now we find out all our servers are infected." He paused. "As a matter of fact, we are investigating the MATRIX software attack as the link among all these things."

Nicholas thought the look that registered on Ardelean's face was sheer horror. Getting on the wrong side of the Security Services wasn't a path for success; to have Radulov tied to the assassinations would be his downfall, whether he had anything to do with them or not. That Ardelean planned to go public with this breach was the smart thing to do, and would probably restore confidence.

Harry continued, "I see we've surprised you with this information."

Ardelean sat forward, his hands clasped between his knees. "You have. Mr. Drummond, let me assure you there is no way our software could be hacked and used to spy on you. I wrote the code myself. It's built to protect against that possibility. There's no way."

Nicholas said, "Yet it's happened. Someone is inside the system and is tracking us. And, quite possibly, was tracking the victims who were assassinated, as well."

He didn't mention Adam was currently reverse-engineering the code to find where the spying was coming from. He wanted to see what Ardelean had to say first.

"Why would anyone do that? Well, all right, certainly there are nation states who would be very interested in the information in your servers. Everyone knows Russia and North Korea are pushing malicious code into every computer they can. But that's why you use MATRIX, sir. We take every precaution to make sure none of the components of the software can be tampered with." He paused. "The assassinations. You honestly think they're tied together? That something in your servers was stolen and, as a result, these people have been killed?"

He was shaking his head, back and forth. "It is difficult to accept. I will personally start an investigation—another investigation—immediately."

Harry said, "That would seem the proper course. You say you addressed the issue of the ransomware in MATRIX, Mr. Ardelean—"

"Roman, please."

"Roman. How, exactly, did you address the

breach that led to the ransomware attack? Because clearly someone got inside your code, or else they wouldn't be able to hold all these computers hostage. And if they can see what's inside them—"

"I'll be honest, Mr. Drummond. The ransomware, we already know that breach was the Russians. We were able to trace the upload to a flat in Kiev, and the hacker was arrested by the Russian authorities. We issued the patch the moment we saw the breach, and trust me, it's secure as ever now."

That's not right. Why is Ardelean lying? Nicholas said, "If one hacker can get in, so can another."

Or the same one. Temora, Temora. "No, no, we've locked it all down, pushed out a special update. And I've personally offered a bug bounty to my employees to see if any of them can penetrate the new software. And I have some of the best talent in the world on my team."

Harry said, "I wish we were as certain as you, Roman. As it stands, the Home Office can't take any chances. We're going to have to explore the security of MATRIX and make recommendations on our findings."

Roman looked over at Nicholas. "Have you found something else? Something in the code we've missed?"

"No. Not yet."

Ardelean breathed out. "Good. That's good." He tapped his briefcase. "Now, if you'd allow me a few moments with the servers, I can update the software personally, and I guarantee, nothing will get through after that."

Nicholas asked, "Do you need access to the mainframe?"

Ardelean held up a small thumb drive. "No, I have it all here. I can access the software from any terminal."

Harry waved toward his desk, where Ardelean sat down, toggled the mouse on Harry's computer, then inserted the thumb drive.

Nicholas watched Ardelean work. He was fast, smooth, but why had he lied about the Russian hacker? Another thing, he was too smooth, too deferential to Nicholas's father. Nicholas's personal experience with brilliant business moguls was the opposite—he would have trusted Ardelean more if he'd acted like a conceited ass.

Granted, losing the Security Services would be a massive blow to the proprietary software development Radulov was contracted for, because if he lost one government agency, he'd lose them all. And variations of MATRIX and other Radulov software were on practically every government computer in the free world. He couldn't afford the blow to his company. Given that, maybe Nicholas would be as apologetic as Ardelean. What was going on here? There was something more.

Still, the Radulov reputation was stellar. Ten years of high-end security, tight as a drum, unbreakable. The world had turned to Radulov when Kaspersky and Norton failed them.

Until last month, when so many of the computers using the software were hacked. Strange, the attacks on the politicians had begun so soon after.

Mike had checked out entirely. For some reason, she was staring at her phone as if it held the Rosetta stone. But his father was watching Ardelean closely, too, which made him even more curious.

They met eyes, and Harry shrugged. What had his father seen?

A moment later, Ardelean was rebooting the machine when a knock sounded on the door and Adam came in. Nicholas knew it wouldn't do to laugh, but he looked like he'd rolled around on the floor and stuck his hand in a socket—his hair was standing on end, his clothes were rumpled, and there was a big coffee stain right in the middle of his *Star Wars* T-shirt. Nicholas knew by the manic smile Adam had made a breakthrough.

"Can I interrupt? I've discovered a back door into the software you need to see."

Ardelean's head came up in a snap.

Nicholas said, "Roman Ardelean, meet Adam Pearce. He's a consultant on our team."

CHAPTER THIRTY-FOUR

Adam could only stare, starstruck, at one of the best computer minds of the century, but he quickly recovered. "I'm a big admirer of your work, Mr. Ardelean." He held out his hand. "I'm Adam Pearce."

"A pleasure to meet you."

"No offense, but someone's making a mess of your code right now. Look."

He set his laptop on Harry's desk, and Nicholas and Roman leaned in to see.

Harry Drummond watched for a moment, but Nicholas and Adam and Ardelean were off into a parallel universe, one he didn't understand and couldn't easily follow. He marveled at his son's incredible skill, not inherited from either him or his mother. Or his grandfather. And Adam, the young man was a *phenom*, a word Mitzie liked to use.

Nicholas pointed a finger at the nonsense on the screen and said, "There. There it is," and Ardelean sucked in his breath in surprise. "Bugger me, you're right." He straightened. "I don't understand how this door was opened. I coded this to allow my people to be able to slip into our systems and push code out. Internally. Only from inside Radulov. No one from the outside could have possibly gotten in. It's a one-way pipe—"

"No offense, Mr. Ardelean, but it's a two-way pipe now," Adam said, "and they did get in, big-time. Look at this. I created an animation of the bug flowing through the systems from the Radulov servers to the infected computers, and this is what I found. It's a small hole, sir, but it's a hole. That's how the software was taken advantage of, and how they can defeat it again."

Nicholas saw the screen light up with what looked like a moving bar chart, knew it must be the paths the data packets had followed.

Mike set down her phone and said, "Adam, can you explain it in lay terms?"

"Sure. Essentially, with this capability, whoever is behind this can spy on every computer that houses Radulov's software and MATRIX. They can do keystroke analysis on any computer that runs the software—which is pretty much every computer out there—so they can follow every text, every file, every email.

"Here's the kicker: not only is it on the computers themselves, it's also tied into any device that shares the systems' Wi-Fi network. So, for example, when we come into these offices, we're given a Wi-Fi password to log into the systems, one that's secure and encrypted and only given to outsiders, not used in-house. When our phones attach to the network, the bad code downloads onto it through the connection. Then they have keystroke and audio on those phones, too."

Harry said, "Governments have this capability, too, though, yes?"

"Sure. On our end, the NSA and FBI can do this with ease, though we aren't supposed to. To use any of it to prosecute criminals, we have to work directly with Apple or Microsoft—or Radulov—to get warrants for the information that's been traced if they want to use it legally. We have to trust they will not use the information they obtain against us without due process.

"But Radulov's vulnerability is now available to any hacker who wants it if they're given the appropriate code through the dark web. Sorry, Mr. Ardelean. I hate to say it, but you're screwed. You're going to need a complete overhaul of MATRIX and your other software packages to make them safe again, then you'll need to convince everyone who owns the software to upgrade to the newest version. Vulnerabilities could float around for years on old computers. This is a mega leak, sir."

Ardelean was shaking his head. He looked incredulous. "But we found the hacker, and he's been arrested. We pushed code in to halt the attack. We contained it."

"You did, absolutely, and your block of the manipulated code was handled perfectly. Exactly what I would have recommended, step by step. The problem is, you were too late. The code is still out there. I saw it—"

Nicholas shook his head, and Adam stopped talking immediately. No need to let Ardelean— or his father, for that matter—know the details of how he and Adam worked on these projects, that Covert Eyes had a hacker in place to do such things. Adam and Nicholas thrived on manipulating the vulnerabilities of software programs. Yes, better to keep those facts off the table.

Nicholas said, "Mr. Ardelean, do you have any disgruntled former employees who might want to take you down, who might want to see your company suffer, or who might be trying to ransom your code?"

Yes, that traitor, Temora. Ardelean rubbed the bridge of his nose, effectively hiding his eyes. He wanted a microdose. No, no, he had to keep it together. He wasn't about to tell them about Temora. He looked up again, in control. "We have very little turnover. My people are under the strictest confidentiality agreements, of course, and can be prosecuted for any breach of those contracts.

"I will compile a list of our terminated employees for you to start investigating. I assume, Drummond, that you and Agent Caine are starting an investigation into this, which is why you're here in London?"

Nicholas nodded. "A breach of this magnitude needs several sets of eyes. A list of your former employees would be a great help. I'd say you need to look back at least three years."

"Of course." Ardelean was still staring at the code. He couldn't wait. He pulled a small box from his pocket and slipped a mint into his mouth, but it wasn't a mint, it was a microdose. Almost immediately he felt it focus him. He nodded to all of them.

"I must go, immediately. I need to deal with this." He stopped, shook Adam's hand. "Thank you for finding this." And to Harry, "Sir, I will do everything in my power to make your servers safe again, as quickly as possible. I have another patch that should hold them off while we work on a permanent solution. I'll put it into the terminal myself the minute I get back to the office. Give me an hour before you reboot the machines in the office."

Harry asked, "And it will fix things for how long?"

"It should last indefinitely, though there will be more to come." Ardelean laughed and ran a hand through his hair. "I thought the update I put in was the permanent fix, until now. Mr. Pearce, I am dead serious. If you ever decide you want a job, please don't hesitate to call. I'll pay you triple what you're making now."

Adam grinned. "You hear that, Nicholas? I want a raise."

CHAPTER THIRTY-FIVE

Once Mike was sure Ardelean was out of hearing, she said, "The minute the three of you landed your starship on computer-land, you lost me, so I went ahead and put all the data on these drone assassinations into ViCAP, to see if there is anything similar in our jurisdiction."

Harry shut the door and said as he turned back to them, "You weren't alone, Michaela. I, too, got lost in, what did you call it? Computer-land. Well, that went well. At least we can be assured the systems are safe now, and we can start communicating properly again. I hate cloak-and-dagger stuff, gives me a headache. How long will it take to hear from your ViCAP?"

Nicholas said, "Not long. I was glad to see Ardelean take responsibility, though I'm convinced he lied about a Russian hacker—when in doubt, blame someone who isn't there I guess was his thinking." He gestured toward his father's desk. "May I? I'd like to see the details of the patch he installed."

"Certainly. Be my guest. What are you looking for?"

He glanced at Adam. "You want to tell him?"

Adam nodded. "I told Nicholas right before the meeting there was something strange about MATRIX. When I was looking at the tracking code, it felt wrong, like it was written in the same language as Radulov's software."

"So," Nicholas said, "I'm assuming Ardelean has someone on the inside determined to bring him down. Disgruntled, former, who knows. Regardless, I have a tracker in the system that will look at the patch he provided, to be sure it's totally clean. No sense reinfecting all the terminals if the code's not perfect."

Harry waved to his computer. "Take a look."

Nicholas inserted a thumb drive into his father's terminal, booted up. Adam came to stand behind him. The program launched, and the two men watched the screen.

Nicholas said, "This patch is complex. I've never seen anything like it. Wait, how can this be possible? The numbers four-zero-eight keep cropping up. Is it the hack, Adam?"

Adam tapped a few keys, and the numbers

showed very clearly now, repeating over and over inside the zeroes and ones.

Nicholas sat back. "We know Roman Ardelean's a genius, and that's why his software is normally impenetrable. It's not based on normal code, but something new, and I'll bet majorly proprietary. This new protocol would be worth billions on the dark web, given what it can do."

Harry said, "And someone in Ardelean's company knows about this?"

Adam nodded. "They have to know some of it, definitely. But the bigger problem is, the code still allows for keystroke analysis, which technically means Radulov software can still spy on any computer using it."

Mike asked, "Doesn't Ardelean have to know? He just installed the patch himself."

Nicholas looked thoughtful. "It's possible, I suppose, that he doesn't know. He certainly seemed shocked. And angry." He leaned back in his dad's chair. As he did, his knee clipped the underside of the computer keyboard drawer. The wood slid out and bashed him in the thigh.

"Bloody—what's this?" He broke off. He saw a tiny black dot on his pants leg.

Adam said, "What's—" But Nicholas sliced a hand across his throat, then grabbed a notepad and wrote a single word.

BUG!

CHAPTER THIRTY-SIX

Once your bird tames down some, you can try putting it on a screen or pole perch unhooded for brief periods. Don't leave it unsupervised during this time. Give it a chance to regain the perch on its own before intervening. Most figure it out fairly quick.

—*American Falconry* Magazine

The moment Roman was out of London proper, he rang Radu, his first words, "FBI agent Drummond obviously wasn't killed by the drone. I just spent the better part of an hour with the bastard. What happened, Radu?"

"I sent the second drone after Drummond, as you wanted, but the drone ran out of battery early. I don't know what happened."

Roman felt the rage begin to pound in his head, louder and louder. He thumbed a microdose, calmed. "Our drones eliminated Donovan, Hemmler, and Alexander. But not Drummond, and this was your second try. Why are these people so hard to kill?"

Roman could see Radu shrugging. "They

know about the drones, they are on the lookout since the attack on them yesterday. I didn't want another Aire Drone to get into their hands, so I had Lauderdale intercept."

"Well done. Is it possible Lauderdale was seen?"

"The FBI agents gave chase when the drone left the scene. As I said, its battery was running low, so it was slow enough to follow, which was why I sent in Lauderdale."

Roman heard Radu draw a deep breath, then he spit it out. "Yes, I'm afraid they saw the capture. They saw Lauderdale fly away with the drone. Both are safe here now."

Roman was calmer now, the pounding in his head lessened. "Good. They don't know anything more than they did. Now, have you heard of a young American hacker, Adam Pearce?"

"No. Why?"

"I saw him in action today, along with Drummond. They know about the break in the code that allows us to spy on government agencies."

"What are we going to do? How long do you think it will take them to trace the source of the code back to me and not that stupid Russian hacker you made up?"

Roman was quiet, his brain examining all the problems he was facing.

Radu said, after a moment, "What if they discover your drone army, the plan with Barstow? Roman, I'm frightened. Tell me what to do."

He was his brother's keeper. He felt calm flow over him, through him. "Radu, the most important thing is to take the lost pages of the Voynich and the woman so you can be cured. All the rest of it? Do not worry about it. I will take care of it." But all he could think about was the quire, page 74, the woman who was Romanian. And he asked, "Dr. Marin, what do you know of her?"

Radu told him what he already knew, then added, "She did have a twin, who died at the age of four. No cause of death given."

"Ah, so it makes some sense why she can read the Voynich."

"Yes, it does."

He felt victory close, within his reach. His heart sped up. A search of a lifetime, if only— He slipped another microdose in his mouth. He needed to think, needed the calm it brought him. The drug hit his system, and a low, warm hum started through him. He took a deep breath, then another. He rang off and immediately called Raphael in Scotland. "You will begin work immediately on a new patch." He dictated a statement to be released to the press, then another longer blog post to the Radulov website, explaining each step of the situation and the remedies they were providing.

Raphael took the notes silently, then asked, "Should we open a bug bounty to the outside community, sir? Offer five thousand pounds?"

"And have every hacker in the free world attacking our software? No. But you can say we're hiring new software engineers to specifically work on this issue."

"I'll get HR on it, sir. I will say, we've been receiving a great deal of external activity, mostly routing through the United States and Britain. The U.K. and U.S. governments are probably looking at us, trying to see if we're secure."

"They'd be idiots not to. Add a note to the press release that we are cooperating fully with the U.S. and U.K. investigations into our breach, and rest assured the software is safe to use once the update is installed, blah, blah, blah."

"Yes, sir."

"Now, you handled our other little issue, yes?"

"Yes. Everything is secure and safe, loaded on the ship, waiting for your word."

"Excellent. Good work, Raphael. If you keep this up, I won't even hold Temora's breach against you. Get the press release out as soon as possible, and upload the blog ten minutes after the release is public. Oh yes, send that prick Nicholas Drummond a list of our recently terminated employees. He thinks the breach is coming from the inside, and it will keep them busy. Go ahead and put Temora's name on the list, maybe they can catch him."

"But—"

He hung up. It was odd. Part of him was fully aware he should be very worried indeed that the company he'd spent years to build might collapse. But another part, the greater part, was consumed with the pages from the Voynich and finding the cure for Radu.

If only Drummond had died like he was supposed to. And that made him think about his escape plan. He had a plane ever on standby. Take Radu and the cast to the small island in the South Pacific he'd prepared for just this occasion. Stage his death—he planned to drown off the coast of Scotland, everyone would assume he killed himself after his company's implosion—and make his way to his family.

Simple, straightforward. He hoped he wouldn't have to, at least not yet. Moving Radu would be difficult at best, and Roman wanted to find a cure before he had to do so.

His mobile rang. It was Barstow. Roman listened, and then he hung up, without saying a word.

From one minute to the next, it seemed everything was unraveling, and none of it was his fault. He remembered the Money's enthusiasm, their optimism, their commitment to Project Cabal seven months before, after his demonstration in the Nubian Desert. What had happened? And there was Temora, thumbing his nose at him, destroying Radulov, and the Voynich, always the Voynich, and Dr. Isabella Marin.

Focus, focus. He would act, he had to act. And another would pay for betraying him. And Barstow. He'd be a fool to trust him.

CHAPTER THIRTY-SEVEN

Govan Shipyards
Glasgow, Scotland

Paulina Vittorini stood on the docks, a hand to her eyes, the wind off the River Clyde plastering her long, wide-legged pants against her. Though the day was gray and overcast, the shipyard was humming with activity. Massive cranes moved through the sky, hundreds of workers swarmed the partially built Type 26 frigate in dry dock, Britain's newest line of maritime defense.

They were doing a stellar job on the naval contract. Delivery early and under budget—that was always her goal, and her success had made her shipyard renowned throughout the world. When this contract was done, she knew the navy would come begging for more. And she whispered, as she always did, "You taught me well, Father."

She'd loved the shipyard from the moment her father, Sir Atlas Giltrow, had carried her on his shoulders when she'd been a little girl of five. Even now, as she looked out over what her father had built and what she'd added to their legacy, she felt humbled. After that first day, her father had brought her with him every day. She remembered so clearly that first steel monstrosity, the skeleton of a monster, she'd whispered to him and he'd laughed and told her to keep watching. And she had. Every day the skeleton added flesh, larger and larger, until she believed it would reach the sky. And when she'd seen that incredible ship sail out of dry dock, she'd known she wanted to be like her father. She wanted to build ships.

By the time her father died, Paulina had earned an engineering degree, married Paolo Vittorini, an Italian shipping magnate, thus combining the power of their two families, and was on her way to leading one of the most successful shipbuilding firms in the world.

Her son and daughter would follow her. She whispered into the furious wind, "You would be so proud, Father, I'm going to help save a country." Well, she would, once she helped deploy into Africa the drone army Roman Ardelean had built. Her name would go down in history as a visionary, a patriot, a humanitarian.

She already had supplemental arms on board the ship to accompany the drones, ready to go. But where were her drones? She'd paid Barstow months ago, two massive installments, 150 million each time. He assured her the drones would be coming, several times, telling her Ardelean had run into a few design problems but not to worry. But they still weren't here. She would call him again, and this time she wouldn't accept any more of his excuses for Ardelean.

Her assistant, Sabriel Coes, came to her side. "Ma'am, we have to go. You're speaking at the Women in Engineering awards luncheon in an hour. I have seen to your luggage on the plane. Following the luncheon, you will fly to Rome."

She took one last glance at the frigate, wondered once more, *Where are my drones?*, and started for the car.

The sting in her neck was brief, and she swatted at it. "Ouch! What was—"

Sabriel watched her boss go down, hitting hard on her side, her hair whipped loose by the wind, now covering her face. What had happened? She ran to her and went down on her knees, suddenly afraid. She smoothed the hair from her face and screamed when she saw the froth coming out of her boss's mouth.

CHAPTER THIRTY-EIGHT

MI5 Headquarters, Home Office
Thames House
12 Millbank
Westminster, London

Nicholas carefully put the bug on the desk.

Mike eyed it, gave Nicholas a small salute and a grin. She said in a laughing voice, "You know, I haven't had anything to eat for hours. And Adam certainly hasn't had a chance for anything healthy. You promised you'd find me pizza. Let's eat. Harry, do join us."

Harry said, "Pizza, or curry? I think we know where I stand on this."

"Curry it is, then," Nicholas said, winding his finger in the air. "Let's go."

Harry shut and locked his door, wrote a note— DO NOT ENTER, COMPROMISED—and another for Ian, whose face went white—FOUND ANOTHER BUG, GET IT HANDLED. GOING

OFF-SITE TO DISCUSS—and they headed out into the street.

"We'd better follow through," Nicholas said. "There's an excellent restaurant, *Millbank Spice*, down the way. They usually need reservations, but with you with us, Father, I'm sure we can get in."

At the restaurant, they were immediately seated at a table for four by the window. They placed orders for samosa, chicken tikka, and tandoori prawns, which Nicholas knew were his father's favorite.

When the waiter weaved off through the tables, Adam was the first to speak. "Any idea what happened? How did a bug get through the sweep?"

Harry was already shaking his head. "Impossible. Simply impossible. A bug like that, I've never seen anything like it. The technology we have isn't capable of detecting it."

"Which means everything we spoke about with Ardelean is in our enemy's hands. This isn't good. First, Ardelean's company is hacked, then someone listens in on our conversation."

Harry said, "I need you to figure out who's behind the three assassinations, Nicholas. My group will handle investigating Ardelean and his possible enemies."

Nicholas fiddled with his napkin. "I have a feeling they're tied together somehow. I'm willing to bet someone was using MATRIX to spy on the Security Services and the victims. And if they're using Radulov software to do it, then Ardelean is a target, as well. We need to make sure he isn't murdered before we figure all this out."

Mike said, "We need a safe place to meet. If MI5 is compromised from within—"

Harry nodded. "Should it become necessary, we have a safe house that will do. It's in Bayswater. I'll have it prepared."

There was a television in the corner of the bar, and Mike sensed rather than saw heads begin to turn. A jolt of adrenaline went through her. Not again.

She pointed to the television, where a red bar along the bottom screamed *News Alert*.

The TV was closed-captioned, so they read the words: *Shipping Magnate Dead in Glasgow, Possible Assassination.*

And then: *Does Britain Have a Serial Killer on the Loose?*

Adam said, "Who is Paulina Vittorini?"

Nicholas said, "She's one of the foremost shipbuilders in the world. I believe her shipyard is currently building the latest warships for the British navy."

Mike leaned forward toward Harry. "Sir, does she have ties to Terry Alexander?"

Harry nodded. "He was the Secretary of Defense. No way she wouldn't have had contact with him since the naval contract was awarded. The media isn't stupid. They're going to go ballistic."

Like Mike, Nicholas leaned toward his father,

his voice low, "Did Heinrich Hemmler or Donovan Chapman have anything to do with the British military?"

"I don't know," Harry said. "But we'll certainly have to find out."

Adam chewed on his samosa. "Sir, this is very good. I don't guess we'll be having more lunch now, will we?"

Nicholas rose. "Everyone stay and eat. I've got to call Penderley. Don't eat it all, Adam."

Penderley answered immediately. "I know why you're calling, and I don't know. This belongs to the CID blokes in Glasgow. If you can get on-site quicker than my people, let me know."

Nicholas said, "Copy that," and hung up. To his father, he said, "Any chance you can get us on a chopper to Glasgow?"

"I can. Is that the best use of your time, though?"

"I'll go," Mike said. "You and Adam need to work on fixing the code."

"I've got the code," Adam said, forking down a prawn. "You two can head north. Trident and Clancy are still at Northolt. They were going to stick around in case we needed to send messages back to New York, but I think Trident really wanted to visit the Tower of London. The G5 will be faster than a chopper."

"Mike's right, Adam, this job needs both of us. We've got to restore secure comms to Security Services, and that will take a while." He sent a quick text to Clancy. It was Trident who texted back immediately:

We're still here, we're gassing up.

"Mike, they're with the plane, not off at the Tower of London. Take Ben, I'll have him meet you at RAF Northolt."

"If I recall, the last time we flew to Scotland, we had to take the prime minister's Hawker."

Nicholas gave her a smile. "As I recall, we had quite an adventure," which made her roll her eyes.

She looked at the television again. "Whoever is doing this is showing off, or it's a massive payback."

"Payback?" Harry repeated. "Why do you think that?"

She shook her head. "It just popped out."

"Or maybe revenge," Adam said, and ate another prawn. "If it is revenge, it's mighty harsh."

"Well, whatever," Mike said, "it's high time to stop them."

Harry said, "Michaela, you must promise to be careful. Scarves around your neck, no exposed skin. And I want you in protective gear. Please make sure the pilots have everything before you take off."

"Don't worry, Harry. I'm not in the mood to

be attacked again. I could go the rest of my life without seeing another drone. But we do have all the proper gear on the plane. As for you, Nicholas, finish your lunch, and as Superintendent Penderley says, you and your dad get this sorted. I'm calling Ben, time to get him in on all this."

CHAPTER THIRTY-NINE

RAF Northolt
London

Forty-five minutes later, Mike met Ben at the private terminal at Northolt. Ben was admiring the lineup of jets on the tarmac. "This place is certainly convenient. They fly private jets and their military Typhoons out of here?"

"They do. They keep the Royal Squadron here, too, to fly the Queen and other VVIPS."

"VVIPs?"

"Very, very important people."

Ben laughed. "Fitting." Across the tarmac Mike saw Trident walking around their G5 with its American flag on the tail. Clancy was inside, sunglasses on, readying the flight plan.

Mike gave Ben a hug. "Sorry to pull you away from vacation. Melinda doing well?"

"No worries. She said four assassinations in three days justifies it, so I'm here with her blessing and her warning I'm not to get myself dead. Seriously, she's really worried about what's happening. Do we know what the link is between the victims, yet? And how this Vittorini woman in Glasgow fits?"

"No, not yet. I'm hoping we will have a better sense of what's happening once we get up there. Someone's trying to spy on MI5, and it has to be connected to all of these murders. I'll brief you on the plane."

Trident met them at the bottom of the stairs. "Good timing. I'm finished up. We'll have you to Glasgow in a heartbeat. Climb aboard."

The shipyards reminded Mike of the Brooklyn Navy Yard, one of her favorite distance running paths. She loved running through the yards, looking over the river, at Manhattan. But it had been decommissioned for actual shipbuilding sometime in the sixties, she knew, while the Govan Shipyards was one of the premier shipbuilders in the world.

A partially assembled Type 26 frigate sat in dry dock, cranes draped over it like metal blankets. The entire shipyard felt empty and quiet, eerily so. Mike knew they'd closed down to honor their owner, and she could see the devastation on the faces of the workers as they hung together in quiet knots.

She also saw a similar group of people twenty

feet away, on the edge of the water, outfitted in the now-familiar fluorescent yellow POLICE reflective vests. Two plainclothes cops stood with notebooks open. A crime-scene photographer snapped shots from all angles, and, unlike the scene in Notting Hill, Mike could easily see the long hair of their victim spread across the dirty ground.

They walked to the detectives focused on a young woman who was crying. As they approached, Mike heard the detective saying to her, "Ms. Coes, run us through it again, if you please."

She said low to Ben, "Let's listen."

The young woman's voice was high-pitched and shaky, her accent deeply Scottish. "She—Mrs. Vittorini—was standing there on the edge of the dock with her eyes shaded, looking at the naval ship we were building. I had to remind her it was time to leave for a luncheon. We started toward the car, and—" Her voice broke. She shook her head, gulped. "She went down. It's so windy today, well it usually is here, and I saw the wind had tossed her hair across her face. I didn't know what had happened, so I went down on my knees beside her. I pulled her hair back, and I saw the froth on her mouth. She was dead." She drew a breath, and tears trickled down her face. "I don't know what happened. I didn't see anything, hear anything, but it's loud here, as you can imagine. Who's that now?"

The group turned to see Mike and Ben standing some six feet away, listening. A young detective stepped toward them.

"Ah, you must be the folks from Scotland Yard. Got here quick. I'm Chief Inspector Graham Mackenzie, head of CID for Glasgow."

Ben stuck out his and Mike's creds. "Special Agent Ben Houston and Special Agent Michaela Caine, American FBI. Superintendent Penderley sent us here. We're working the case with a special team."

"You're Yanks then. Well now, we're not adverse to having Yanks on our soil. Welcome aboard. We hope you know something we don't."

Mike said, "Chief Inspector, we need everyone to stop exactly where they are. We need a magnet." She saw him blink and added quickly, "We're looking for a needlelike object. We believe this murder is tied to three others in London over the past couple of days."

Mackenzie said, "Let me find a runner, have them bring a magnet."

"There's no need for a magnet," Sabriel Coes called. "I saw something metal in her scarf."

Mackenzie said, "Shall we have a look? We're still waiting on the coroner."

Mike and Ben followed Mackenzie into the perimeter. The dead woman wasn't beautiful, not anymore, but Mike could see she had been, high cheekbones, a straight nose, full lips, now drawn back in a rictus smile.

Mackenzie said, "Paulina was a popular lady around these parts, grew up in Glasgow, was passionate about the shipyards from the time she was a wee lass. She had great civic pride, was generous with her donations. But most of all, she gave jobs to those who might have gone without. She's famous, you know, throughout the world. Word had it she was going to try a political run, try to reboot the Scottish independence vote, especially now we've seen the back end of Brexit. It's a profound loss to us, a bitter loss, since it appears she was killed."

Mike put on nitrile gloves, leaned down, and gently moved the scarf. She saw the tiny red puncture on Vittorini's neck and the needle lying in a fold of the scarf.

Mike looked up. "We believe she's been shot with a drug called epibatidine. Tree frog poison. We think the needle is the delivery mechanism."

Ben said, "Did anyone around see or hear a drone flying overhead before or after the murder?"

"A drone? We'll canvas the scene and see, but no one's mentioned it. You mean someone flew in a drone with a poisoned needle, shot it into her neck, and killed her?"

"It's how the last three murders were committed in London. Do you have an evidence bag for this needle?"

Mackenzie snapped his fingers, and a crime-scene tech in a white Tyvek suit appeared.

"We'll take care of it. Sorry, I can't hand a

murder weapon to the FBI and let you walk off with it."

Mike grinned. "If you did, I'd report you to your boss. But we do need it sent for analysis immediately. Scotland Yard has the information. You can get in touch with Superintendent Hamish Penderley—he's the head of London CID—and he'll give your lab instructions."

Mackenzie relayed this information, and the chain of custody was established so they could rush the needle to the lab. That done, he said, "Walk with me."

He led them downriver twenty yards, back into the silence of the shipyard. When they stopped, Mike said, "If you're about to tell us something important, you need to turn off your phone."

Mackenzie didn't hesitate, turned it off, and shoved it back in his pocket, then asked, "Why?"

Ben said, "Comms in London are compromised. We can't take any chances that yours are, too."

A dark eyebrow went up. "This sounds like a right proper cock-up. Now, given this is clear-cut murder, we had a look around. There's a warehouse on the edge of the shipyard locked up tight. Ms. Coes told us no one was ever allowed in there but Mrs. Vittorini. I believe you should have a look."

CHAPTER FORTY

MI5 Headquarters, Home Office
Thames House
12 Millbank
Westminster, London

"We've swept everything again, sir, and there's nothing else."

Harry dismissed the aide and shut the door. As Nicholas watched, his father walked to the bar and poured a small finger of Scotch. Harry tipped the bottle at him in question. Nicholas wasn't used to seeing his father drink during the day but was perfectly happy to join him. Adam had no choice but to agree. With three drinks poured, they took their spots at the table and sipped, Adam making faces as he sipped the Scotch.

Harry stuck out his glass. "Come on, lad, puts hair on your chest. Drink up."

"That's what I'm afraid of," Adam said, then brightened. "I wonder how Scotch tastes with

Red Bull in it." He poured the rest of his can in the glass while Nicholas and Harry looked on in horror.

Adam took another sip, and a big grin came across his face. "Much better." He opened his laptop. "I'm going to keep working our patch so we can get comms up and running. I don't like being blind, deaf, and dumb with the rest of the team."

Nicholas nodded. "Mike and Ben should be in Scotland shortly. With luck, we'll have things working by the time they're ready to report in. Now, how did your people miss the bug earlier, Father? Was it different than the earlier listening devices?"

"It was. Much smaller. Ian told me it was a different technology. We weren't equipped to find it. No excuse, I know."

"Are there cameras in the office so we can see who might have placed it?"

"No. We've never spied on ourselves, which means we've created a perfect system for someone to infiltrate. They know they won't be seen." Harry rested his forehead in his hand for a brief moment. "Either way, I believe it's time for me to report to the home secretary and explain our vulnerabilities. You'll excuse me?"

"Certainly. Adam and I are going to do some more patching on your servers so we can be assured no one from the outside is looking in. With your permission, we'll also begin looking terminal by terminal at possible breaches, uploads, and malware that could be responsible for the breach. The MATRIX software is powerful, but we have a few tricks up our sleeves. We might be able to put all of this to rest shortly."

"Thank you, Nicholas. I will let the home secretary know you're working on this for us. Better to have someone from the outside, since we're not sure who we can trust in-house."

Nicholas and Adam got to work, sweeping through the servers and into the individual terminals—of which there were thousands of possibilities.

Adam said, "I wrote a program that looks for the vulnerability. I thought you could piggyback on it with a variation that looks for those strange numbers, four-zero-eight, in Radulov's base code."

"That's an excellent idea. Let's get to it. You install your program, and I'll work on a secondary sweep. When we disengage the code, we can upload our own, and we should have a fully encrypted communications system back online."

Adam started typing furiously. A few minutes later, he said, "Uploaded. Ready for your code."

Nicholas wasn't quite ready, held up a finger to say wait, and Adam grinned at him. "Getting slow in your old age?"

"You know I can have you arrested, don't you? I'm trying to understand the base code without the usual markers from our normal computer languages. It is genius, isn't it?"

"It is. To develop a new system is advanced stuff, to rewrite the world of code is another level entirely. I can't say I understand it all yet, though I can admire its architecture."

"Ready," Nicholas said, pressing the button that would launch his code to follow Adam's into the system.

The terminal blinked, then went black.

"What's this?" Adam looked at his screen.

They could hear voices in the hallways, people shouting. Nicholas went to the door, opened it, as Adam shouted after him, "A kill switch. They have a kill switch, and we triggered it. It's melting down the entire system here. Oh, man. We are in serious trouble."

And the lights went out at MI5.

CHAPTER FORTY-ONE

The peregrine, wrote W. Kenneth Richmond, is a bird of "perfect proportions and finely cut features, daring and intelligence, spectacular performance in the air and matchless execution in the chase—a natural aristocrat."
—Helen Macdonald, *Falcon*

The Old Garden
Twickenham
Richmond upon Thames, London

Roman was in Radu's suite looking at the computers when he saw the black spot start to filter through the Internet.

Radu poked his fist in the air. "Roman, they've activated the kill switch."

"Good. *That one's for you, Drummond. That should keep you busy for quite some time.*"

"But we are rendered blind, as well, now," Radu said. "And they are aware of how we've killed. They know MATRIX is compromised. I'm afraid, Roman. After they figure out how to turn things back on, they'll figure it out and they'll come."

Roman saw his twin's fear, his face pale, his restless hands wringing in his lap, and set himself to soothe. "They will have no idea we're involved, Radu. I've taken care of it all. When—if—they manage to get the systems back, everything will be wiped. There will be nothing to lead them to us. And the install I did will confuse them."

Radu was shaking his head, his oily hair slapping his face. "Nothing seems to be going right, Roman. How can you simply sit here doing nothing and hope the FBI and Scotland Yard and MI5 look elsewhere?"

"I'm not doing nothing. On the contrary, they'll be looking elsewhere very soon now. And while they do, I'm going to secure the lost pages for us. Then, Brother, we will have the means to cure you. It's the only thing that matters to me. I am happy to let Radulov burn to the ground if it means your blood will be clean."

Radu saw it—Roman slipped a microdose into his mouth.

"How much of that are you taking?"

"It doesn't matter. I'm in control. I'm always in control. I need a new batch made, by the way, with your special formula."

"Roman. That's two weeks' worth of LSD

you've consumed in two days. Even with the alterations I made in the formulation, you can't keep this up. If you're dead or in jail, having a cure won't matter."

Roman reached to touch his brother's arm, stopped when Radu pulled away.

Roman turned and punched a number into his mobile. "Cyrus, it's time. Yes. Yes, that's right."

He punched off, saw Radu was shaking his head.

"What do you have Cyrus doing? I don't like him. He thinks I'm crazy, but I'm not. Roman, we don't need him."

"We do need him. Trust me. No one in MI5 and MI6 will be thinking about vulnerabilities in MATRIX—or us—after this. And Drummond will be elsewhere. It's perfect."

CHAPTER FORTY-TWO

Govan Shipyards
Glasgow, Scotland

Mike and Ben followed Chief Inspector Mackenzie to the far end of the shipyard to a huge building with no windows, no activity at all, and a brawny cop standing in front of the door, his hands behind his back.

He came to attention. "Sir. No one's been around. The lock hasn't been disturbed."

Mackenzie said, "This is Inspector Lloyd Westcott. He and I will be handling this investigation. Caine and Houston, FBI."

Westcott's accent was thicker than Mackenzie's, and he spoke quickly, so Mike had a hard time keeping up.

"Good to meet you. Chief, we've swept for booby traps, have put a camera under the door—all surreptitiously, though no one's been around here. If they're watching, it's not obvious. Let's go in, shall we?"

At Mackenzie's nod, Westcott picked up a massive pair of bolt cutters. With a single powerful snap, he cut through the lock, catching it before it fell to the ground.

"In we go."

And he lifted the latch.

It was pitch-black inside the warehouse. It smelled musty, with a thick overlay of oil. Nothing unusual for a shipyard warehouse.

Mackenzie raised a Maglite to shoulder level and thumbed it on.

Mike blinked. "All I can see are crates. There must be hundreds."

"This warehouse is about sixteen thousand square feet. Not so big for the area, but big enough." Mackenzie gestured to the first crate, and Westcott used a pry bar to wrench it open. It was packed with what looked like shredded cardboard.

"Oh-ho. What do we have here? Five guesses," he said, pulling it aside, letting Mike and Ben look.

The crate was full of weapons. Automatics. Westcott moved things around carefully. "M4 carbines, twenty, twenty-five to a crate. I assume that's not our only weaponry, considering we have variable-size crates in here." He looked at his boss with a crooked smile. "Bugger me, mate. It would appear Paulina Vittorini was running guns right under the navy's nose."

They sat down with a pot of tea inside the Govan Shipyards offices. Mackenzie said, "The full assessment of the warehouse will take days, and we can start taking apart Vittorini's books in the morning. I have a forensic accountant who is practically magic. If anything's hiding in the company books, we'll find it." He shook his head. "I don't want to believe this, I mean, Vittorini is a patriot, a local legend. I've always believed her above reproach. I can't believe she'd be running guns to terrorists or countries that run counter to our beliefs."

Mike asked, "Could she have been holding the guns for someone else? What we have to find out is where the guns were headed when they left the warehouse and who they were being sent to. When you find out, please notify us."

"Yes, all right. When will you head back to London? Or are you going to stick around and lend a hand?"

Mike saluted him with her teacup. "As soon as we get confirmation of the poisoned needle and finish the tea, sir, we must be on our way back to London. We have to discover how Donovan, Hemmler, and Alexander fit with Vittorini."

Ben said, "And we know they fit together. They all crossed the wrong person or people." He started to pull his cell phone from his jacket, then shook his head. "It's very annoying not to be able to pick up a cell or the phone and call, update my team on what's happening."

Mackenzie laughed. "It'll turn you youngsters into old-fashioned gumshoes, like I used to be."

The phone rang, and Mackenzie, startled, answered it. He listened for a moment, then hung up.

"You can leave now, agents. The poison has been confirmed. As you said, the cause of death is the same as the other three. Tree frog venom, of all things."

Mike finished her tea and rose, Ben following suit. "Thank you for your help, Mackenzie. We will be in touch."

"Good. Let's get you back to Prestwick and your plane."

Clancy and Trident were waiting for them, but the jet's engines weren't running. Clancy said, "There's a major power outage in London. We're grounded temporarily. We can't fly in. Air traffic control is in emergency-operations mode, trying to get the planes in the air onto the ground without proper communications. Even with generators, the entire airspace is messed up."

"Do we have any way to communicate with Nicholas?"

"We can encrypt a call through the plane's system and give it a try. Though if there's no power, there's no cell service, and the landlines will be out, too."

"How did the power go out?"

"No idea. Radio traffic said it all went black, and—"

There was a squawk from inside the plane. "There's good news. Someone's trying to reach us." They ran up the gangway, and Mike watched Clancy sit in the pilot's seat and put on the headset.

"It's Nicholas. He's asking for you, Mike."

He gave her the headset. "Hey, what's going on?"

"Nothing much really, only a minor glitch. Adam and I may have melted down London's grid, but we're back up and running now."

Mike burst out laughing. "You're the reason London has no power? Why does this not surprise me? Those hoots and laughs you hear in the background is the team laughing at you."

Nicholas called out, "All right, you baboons, why don't one of you guys try to single-handedly—well, okay, double-handedly, since I have to include Adam—restore the Internet to a pristine state? Mike, I'll explain it all when you get here. Our comms are now officially secure. We purged MATRIX off MI5's servers entirely. Plug in your mobile and get back here right away."

"If this is a secure line—"

"It is."

"We found a massive cache of weapons. It appears Vittorini was running arms."

"Was she now? My father will be interested in this news. Come on home. I'll meet you at the house. We have all sorts of things to discuss."

CHAPTER FORTY-THREE

MI5 Headquarters, Home Office
Thames House
12 Millbank
Westminster, London

Harry Drummond was packing his briefcase to head to Clapton House, the flat he kept in Bayswater, when a knock sounded on his door, and an old friend's face appeared.

"Harry, how are you? Do you have a moment?"

"Corry, I'm fine. How are you? How is June?"

"She's bursting with health, as always. In Cornwall, at the manse. Mitzie?"

"At home, as well. Say, you look a bit peaked, are you coming down with something?"

"No, no, all's well. What a few days. Terry Alexander, Chappy Donovan? Who would have thought they were capable of getting on the bad side of someone? Now Hemmler I never liked, he was a bad man, so I hear. But Alexander and Donovan? Ah, it's scary times we live in, Harry."

"And now Paulina Vittorini was killed up in Scotland, in Glasgow, at her shipyard—"

"*What?*"

Harry grabbed Corry Jones's arm. "You hadn't heard? So you knew her?"

"Yes, of course, most of us knew Paulina. This is horrible, Harry. Was it a drone, like the others?"

Harry still held his friend's arm. "We believe so. Was she a friend of your family?"

Corinthian Jones, Lord Barstow, slowly shook his head. He made his hands tremble, his face pale. He wanted to send his fist to the heavens. Another down, another 150 million pounds for him. It was too easy manipulating Ardelean. He was so bloody predictable, so eager to kill when he believed he'd been betrayed.

Would Ardelean decide to cut his losses and kill him next? What if June were his next kill? No, he would decide how to get the drones to Africa, he would decide how to eliminate Ardelean before he figured out he'd been scammed. Maybe he would give Ardelean some of what he considered to be his own money, get him to turn over the drones, then he could kill him. He'd figure something out, something better. He always did. He thought again of his magnificent idea, an idea to make his ancestors proud, one to make him the most heroic, not to mention, the richest of them all.

He looked at his supposed friend, made his hands tremble a bit more, the older man so upset he couldn't control himself. How he'd resented Harry Drummond all their lives, since they'd been boys at Eton. Smart, liked by everyone, the apple of his father's eye, the sod. Tall, trim, good-looking, and holding up well.

Ah, remember what you've accomplished. You're far more impressive than Harry Drummond. And smarter than the vaunted Roman Ardelean.

Barstow said finally, shaking his head, as if dazed, fully aware Harry Drummond was staring at him, "It's simply too much, Harry, too much. I don't know how much more of this insanity I can take. It's simply so shocking. And all the terrorist attacks, the bombings, cars plowing into crowds, and now drones assassinating people—it doesn't stop, doesn't stop." He fell silent, the picture of a man trying to pull himself together.

Harry cocked his head to one side. Certainly Corry was shocked, to be expected, but this? The look on his face, it was somehow too much. What was going on here?

Barstow drew a deep breath. "Well, I've worried you, I see. I was coming by simply to tell you I've put in for leave. I thought I'd take June to Italy. She's been after me for months to take a break, says I'm working too hard."

Harry nodded, searching his old friend's face. "Perhaps she's right. Perhaps a change of scene would be good for you. I know personally I'm working harder now as a consultant than I did as an employee of the Crown. It appears you are, as well."

"I'd wondered why you came back, Harry."

"The PM convinced me I was needed, supposedly to relieve some of the pressure on the home secretary, help with the fallout from Brexit and the new terror norms. But that has taken a back burner. Turns out our systems have all been hacked—"

"I wondered about the sudden blackout. You know what happened?"

Harry shook his head. "I know it's fixed now, my son and one of his team, both computer geniuses, sorted it. There's so much more, but it needn't concern you. How are things in MI6 now?"

"As insane as they are here, of course. Speaking of, I should be on my way." Barstow stopped at the doorway. "It's good to see you, Harry. We should do lunch sometime soon. Or you could come out to Cornwall, bring Mitzie. She and June could rattle around, and we could go fishing. It's been too long."

"Yes, it has. When things calm down, I'll be in touch."

"Good, good."

But he lingered, and Harry watched him for a few moments. He'd been pale, upset, but now he looked once again a man in charge. Barstow went out the door, his step quick and firm, shoulders straight, and disappeared into the hallway.

What was that all about? Harry's phone began to ring. He recognized the extension. The home secretary.

"Drummond, there's been a bombing in Kent. Near the Folkestone station. Apparently, the train had just left the station when the bomb went off."

No, surely not— "It was heading into the Channel Tunnel?"

"We don't know yet, still assessing, no way to get figures without someone on-site. I've activated the emergency network. I trust you'll know more shortly. The first responders are on site. Terrible few days."

"Thank you for informing me. I'll be in touch as soon as I know the extent of the attack. Is anyone claiming it?"

The home secretary sounded tired, harassed. "No one yet. I'm sure that will come soon enough."

Harry punched off. What was happening? Vittorini murdered in Glasgow, and now a possible bomb on the Chunnel train?

He locked his safe, an automatic reflex, and ran out of his office, toward the command center. Barstow was by the elevator. "What's happened?"

"Bombing in Kent. Eurostar train."

Barstow stilled. "So much for leave—I'd best go check things out. Will let you know if I hear anything of use."

Barstow stepped into the elevator, his brain

screaming. *Roman, who did you want dead now? Who? Or have you figured it out? Is this your final warning? Next, it's me if I don't get you the money?*

In his gut, Barstow knew it was Roman's doing—and what if the train had exploded in the Chunnel? To have a bomb go off 150 feet underwater? Barstow shuddered at the thought. It was bad enough to have a Eurostar be blown up as it was leaving the station, but add to that the damage to the infrastructure. *You deserve to die for this, Roman, you deserve it. Now I have to figure out how to make it happen.*

Harry looked back once as the elevator closed on his friend Corinthian Jones. What was wrong with the man? No time to worry about it now. When he walked into the command center, images were flooding the wall screens. It was a nightmare scene, twisted metal and shattered glass, the train bent and on its side. Harry didn't interrupt the frantic group of people to announce his presence. They knew what to do, had been well trained. He listened to the varied accounts as they came in, assembling a timeline in his head. Ian came to stand beside him, taking notes.

"First reports of injuries are coming in, sir. Miraculously, only a few people are injured, though two have been taken to hospital with burns and are listed in critical condition."

"Someone's saying the bomb went off outside the train, which is good luck for us."

Harry said, "Outside the train? Was the bomb beside the tracks, like an IED?"

"No, what I'm hearing is it was dropped onto the train."

"Hey, we have a witness, a videographer, can you believe it? The photos are being uploaded right now. He says he saw something fly over the train, then it exploded. He has it all on film. He was doing a promotional video shoot for Eurostar. Here it comes."

The multiple screens coalesced into a single view of the handsome white-and-yellow sloped nose of the train, flashing into view and then out of it, then an earthshaking blast; the camera wobbled and the train screeched as it flew off the tracks and came to rest on its side. Harry watched, mesmerized, as the video replayed again and again, slowed down frame by frame until, finally, a small black object could be seen entering the frame and making contact with the train.

"There it is," he said. "Enhance and enlarge."

Ian stood next to Harry, watching the video loop over and over again, the bomb going off in slow motion, the top of the train coming apart and blowing metal out of the frame.

He said, stunned, "Someone dropped a bomb on it from above. How is that possible?"

Nicholas stepped into the room and caught his father's eye. "A drone. That's how."

CHAPTER FORTY-FOUR

My falcon now is sharp and passing empty,
and till she stoop she must not be full-gorged,
for then she never looks upon her lure.
> —William Shakespeare,
> *The Taming of the Shrew*

Dawson Place
Notting Hill, London

Isabella was humming as she put the finishing touches on her face—there, a bit of red lipstick—and shut off the light in the bathroom the very moment the doorbell rang. Perfect timing. Gil was always prompt, bless him. He'd been gone for a week on a shoot, and she couldn't wait to see him. Though why he was ringing the bell was beyond her. This was his place, too.

She hurried to the door, flung it open.

"Hello, sexy lady."

She saw the flowers in his hand, the bottle of wine tucked under his arm, and grinned.

"My arms were full. I couldn't get my key out."

"Get in here so I can hug you. Now."

"You get one press conference and suddenly you rule the world. Grab my suitcase, and I'm all yours."

When she got the flowers, the wine, and his suitcase out of the way, she threw herself into his arms. She loved his kisses, and this kiss, she thought, he smelled of the sea. It was hard to pull herself away, but she did, finally, knowing the lipstick was already gone, and she wondered why she'd bothered in the first place.

She reached for the wine, but he put the flowers in her hands instead.

"You take care of these. I'll handle the wine."

"How was the trip?"

"Long. Remind me not to get a wild hair to go deep-sea fishing again anytime soon. Those guys are nuts, but man, I got some photos that are going to blow your mind. I'm telling you, babe, these are *National Geographic* worthy. I'll upload during dinner, so you can see them in real time before I start the edits. There are some pretty awesome shots."

He popped the SD card into the computer, and the photos began uploading. She joined him at the desk.

"This is going to take a while." Gil started playing with her hair, brushing it back off her face, and kissed her again, slowly. "Whatever you have in the oven smells terrific, but if you don't mind—"

"It's chicken tetrazzini, the oven is already on warm, and it will keep just fine."

An hour later, the tetrazzini finally made it to the table. They toasted each other and drank. "Perfect, absolutely perfect. What more can I ask? We made love, we're about to eat my amazing tetrazzini. A perfect end to the day."

He looked oddly excited, almost hyper, which wasn't like him. "Gil, when do you have to ship out again? Don't tell me it's tomorrow morning."

"Oh, no, I'm here for at least two weeks. I have some things I want to do." He looked away, toward the door, and she felt a jolt, a strange disconnect. What was he thinking? What was going on here?

He pushed his plate away.

"Isabella, I—"

The doorbell rang.

Gil waved toward it. "Ignore that. I want to talk to you. I missed you, Isabella, so much. I don't want to be apart from you like this ever again."

Her smile probably lit up the whole room, maybe even the block. "What are you saying?"

"I'm saying I want to make things official. You're everything I have ever wanted. You're, well, you're everything to me. You make me so happy."

The doorbell dinged again, and he looked at

his watch. He cursed, unusual for him. "They're early."

"Who's early? Gil, what's going on?"

Gil dropped to one knee, reached into his pocket, and pulled out a diamond ring that glittered and winked in the light.

Isabella gasped, then dropped down next to him, threw her arms around him.

"Yes!"

Gil started to laugh. "I didn't ask you yet."

"So ask already," she said, nuzzling into his chest. He did smell of the sea, and hope, and vanilla and something cedar, and of her and them, and she was never going to forget this moment, never going to forget how his beard tickled her cheek.

Gil put a hand under her chin, drew her face up so she could see his eyes. He whispered, "Will you marry me? Because I want to marry you, Isabella."

"Yes, I will marry you."

He kissed her, a contract sealed, then put the ring on her finger. It was a perfect fit, he'd borrowed one of her rings a month ago to make sure the size was going to be right. He was so happy he thought he might burst, and Isabella was moving her hand this way and that in the light to make the diamond sparkle.

The door rang again.

Laughing now, Gil shouted, "Okay, okay, I'm coming."

"You probably have some weird mariachi band out there, ready to burst in and serenade us, don't you?"

"Not exactly, no. This particular moment was meant for us alone." He kissed her on the nose and went to the door. "But now——"

He flung open the door. He hadn't hired a mariachi band but a photographer to show them photos of the engagement from the video camera he'd stashed in the kitchen, then take a few more for posterity. He'd been planning this for weeks. The photographer was early, but who cared?

But it wasn't the photographer on the other side of the door. He didn't recognize the man standing there—tall and swarthy with round gold glasses, a brown beard, and sandy-brown hair. But Isabella put her hand on Gil's back and said, "Dr. Bruce? What are you doing here?"

Roman Ardelean had flowers in his hands and a wide, welcoming smile on his face. He took in the scene—the candles, the dinner dishes on the table, the flowers in their blue vase. His smile faded. "I wasn't expecting you to have company."

Gil stuck out a hand. "Gil Brooks. I'm Isabella's fiancé. Well, her fiancé since two minutes ago."

If she could, she'd slam the door in his face. Whatever did this disturbing man want? She said, trying to hide the distaste she felt, "Gil, this is Dr. Bruce, a Voynich scholar and friends with Persy.

We met yesterday at the museum. Is there something I can help you with, Dr. Bruce?"

Even though she made no move to invite him in, tension bled into the room. Gil's back straightened. "We were just finishing dinner, or we'd invite you in. Surely you can discuss this tomorrow. We're having a bit of a celebration."

Bruce's voice was formal and remote. "I'm sorry to interrupt. Yes, since I see you're very busy now, we can certainly discuss the issue tomorrow at the museum. Before I go, I'd love a glass of water, if you wouldn't mind. I have a long trip home." He shook his umbrella to make the point, scattering water on her foyer floor.

Isabella didn't want him in her apartment, didn't want him anywhere near her, ever again, but Gil said, "Sure, it's in the kitchen. Come with me."

Without hesitation, Bruce was through the door and heading to the kitchen as if he knew exactly where it was. But this man wasn't supposed to even know where she lived, much less how her flat was laid out. Something was wrong. She shut the front door and followed the men.

She caught sight of a glitter, and after another glance and a smile at her left hand, walked down the hallway. Spring, they'd be married in the spring. She wished her mother were still alive. She'd like Gil.

There was a loud grunt from the kitchen. She rounded the corner, but her mind couldn't catch up with what she was seeing. Gil, on the floor, blood on his neck. Dr. Bruce standing over him, a manic grin on his face, blood on the lenses of his glasses. She was rooted to the spot, staring at Gil's pale face. He wasn't moving, his lips bubbling with a froth of red, eyes already staring. She yelled, "No!" and then Dr. Bruce struck her cheek, and she went down hard on her back, something sticky running down her face. She registered that he'd struck her—but then Gil, no, not Gil. She saw Dr. Bruce standing over her, a horrible smile cracking his face in two, before the darkness took her.

CHAPTER FORTY-FIVE

Drummond House
Barton Street
Westminster, London

Mike and Ben snacked on the nuts and crackers Nigel had brought them and watched the news about the train bombing while waiting for Nicholas to come home.

She popped an almond, chewed, then, "Ben, it's nuts, no pun intended. All these murders and now a terrorist attack on a Eurostar? Do we know yet if it was heading for the Chunnel?"

"Yep, it was."

"What in heaven's name is going on?" She hit her knee, winced.

Ben drank down some of his ale. "Don't jump the gun, Mike. They haven't said it was terror-related."

"What else could it be?"

The dining room door opened, and Nicholas

and Adam came in the room. "It's not a terrorist attack, not ISIS or Al-Qaeda, anyway."

"Then what is it?" But Mike knew what had happened even before Nicholas said, "A drone. Watch this. We've managed to keep it from the media, though I don't know how long we have before it leaks."

He set his laptop on the table and showed them the feed. Mike was amazed at the precision of the drone strike.

"Bombed by a drone," she said, shaking her head. "No, not terrorism. It's more of the same, all part of an insane script."

"Script? Interesting you'd say that. And this train bombing is a splashy attack, draws everyone's attention."

Adam grabbed a handful of pistachios, out of the shell, so he couldn't resist. "Are you saying all the murders, the computer glitches, and now the train bombing, these attacks are all tied together?"

Nicholas said, "I'm assuming there was someone on that train who was a specific target, someone who has ties to Donovan, Hemmler, Alexander, and Vittorini. We're waiting on the manifests. Two people have died, tourists from Australia. No one related to the government. But I don't understand, it's always been one victim at a time, but now? A whole train of innocent people?"

Mike felt numb. "Maybe it's a different message."

Adam said, "Tell her the good news."

"*Good* is a relative term. We're all up late tonight. The hard drives of the victims' personal computers are in. Let's have some dinner and get started. We have to find a link between the murders, and find out who was being targeted on that train." He looked at Mike. "If there was a specific target on that train."

Mike shrugged. "Let's go to Vittorini. We know she was running arms through the Govan Shipyards, maybe those are the bread crumbs we need."

It was three in the morning when Mike saw it. She sat up, scratched her head, pushed her glasses up her nose, and shouted "Eureka!"

Tired, blurry eyes stared at her. Nicholas asked, "Eureka? Does this have something to do with the water level in the tub?"

"No, no, I have it. I've found the link between them. And you aren't going to like it."

CHAPTER FORTY-SIX

Ambition is to the mind what the cap is to
the falcon; It blinds us first, and then com-
pels us to tower by reason of our blindness.
—Charles Caleb Colton, *Lacon*

Gradara Castle
Near Venice, Italy
1812

All knew the march to the Russian border would
be long and hard, but there was excitement in
the ranks, thoughts of pillage in this strange land,
of killing heathens and those fierce warriors called
Cossacks.

General Barclay de Tolly and General Bagration
had planned to stop this fine day for provisioning in
northern Italy. Napoléon was given hospitality at a
grand castle with views of the Adriatic. It was called
Gradara, old and wealthy and filled with treasures
Napoléon would not take, for the master was an ally.

It was at Gradara Napoléon read the courier's message from the front. He walked to the ramparts, gazed beyond, to the Adriatic Sea, a beautiful sight, opened the message, and smiled. Czar Alexander was mobilizing two of his armies to meet them. He said aloud, his words blown away by the wind, "Let him bring every cursed soldier in his lands, it matters not. I will prevail. I will burn Moscow to the ground and dance in its ashes and blood."

He was still smiling when he walked back into the great hall of Gradara. He drank and dined on fresh pheasant and newly butchered boar, listened to his generals boast of the destruction they would visit upon the Russian upstarts.

At last, Napoléon struck his knife against the wooden table and shouted, "I wish no more talk of war this night. Entertain me."

The generals glanced at one another, brows raised, not knowing what to do. Suddenly, an old man appeared and walked forward to stand before the emperor. "I am Gradara's bard."

Napoléon looked him up and down. "Look at you, your hair's as white as snow, your beard nearly touches your bony knees, and your eyes are filmed to near blindness. You are so old, how can you remember a single song? A single tale?"

The old man said in a strong, firm voice, "Ah, but I do, sire, I have a grand tale for you."

Napoléon nodded to one of his generals, who

threw the old man several coins. "I do not wish to hear the usual swill of a fair damsel and a valiant warrior, bard. I want something dark, something to make my belly tight. I will give you another coin if you please me."

The old man nodded and began, his voice strong and loud, reaching every corner of the great hall. "Sire, what I will tell you is true. It is about two brothers who lived not the normal life span allotted to most men, but for hundreds of years, perhaps more. They lived here, in this very castle, for a time.

"The brothers were born on the same night, arms linked together, in a shared caul. From birth, one was strong, and one was weak. The strong one loved his brother very much and would do anything for him, carrying him to the woods, saving the finest bits of meat from their suppers for him.

"One day, the strong brother went into the woods to hunt, hoping to kill something to please his brother when a great storm blew up. He was separated from his friends, forced to light a fire under a great oak tree and cook a squirrel from his game bag.

"A great falcon came down from the skies and ripped the dead squirrel from his hand. The brother called after the bird, 'Please don't go. I'm lost and hungry. I'll share the squirrel with you.'

"And the great bird wheeled around and returned, dropping the squirrel at his feet. True to his word, he cut the squirrel in half, giving the bird the slightly larger piece. It was then the brother realized he could hear the bird's thoughts.

"'Thank you for your kindness. I will share one with you, as well. I know of a cure for your brother. Spill my blood in a cup and give it to him to drink at the full of the moon.'

"The brother drew back, horrified. 'I cannot kill you. You shared your meal with me.'

"The falcon thought to him, 'You must trust me. Bring me back to your home, and when the time is nigh, spill my blood. Your brother will drink and be cured.'

"The falcon showed the brother the way home. And remained a friend to both brothers, and they could hear the falcon's thoughts, the falcon theirs.

"Moon cycle after moon cycle passed without the brother honoring his promise. Finally, on the third full moon, the bird thought to him, 'You must kill me this night, or the cure will no longer work.'

"The weak brother, who by this time was barely able to move, heard the falcon. 'Please, no, Brother. I do not want to lose our friend.'

"But the stronger had promised, and he knew his brother would die if he didn't. So, when the moon was full, the falcon presented his neck, and the brother sliced it open, catching the ruby blood in a pewter cup. He gave the drink to his brother. He drank it down. The two brothers mourned the bird, buried it, and slept. In the morning, the weak brother was strong.

"He bowed to his brother. 'I have long wanted a human body to live in. Thank you.' And the stronger brother saw that his brother's eyes now glowed red. And he realized his brother had spoken in the falcon's strange tongue.

"'What do you mean? What evil is this, to possess the body of a bird, and now of my brother?'

"'A priest banished me into the body of a falcon many years ago. I did not sleep, and blood was my only succor. Ah, it feels good to walk again.' He left the castle but returned a few hours later. He showed the brother a sheaf of strange pages. 'Now, I need your help.'

"The stronger brother had no choice but to comply, for he still loved his brother, though he knew this was unnatural and wrong.

"'You must bring me a virgin before nightfall. I must drink her blood. Only then will I have the strength to live through the night.'

"He brought his brother a virgin from the village, and the next night another, until the village was emptied. He grew strong, and soon, the two were feared throughout the land. They fled to a dark castle, deep in a forest. It is said they experimented with many things, with blood and herbs and silver, to find a way to make themselves live forever. Did they succeed? I do not know."

Napoléon rose to his feet. "Bah. Blood drinking and talking crows. Ridiculous. Off with you."

The old bard cackled a laugh, then leaned in and whispered to Napoléon, "It was a falcon, sire, not a crow. One truth I do know: the brothers brought the magic pages they used to divine this spell back here to Gradara. This is where a sainted ancestor found them, many years ago. They are mine now, though I do not understand them. But as I said, the brothers understood them very well."

"I don't believe you. Show me these pages."

The old man pulled the pages from inside his shirt. Napoléon grabbed them, but he couldn't read the pages—all he saw were strange symbols and writing, and puzzling drawings that baffled him, the red and green ink still vibrant. What did it mean? And then he knew. The pages were magic. They would give him the power to defeat the Russian czar. It mattered not he couldn't read them.

Napoléon said to the old bard, "These pages were ripped from a book. Where is the book?"

"I know not, sire."

"Then I will keep these pages. This legend you told me—I know now it is a portent of the blood I will spill in accursed Russia. Mayhap I will show them to the czar as he bows before me."

The mighty army marched away in the morning and into disaster. Nearly half a million soldiers were lost to a bitter winter, to starvation, to people who would rather die than accept Napoléon's boot on their neck.

Months later, Napoléon looked at the pages and realized the portent he'd believed to be his mighty victory and the blood of the Russians was his own soldiers' blood and bitter defeat. But he could not destroy the pages, for fear of their curse staying with him.

And so it was that somewhere near Smolensk, a tinker found a saddlebag lying in a pile of bushes. There were only loose pages within. He had no idea what they were but kept them. Perhaps they had value, perhaps someone would pay him for them.

THE THIRD DAY

THURSDAY

Cabal: a private organization or party engaged in secret intrigues; also, the intrigues themselves.

In England the word was used during the 17th century to describe any secret or extralegal council of the king, especially the foreign committee of the Privy Council. The term took on its present invidious meaning from a group of five ministers chosen in 1667 by King Charles II (Clifford, Arlington, Buckingham, Ashley Cooper [later earl of Shaftesbury], and Lauderdale), whose initial letters coincidentally spelled cabal. This cabal, never very unified in its members' aims and sympathies, fell apart by 1672; Shaftesbury even became one of Charles II's fiercest opponents.

—*ENCYCLOPAEDIA BRITANNICA*

CHAPTER FORTY-SEVEN

Falconers are a fortunate breed. Not only do
we have the pleasure of our current hawk, but
also, increasingly over the years, the memory
of former hawks, which were dear to us and
individual flights, which are etched in the
memory forever.
—Emma Ford, *Falconry: Art and Practice*

The Old Garden
Twickenham
Richmond upon Thames, London

Isabella woke in darkness. She didn't know where
she was or what had happened. She touched
her fingers to her throbbing face. He'd struck her.
Why? She stilled. Something was terribly wrong.

Fear swamped her, she was inside a tomb,
something black—she was dying.

And then she remembered, saw it all again,
and—no, no.

Gil was dead, lying on the kitchen floor, dead, dead, dead, and that obviously insane Laurence Bruce had murdered him and struck her down.

She couldn't accept it, simply couldn't, but there was blood, so much blood, and Gil was on his back, his beautiful eyes staring unseeing up at her. His throat, something was wrong. So much blood. And Bruce had struck her. She vaguely remembered the jostle and rumble of a car. The smell of gas and asphalt and—

"You're awake."

She jerked her head toward his voice. She tried to scream, but nothing came out. A gag, she was gagged. She was tied down and gagged.

"Don't struggle. If you fight, he won't like it. He might punish you."

The man who'd spoken came into focus. Who might punish her? Dr. Bruce? Yes, of course. But who was this? He stood by the door, hair long and unwashed, his jeans and black T-shirt rumpled and stained. His skin was pale, and he was thin. The words coming from his mouth were no language she'd ever heard aloud, strange garbled sounds that held no meaning, only they did. She realized, somehow, she understood them.

She began twisting and fighting, but the man didn't move to untie her. He stared as if she were a butterfly pinned to a board. She shuddered. She knew she was as good as dead. As Gil was. Her brain shied away from him lying so still, and all the blood. No, no. She didn't want to see it again. Was this strange man, his face so pale he was nearly translucent, here to kill her? She swallowed tears, looked away from him, up, at the ceiling. Tall, at least twelve feet, timber beams running across it. Everything was white: the walls, the ceiling, the man's skin. He still stood silently, watching her twist and turn.

"I was looking at your face. You can understand me."

She began shaking her head. She could smell him, from that far away. Garlic, cedar, patchouli cologne. And blood. He smelled of blood.

Where was Dr. Bruce? What was happening? Panic rose, and she fought it, hard. She needed to stay in control, or she'd die—like Gil. *No, Gil, no.*

The man moved even closer until he stood next to her, looking down at her. "How is it you can speak our language?"

Of course she understood him, but she shook her head, felt tears burning her eyes, swallowed. She was gagged, so how could she explain he was speaking Voynichese, the language of the Voynich manuscript?

She hadn't heard it since her twin sister had caught a flu virus and died, so small, shrunken in the hospital bed, covered with white sheets. *She shouldn't have died,* the hospital had said, *she shouldn't have, we did everything we could.* But their words were meaningless. Kristiana was dead.

He leaned down and took off her gag. "Speak to me."

She looked up into that pale, intense face. She knew instinctively there wasn't something quite right about him. She said, "I was a twin." A special twin, she thought, but didn't say it aloud, because, quite simply, she didn't know what it meant. To him. "Of course I understand you."

He looked pleased. "And your mother and father were Romanian. Roman was right, perhaps you are the one."

The one what? Isabella heard a flurry of movement in the hall, and she turned quickly and shrank back.

It wasn't Dr. Laurence Bruce—no, wait, she recognized the dark intense eyes, before hidden behind the thick lenses he'd worn. No brown beard and hair now. His hair was black, and he was straight and tall. And perched on his wrist sat a small raptor bird. He wore a leather glove that covered his wrist and arm up to his elbow, and the bird was wearing a matching leather hood, with a small plume on top. He gave Isabella a long look, then turned to the pale man who held her gag in one hand and spoke in the same guttural language, twin talk. She knew these might be the last moments of her life, yet she listened as he spoke.

"Look at her, Radu, the one who had our pages. She did not find them by accident. My question is, why did she make such a big production of it at her press conference? What do you think?"

"I spoke to her, Roman. We were talking. She understands me."

Radu? Roman?

"That's good, very good. Radu, I need to speak to her now, alone. Please leave us for a moment, all right?"

"But, Roman—"

"Please, Radu, it is important." He said nothing more until the pale thin man called Radu left the room.

"Now, let's see." She watched him take the hood off the falcon and say, in an almost offhand manner, "This is Arlington. She's a particular favorite of mine."

Isabella heard him give a whispered command—in Voynichese. The bird spread her wings wide, turned her head, a yellow eye fixed on Isabella. He threw something on her stomach. Then the bird hit Isabella's belly, a flurry of wings and claws. Sharp talons raked her through her slacks, ripped up her belly. She screamed, tried to pull away, but she was tied too tightly.

He watched her as a scientist would watch an experiment, with only mild interest. He tossed another piece of meat on Isabella's chest. Arlington was more delicate about it this time, but Isabella still got a full face of feathers. The strange, smoky scent of the bird and the tang of the raw meat made her gag.

The bird stood heavy on her chest, staring at her with its head cocked, and Isabella fought down bile, fought against the fear.

With another scrape of talons, the bird launched herself into the air and landed gracefully back on his gloved arm.

"That demonstration was so you understand I am perfectly serious. If you lie to me, Dr. Marin, I'll cut you open and let my entire cast in to enjoy a morning treat."

She was trying to suck in breaths, but the pain in her belly and her unreasoning fear made it difficult. Finally, she stared up at him, silent, as Gil was silent, no, no, she couldn't think about Gil. But this man had murdered him. "Who are you?"

And suddenly he smiled. "No, I am not Dr. Laurence Bruce, a silly, pretentious little man who has served me well in the past. I am Roman Ardelean. Now, I will ask you only once. How did you come by the lost pages of the Voynich?"

She whispered, "Who is Radu?"

He raised the hood from Arlington's head.

"No, no, please!"

He studied her terrified face, shrugged. "Very well, I will tell you. Radu is my twin brother. He doesn't do well with crowds or the outside world. He stays here, where he is safe. He has a good life. He enjoys himself. His computers are his window to the outside world. Though I must say, I was impressed to see him speaking to you. Radu does not like strangers. Now, answer me." He stroked the neck of the bird, and she preened for him.

"Please, just one more question, and I will tell you what I did. Did you steal the Voynich last year from Yale?"

"No, I did not. Nor do I know who did. I wish that I had now, but of course it's far too late. No more, tell me how you came by the pages."

She couldn't tell him the truth, she wouldn't, but she knew she had to convince him. After all, she'd practiced her lie so often, it came out smoothly, without hesitation. "I found them inside a book in the museum's library. The pages were inside *Meditations*."

He regarded her for a moment, then said, "That's a lie, but I will let it go for the moment. How can you understand the language of the pages? Tell me, and don't lie."

She realized he'd switched from English to Voynichese. She wished she could pretend she didn't understand, but it was too late for that. "I can't explain how I know it, I just do. You know it is twin talk."

He continued to stare at her, a finger stroking Arlington's head.

She said, "You are a twin. You can read the Voynich as well as I can. It's an early medical manuscript, written by twins who were geniuses, twins of Vlad Dracul's line, one ill, one strong. The entire book is a discussion between them, conversations, about the earth, about herbs and flowers to heal and to maim, and the alchemic relationship between metals and matter, astrology, women, fertility, everything. You know it explains the way blood works in the body, how it nourishes the organs, the brain, the heart. You know it's an herbal, but it's also a code. It says for some, drinking blood, if a potion is given first, is necessary to live. I believe the writers, these twins, were probably very misunderstood and very isolated. Feared, most likely because no one could understand them. You and your twin, Radu, are the first I've ever met in my life who could read the Voynich and speak Voynichese."

"I agree with you. I've already done your research—I have given the manuscript to many other sets of twins. There was no recognition. The best cryptographers approach it as if it's a cipher. They look for a key, a code, when it's a unique language. Your press conference on Thursday—how do you believe your announcement will be received by your peers and other so-called Voynich experts? And your claim that page seventy-four provides a sort of key to help the lay reader understand the manuscript?"

"They'll probably laugh at me, about all of it."

"As do I, at least about page seventy-four. I have examined all the loose pages, including page seventy-four. They are more of the same. Why were they torn out? Why was page seventy-four cut out? I have no idea, nor have I been able to find a single clue about it."

He took a step toward her, and the falcon on his arm leaned toward her, as well. Isabella couldn't move. "Yes," Roman said, "Arlington would very much like to visit you again for a bite to eat. A reminder you will continue to tell me the truth. Now, before you tell me why you lied about where you found the pages, tell me, do you believe the twins who wrote it were mad?"

"No. Of course not. They were as sane as I am."

He slowly nodded.

She was scared, desperate. "Please, you took the pages from my apartment, you killed my fiancé, why did you bring me here? What do you want of me?"

"We need you," Radu said from the doorway, obviously listening. "We want you to help us."

Isabella pulled up as far as she could to see him. "How can I possibly help you? I've told you everything I know. I'm a twin, I can understand Voynichese and read it, just as you and your brother can. So we are special twins, I suppose, but there's nothing more I can say, nothing more I know."

Roman moved closer to her. Arlington spread her wings again, sharp beak clacking at the noise. "Oh, you'll help, Dr. Marin. Or you'll wish you were dead, like your unfortunate fiancé."

CHAPTER FORTY-EIGHT

MI5 Headquarters, Home Office
Thames House
12 Millbank
Westminster, London

Seven in the morning. The team, with the exception of Adam, sat around the private conference room with cups of hot black coffee in their hands. Except Harry Drummond, who was drinking his favored oolong.

Nicholas sat forward. "Father, Ian, sorry it's so early, but this is critical. Mike found a common time and location on each victim's calendar, and we spent the night pulling it all together."

Mike said, "We think it's more than a theory, sir. Look at this." The screen filled with a series of letters and numbers.

Mike took another sip of her coffee. "As you can see, these are GPS coordinates. 21.0976° North, 33.7965° East. They correlate to the Nubian Desert in Sudan, south of the Egyptian border. The coordinates show in every victim's calendar on the same date, seven months ago, December. We looked at the recent history of the area, and there's been nothing in the news, nothing happening, no attacks, no people. It's sand."

Nicholas said, "So we accessed the satellite footage from that day, for those specific coordinates."

"Do I want to know how?" Harry asked.

"Quite aboveboard, Father, don't worry. We sent an emergency request to the NSA—Adam has a friend there." He gave his father a sleepy grin. "We didn't hack them."

"I'm glad to hear it. So what did the satellites show?"

Ben forwarded the slides. "This is the area represented by the coordinates the morning of December second. You can see a small village on the dunes. It's not on any maps we could access, but this is a desert area, things shift and change. Nomads set up shops. Sandstorms blow through. It's an ever-changing environment. Lidar, short for light detection and ranging, that allows for measurements below the land's surface area, doesn't show any permanent structures, no deep foundations. This was all on the surface, temporary. The satellite itself wasn't trained on it—it simply flew over that area once a day. We're lucky it was nearby.

"Now, this is the morning of December third."

Harry could see the village was no longer standing. There were pieces of it in different places, though, scattered like toothpicks across the reddish sand.

"Storm blew through?"

Nicholas said, "No, sir, we think this was manmade destruction. We think this was a proving ground for a weapons test. We checked with all the services we could and no one had any assets in this area. There's no knowing exactly what happened between the second and the third of December. But—"

Ben flashed up another slide. "Here we have a shot from two weeks earlier. There's nothing. Now, watch the progression."

They watched a village slowly take shape, day by day, rising from the desert sand. The footage was clear, easy to pick out the details.

Ian said slowly, "So someone builds a village only to blow it apart. Who does that?"

Mike said, "Someone who had a show to give."

Harry sipped at his oolong. "And with what sort of weapons?"

Nicholas flipped closed his laptop. "I'm going to bet it was drones. We know whoever is behind this has an army—from tiny drones that can shoot poisoned needles into people's necks to large ones that can drop bombs on trains. I think this was the demonstration to the people they wanted to fund the drone army, to get them on board. It might be legitimate, it might be off-book. I don't know. I would assume the victims were a party to this, though if they were funding it, I don't know why they'd be murdered. Father, have you heard anything about the victims' possible involvement in building an army of drones?"

"I haven't, but we can look deeper, ask around. Perhaps Barstow knows. He stopped by yesterday, seemed like he wanted to talk, but that didn't happen. I'll call him after this meeting."

Mike sat forward. "This isn't only about drones. Paulina Vittorini had a warehouse of weaponry, enough to arm a small country. Someone's created their own private army."

Harry said, "All right, all right, say this is a black-ops program. Who were they planning to attack?"

Nicholas's phone rang. "A moment, Father. It's Adam. Adam? You're on speaker. What's up?"

"I've found another link between the victims. You aren't going to like it."

Mike called out, "Come on, Adam, we can take it. I hope."

"Okay. Not surprisingly, all of the computers use MATRIX. But they all also have an encrypted email system with its own private VPN, housed in a separate portion of their hard drive, where MATRIX can't access. The four victims were communicating in a completely secret, bespoke private system. It's built on a new computer language."

"Ardelean's, I presume?"

"Yes. It's not exactly the same, some parts have newer language, but his markers are there, those same numbers as the base code, four-zero-eight. That's not all—the victims were all talking to the same person. Lord Barstow."

Harry felt a punch of adrenaline. "Go on, Adam."

"It looks like they were funding him. Barstow is the one who is behind building this army."

Harry closed his eyes against the enormity of it. "Oh, Corry, what have you done?"

Nicholas said, "Adam, was the bespoke email for this group designed specifically by Ardelean? As in he was hired to find them a secure way to communicate?"

"I'd say so, yes. It makes the most sense."

Harry said, "So he may know more about this than he claims. Good work, Adam. We need to get Ardelean back into the office and have another chat. I certainly hope he was only hired to build a secure communications system for this team of renegades, and nothing more."

A voice came from the corridor. "There won't be any need. I'll be happy to explain what's happening."

The man Nicholas knew as his father's friend and his counterpart at MI6—Corinthian Jones, Lord Barstow—stood in the door of his father's office.

Harry slowly stood. Mike saw his hands were clenched at his sides.

"Corry, what the bloody hell are you thinking, man? Raising funds for a private army?"

Barstow shrugged. "Since you've stuck your nose in, Harry, I'm forced to explain. This is a black-ops program run by MI6. I am overseeing it. That is all you need to know. I need you and your team to stand down. I have this situation well in hand. Don't stand down, and we will have a serious problem."

Nicholas said very quietly, "People are dead, and we've been tasked with uncovering the truth behind their murders. If your off-book drone army has gone rogue, we need to know."

Barstow heaved a sigh, and Nicholas saw a bulge under his coat.

He slowly rose. "Why are you wearing a weapon? I thought you had lackeys to kill for you."

"Nicholas," Mike said, a hand on his arm.

Barstow said, "Yes, Nicholas, listen to your partner. Sit down and shut up. You've caused me a great deal of grief these past two days. You would have done well to stay in America. We don't want or need you here. I'd have thought Afghanistan made that clear enough."

Harry said quietly, "Yes, sit down, Nicholas." And to Barstow, he said, his voice formal, "Corry, are you admitting to killing the people who helped you build your private army? I assume you couldn't get the funding from Her Majesty and had to find your own sources of income? Is that how you managed to get tied up with Heinrich Hemmler? Was Paulina Vittorini running the guns for you? And Chapman Donovan, you've never been a fan of his, but Terry Alexander, man. He was your oldest friend."

Barstow said through gritted teeth, "I didn't kill them, none of them. I'm trying to make sure no one else is murdered, which is why I need you to back off."

Mike saw his hands were trembling. He was frightened, understandably so. He was in a room of sharks. *Make him lose it.* She gave him a push, put some bitch in her voice. "Why should we back off? Can't you tell whoever's been killing those funding you to stop? Or are we next? How are we to know you don't have one of your drones positioned outside, or the birds you've been using to spy on us? How did you manage to corrupt MATRIX? You don't seem smart enough for that. If Roman Ardelean doesn't know you were behind the breach, he soon will, you know it." She added extra bitch. "You're finished, sir, it's only a matter of time, very little time—"

Barstow started to laugh, a strained laugh, an ugly laugh. He laughed so hard he nearly choked. "You think he isn't a part of this? You stupid girl, you—"

Nicholas was ready to jump at Barstow and

beat him to a pulp. Barstow's eyes grew wild, and in a flash, he'd drawn the gun and was pointing it at Nicholas.

The room erupted in shouts.

Nicholas ignored the yelling, felt his father's elbow gently nudge his arm, saw the slight nod of his head. Nicholas in turn nudged Ben with his knee. Harry dove to one side, Ben ducked away, and Nicholas kicked out of his chair and launched himself at Barstow.

CHAPTER FORTY-NINE

Barstow saw Nicholas move a second too late. He fired as Nicholas crashed into him, knocking him over backward.

Nicholas felt the sting of a bullet against his side, right above his belt, heard the shouts, but ignored everything, flipped Barstow over on his stomach and pinned his arms behind his back. He knew he was bleeding, prayed it wasn't too bad, and then Mike was there with the handcuffs she always had latched to her belt. She clapped them around Barstow's wrists.

"Cover me," Mike shouted to Ben, darting into the hall. Ben was right behind her. They were back in a moment, Mike panting. "Looks like he came alone." Then she saw Harry kneeling beside Nicholas. He'd pulled his shirt up and pressed his handkerchief against his side. "Harry, is it bad?"

"I can speak, Mike. No, it's not bad, is it, Father?"

Harry looked up. "I think he missed the important bits."

"Why is Barstow unconscious?"

Harry said, "I hit him in the jaw for shooting my son."

There was shouting from outside the conference room, and Ben ran out. Nicholas started to follow, but Mike and Harry held him down. "Listen to me, lamebrain, all you have to do is stop yourself bleeding, all right?"

"You said that perfectly, Michaela."

"Don't worry, Ben's in control. He'll call if he needs us. He can handle things while we check you out." Harry lifted the handkerchief, and she lightly probed the wound, then sat back on her heels.

Barstow groaned.

Mike tapped him on the side of the head with the heel of her hand. "Stop making noise. We'll get to you in a minute."

And to Nicholas, "As for you, it's a nasty scrape, but it won't need stitches. Through and through, lucky you. I really don't like this, Nicholas, curse you. It could have been another of your nine lives down the tubes."

Harry rose, looked down at his bloody hands. His heart was pounding and he knew such fear and rage, it was hard not to kill Barstow with his bare hands. So close, too close. He managed to get out "one moment"—and he disappeared into the bathroom adjacent to the conference room.

Harry came out, handed Mike a hand towel and three washcloths. Thankfully, he had himself in control again. "These should do it." Together they bound him up. She said, "There, better, we'll get you to the ER later."

Mike helped him up, and he pulled her close for a moment. She squeezed his back, whispered, "Stop being a frigging hero, okay, James Bond?"

"A statistical impossibility, Agent Caine. I can't seem to stop showing off for you."

Barstow moaned again. Mike said, "Good, his lordship is with us. Time to see what he has to say."

They settled Barstow in a chair in the command center, hands cuffed behind him. Harry got right in his face and shouted, "Tell us what you've done, you old fool." Nicholas didn't think he'd ever seen his father so angry before. Harry Drummond had a long fuse, and Nicholas rarely saw it lit. It was lit now.

Nicholas asked, his voice calmer than his father's, "Yes, tell us what you've done."

"What have I done? I'm trying to save lives, you idiots. I've had a plan on the table for more than a year, a plan to help arm the patriots in Africa who are trying to fight the incursion of terrorism. And it's been going gangbusters until you lot got involved."

"Tell us who you talked into building the drones for you."

Barstow yelled, his face now alarmingly red, "How dare you treat me like this?"

"Talk now or I'll call the home secretary, tell him I have you here in handcuffs ready for a march through Fleet Street."

"All right, curse you. We hired a man to build us a drone army. Six patriots gave him a total of one billion to start, one billion on delivery. Then they refused to make the final payment until he delivered the drones. He refused. We were at a standoff. That's why people are dead. He's furious and killing every investor who hasn't given their money." He sucked in a breath. "I'm next, maybe June, my children. He'll kill all of us."

Mike said quietly, "Who is he, Lord Barstow?"

Barstow sneered. "The lot of you think you're so bloody smart. He's fooled you like he's fooled the world. He's ruthless, a psychopath, and the LSD he's taking has pushed him over the edge. Still don't know? The wunderkind of technology, the only man in England capable of building a drone army."

Nicholas stared at him. "Roman Ardelean? He's been building an army for you?"

"Yes, thousands of drones to kill the bloody terrorists. I believed the man a true patriot, but he's not. He's a common murderer—my wrists hurt. I need some water."

CHAPTER FIFTY

It was obvious to all of them that Barstow was scared to his soul of Roman Ardelean, but something wasn't right. Even though Nicholas's side ached, he wasn't about to admit it to Mike, who gave him the eye every couple of minutes.

"This is everything, Corry? You've told us the entire truth? Roman Ardelean has killed these people because they refused to pay him their final payment for the drone army?"

"Yes."

Harry motioned them into the hall. "Ben, Ian, I trust you've located him?"

Ian said, "Actually, sir, we can't find him. No one's answering at his home, his mobile is off, and his offices claim they haven't seen him. His jet is at Northolt, in the hangar, unused. But Ardelean himself, we don't know."

Mike said, "Ardelean wants his final payment. I'm thinking Barstow can get him to come out if he offers to pay him."

Harry rubbed his chin. "I daresay you're right, Michaela. Let's approach him."

Barstow looked exhausted. He was no longer handcuffed, but they knew he wouldn't try to run. That wasn't an option.

Harry asked, "Where is Ardelean?"

"I don't know. I told you the truth, he's gone mad, uses LSD like I told you, at very low levels to keep himself in check, a special formula he mentioned once. I think he's now become dependent on the drug, and it's making him extremely reckless. He must be stopped. You must stop him. If I could, I would."

"How do you propose we do this?" Mike asked him.

"Kill him. We have to kill him. It's the only way."

Nicholas said, "We're not assassins."

"You were," Barstow said, a sneer marring his mouth. "And quite good at it, if I recall."

Harry leaned over Barstow, his voice quiet and deadly. "Listen to me, Barstow, one more accusation out of you about my son's past and when I find Ardelean I'll feed you to him."

Mike wanted to kick this miserable immoral ass into the wainscoting. Nicholas stared at his father, saw his rage at Barstow—and it was for him. He swallowed.

Nicholas laid his hand on his father's arm, said, "We won't execute your problem for you. But we will arrest him, make him pay for the four people he's murdered. Ah, and the Eurostar he bombed with one of his drones. Two Australian tourists died."

"Yes, yes, he did that, too, to put the screws to me more, that, and I'm sure he wanted to distract you. Harry, listen to me, if you eliminate Ardelean, the drone army he's built can go to Her Majesty's government. He's the head of the hydra. Kill him and the whole nightmare comes to an end, and perhaps, since I've told you everything, there will be leniency for me."

"One more chance, Corry. Where might we find Roman Ardelean?"

Barstow said, "I didn't lie. I know he has a flat in Belgravia. Search there. There's where I usually met him, before."

Ben spoke up for the first time. "Belgravia? I thought he had a country estate north of London, that's where all the articles say he lives."

"He owns multiple homes."

Nicholas said, "Ben, please get Adam on it."

Harry asked, "And what of the one billion pounds you owe him for building your army?"

"I couldn't put him off any longer. To buy time, I told him I would pay him today. I realized it wouldn't work, that he would kill me next. You have to kill him."

Mike said slowly, "You said you aren't able to pay him the rest of his money because the investors haven't paid you? Or him? It's you, isn't it? They were to pay you, and you were to pay Ardelean."

"Yes, of course. I'm running the program."

It was then everything clicked into place. Nicholas said, "No wonder you want us to kill Ardelean. You can't do it yourself." Nicholas leaned over right in his face, his hands on the chair arms just as his father had done. "You know what I think? You decided to screw him out of his final payment. You kept his one billion pounds."

"Of course not! The investors refused to pay, they—" Barstow stopped cold when Nicholas laughed at him, straightened and crossed his arms over his chest.

"You're a paltry human being, my lord. Did you ever have a grand notion of saving the nations of Africa, of shipping them arms and a drone army to fight off radical Islam? ISIS? Or was it always about getting yourself really, really rich? One billion pounds is a lot of money."

"Don't you dare speak to me like that! I wanted the drone army! Do you hear me, I'm a patriot. I love my country, all my ancestors have loved England, served England. My family is in all the history books. I wanted to join them—I would have been the best of them. I would have saved a country! None of this is my fault. Ardelean is the one, the only one!"

He was heaving. Harry said, "You're going to call him, Corry. You're going to reaffirm your promise to pay him. You'll set it up for tonight. And we're going to arrest him, not execute him."

Barstow, calmer now, said, "He's probably with his brother, but not at the flat in Belgravia. From what I gather, the brother, his twin, has some sort of rare disease. Roman won't ever say, but I know his twin never leaves the house."

Harry said, "His twin brother? I didn't know Ardelean had a brother."

Nicholas said, "Adam will find Ardelean, and he'll find his brother, too." His mobile rang. It was Penderley.

"Sir?"

"Drummond, we have a problem. Another murder. No, not a drone murder with poison fired into the neck, but listen to this. When our people interviewed all the neighbors, an older man reported seeing a falcon perched on the windowsill of the apartment. He thinks it's the same apartment where the murder occurred. I didn't like the sound of it. The murdered man is an American. The manner in which he was killed, it is unusual. You'll see when you arrive. I have a very bad feeling about this."

Nicholas looked back into the conference room. Adam would locate Ardelean, his father would deal with Barstow. "A falcon? The man was sure?"

"Yes, he was."

"We're coming. Where shall I meet you?"

"Dawson Place, Notting Hill, W2. Oh, Drummond? Have you got the murders sorted yet?"

"Yes, sir, I believe so."

"Ah, excellent. Oh yes, DCI Gareth Scott is the lead."

He punched off to see Mike beside him, a brow raised. "What was that?"

"Are you in the mood to divide and conquer? Because Penderley needs us, says an American has been murdered in Notting Hill. A falcon was reported sitting on the windowsill. Penderley thought we'd like to get involved. He said something about the manner of the murder was unusual."

"There's no 'we' in this. I'll go. You are going to the hospital. No, no arguments."

He started to argue, but a fierce shaft of pain went through his side. "You're sure? This could be big, Mike. I really don't need a doctor—"

"No arguments, or I'll tell your father."

"Come back as soon as you can."

"You promise you'll go get checked out at the hospital?"

"Actually, there's usually a physician here."

"All right, I believe you. Don't make me hurt you, Nicholas. Now, I'll catch a cab. How far is it from here to Notting Hill?"

Ian had stepped out of the conference room

and had obviously overheard the discussion. "Mike, I'll drive you. It will be faster. Really, a falcon?"

"Yes, I appreciate that. We should go." She gave Nicholas's hand a warning squeeze. "Physician, now. Oh, and Nicholas, don't shoot Barstow—excuse me—his lordship."

"That I can't promise I won't do."

"Then do it so we won't be caught." And she and Ian were gone.

CHAPTER FIFTY-ONE

The quality of decision is like the well-timed
swoop of a falcon, which enables it to strike
and destroy its victim.

—Sun Tzu, *The Art of War*

The Old Garden
Twickenham
Richmond upon Thames, London

Roman soothed Arlington, lightly rubbing her
feathers, which he knew the falcon loved. He
hated having to need anyone, but he knew he
needed this woman who lay terrified, her stomach bleeding. He set Arlington on her perch and
turned back to her. "You are Romanian."

"Yes, you know that."

"Your mother?"

"Didn't I tell you? She was a gymnast, from
Walachia. She's dead now. You can't hurt her."

Walachia. The birthplace of his ancestors.

It had to be true, she was of his line. But her last name—Marin.

"Your father is American?"

"Yes."

He felt excitement, a sense of victory, very close now. "Hold still and it won't hurt. I've become very good at this." He pulled out a kit to take her blood, swabbed alcohol on her tethered arm, then expertly drew off a vial. He needed to run it immediately.

"What are you doing?"

Roman said, "You're the daughter of a gymnast from Walachia—is your mother Nadia Gabor?"

"Nadia Gabor Marin."

He pulled up a chair beside her. "She was Gypsy stock."

Isabella said nothing, stared as he ran a long white finger down the length of her arm. A fine red drop of blood sat in the crook of her elbow. "What are you going to do with my blood? What is this all about?"

"How far back do you know your bloodline?"

"What?"

"Answer me!"

"I don't—not very far. If you're at all familiar with Romanians, you'll know many of the records are lost. The only way we can find each other is through online DNA testing, which of course we've done as most everyone has. It didn't reveal very much, only a few matches."

"Excellent. I will look on your computer and see what I can find. I want to see every match you've made."

"Tell me what this is all about. You're taking my blood and you're probably going to kill me anyway. Why not tell me why you're doing this?"

Roman smiled at her, patted her arm right above the Band-Aid he pressed down. "You won't die, not for a long time." He studied her a moment, recognized her on some very deep level.

"Why not tell you the truth? My brother, my twin—Radu—suffers from a rare form of hemophilia, one untreatable by modern medicine. The Voynich tells how to cure blood illnesses, but there were missing instructions, missing ingredients. I've read the pages you supposedly found, and you know what? The instructions are now complete. I can mix the potion and know it's correct. But I always knew Radu's illness was different from the others in our line, not like the blood diseases discussed by the twins in the Voynich. When it became clear that only blood from our line would help him, I began a search all over Eastern Europe. It appears Romanians live everywhere. Wherever I've traveled, I've taken Romanian blood, but have never found a perfect match.

"And now I have you. If you are my perfect match, then with the final instructions in the pages, the potion, and your blood, we'll cure Radu."

Her pages held the final answers? Her blood was his perfect match? No, it was crazy. He believed she was of his familial line? "Why can't you use your own blood?"

"Because my blood has the same defective gene within it, though I don't suffer from the disease. As I said, I need blood from our familial line."

"What line are you talking about?"

"And here I thought you were clever. Whose do you think?"

She shook her head.

"You and I and Radu, I believe we are all direct descendants of Vlad Dracul III. And once I've tested your blood, I will prove it."

She was afraid, her stomach hurt from the falcon's sharp claws, and yet this astounded her. "You know he's not really Dracula, don't you?"

He wanted to strike her but didn't. Other than Radu, she was the most important person in the world, at least her precious blood was. He managed to shrug while he thumbed a tab onto his tongue. "And how do you know? We are living proof—direct descendants, one with diseased blood, another, the stronger, who will cure him."

"So you think you're a vampire?"

"You stupid woman, you think I'm mad? Of course I'm not a vampire in the movie sense, nor is Radu. I told you, Radu and I are descendants of Vlad Dracul, a very real man. Am I born to blood? Do I drink it?" He smiled at her and shrugged again.

She wanted to scream, she wanted to curse, but she was helpless. If she was a match, if he proved she was in the direct line, no, he wouldn't kill her, he'd keep her around as his permanent blood bank for his brother. She felt grief flood her, grief for herself, grief for Gil, never to take another amazing photo, never to know a life with her, never to have children. She wanted to weep, but instead, she whispered, "Why did you kill Gil, my fiancé? He had done nothing to you. You cut his throat. Why?"

Roman lightly ran a fingertip over her eyebrows, smoothing them. "Ah, I suppose because he was there. I didn't cut his throat, by the way, not exactly. Truth is, too, I am rather used to killing. I suppose you could say it's second nature to me, my own special way. And he would have presented complications. Now, you'll excuse me, Dr. Marin, but I have other things to attend to. I will be back, don't worry about that. Ah, don't try to escape. There is no way." He waved the vial of her blood at her, smiled. "Think of all the beautiful blood you will give Radu."

She heard Radu shout, "Roman. Roman, come, now!"

Roman bolted from the room, rushed to Radu's side, where he sat hunched at his bank of computers.

"What, what is it?"

"Look, we received an email with a video attached. You need to see this."

"Play it."

There was no sound, and the composition was grainy and dark. There were two people in the frame.

Radu said, "Look, he's handcuffed to the table. He's a prisoner. Who is the other man, the one with his back to the camera?"

Roman looked closer. "Is that—Caleb Temora in handcuffs?"

"Yes. And look, the standing man turns, you can see half his face now."

Roman watched carefully, felt his heart kick, felt adrenaline flood him.

"Roman, is that—"

"Barstow. That's Barstow. Why does he have Caleb in custody? Why are they alone? When is this dated?"

"There is no date. No identification."

"Who sent it?"

"The address is gibberish. It will take me time to decipher."

Roman thumbed a tab in his mouth to calm his mind so he could think clearly, rationally. Barstow and Temora?

He said slowly, "So MI6 captured Temora where? In Syria, probably, in an ISIS camp, and Barstow brought him as a prisoner to London. I wonder if Barstow made him hack Radulov or if Temora volunteered to take me down."

Radu said, "You have the drones hidden in

Scotland, Roman. Only Raphael Marquez, Cyrus Wendell, and I know they're there. I think Barstow wanted Temora to find them so he could get ahold of them, cut you out. Maybe he also wanted Temora to hack MATRIX in order to distract you, and Caleb decided he would try to destroy you instead."

"By bringing down Radulov." Roman felt a surge of rage and thumbed another tab onto his tongue. "Perhaps Barstow forced Caleb to write the hack on Radulov. Maybe Barstow didn't only want the drone army location, he wanted me ruined and destroyed." He paused a moment. "It's all about the billion pounds, Radu, all about money, or what's left of it."

Radu said, his Voynichese even more guttural because he was upset, "Barstow is smart, but that would be beyond him, I think. No, I think Caleb wants to destroy you."

"Why send the video then? Why show me he's Barstow's prisoner? Make me think he's a hero?"

Radu shrugged. "Caleb worshipped you, Roman, but he also resented you. He saw you as the alpha male he had to defeat. When you stopped his pet project, he had only one goal—to prove he was better than you. I think he wanted you to figure this all out and recognize him as being the victor, so now he was the alpha. He sent the video to taunt you. I think he's laughing at you, Roman."

Roman nodded slowly. At last he understood.

Barstow had wanted the drone army to swarm through Africa and defeat radical Islam, so he'd go down in history as a hero, like his blighter ancestors. But that was only a part of it. He thought again, Barstow wanted the money. Which had he wanted most? Roman had to laugh. A clever plan, but Temora's video, regardless of his motives, was proof of what Barstow had done. He gave a moment's thought to Vittorini, Alexander, and Donovan. He realized now they probably paid their share, and Barstow had kept it. He gave a moment's regret to killing them. He lightly patted Radu's shoulder.

"Of course you're right, about all of it. It's all so simple, really. The moment Barstow knew I had the drone army ready, the moment I told him he had to pay me, he had Temora hack into Radulov to find where I was storing them. What would he do? Send a special-ops squad up to Scotland to steal them?" He paused, stood. "Do you know, I really don't care why Temora sent me the video. He is what he is, curse him to hell."

"What will you do?"

"I must think, Radu. Something fitting for both Barstow and Temora."

CHAPTER FIFTY-TWO

Interpol Orange Notice: To warn of an event, a person, an object, or a process representing a serious and imminent threat to public safety.

—Interpol.int

Dawson Place
Notting Hill, London

The street ahead was lined with cars. A crime scene was a crime scene no matter what country you were in. A falcon seen on the windowsill. Was it Ardelean? Had he murdered whoever this man was? And why?

Mike flashed her credentials and was through the line and up the stairs to the flat in moments. As she entered, she looked around—so familiar, so normal—aside from the forensic techs in white Tyvek jumpsuits.

A woman was seated on the living room sofa,

blank-faced, in shock. She had tissues in one limp hand, a photography bag at her feet. Shouldn't she be the one taking photos? Not a crime-scene tech, then. A witness, perhaps. But what was she still doing here?

"Mike!"

Mike turned to see Nicholas's former second-in-command, Gareth Scott, walking toward her. He whipped off his gloves and held out his hand. They shook. "It's good to see you. Penderley said you'd be along. Thanks for coming so quickly." He waved a hand around him. "This whole thing with the falcon on the windowsill, Penderley said it had to do with the case you and Nicholas are working here in London. And the poor lad found on the kitchen floor was an American."

"Good to see you as well, Gareth. And yes, the falcon—it very likely does tie in with our case. Gareth, this is Ian Sansom, MI5. Ian, this is DI Gareth Scott."

A big smile bloomed. "It's Detective Chief Inspector now, Mike, papers signed last week. Sansom? MI5, you say? A pleasure." And the two men shook hands.

Ian said, "I'm here more as her escort. I'll not be in the way. Hey, congrats on the bump—the big bump."

Mike said to Gareth, "He's all right, Gareth, he works for Mr. Drummond. You removed the victim last night?"

"Very late, yes, but we've preserved the crime scene for you. Come this way. And I have photos."

Gareth led them to the kitchen. She quickly registered the scene as she'd been taught, surroundings first—dinner remains on the counters, the table set with plates and flowers, food still uneaten, candle wax overflowed onto the tablecloth. Evidence placards littered the scene. Gareth pulled up the original crime scene shots on his tablet, showed her the victim's body.

"His name was Gil Brooks, thirty-two years old. He was a freelance photographer."

Mike saw the man's body was contorted, saw blood pooling under his head. "His neck," Mike said, "Nicholas said the manner of death was unexpected, strange. What am I looking at here?"

Gareth swiped to a close-up of the wound. "You can see the two small holes, right over the jugular? We don't know what the killer used, but he knew exactly where to strike. He bled out very quickly."

Mike looked through the photos, looked into the young man's sightless eyes, the bluish bruising around his neck, the two narrow holes. She looked up. "But he wasn't exsanguinated?"

"No," Gareth said. "Superintendent Penderley and I briefly discussed the Vampire Killer who's been roaming over Europe the past couple of years. As far as we know, this is his first stop in the U.K. But why this man? He's not Brit, he's not

Romanian as most victims have been, no, he's an American. What do you know about this, Mike?"

"All I know is what I happened to see in an Interpol notice, a killer poking tubes of some kind into victims' necks and draining their blood—the Vampire Killer, or Dracula."

Gareth nodded. "But as you said, this victim wasn't exsanguinated. Do you think it's the same killer?"

"Yes," Mike said. "I do."

"Well," Gareth said, "I've never seen anything like this before. And it gets better. The lady on the couch is a wedding photographer. She was hired by our victim to show up to take engagement photographs. She came promptly at ten o'clock last night. The door was cracked open, and she found him."

"He was engaged? Where is his fiancée?"

"We don't know. I spoke to the photographer last night, but she was rattled. She agreed to come back to meet with you. Let's see what you can get out of her."

Her name was Becca Chance. After introductions, she turned her beautiful brown eyes to Mike. "You're FBI, like in America?"

"Yes, that's right. You were here to take engagement photos? Were you a friend of the deceased?"

"He's not—he wasn't a friend. Mr. Brooks is—was—a client. He hired me to come take photos of him and his girlfriend. He said he was going to propose right before I got here. He was so excited." She paused, closed her eyes a moment. Mike lightly laid her hand over hers. She swallowed, straightened. "I'm all right. When I got here, the door was open, and I came in, called for him, and I found him. He was dead on the floor in the kitchen." She took a deep, shuddering breath. "There was so much blood. How could she do this?"

"She?" Mike asked.

"His girlfriend. Who else?"

Mike glanced around. There was a single photo of a couple on the coffee table. She pointed at it.

"Do you have her name?"

"It's Isabella Marin. She's a doctor of some kind. I didn't ask. Why? Mr. Brooks was very nice, a lovely man."

A cop stuck his head in the door. "DC Scott? Landlord is here, finally, says he has the rental contract. He told us about the security camera in the stairwell and the lift. It's concealed, and he's pulling the tape for us. Five minutes."

Mike said, "There's luck. Ms. Chance, did you see anyone as you came in the building? Did Mr. Brooks ring you in, or did you come in yourself?"

"As I've already said to DC Scott here, the apartment building front doors were open. I let myself in the foyer and came up the stairs, and no, I didn't see anyone. It felt strange, though. I remember feeling the hair stand up on the back of my neck right before I knocked. It felt like someone was watching me."

Mike said, "We'll see what the cameras show. One last thing. When was this gig booked?"

"Over a month ago. I'd have to check my calendar for the exact date."

"Thank you for being so clear and concise. I appreciate your coming back to speak to me. I'm very sorry you had to be here. This is all very difficult."

She and Gareth moved to the door together, and the cop standing there led them to the first floor. "Landlord has the video queued." He took her arm. "Mike, the falcon seen on the windowsill, why is this so important that Penderley asked you specifically to come here?"

"As soon as I can, Gareth, I'll tell you all about it. Please, be patient."

The landlord was older, midsixties, no-nonsense, and short on words, something Mike appreciated.

He nodded to her, and all he said was, "Here," and pushed the small television toward Mike and Gareth.

Mike could see the camera footage was black and white, the angle geared for the stairwell, but the elevator foyer was visible.

They watched for a few minutes—empty hallway, empty elevator—then a man's head came into view. She could see sandy-brown hair but not his face. He turned to step into the elevator, and she caught a glimpse of glasses. The video went blank when the elevator doors closed.

Mike asked, "Wait, Gareth, did you see a beard?"

"Yes—dark brown, darker than his hair." Gareth said to the landlord, "Is there a full frontal shot of his face on this?"

"Keep watching. I'm gonna speed it up."

Twenty minutes later, according to the time stamp, the elevator door dinged, and Mike saw the man exit, still without a good shot of his face, but now, there was a girl on his arm. She was walking slowly, heavily. The man was almost dragging her along.

"Oh my, that's Dr. Marin," the landlord said, rising out of his seat. "What's he doing to her?"

Mike watched them walk out of the shot, and almost right away, Becca Chance, the photographer, appeared in the foyer.

The killer had been in and out in less than twenty minutes.

Gareth said, "Doesn't look like Dr. Marin murdered her fiancé. She looks drunk, or drugged."

Gareth said, "The garage is beneath the building, so he lucked out that no one was around to see anything."

Mike turned to the landlord. "Can you give us all the information you have on Dr. Marin?"

"Already did, to this gentleman here." He shook his head. "Poor lady, whatever happened—

well, sure, she's been a good tenant, her boyfriend, too, both on the lease."

"Here, Mike," Gareth said, and handed her a file.

Mike said, "I see Isabella is American, from Florida, works at the British Museum."

The landlord was shaking his head. "Both of them, nice kids, quiet, rent's on time, paid in full. Mr. Brooks travels. He's a photographer for the *Globe*. Nature, war, that kind of stuff. What's wrong with people?"

Gareth asked Mike, "Any emergency contacts on the paperwork?"

"Looks like a three-eight-six area code and the name Nadia Marin. That's Florida. We'll have to get in touch as soon as we know what's happened."

"Pretty clear to me," the landlord said, and now the man once short on words, spewed. "Mr. Brooks's been murdered, right here in my building! And poor Dr. Marin's been kidnapped. Who would do this? A maniac, I know it's some crazy. Do something."

CHAPTER FIFTY-THREE

Mike stepped into the hallway and called Nicholas. "You answered your cell so you're alive. What did the doctor say?"

"I'm fine, Mike, it's just a flesh wound." He paused, and she could see his grin, then, "Don't worry. Talk to me."

"Gareth verified there was, to the best of his knowledge, a falcon spotted on the windowsill of the apartment. He interviewed the man himself who saw it. Penderley asked him to."

"Which brings to mind Roman Ardelean."

"Unfortunately, the video we saw did show a man coming in and dragging Isabella Marin out, but it wasn't Ardelean." She gave him the description of the man, told him about the two puncture wounds in Gil Brooks's neck. "But he wasn't exsanguinated, Nicholas, not like the Vampire Killer, or Dracula, Interpol is looking for.

"The man—who isn't Ardelean—hauled the woman away, probably downstairs to the apartment garage. Nicholas, she looked like she'd been drugged or smacked hard. She works at the British Museum. I'm heading there right now. Oh yes, Gareth says hello."

"Hello back to him. Now, Barstow has called Ardelean three times, and he's not answering. We've sent a team to watch over the Belgravia flat. Adam is looking for any possible addresses for Ardelean outside of Belgravia, and so far we're coming up blank. We may start tapping into CCTV and see what we can find from yesterday. Ardelean had to come to us from somewhere, perhaps we can follow him back out."

"Was he driving or walking?"

"I don't know. Why?"

"Remember the article you showed me about the Internet of Things and how easy it is to hack someone's personal information out of the devices they're using for their home and for their car? You said it was possible to hack into a car's GPS system and see addresses. If you can find his car, maybe you can find an address that way."

"Mike, you are brilliant. We'll get on it right

away. We have to find his car, obviously, but they'll have a record of its make, model, and vehicle registration plates in the parking garage."

"Glad to help. Why hasn't MI5 released his information to the media?"

"My father wants to capture Ardelean quietly. It won't do for the public to get wind of his and Barstow's actions. We're talking a big scandal in the government, not good."

"Barstow set the train wreck in motion, and now people are dead. They won't be able to cover it up forever."

"I agree, but this isn't my call. We will certainly go public if we need to, but for the moment, since Ardelean has means to flee the country and disappear, we want to try to keep this quiet. If he is as unstable as Barstow claims, and it goes public, he might retaliate with more attacks."

"I'm off to the British Museum. Nicholas, you'll find him. Have faith."

"Will do. You keep me up to date, as well. And, Mike? Be careful. If Ardelean gets wind of us looking for him, I don't think he'll hesitate to come after us again. If he knows where you are—just be careful."

Nicholas hung up with Mike and started typing again. Adam had imported all the CCTV feed from the surrounding area, and Nicholas had tapped into the garage system so he could pull up the car and registration plate. All the while, the back of his mind was spinning.

Who was Roman Ardelean?

"Ben, do me a favor. Find Ardelean's history, his whole backstory. We're missing something here."

CHAPTER FIFTY-FOUR

There are around 2,000 people with severe haemophilia A in the U.K. A hereditary genetic condition dominantly affecting men, people with severe haemophilia A have virtually none of the protein factor VIII, which is essential for blood to clot. It puts those affected at risk of excessive bleeding even from the slightest injury, as well as causing spontaneous internal bleeding, which can be life-threatening. . . . [T]here is no cure.

—MedicalXPress.com

Radu watched from the window as Roman strode down to the dock.

He could tell things were unraveling, had a terrible feeling in the pit of his stomach. All the work they'd done, all the planning, the years of searching, and they'd finally found the person who could cure him. But Roman was unstable now, furious and impatient, and betrayed, so betrayed, by the man he'd thought was his friend—and Radu had believed was his friend, as well—Caleb

Temora. And what of Barstow, once his trusted partner?

Iago came to the window with him. "I will let the cast out to follow him. They always calm him."

"What do we do, Iago? I'm afraid for him."

"We trust in him, wholeheartedly. He is the last hope for you, for this family. He has never wanted anything more than to see you well, to see you cured. You must have faith, Master Radu. And you should speak with the woman. She knows things in the way Roman does, knows Romanian, knows the ways of our people. If it is her blood that will cure you, you need to establish her trust."

Radu glanced at Isabella Marin. She was staring at the ceiling, unblinking. Iago was right, but speaking with other people frightened him. But at least she could both speak and understand his mother tongue.

"Go, Master Radu, go, you must."

He crossed the room and sat next to her. He didn't look at her, but he said in Voynichese, "Our people have been subjugated for years. Feared. Misunderstood."

"Our people?"

"Vampires."

Isabella looked up at him. She hadn't realized before, she'd been too frozen with fear, but now she saw this twin was ill, very ill, and he was uncomfortable with her. Because she was a woman? Or because he wasn't comfortable with people?

Now he believed he was a vampire? She said, her voice flat, "You're a man, not a vampire."

"I am a descendant of Vlad Dracul, and I think you are, too. I come from an illegitimate line of men who are drawn to blood. This blood disorder runs in the family. It always appears in the twins. One has it, and one does not. One twin is strong, the other weak. You have no idea what it's like, either."

"Tell me."

"There's a burning inside me. It's hard to explain, but it's there, always there. Roman and I have experimented with so many ways to transfuse, even drinking the blood of possible matches, as the legends say. Nothing has worked to heal me, but it's kept me alive much longer than any of my predecessors. Of course, I've been developing new treatments for years. None have benefitted me, but we do share them with the world. I've saved countless lives."

"You've killed people before me to take their blood?"

Radu said simply, "It is the only way. Roman researches and selects Romanians who seem possible, he brings me their blood, and we experiment."

Isabella couldn't help herself. "I know you are ill, that you are afraid of dying, but so am I. So was the man I was supposed to marry, yet your twin murdered him, in cold blood, for no higher reason than he was there! And all the other people your brother has murdered for their blood? Do you believe your life is more important than theirs? Than mine?"

"Roman says I cannot die, I am too valuable to humanity. Every human we sacrifice is to provide me longer life to continue with my work. This man with you last night, he wasn't really all that important, now was he?"

If only she could have leaped on him, killed him with her bare fists. He believed what he'd said as he believed his brother, utterly. Another tack then. Isabella said, "Surely you must know by now I've been missed. My employers will have reported my absence to the police."

He shrugged. "It is nothing to us. Roman has eyes and ears everywhere."

"You can't be serious."

"You think I'm lying? Our software is on every computer that matters. We can look into any of them, at any time. We own you. We own the government. We own the world."

"And yet here you are, locked away, shuttered inside these rooms, unable to leave, or love. I think the world owns you."

He shrugged. "Who needs to move in the real world? It's dirty and cruel. I live in cyberspace. I live in the crevasses most people forget. When they stopped worshipping in churches and started worshipping their screens, I became their god."

"Like your brother, you are mad."

"I am far from mad. I told you: I've spent my life looking for a cure for this affliction, my family affliction. So many generations with twins, one strong, one weak. How did you really come by the pages, Isabella?"

"You heard everything I said to your brother. It's all true."

"It is not. We both know you're lying." He walked to the far counter. He brought the loose pages back to her. "Tell me where you got the pages."

She saw the pages, knew his brother had stolen them from their lead box in her bedroom. She was shaking her head.

"Tell me." He held the pages close to her. She couldn't bear it. The pages were singing, speaking to her, they wanted her. No, they wanted him, too—they wanted Radu. She said nothing. He said, "The pages speak to you, don't they? And that is why you put them in the lead box. They do to me, too."

"What do they say?"

"They tell me things. And they cry for the rest of the book. You're not mad, Isabella. If you're worried I'll think you're crazy, I know you're not. The pages are special."

She took a deep breath. "The pages were in my mother's keeping. I was the strong twin, my sister the weak. Did she have the affliction? She died before it was known. But she heard the pages, too. My mother saw the pages upset me. And one day, soon after my sister died, she buried them so I wouldn't hear them anymore.

"I found the pages after she died."

"That is not the whole truth, Isabella." Radu shrugged. "We can control so little in our lives, but through the Voynich we've gained unimaginable knowledge. It gave you power, didn't it? Gave you precious knowledge no one else had? And in the back of your mind when you studied and deciphered, you knew you wanted greatness."

"No, no, of course not."

But they both knew she was lying.

The rapid PCR—polymerase chain reaction—machine testing Isabella's DNA started to beep. Radu's heart leaped into his throat. The printer kicked in with a mechanic whir, and a single sheet of paper slipped out.

He rushed across the room, held the scroll up to the light. He couldn't believe what he was seeing. It was everything they'd hoped for, for so long.

He shouted in English, "She's a match. Iago, she's a perfect, exact match. Get Roman in here."

CHAPTER FIFTY-FIVE

The British Museum
Great Russell Street
Bloomsbury, London

The entrance of the museum reminded Mike of the Parthenon, with its huge columns presided over by a triangular frieze. The massive courtyard was full of people; tourists and students, many segregated into groups with leaders, speaking different languages—a polyglot babble of voices.

Inside the glass doors was another large courtyard with walls painted a calming shade of green, lined with marble busts of Roman leaders. She wondered if they were replicas like they'd seen in Italy, with the real pieces stashed away where thieving hands couldn't steal them.

The interior was stunning under a clear honeycombed metal roof, the huge white cylinder in the center.

Mike saw a young woman with a blond bun

and glasses approaching her, saw the woman had been crying. How much had Ian told her?

"You're the investigator from Scotland Yard? Please come with me."

Mike didn't bother to correct her, or show her creds. She followed her deeper into the museum, past the gift shop, past the donation box signs Mike read as they passed—*The British Museum, free to the world since 1753.*

There was a private elevator behind the stairs, staff only, Mike saw. The woman pressed the elevator button.

When the elevator doors shut on only the two of them, it was suddenly eerily silent. The woman turned and said, brow arched, "You're not Scotland Yard."

"You're right. Special Agent Michaela Caine, FBI." She pulled out her credentials, flipped them open. "What gave me away?"

"The gun. Plus, none of our Scotland Yard detectives have quite your style. I like your motorcycle boots." She put out her hand. "I'm Phyllis Powers, Dr. Wynn-Jones's personal assistant, have been for almost ten years now. What's happened to Isabella?"

"We're here to find out. I see you're upset."

"Yes, of course I'm upset. Everyone is horrified at Gil's murder and her kidnapping. It's too much, simply too much, and no one knows what's going on."

The doors opened, and Mike followed Powers down the hallway, up the stairs, and down another, smaller corridor.

Mike smelled the familiar, comforting scent of tea, and, sure enough, inside the office, there was a pot waiting. "Persy had to jump into a meeting, but he's given me permission to share all we have, to help in any way. Tea?"

"Yes, please."

Phyllis poured tea into a souvenir mug from the gift shop with BRITISH MUSEUM stamped on the side and handed it over. "Sugar, milk?"

"This is fine. I'm going to get right to it. We need as much information about Isabella Marin as you can provide—what she was working on, who her friends were."

Phyllis Powers said very simply, "Isabella is a sweetheart, exceptional, frighteningly brilliant. She's been working here for almost a year now, and she's been a huge asset to Persy. She also had her first presser this week, on the newly discovered Voynich pages. It is ridiculous to think someone inside the community would attack them, but she was on television and all over our media resource page. Some disturbed person must have seen her and decided—"

"Hold up, did you say the Voynich?"

"Yes, I did. Isabella is a Voynich scholar. Finding the lost pages was a huge break for her, the kind that makes careers."

"How did she find pages of the Voynich?"

"She was in the ancient Rome archives, archiving a shipment of books. She pulled a book from the box, the quires fell out. An amazing co-incidence."

"Yes," Mike said, thinking about Ben and Melinda, "that surely is an amazing coincidence. What book were the pages in?"

"*Meditations* by Marcus Aurelius. Surely you understand this is a once-in-a-lifetime discovery."

"Would Isabella normally be cataloging books?"

"Not normally, no, but this was a priceless collection that came in from a major collector. It needed the utmost care, and she offered. Wait, are you saying you think Isabella planted the quires?"

"Yes, I am."

Mike's phone beeped. She glanced at the screen. A text from Gareth.

> Big surprise! We have the murder on video. The crime scene crew found a small camera hidden in the kitchen. We guess Gil Brooks was taping the engagement. My tech ran it. Sending screenshot of the suspect now.

A photo scrolled in, an almost perfect profile shot of a man with sandy hair, a beard, and glasses, his black eyes dead in the pixels. Mike felt a punch to the gut looking at the vicious smile on his face. Wait, there was something about the profile that looked familiar to her.

Mike turned the phone around.

"Ms. Powers, do you know who this is?

Mike watched Phyllis pale. "No, it's not possible. How could it be? I mean, that's Dr. Laurence Bruce."

CHAPTER FIFTY-SIX

Mike called Gareth Scott immediately.

"The murderer's name is Dr. Laurence Bruce. I'm putting you on speaker with Phyllis Powers, Dr. Wynn-Jones's personal assistant. He's Isabella's boss. I'm hearing all this for the first time, too. Please, Phyllis. Go ahead."

"He's a colleague of Persy, I'm sorry, Dr. Wynn-Jones. He's a Voynich scholar, always around when discoveries are made. He's multipublished, well known in the field. He was one of the first calls we received on Tuesday after the announcement. He was in town, as I recall, wonderful timing for him, as he's based in Rome. He came to see the manuscript and spoke at length with Isabella."

Gareth said, "Please tell me you have cameras, Ms. Powers."

"I'm sure security at the museum would be happy to help. Shall I take Agent Caine to them?"

"Yes, and thank you for being such a help. We'll be in touch. Mike?"

Mike turned off the speakerphone and put her cell to her ear.

"Hey."

"This is quite a break. Let's get as much information about this man as possible and figure out where he is. If we can find that, we might have a chance to save Isabella Marin's life."

"I'll get back to you as soon as I have something."

"Thank you. I'll get my people working on his Rome connections. Keep me apprised."

"Will do." Mike punched off and said to Phyllis, "I need everything you know about Dr. Bruce, especially where he might stay when he's in London, and we need to get with your security folks and get a visual on him if at all possible."

"Give me a moment."

Phyllis picked up her phone, said, "Charlie? We have an emergency. We need all the video pulled from two o'clock to three o'clock Tuesday afternoon for the third-floor corridors and my office. Thank you. We're on our way down."

"Phyllis, where is your boss?"

"He was, well, honestly, he was distraught. I

encouraged him to go home, or we would have been sobbing together all afternoon."

"I see. Oh, and Phyllis, can I see the pages Isabella found? We will need to photograph them for evidence."

"Of course. Let's get them. It will give Charlie a moment to pull together the video."

She led Mike down the hall. "Isabella's office is small and cramped, but at least she has one. Many of our people share or are in cubicles upstairs. It's a requirement that I have access to all the associates' safes." She consulted her notepad, then knelt down and inputted the combination, following with a key. The door opened, and she reached inside. Mike watch her riff through the papers inside, then she frowned. "They aren't here. Surely she didn't simply file them."

Mike started going through the paperwork on Isabella's desk while Phyllis checked the filing cabinets.

"Perhaps they're in Persy's safe. I have the combination. Let's check, shall we?"

They hurried back to Dr. Wynn-Jones's office. She unlocked the safe hidden behind a beautiful Renaissance nude statue. She spun the dial, opened the safe. The pages weren't there. "But this doesn't make sense. She wouldn't take them with her. They are far too valuable."

Phyllis looked at Mike. "But she must have.

Now that I think about it, I thought something was wrong with Isabella after her conversation with Dr. Bruce. Do you think he took Isabella? Do you think he might have the lost quires, too?"

CHAPTER FIFTY-SEVEN

Scotland Yard: The name derives from the
location of the original Metropolitan Police
headquarters at 4 Whitehall Place, which
had a rear entrance on a street called Great
Scotland Yard. The Scotland Yard entrance
became the public entrance to the police station, and over time the street and the Metropolitan Police became synonymous.

—Wikipedia

New Scotland Yard
4 Whitehall Place
Westminster, London

Armed with the videotapes Charlie had recorded
for her at the British Museum and a trove
of Laurence Bruce's scholarly papers Phyllis had
printed out for them, Mike took a taxi to Scotland
Yard.

She called Nicholas to fill him in on what had

happened. "I'm meeting with Gareth and his team. Can you make it?"

"Sorry, Mike. Remember when Adam and I accidently hit the kill switch and all the systems fried? Some are still on the fritz. Keep me posted."

She stood under the rotating silver sign for a moment, then headed in. Gareth Scott was waiting for her in the lobby, as promised. He got her signed in and through the extremely tight security, then took her upstairs, walking her through a crowded bullpen that made her feel right at home. She relaxed. Cops were cops regardless of the locale. Where, she wondered, were the doughnuts and bad coffee? Not a whiff of either. People were on Mike's heels, ready to be briefed.

Gareth showed everyone into his office, standing room only for most of them. She saw files stacked everywhere and a whiteboard organized by case numbers and dates. Gareth said, "No word yet from our friends in Rome. They're tracking down everything they can find about Laurence Bruce."

Mike said, "Phyllis called while I was on my way over. She thinks Bruce stays at the Savoy when he's in town. Said he likes their afternoon tea. We should get an officer over there right away to see if perhaps he was stupid enough to take her there."

"On it." He pointed a finger, and a female

officer peeled off. Gareth's mobile rang, and he picked it up. He punched off a moment later, and Mike dropped the rest on him. "Bad news, the lost quires are apparently lost again. They weren't in either Isabella's or her boss's safe. You didn't see anything related to the museum in Isabella's apartment, did you?"

"No, but I wouldn't know what to look for. There were a ton of pages on her desk, but she's a scholar. I will call and have them cataloged. The last thing we need is losing something stolen from the British Museum."

The female cop stuck her head back in. "No one by that name at the Savoy, but I'll take a run over and have a look at their registration, show his photo around. Also, nothing remotely ancient on the desk at the crime scene. Everything was basic correspondence, pay stubs, and notes. Nothing relating to the Voynich."

"Thanks, Ingrid. Keep us informed." And to the rest of them, "You've all met Special Agent Michaela Caine. For those who might not know, she inherited Drummond from us, so we all owe her a huge debt of gratitude."

Laughs all around, and she relaxed a little more.

Mike said, "Yes, it's as bad as you think. He's insufferably good at being an FBI agent."

Gareth raised a hand. "Moving right along. Here's what we know. Dr. Laurence Bruce came to the British Museum Tuesday to see the lost quires of the Voynich manuscript that Isabella Marin discovered. We'll have to track down his movements once he left the museum. Did he look up her address before he left Wynn-Jones's office or do research on her afterward? I don't know, but it might help us discover if this is a crime of passion or one of motivation. The killing of Gil Brooks might have been an end goal, he might have been an impediment, or he could have been the target all along. Though my instinct says Isabella was the target and Gil was an unfortunate bystander, we need to look at all angles.

"The second issue is the quires the museum announced are now missing, as well. Logic says the two are related, since Dr. Marin is the one who discovered the quires and did the press conference. Since both are now missing, we're going to work from the premise that they're tied together.

"A bit of background. The Voynich manuscript was stolen from the Beinecke Rare Book and Manuscript Library at Yale University last year. At the end of her press conference, Isabella Marin made a plea for the thief to return the manuscript so it could be reunited with the lost pages. I believe Dr. Bruce stole the manuscript and decided he wanted these papers, too. Why did he graduate to murder and kidnapping? We don't know yet."

Gareth paused a moment. "As you already

know, there was a very strange signature at the crime scene—the dual holes in the victim's neck, directly into the jugular vein. It matches a number of European murders by someone Interpol calls the Vampire Killer or Dracula. All the victims were exsanguinated. However, in this instance, Gil Brooks wasn't. Didn't the killer have time? We don't know. Dr. Bruce is now our leading suspect for these crimes, as well."

Mike said, "Gareth, do you have access to a facial recognition system? I'd like to run the photograph of Bruce through and see if anything pops. Something about him feels familiar to me."

Gareth nodded. "We do, but our Police National Database is more limited than yours in the FBI. Though if I have a direct match, I can certainly use it as confirmation. That said, I'd be happy to let you send the photo to your folks if you'd like."

"I would, Gareth, thank you. The NGI database is cutting-edge and can work with a profile shot. I'll send it in immediately if you have a computer I can use."

"Use mine." He unlocked the machine, and Mike got to work. The photo was uploaded into the system in a matter of minutes.

She said, "And now we wait."

They didn't have to wait long. The computer flashed a match two minutes later.

No wonder the photo of Dr. Laurence Bruce

in profile felt so familiar to her. The falcon on the windowsill, it all made sense.

Gareth was looking over her shoulder when the match appeared. "Holy crap."

They looked at Roman Ardelean.

CHAPTER FIFTY-EIGHT

Mike called Nicholas immediately. "Roman Ardelean murdered Gil Brooks and kidnapped Isabella Marin. I ran a photo of the man from the apartment video through NGI. Ardelean's been posing as a Voynich scholar using the name Laurence Bruce for years—and, Nicholas, he also has the Voynich pages Isabella found at the British Museum."

He was silent for a moment, then, "Despite what my father says, it's time to go public. I'm going to have Ian put together a release, and meanwhile, we will double our efforts to find where Ardelean lives. Anything on the tape that might help?"

"No. You're going to have to work fast, Nicholas. Wherever he took Isabella, the quire is, as well.

We need to find her, but we need to be careful. We don't know what he wants with these pages from the Voynich, but he wanted them badly enough to kidnap her and kill her fiancé."

Nicholas said, "Do you think he committed the vampire murders in his search for the pages?"

"I don't know, but all I know is we've got to hurry. Why would he keep her alive if he's got the pages? If that was his purpose?"

She heard Adam's excited voice in the background. "I think I've got something. Nicholas, I'm sending it to your screen. Mike was right. The car was the key."

"Hold on, Mike, let me see what this is."

Adam had the video from the garage up and running. "Here's Ardelean's BMW i8. You can see him turn left out of the garage. Mike's idea was brilliant. I cracked his GPS system and downloaded the last several days' worth of coordinates. I can find him."

"You heard that, right? Mike, get back over here as soon as you can. The moment we know where Ardelean is, we'll go in."

"On my way." She hung up. "Gareth, any chance you can get me a lift to MI5?"

"I'll take you myself. Let's go."

The command center of MI5 was up and running when Mike returned with Gareth Scott. She saw a large glass room with screens from top to bottom, advanced telemetry and visuals from overhead drones, CCTV feeds, and multiple people in headsets. Harry and Nicholas stood against the back wall, both with arms crossed, both looking deadly serious, ready to lower the hammer.

But when Nicholas saw Gareth, his smile was huge. "Good grief, why'd she haul you along? Mate, it's been too long."

They hugged, slapping each other's backs. "That's what happens when you run away. Have you found him yet?"

"We're narrowing it down. Adam and the team are looking at the last-known GPS location from the car and plotting it on a map. We're up to yesterday—"

Adam shouted, "Got it. Richmond—East Twickenham. On the river. He's been at this address several times in the past week. It's not in his name—it's owned by a private LLC. This could be his place. I'll have to do some more investigating."

Nicholas said to Mike, "If it's him, that's forty-five minutes southwest of our current location."

Adam said, "Wow, this place is huge. It backs to the Thames. Good, we have a river entry. Pulling it up now."

Adam pinched his fingers on his screen, then opened them wide, and the house took over the four main screens.

Mike was astounded. The house was elegant

and massive. "It looks like a mini White House, Nicholas."

"It does. It's designed in the same Palladian style," he said, gave her a tap on the shoulder. He saw she was staring at his side, the heavy bandage obvious beneath his shirt. "I'm all right, forget it. The nurse got carried away. A Band-Aid would have been fine."

"Yeah, right." She turned to Gareth. "James Bond here got himself shot this morning."

"It's nothing," Nicholas said, "forget it."

Mike said, "How do we confirm it's his place, and how do we know this is where he took Isabella?"

Adam said, "The GPS on the car. He was in Isabella's neighborhood the night she went missing, close to her address, probably in an underground garage. The next coordinate is this house. It's thin but possible. Whoa, considering the security, I'd upgrade that to probable."

Harry said behind Gareth, "I assume its security rivals Kensington Palace?"

"You better believe it, sir. Look at this." The screens went black, and a series of blue lines appeared. "There's a laser field across the lawn and the driveway. The minute an unauthorized person steps onto the property, those will go off. The walls are concrete, and there are cameras all over the place, though they're well disguised, in trees and bushes. Which means they have video, and I'm going to guess thermal, as well. You wouldn't go to this extent unless you had something to hide."

Nicholas said, "I don't see dogs, that's good."

Mike was shaking her head. "But a place like this—it's going to be fortified inside, too. We have to confirm Marin's there before we try an assault."

Gareth had a screen open on a desktop. "CCTV from the Richmond Bridge shows someone in the car. Can't tell if it's a male or female, but, for sure, he wasn't alone."

"It's got to be Marin," Mike said.

Nicholas turned to Harry. "What do you think, Father? Enough to go in?"

"Yes." His dark eyes glittered. "Let's do it."

"Good. If we go in predawn attack, we'll have enough time to prepare and find out who else might be in there."

Mike said, "We can't exactly take a team to the front door, even at predawn."

"No, and that means coming in from the air. Adam, give us the top of the house."

The screen twisted and shifted until the roof-line appeared. Nicholas shook his head. "Not good enough. We'll need to get a better look. Let's get a satellite pass."

Harry snapped his fingers at one of his techs, who immediately grabbed a phone and made a call.

"Nicholas, if it's this well guarded electronically, wouldn't they have physical security as well?"

"You'd think. I haven't seen anyone moving about. But if he has drones on-site, they can be controlled remotely to attack, and might be better than physical security."

Harry's tech called, "Satellite's rerouted. Putting it on screen in three minutes."

Adam was typing furiously. "There are work orders for this address at a security installer based in London, and bless their hearts, they listed all the upgrades. The place is a fortress. Doors are bulletproof, windows are ballistic glass, there's an internal core safe zone that takes up a whole section of the bottom floor. The wine cellar in the basement is also bombproof—in case of a dirty bomb, it has a separate ventilation system with scrubbers that will allow them to hide out for a couple of weeks if necessary. Man, Ardelean is seriously paranoid."

Mike said, "Makes you wonder what, exactly, he's doing inside of the house."

Nicholas said, "I think we know the basics—he's been building minidrones and distilling epibatidine."

Adam said, "Hey, here's something interesting. When the house was purchased back in 2004, Ardelean had a sophisticated lab built inside. We're talking high-end, pharmaceutical-grade testing equipment. A clean room with PCR machines, thermocyclers, centrifuges—I get the epibatidine would need specialized equipment, but this?"

Mike said, "PCR—polymerase chain reaction—

that's for DNA analysis, right? He's doing DNA testing in a home lab?"

Gareth said, "Maybe he's trying to code the epibatidine to specific people?"

Mike shrugged. "Or he's running a side business identifying baby daddies. This is too weird. The house is a fortress. He's running a lab inside, he's murdering people using drones and close-up and personal—Roman Ardelean is much more than a software genius, isn't he?"

Harry called out, "Satellite's ready. Here we go."

CHAPTER FIFTY-NINE

In November 1917, radical socialist Bolsheviks . . . seized power in Russia from a provisional government, establishing the world's first communist state. The imperial family was sent to live under house arrest in Siberia. In the late night or early morning hours of July 16–17, 1918, the imperial family (Czar Nicholas II, his wife Czarina Alexandria, their five children Olga, Tatiana, Maria, Anastasia, and Alexei) and four attendants were executed in Yekaterinburg, a city on the eastern side of the Ural Mountains.

—History.com

Byelovvyezh Hunting Lodge
Spala, Poland
1912

He appeared before her as he always did—long, filthy black hair, beard tangled and crusted with dried bits of food, his black robes slovenly.

Alexandra did not care he was called the Mad Monk, a debaucher, a drunkard. Even now, she smelled vodka on his breath, and his robes smelled of sweat and sex. It mattered not. He was holy, he had mystical powers no one else had. She believed to her soul this strange mystic was sent to her by God, and she trusted him implicitly.

Rasputin bowed low to her. It was an improper audience, he knew, but the czarina had bid him to come alone to the lodge, and in secret, away from the czar. She gave him her pale hand. He said in his soft, deep voice, "I understand the czarevitch is ill from the journey."

Her hand tightened in his, and he saw the fear in her eyes, a familiar sight. But he saw now she was even more frantic than usual about her son. Her words burst out, "A friend, a trusted friend, has told me you have a new method to help Alexei. Is this true?"

Rasputin said slowly, "Yes, I have learned I can do more, perhaps heal him entirely."

He'd saved Alexei before through his prayers, at least temporarily, and now he could heal him? Her heart leaped. "He is the future czar, my only son, among all the gaggle of girls. You know the physicians say there is no cure for his hemophilia, yet you say you can cure him? They say there is no hope, that soon he will die." She clutched his black sleeve. "I cannot bear it. He must live—he is our country's future." She leaned close. "Tell me what you mean, what is this method you say will cure him? Is this really true? Why did you not tell me sooner?"

So many questions tumbling over each other. Instead of answering, Rasputin pulled a sheaf of papers from his coarse woolen bag.

Alexandra saw Alexei's head snap up, his eyes on the papers.

Rasputin said, "Your Highness, the physicians know only what is of this world, what they see, what they can understand. But you see these pages? They hold the answers. They were found last year by a family in my village, in the old grandmother's trunk after she died. The family's father assumed they were gibberish, for he doesn't read, and he found the drawings disturbing. He was talking about them at the inn in the village. I looked at them and I knew they were important, no, more than important, they were sent to me from our Holy Father.

"He gave them to me. I have studied the pages, and I have experimented with what I believe are ingredients from the plants drawn on the pages. And there are other things I didn't first understand, but then slowly I came to realize the book was telling me how to cure the hemophilia." He lowered his voice. "I tried it on another last month in a neighboring village. It worked. The child thrives. But Your Highness, word has gotten out. There are cries of evil and blasphemy, and threats of death against me. You must swear to stay silent."

"I swear. Of course I will not put you in harm's way, but what do the pages tell you to do?"

Rasputin looked over at the boy, precocious, studious, too old for his age. The fear of death around every corner had made him thoughtful beyond his few years. Rasputin saw Alexei's eyes were still fastened on the pages he held in his hand. He said nothing, merely turned to show the czarina the pages. She couldn't understand the symbols, the letters, of course, and the strange drawings in muted reds and greens resembled nothing she had ever seen.

He hadn't been able to read the strange language or understand the symbols, the bizarre drawings, either, until one night when he was nearly insensible from drink. He'd thought of the czarevitch, and suddenly he saw meaning in the strange letters and had recognition for the drawings; he saw herbs he'd never seen before, and he recognized them. It was further proof the pages were from God.

The next day he'd collected the herbs and begun to experiment. And he came to understand that whenever he thought of the dying boy, the pages somehow made it possible for him to read and understand and learn. He said to the czarina, his voice even softer, lowered now to a near whisper, "My method, it is unorthodox, but it will work. Your son will not only grow strong, he will live a very long life."

She whispered, "Is it witchcraft?"

He immediately reassured her. "No, no, it is not, my lady. It is science. Proven science."

But she was shaking her head at him. "You misunderstand me. I care not what you call it. I do not care if it is witchcraft. Will it save my son? And saving him will save Russia? How does it work? What must you do?"

Rasputin leaned close and whispered to her. She jerked back, her face draining of color. "No, that is worse than witchcraft, that is blasphemous, barbarous. It is—evil."

Only at rare times had he seen her go stubborn, not that he could blame her, not this time. He found it exciting, the passion in this beautiful woman. He set out again to soothe, to calm her. "Your Highness, I will admit the cure is esoteric, yes, but it cannot be evil, because I know God sent me the pages." Still she sat frozen, staring at him.

He said, "There is a potion first, and it is not dangerous nor is it witchcraft. Then we will do what we must. As I said, I have witnessed its results. I will be discreet, naturally. No one will know but you and me."

"And Alexei. He's the one who will be taking this—treatment. He will not abide such a thing—he won't."

"Even to be healed, once and for all? To know that he must rule after his father, so Russia will grow in strength and power under his hand?"

The czarina paced, at last coming to a stop at the window. She looked out upon the courtyard. Only her coachman was there, feeding the horses. If she agreed to this, would she be cursed into eternity? Yes, she knew she would, it was horrifying. How could she allow such a thing, how?

The young boy said from the chaise set close to the fire, "Mother, I do not want to die, and you know I will. One careless prick, and I will bleed to death. Please, Mother, I do not know what this method is, but I wish to try it. Let him."

She hadn't heard Alexei speak with such passion for a very long time, her poor boy, weak, pale, his skin stretched so tightly over his bones. To look at him smote her. Some days she didn't think she could bear it another minute, another hour. He wanted this? But he didn't know. She went to him, kneeled beside the chaise, and took his small wasted hand. "Alexei? You don't know what it is you ask."

The boy said simply, "I want to be well. I am tired of being ill. I am willing to try anything."

"But this method, it is wrong, it is accursed."

Alexei sat up, his pale face filled with excitement, with determination, and in that moment she could see the future czar. "Mother, you will listen. I have decided. I do not want to die. I do not care if the method is cursed. Do what you must, Rasputin. And give me the pages. I should like to read them."

Rasputin stilled. He said slowly, "Most cannot read them, they are a mystery. Do you think you can?"

Alexei gave him a faint smile, and her boy's voice sounded suddenly full of conviction. "Of course I can read them. Even now I can hear them speaking to me from across the room."

The man called the Mad Monk, demon, and spawn of Satan, bowed his head. He believed the boy. Hadn't he only understood what herbs to mix when he thought of him? And the blood, its directions so clearly coming into his mind?

He watched the czarina slowly get to her feet. She looked at him. Slowly, she nodded.

Rasputin bowed to her. "It will be done. I will come to you at midnight." He was aware the boy stared at the pages as he placed them back into his black bag.

It was only after Rasputin left that Alexandra explained to her son what Rasputin would give him. She'd fully expected him to draw back, horrified. To her shock, he had not. He leaned close. "The pages, Mother, they already told me what I must do. If the monk were to bring me a goat, it wouldn't matter." He smiled at her, took her hand between his thin ones. "I will drink the potion, I will drink the blood, and then I will be well, Mother. I trust the pages. I will be well."

And she said nothing more, but he saw a tear running down her face.

"Mother, I know you do not wish to believe in magic, and thus you believe me mad to claim the pages Rasputin has brought speak to me." He shrugged a thin shoulder. "If I hear the pages speaking, then they can hear me, they understand what is wrong with me. The pages tell me I can be cured."

Still she fretted and paced, wondering how such a thing could be possible. Alexei hearing pages speaking to him? It was his illness, finally it was in his head, in his brain, yet he had spoken with such clarity of thought and so logically. Were the pages telling him what to say to convince her?

When she turned back to him, he said, "Mother, I feel so weak, I know I will die. How can I lead our magnificent country if I am dead?"

She had no more arguments. Though her fear, her revulsion, was great, at the appointed time, she took her son to a small room in the basement of the lodge, far away from the servants and the guards.

Rasputin was there.

The girl with him was pale as fresh cream, with dark hair and fear in her glazed eyes. Alexei stared at her, felt something deep inside him stir. He heard the pages, softly singing to him. He knew what he would do to her. And suddenly, he wanted it very badly.

He said in a formal voice, "Mother, I wish you to wait outside. When it is done, I will come out to you." Rasputin opened the door, waited for her to slowly walk from the room, one last look at the girl and her son. When she was gone, the door locked, Alexei said simply, "Let us begin."

Her blood was so warm, like heated silver and salt. Rasputin had fed her opium to keep her calm, and so she was. The very pretty young girl sagged against Alexei as he drank, and drank, and drank from the cut in her neck. The opium in her blood went to his head, making him dizzy with swirling colors bleeding into each other, colors so bright they burned his eyes, and suddenly he was flying in bright skies filled with low-lying clouds dripping golden drops of rain to the fields below. And birds, so many he didn't recognize, in all colors and shapes, were all singing to him. And it was beautiful, and he was happy.

Just as suddenly, Alexei felt himself thrown from the present back, back, into the past, where a French soldier, no, he was far more important than a simple soldier, he was a long-dead emperor and he was listening to an old man with a white mane of hair and brilliant blue eyes telling him a tale of two boys, twins, one strong and one weak with the blood disease, like him. And then he saw piles of dead and fires burning entire villages, heard screams and saw the emperor's face, pale as death, and he was riding away, surrounded by soldiers.

Then he was thrown into the future, but he saw nothing at all, only whiteness, but he heard clearly the pages singing to him as he drank. Of life, of death, of simply being. And he rejoiced. It seemed to take forever, but perhaps it was only moments, Alexei did not know.

When it was done, and the girl was dead, Alexei didn't want to let her go. She was part of him, her lifeblood filling him, giving him a future. He rocked her against him, kissed her white slack mouth. Rasputin finally pulled her away.

He studied Alexei. So little amazed him, but this did. The pages, the pages had wrought this miracle. The boy glowed with health, his cheeks were fuller, his eyes bright, his shoulders straight. He was weeping. "Please, don't take her away, not yet."

"I must," Rasputin said. "I will see she's properly taken care of."

Rasputin then examined Alexei, listened to his heart and lungs, checked his pupils. He stepped back, nearly tripping over the girl's body.

"It is good, Czarevitch. You are healed." And he carried the young girl over his shoulder, past Alexei's white-faced mother, through the back of the lodge, deep into the forest.

And for some time, Alexei was healed. He was strong and able to play without worry of falling and having blood flow out of him, and not stop.

Eventually, though, he sickened again. He came alone, not telling his mother. Rasputin brought another girl, a blond china doll this time, younger than the first. Alexei didn't like the taste of her as much. He much preferred the third; even with the drug Rasputin had forced down her throat, she fought and screamed. He thought of her as the fighter, with raven hair and blue eyes. Rasputin finally bound her. She was helpless, and the horror of him and what he was doing made the blood taste tart and rich. And he flew again back, back to a long-ago castle in a faraway land and he saw two young brothers, one well and one sick, like him. And they had the pages. And they spoke to the pages, and the pages spoke to them, sang to them, and wept when they were parted.

And then he was flung into the future, only this time there wasn't only blank whiteness. No, he saw a peasant boy kneeling by a rowan tree. He saw him pull out the pages from his shirt and wrap them carefully in a dirty woolen cloth. He dug a hole and buried them there, beneath the rowan, and he ran, never seeing the small girl from the nearby Gypsy encampment watching him.

Two years later, Rasputin, fearing the nobles had discovered what he had done, knew he had to rid himself of the magic pages. He was deaf to Alexei's pleas that he have them. He sent them off with a young boy, an acolyte, cautioning him to take them away as far as he could and bury them under a rowan tree.

He didn't have to tell Alexei what he'd done,

the boy already knew, because he could no longer hear the pages sing to him. They were too far away. He was inconsolable.

When Rasputin finally met his end, his last thought was of the magic pages buried under the rowan tree, and the boy.

Without the potion given him to drink before he drank from a girl, Alexei weakened. He dreamed often of the now-silent pages, so far away from him, buried under a rowan tree. And he dreamed of the small gypsy girl watching, and wondered.

His end came on a hot evening in July.

His exhausted blood was no match for the bullets.

THE FOURTH DAY

FRIDAY

Bitcoin is a digital cryptocurrency with a mixed reputation. At worst, it's the currency of hackers and criminals, at best, a lively new free market that allows anonymity, security, and lack of government oversight. With its value all over the map and raiders regularly stealing it from other "wallets," this new digital currency has moved beyond a techie playground and is now a speculative investors' nirvana.

—J. T. Ellison

CHAPTER SIXTY

You don't need to tie a big chunk of meat to the lure, a tidbit the size of the end of your finger will do. Start by putting your hooded bird on the floor inside the house. Put the lure, garnished with the tidbit, on the floor about a foot away from it, then pop the hood off.

—*American Falconry* Magazine

The Old Garden
Twickenham
Richmond upon Thames, London

Roman leaned back against the wall, wiping the sweat from his brow. The delivery had gone well. The drone army was now in London, safe, and even better, accessible. Ready to use. Against Barstow? Possible. Very possible.

Back in the house, he went first to the cast. They were hungry and ready to fly. He pressed the button that exposed the roof to the sky, untethered them, and watched them take off, one by one. The eagles went last, their massive wings helping them soar straight into the sky.

"Good hunting, my lovelies. Be back before dark."

They would, he knew. The cabal would hunt on the grounds and come back to him, sated and happy.

He left the roof open and went to the lab. Radu was standing over Isabella Marin, talking animatedly. Roman was shocked. Radu willingly talking to a stranger? Of course, she spoke Voynichese, and perhaps that made the difference. He wondered if she were indeed a blood match, how long she would survive, being exsanguinated over and over again.

Radu saw his brother enter and signaled for him. He went to the lab, and Roman followed.

When the hermetically sealed door hissed shut, he whispered, "She's a match."

"Why are you whispering?"

"Excitement, perhaps? We should do the transfusion now."

"She may have diseases. She may have anomalies."

"No, Roman. The blood is clear. She is perfect. She is a descendant, as we are. She is the cure. The pages spoke of an angel who would come in the night. She is our angel."

"I don't think I've ever seen you quite so excited, Brother."

"It's hard not to be thrilled, after all these years. And she speaks our language, not unexpected, since she, too, is our own familial line. Let's hurry, Roman, I want to move ahead with the transfusion immediately."

"We don't have time right now. I must deal with Barstow." Roman shrugged. "If he fails to give me my money, I will kill him." As he walked away, he reached into his pocket for a tab of LSD, thumbed it onto his tongue. To his astonishment, Radu exploded.

"Barstow's been stringing you along for seven months, and you chose to believe him. And what has he done? He had Caleb Temora hack Radulov to ruin your company to destroy everything we've built. You know he won't give you your money. He never intended to give you the billion pounds. He wanted it for himself.

"Look at you! Another microdose of LSD? And your wretched savior complex. Who cares about the terrorists taking over Africa? You tell me over and over I'm the most important thing in your life, to cure me is your highest priority. Well, prove it.

"We have our cure, and I'm ready. Save me, Roman. You know time is running out, we may not get another chance."

"Calm yourself, Radu. We have all the time in the world. No one knows we're here. No one knows where she is. As soon as I've dealt with Barstow—"

Radu shook his head. "You've lost all sense of reality, Brother. You murdered Isabella's fiancé. It's all over the news. They're looking for her, everywhere. Looking for you, too, though they only know the name of your alter ego, Laurence Bruce. I refuse to lose my chance to be cured because you've acted recklessly, yet again. We're going to do this my way. I know exactly what I'm getting into, and I want you to give me this one small thing. And then you can go after your filthy money, I care not."

Rage built inside Roman. "That filthy money is what's allowing you to have this home, away from all stimulation that might upset you. It's what paid for your lab, to search for this cure. Do you not understand, Radu? All I do, I do for you. Everything I've done, always, is for you." He was panting, he was so enraged, nearly beyond himself, and now his brother was questioning him?

Radu touched his brother's arm, his voice calm again. "Then hook us up. I can hear her blood singing to me, Roman, like the pages sing to both of us. I've never felt this before. She is my life's blood. She is the cure. We've been wrong all along. The Voynich, the pages, they're only part of the story. It is Isabella: she is what we've looked for all this time. Roman, listen to me. Blood doesn't lie. Isabella's blood will save me. Now, stop making excuses, stop putting everything above me, and start the transfusion. Iago can watch over me while you go play with Barstow. It will take hours. You will have plenty of time. She really is my gift from God."

Roman stared at his brother. He was right. "All right, Radu. Prepare yourself. I will ready Isabella."

When Radu hurried out of the room, Roman rubbed his forehead, then slipped another dose into his mouth. He stopped by his office for his notebook. Like Radu, he kept notes on every experiment, on every observation. And this one would surely be the most important.

A small red light was flashing on his computer screen. He bumped the mouse and saw camera footage, knew immediately it was the flat in Belgravia. The flat's perimeter sensors were activated. Someone had gone inside.

Something else to make him crazy. He calmed himself, scanned the flat but saw nothing. A system failure, a short circuit? No, he knew better. He flashed to the external cameras. There were two men in a black SUV sitting across from the entrance.

He said aloud, "Barstow. What are you up to?"

The light flashed on his desk phone, the speaker turning on with a gentle click. His brother said, "Where are you?"

"I'm coming." He turned off his computer screen. If what Radu said was true, it didn't matter what Barstow was planning. Roman had plans for this man he'd once believed was a patriot, like himself. A man, he'd realized too late, who had drawn him to a vast humanitarian project that was all based on lies. A billion pounds, that was Barstow's only goal. He rather hoped Barstow would kill Temora, save him the trouble.

As he left his office, he saw the shadows flitting through the sky. The cast was returning.

He detoured up the stairs to the falconry, waited for his brethren to land back in their places, claws and beaks red with blood, then closed the roof and went to give his brother the potion, then Isabella's blood. Two strong brothers, not one strong and one weak. Not after tonight.

CHAPTER SIXTY-ONE

The satellite is going overhead right now. We will capture as many shots as we can."

Harry's technical team was top-notch. Nicholas enjoyed listening to them run through the satellite imagery. When they had it all uploaded, they started tearing it apart.

"We have a helipad up there, not a huge surprise for a house of this size."

"I'm not seeing any antiaircraft battery—that would be bad news. So we should be able to fly in, but we'll have to shut down the security systems first. Knock out their power grid. Though I'm sure they have generators, we might have a few seconds opportunity when the power goes down before the backup turns on."

Gareth pointed to two rectangular openings. "Are those skylights? Can you get closer?"

The satellite imagery enlarged. "Definitely glass. Even if it is ballistic-grade, do you see those hinges?" He circled the two spots with a red laser pointer. "If we hit it right, it will pop. Nicholas, remember the house in Cambridge we infiltrated from the roof? We could do it again, the same way."

"I remember. You hit it with a depth charge, and we fast-roped in. That would work. But in case it doesn't, we need another ingress. Find us one, Adam."

"Working on it. Hey, look at this huge concrete building over here. It has the massive security, too, but it's all external. Might be a safe room on steroids."

"Or he's keeping something nasty inside."

Adam ran through what he had found of the house's schematics. He would kill for a decent set of blueprints, was searching online the whole while, but hadn't found the right ones yet.

"Nicholas, I'm not seeing any other ingress, but the estate is huge. Seventeen acres of land around it, too. We don't have enough time to map it all if we want to go in tonight."

"What's this, right here? Freeze frame, please."

Nicholas pointed to an area to the right of the helipad. "There are edges here. Uniform edges. What is this? Can we get the cameras to pan in?"

Gareth said, "Wait, wait, wait, it's opening. The roof is opening."

They watched in silence as a section of the roof slid back. In the eerie silence of the massive screens, a black rectangular hole gaped open, and birds began flying out of the roof.

Nicholas asked, "Bloody hell. What is this?"

Mike grinned. "They're falcons. The ones that have been watching us, I'll bet, and one of them carried that drone away."

They watched the screen as it cleared. The roof stayed open.

Adam said, "So there is another way in."

"Better yet," Nicholas said, "it's another way out. That bird roof could be on some sort of automated switch. If it's a timer, we're royally screwed, but if it's something we can control, we can get out through there. The roof it is." He looked at Mike. "You ready to go for a ride?"

She grinned at him. "Always. This is a walk in the park compared to dropping onto a ship deck in the North Sea."

Harry said, "I want to try and confirm one hundred percent this is his home. Get Barstow in here. Let's have him try to make the call again, see if we can pull Ardelean out of the house. We can arrest him off-site and, with any luck, the house—and the falcons—won't fight back."

Barstow was alone in the library next to the command center, his wrist handcuffed to a heavy brown leather couch arm. When Nicholas and Harry came in, Barstow looked up. With his free hand he took off his glasses, held up a slim volume showing an oil painting of a house. "Churchill wasted his time on painting. But his book about his passion is quite charming."

Harry looked down at him. He looked older, somehow less substantial, his good-old-boy attempt at normalcy pathetic, really. He said, "We need to find Ardelean immediately. He's murdered a civilian and kidnapped a woman. We have to get her back."

Barstow laughed. "So, he's finally gone barking mad, has he?"

Nicholas said, "He's probably been killing for years. We need to bring him in now. We believe we've found his estate, and we believe he's taken the woman there. It's well fortified, and we are going in to rescue her. But we need him out of the house. We don't need the complication of trying to take him down and saving her. If he's completely off the rail, as you believe, he might simply kill her to spite us. We want her alive. We want him alive, too."

Harry said, "Try again, Corry. Call him now."

Barstow pulled out his mobile. "You know he hasn't been answering . . ." But he put his mobile on speaker and hit a few numbers with his free hand. They waited while the phone rang and rang. Barstow shook his head and turned it off. Moments later, a text appeared.

I'm busy.

Barstow lit up. "Got him."

Nicholas said, "Tell him you have the money, and you'll meet him at the flat in Belgravia."

I have the money. Meet me in the usual place.

Someone is watching the usual place. What have you done, Barstow? Who have you talked to?

I've done nothing. I give up. You've made your point. I have your money. The wire transfers will be completed within the hour, but you have to accept them yourself, in person. I need a thumbprint. You know how this works. Let's be done with this, Roman. Take your money and give me my army.

There was nothing. Nicholas said, "We lost him."

But the screen lit up again.

I won't meet for wire transfers. You get me money, and we'll talk. Call me when you have the cash.

Another pause, then:

And, Barstow, no more games. I know
what you've done.

Nicholas said, "What does he mean, he knows
what you've done?"

Barstow shrugged. "I don't know. But he'll
come if I promise him cash. We can meet at the
theater."

Nicholas asked, "What theater?"

"The Prince Edward. *Hamlet* is playing."

Harry's eyes narrowed. "How much money are
we talking about?"

"You heard me, I promised him the full
amount." Barstow shrugged again. "But it doesn't
matter. You'll take him, and the money won't
matter."

"I suppose you have the one billion pounds,
Corry, stashed in accounts out of the country?"

"No, of course not. I told you, the investors
hadn't paid up. I did keep a bit from their first
payment, only fair. Again, I am not the criminal in
this. I am a patriot who wanted only to fight terrorism. It is Ardelean."

Nicholas looked at his father. His face was
expressionless. No, there was something else—it
was disappointment. In this man he'd known most
of his life.

Harry looked away from Barstow. "Nicholas,
we'll split the teams. You're on the rescue squad. I'll

go with Barstow and another team to take Ardelean into custody. And Nicholas?"

"Sir?"

"Be careful. You've already been shot in the
side. I know, you're fine, you're always fine, but we
have no idea what might be waiting for you inside
that house. I—be careful, Nicholas." Harry cleared
his throat, said to Barstow, "Send the text to Ardelean. The theater it is."

CHAPTER SIXTY-TWO

The Old Garden
Twickenham
Richmond upon Thames, London

Isabella didn't know if it was night or day, nor did she care. The drug they'd given her had sent her into a surreal landscape made up of Voynichese language, but somehow perverted so she couldn't read it. And the drawings, the green women and constellations and bizarre plants, what were they? She faded away, in and out.

Nor did she know how much time had passed, but now she was awake, clearheaded, and being wheeled into a stark white room that felt almost like a hospital suite by an older man, white white skin, his hair pale blond mixed with silver, no expression on his seamed face. She was tied down to the gurney in webbing—arms, legs, and neck. She knew what was going to happen. They were going to take her blood. How much? She saw Roman come toward her and wanted to scream, but no sound came out of her mouth. He leaned over her, lightly patted her face.

"You'll be happy to hear all the tests came back, and yes, you are a perfect match for Radu. He tells me you are his life's blood. Now, relax, this won't hurt a bit."

She felt cold, wet gauze swab over the vein in the crook of her arm. He jammed in a cannula. It felt like a railroad spike. Of course it hurt, but she didn't make a sound.

"That wasn't too bad, was it?"

The older man wheeled in a second gurney. Radu was on it—not strapped down like she was, but sitting up, looking excited, like a child. He was clean as a whistle, too—hair freshly washed, wearing a white gown. She could smell something antiseptic, like medical soap.

Roman smiled. "You're our blood sister. And you brought us the pages. Radu has drunk the potion, and now he awaits the life that should have always been his."

She started to struggle against the webbing. She twisted and turned, nearly displacing the cannula in her arm.

She heard him say, "I should have done this earlier." He leaned over her again. "Here, a little something to make you calm." He injected a needle into her arm. Almost instantly, she felt the fear fade. There was no pain in her arm, no sense of what was going to happen. He was saying, "I hope you can still understand me. We're going to have to take a great deal of your blood, and probably do this two or three times, but the manuscript's directions are clear. If we follow these steps, he will be cured, and you shouldn't be dead."

She looked up at him, blurred now, but she still saw a handsome man, a genius, it was said. She admired genius. She whispered, "All right, but you know, I really don't want to die."

"You spoke to me in Voynichese, did you realize that? Well, I gave you something quite pleasant. Sorry I can't play music for you, Radu doesn't like it. Perhaps he will once he has your blood coursing through his veins. Do you want to hum?"

"Yes, I want to hum." And she started humming, an old Romanian ballad sung by her mother and her mother before her, all the way back to who knew? A sad song about a man and a maid and how they were betrayed and both died. Who cared? She kept humming.

She thought she heard him laugh. Was that Radu's excited voice?

He was leaning over her again, and lightly laid a finger over her mouth. "You're humming too loud. I don't want Radu to get too excited. Transfusions are difficult for him, and we must be so careful. Even the tiniest bit of jostling while the needle is in place could be the death of him."

She whispered her hum, more the sound of a bee now, but she didn't want to jostle Radu.

"It's time. Radu, are you ready?"

"I am. Oh, Isabella. My dearest sister. I am very excited to have you inside of me."

Iago leaned over to insert the needle into Radu's arm, but Roman stepped to his side and took the cannula away. "Iago, I will do that. I don't want any mistakes now."

"As you wish." And she saw the man Iago step out of the way, his face still expressionless.

Iago. Was he named after Shakespeare's Iago? A bad man he'd been. She whispered his name.

A phone started ringing.

Roman cursed.

"Iago. Tend to that."

Tend to what? Oh yes, the phone. Was his sweetheart calling him? No, Iago was a betrayer, he didn't love, couldn't love. She started humming again. She heard Roman murmuring something. To Radu?

No, to her. "It's only the needle," Roman said. "Hold still, and yes, keep humming. It's in place now."

Almost immediately, she had the strangest sensation. She saw a vacuum, and it was attached to her arm, and she could feel the blood being pulled out. Somewhere deep inside, she knew she should be screaming, but she didn't. She closed her eyes and hummed. Was that her mother standing over her? Why was she crying?

She heard Iago's voice, a whisper, yet it sounded loud in her ears. "Roman, you must take this call. It's Lord Barstow. He's texted a number of times and continues to call."

"What does he want?"

"He says it's urgent. He says you must get on the phone immediately."

"Give me that."

Isabella heard a faint snap over her humming and knew it was Roman ripping sterile gloves off his hands.

He sounded angry—why was that? He was going to drain her blood into Radu. Would she die? He said, "What do you want now, Barstow?"

Barstow. She hadn't ever heard that name before. She wondered why Roman was so angry at him.

"Yes, I'll come. I will meet you at the theater. If you don't have the entire amount in cash, I will kill you. Do you understand?"

He hung up, and Isabella saw through a pleasant haze that he was smiling. And then, "Radu, the bastard finally took me seriously and is paying up. All of it. It's a great day, Brother. You will be healthy, and the drones will go to Africa. Iago, supervise the remainder of the blood transfer. I must go meet Barstow."

He laughed again, and both Radu and Iago laughed, too. She wondered about the money. Why give it to him? Barstow, who was he? She wanted to laugh, too, but all she could do was hum.

She saw a shadow out of the corner of her eye. It was Roman, and he was leaving. Well, that was all right, wasn't it? She started humming again, and the world was vague and quite lovely.

CHAPTER SIXTY-THREE

MI5 Headquarters, Home Office
Thames House
12 Millbank
Westminster, London

The team was soon in black tactical gear, strapping on Kevlar vests and securing M4 assault rifles to their backs.

Once Mike was fully armed, she tucked a pair of sticky gloves in her tactical belt, then stashed both a small first aid pack and three extra thirty-round magazines into her bag. No one knew what they were jumping into, so they were prepared for everything. She felt focused, calm, adrenaline on a low simmer. She was saving the big burst of energy for the jump. She was ready to get Isabella back. Mike prayed she was still alive.

Once everyone was geared up, they gathered around Adam for a briefing.

"I found the plans from Ardelean's last renovation. The lab is on the third floor. There's an attic that opens onto the roof on the fourth. If that's where the falcons flew from, I suppose it's the aviary. There is an entire suite of rooms on the second floor, I can't tell if it's a guest suite, or this is where the mythical brother lives. Maybe servants, too, it's roomy. The first floor is reception, kitchen, dining room, and several large, open spaces, living room, den, I suppose. The backyard opens to a pool and gardens. The path down to the river comes off the east side of the house."

Gareth picked it up. "Should something happen, bolt for the river. We'll have Zodiacs waiting. Air reconnaissance will be monitoring for drones and those birds, too. They aren't back yet. The sky door is still open. The chopper is at Battersea heliport and ready when you are. Faster than taking you out to Northolt. We're going to put you in a Gazelle—it's quieter, less chance of being spotted too early. They've plotted a path down the H4 to the house that keeps them in the London heli lanes but allows for a last-second deviation out toward Twickenham. Heathrow ATC has been notified we're doing a training exercise."

Nicholas said, "Too bad it's dark. Flying a helicopter down the Thames can be quite romantic."

Mike rolled her eyes. "You have a bandage over a gunshot wound in your side and you're thinking about romance? Well, what are you waiting for? Let's go do it."

Nicholas and Gareth burst out laughing.

"I meant, let's go get Isabella, you idiots."

Adam called out, "I've sent the schematics to your comms. You'll be able to see what's what on your wrist cams, and I'll be here with Ian—we'll be in your ears. Good luck."

The Gazelle was cramped compared to other choppers she'd been in. Only the two pilots and Mike, Nicholas, and Gareth could fit. But the benefit was the Gazelle was indeed substantially quieter, as advertised.

Since they were wearing helmets with headphones, she could hear the pilots' technical talk as they lifted off and started their run down the Thames. She tuned them out, tuned in her father's deep, calm voice. *You know what you're doing, you're ready to move. Now make sure you're ready mentally. Focus, Mike, make sure you're focused.* She didn't tune in what her mother, the Gorgeous Rebecca, would say.

The pilot said in their ears, "Ten minutes to drop," and Gareth gave them a thumbs-up. They were approaching their target fast, the river a shining ribbon in the darkness below them.

Mike said, "I can't get my bearings. I barely know the city in the daylight. At night, from the air, I'm lost."

Gareth said, "We're over the botanical gardens."

Nicholas said, "Let's run through once more. Mike will go first and cover me as I come down with the explosives. We'll set them on the window hinges and blow them inward, then rope in. The chopper will bank back to the river and be waiting for our call to get us out, hopefully with Isabella."

Gareth said, "It sounds so easy when you lay it out like that."

"It's exactly how things will go. Trust me."

The pilot said, "Three minutes to jump." The copilot said, "Five minutes to explosives, if you please."

"Copy that," Nicholas said, and Mike heard the banked excitement in his voice. He was even a bigger danger junkie than she was. She checked her weapon once more, tightened the straps of her Kevlar vest, then pulled on her gloves.

The pilot said, "One minute. Take your positions."

Nicholas opened the door, and the cool night air rushed into the cabin.

Mike felt the helicopter slow, then hover. She looked down to see the roof glowing white below her. She grabbed the thick black coil, got a good grip thanks to the sticky gloves. She thought of her father, and smiled. *All set, Dad.*

"Ready," the pilot said. She leaned toward the door. Gareth patted her arm and said, "Luck."

The pilot said, "First jumper, fast-rope on my mark—three, two, one—jump jump jump."

Mike went straight down and landed lightly on the roof. She felt the rope tug, saw Nicholas come out the door behind her, fast. She pulled the weapon off her back and began scanning for trouble. With no warning, the helicopter lurched to the right, hard, its nose dipping, the rotors twisting counterclockwise, pushing for air.

Nicholas whipped past her head, only one hand on the wildly swinging rope, yelling, "Move, move, move!"

The chopper was burning, red and orange flames shooting into the sky above her. She heard the boom, realized it was about to land on her.

Everything happened in an instant—Nicholas's horrified face, Mike sprinting hard across the roof, the helicopter tail lashing wildly around toward her. She couldn't get away, so she went down flat on the roof, hands over her head, and prayed. She felt the harsh wind as the tail rotor passed only a few feet above her and smashed into the concrete ramparts on the roof. She smelled fuel, looked up to see the helicopter tip over the edge, the metal screaming, and fall, upside down, out of sight.

The fire on the roof was burning fast and hot. *Please, the pilots got out, please. Wait, where is Nicholas?*

CHAPTER SIXTY-FOUR

To Belgravia

Harry sat next to a man he'd known most of his life, a supposed friend who wasn't a friend at all. Did he believe his own lies? They were silent in the back of a Range Rover, heading at breakneck speed toward the Prince Edward Theatre.

"Once Ardelean is dead, all will be well," Barstow said.

"Do you really believe that, Corry?"

"I have done nothing wrong."

Harry didn't say anything—what was there to say? He was worrying about both Michaela and his son, couldn't help himself, even though he knew to his soul both were strong and smart. But the problem was neither of the two were afraid of anything. Show them a wild tiger, and they'd gladly hop into the pit and take him on. No, he couldn't think like that. *They're all right. They'll do what's needed. They will be all right*, his mantra, he supposed.

He turned to Barstow. "Tell me how you hooked up with Roman Ardelean. How did you know Ardelean would be able to supply your army?"

"Well, why not tell you? It was his falcons. Ardelean spoke once at a British Falcon Society meeting. He mentioned he was training them to attack drones. It's all the rage—the French are doing it, with eagles and falcons, a new line of defense, and we're doing it, as well. Being the genius he is, he built a few drones to let the falcons destroy them, discovered he had an affinity for building them. I saw how quickly he was able to prototype—it would have taken years to go through channels and achieve the same velocity—and realized I had an opportunity.

"The way he talked about the birds—they're an obsession. He's their master, but he's also a hunter like they are. He cares for them himself, makes their hoods, makes them dependent on him, then trains them to see the drones as prey in the sky. It's an incredible sight—the birds all wearing Kevlar, handmade breastplates and covers for their talons—the way they attack the drones."

Both men fell silent. The city swept past. Rain had begun to fall, cold and gray, and the fog curled round the lampposts.

Barstow threw back his shoulders. "Listen, I told you why I did this, and it's the truth—I am a patriot, like my ancestors. I wanted to make my own mark."

Harry said quietly, "But the thing is, Corry, I believe Nicholas. You claim you're a patriot, but what you really are is greedy. It was always more about the money than your love for England, your hatred of radical Islam."

"No, no, that's not true."

"Yes, Nicholas was right. You lied to Ardelean, told him the investors hadn't paid the final payment. You have that money. Where? In a series of accounts outside of England?"

Barstow wanted to kill this pompous, self-righteous sod, but he couldn't. He knew he had to convince him to kill Ardelean, or Ardelean would kill him. He knew it. "You have to listen, Harry. Ardelean can ruin all of us, and he will if he believes it will save him. I had no idea when I took him on as a partner that he knows everything. Think of MATRIX. It's in nearly every computer in the world. Don't you understand? He has access to our files, our bank accounts, the websites we visit. Anytime he wants to know who MI5 is investigating, he can. Ardelean has an email server set up to blast our personal banking records, offshore accounts, Internet history—he has our secrets. Can't you wrap your head around this? Did you learn nothing from WikiLeaks? The Internet, that's the playing field, and the perfect place to hang the threat over our heads. It can never die. Whatever allegations he makes—and he will make them, if you doubt that, you're a fool—generations will be affected by the secrets he will release. Nothing is sacred in his world, and now, he will use everything he has against us. You must end this tonight, Harry. You understand what I'm saying, don't you? You must eliminate him. You must kill him and dismantle Radulov."

"I don't want him dead. I want him brought to justice."

Barstow would have grabbed his arm, but his hands were cuffed. "He's too dangerous—he must die. We're not going to survive this with him alive."

"We've weathered worse."

"You're a blind fool. Roman Ardelean's a murderer. He's the enemy, not me."

The lampposts were a blur outside the darkened glass. The city felt coiled and tense, ready for mayhem.

Harry said, "I do wish you would simply admit what you've done, what you set into motion, and for the basest of motives."

Barstow stared at him, and said, his voice meditative, "I do despise you, Harry, despite everything you are. I suppose I always have. And now you want to be my judge and jury? Why not, he'll kill me anyway." Barstow gave him a twisted smile. "You want the truth? I wanted it all, Harry. The money, the drones, the power that came with saving the world from these animals, these terrorists. You know I come from a long line of military strategists. I thought this was simply another game of chess, with bigger stakes. I had all the moves figured out. I didn't anticipate Ardelean not to be willing to part with the drones until he had the money in hand. I was wrong. So I tried to distract him by submarining his company."

"You were behind the hack on MATRIX? How is that possible?"

Barstow looked at Harry and said with a sneer, "I've always been smarter than you, Harry. I found a former employee who was Ardelean's trusted protégé, a brilliant young man who hated Ardelean so much he was willing to take him down, both him and his precious Radulov."

"Where did you find this genius?"

"You remember we lost several young men to ISIS about four years back? One of them was named Caleb Temora."

"I recall the name."

"He was a coder with Radulov for a few years, brilliant, absolutely brilliant. We picked him up in a sweep while looking for people who might be defecting home from ISIS. They get there and realize the caliphate isn't what they thought it would be.

"The moment we got him home, he tried to hack the security at Buckingham Palace. For ISIS? We don't know. He claims not, claims he was doing it for fun, but we couldn't take any chances. He wanted to make a deal with me. He told me Ardelean built his computer code using an ancient manuscript. A new computer language, he called it. Not zeros and ones but fours and eights, something like that, based on the call letter of the manuscript."

Harry stared at him. "You're talking about the Voynich, aren't you?"

"Yes. He was able to write us code to brute-force attack Radulov Industries and start a waterfall effect of hacks on all the terminals housing MATRIX. I'd hoped it would keep Ardelean too busy to bother with me."

"You, the vaunted patriot, cost the world millions of pounds in lost time and ransomware payments."

Barstow shrugged.

"Does Ardelean know it was you who had someone playing with his code?"

I know what you did. Barstow shook his head. Ardelean couldn't have meant Temora. There was no way he could have found out Barstow had kept him in a safe house for the past year—just in case he needed him, and he had. "You wish to talk to Temora? He's all yours. He'll give you all the details. Oh, here we are, we're coming up to the theater. Harry, you must kill him. He's more dangerous than you can possibly imagine. You should—"

There was a brilliant flash of light, and the front of the Range Rover exploded.

Harry felt the burst of white-hot flame, the window give against his shoulder, the cool night air, then he landed on the pavement, rolling as he hit, to protect himself. He rolled into a gutter, the flames hot on his face, sucking out his breath. He covered his head with his arms and waited for another blast, or gunfire. Finally, he crawled to his knees, then stood, wincing at the pain. His arms were scraped, his ribs—were they broken? Even the smallest breath hurt, but he was alive.

He looked at the mangled SUV, an inferno against the dark sky, and he couldn't see either the driver or Barstow inside.

He became aware of the growing chaos around him, people screaming, shouting for police, some running away, some pulling out their phones and recording videos. One man with a small dog on a leash stared dumbly at Harry, who realized he must look like a war victim.

His mind struggled to catch up. Drone, it must have been a drone, and it dropped a bomb on the car, like the train attack. Only this time the drone did it on the front of the car, blowing off the doors and windows. Harry, not wearing his seat belt, was thrown from the wreckage by the blast. He learned soon enough that Barstow and the driver had not been so lucky.

Harry saw blood running down his arm and pulled out a handkerchief to tie around the gash. He managed to get away from the flames and pressed against the building, scanning the skies as he reached for his phone. He heard the faint noise above him, looked up to see a red eye in the sky.

The drone was searching the scene. It zoomed over, back and forth, seeking, but Harry was hidden in the shadows.

Bloody hell, where was his phone? It wasn't in his pocket. He realized he wasn't wearing his jacket anymore, either, it must have gotten caught in the car. He was also missing a shoe.

He leaned his head back against the building, hiding from the drone, listened to sirens wailing as they grew nearer and nearer and the noise from so many people as they watched the car burn. He heard the faint hum of the drone, flying away now, its pilot satisfied it had done its job.

Fury filled him.

This was war.

CHAPTER SIXTY-FIVE

The Old Garden
Twickenham
Richmond upon Thames, London

Isabella fell asleep humming. When she awoke, her mind was clear, and she realized she was exhausted. Then it came back. Ardelean had drugged her, and he'd drained some of her blood.

At least she was still alive. It was dark in the room, only the lights from under the cabinets shining down on the desk below, onto Radu's notes.

She felt a hand on her arm and jerked away. Iago stood over her, nothing showing on his face.

"You're awake."

"What time is it?"

"Nearing dawn. The cast will need attending. Before I go, may I bring you anything?"

"You spoke."

"Yes. I apologize that my accent is so very strong." Then he shrugged. "Water? Would you like some water?"

"No, I would like my phone to call the police."

Remarkably, that blank face suddenly split into a smile.

"Madam is amusing. And you are no longer humming. A pity." He leaned closer. "You are saving my master. For this I am grateful."

"When will he take more of my blood for your master?"

She heard a yawn close by. Radu called out, "I am still getting your blood, Isabella, only much slower now. He will give you a day to build yourself back up. I don't think he'll kill you since it's possible I will need transfusions from you forever. You will be my private blood bank.

"Thank you, Isabella. It is amazing you came into our lives after all this time."

She struggled against the webbing, but it was no use. She had to think, had to figure something out. She said, "When is he coming back?"

"I don't know. It's nearly dawn, so he'll be back soon, I hope. I want him to see how strong I am."

"I would like some water."

Iago hurried out of the room. Radu said, "When Roman comes back, I'll have him release the webbing around your neck. Are you very uncomfortable?"

Why would you care? "It's very uncomfortable, yes."

"I am sorry. Roman has his ways—I feel good, not the way I really want to feel, but better, with your blood I am so much better."

"Glad to be of service." Where had that come from? She was going as insane as the inmates.

Radu said, "I hope Iago will get you my special water. It is wonderfully healthy, perfect to help you build back up."

There was a loud bang.

"What's that?"

Isabella heard voices and smelled smoke.

Iago came running back into the lab, slamming the door behind him, a biometric code snapping into place.

He crossed himself. "Master Radu, they've come. They're here. Someone's attacked the house! The antiaircraft battery shot a missile. I heard it activate."

Isabella couldn't do anything, so she closed her eyes and prayed. Someone had come to rescue her?

Radu screamed, "Unhook me, Iago. I am strong now. Give me guns. We will fight them off."

The whapping sounds of a helicopter rotor grew louder and louder, and, out the window, Isabella saw an explosion, then felt a crush of flame and glass.

"Iago? Unhook me! We cannot let them come in. We cannot let them take her."

"No, master, no one can get in. The door is barricaded. We will be safe. Hold still, I will unhook you."

"Call Roman. He must come."

"Master, your brother isn't here, but we have the house as a defense. I have the guns. The room is safe. We will be safe."

"I smell smoke, Iago." He was whimpering, like a child. He was afraid, she saw his eyes were wild. Again, he whimpered. "Iago, I'm scared."

"Don't worry, master, you know Master Roman installed a chemical-fire suppression system throughout the house and in these rooms so there could never be any harm to the equipment. We will be safe enough. Nothing bad will happen to you."

"Nothing can happen to Isabella, either! They can't take her from me, Iago. I must have her."

She saw Iago had been moving around the room, setting switches into new positions, filling the magazine of the handgun.

There was banging, and they heard shots being fired. Calls and screams.

"Prepare yourself, master. Here is a gun. All you have to think about is pulling the trigger. That's right, put your finger just there."

The sound of automatic gunfire came through the doors. They all froze, waiting. Isabella prayed harder than she ever had in her life. Iago and Radu had their guns aimed at the door. She heard a noise on the other side of the door and yelled as loud as she could, "Please, be careful. They have guns!"

CHAPTER SIXTY-SIX

The sky around Mike was on fire. As she dodged flying debris, her mind focused on only one thing—Nicholas. She shouted his name again. "Nicholas!" Nothing but the roar of the flames. She remembered an orange glow moments before the helicopter jerked wildly—she realized it had been a missile shot into the fuselage. She thought of Gareth and sent a prayer.

She stood on the roof of the immense house. Where was he?

A man's voice. "Mike!"

She ran to the western edge of the roof to see Nicholas dangling off the side, his body sideways, one arm on the fast rope, which had miraculously hooked onto a window frame. Gareth was alive and cursing a blue streak, hanging on to Nicholas's hand. Both of them had fallen? Below them, the chopper was burning on the grounds.

Nicholas's face was black with smoke. He gave a laugh and a beautiful white-toothed smile. "Hey, so much for a surprise attack. Mike, Gareth and I went over together. Only one problem—I don't know how long this rope is going to hold, and Gareth is getting concerned."

"Hang on."

Mike unwound a tactical rope in her kit and looped it twice around an air vent. She leaned over the roof edge. "The rope won't be strong enough for the two of you at once." She wrapped the rope around her waist and threw the last fifteen feet over the edge. "Gareth, you come up first. Yell when you've got a good hold."

Moments later, Gareth called, "Have it," and she sat on the roof and braced her feet against the roofline.

She shouted, "Go, I'm ready."

She felt the jerk and the sudden load of weight as he let go of Nicholas's hand. It felt like hours before Gareth finally made it up and over the roof. He lay there for a moment, breathing hard, then unwound the rope from his bloody hands and tossed it to Nicholas. "Mike, let's do him together." He wrapped the rope around his hands, and the two of them held steady as Nicholas climbed up the side of the house to the roof.

When Nicholas rolled over the edge, onto the

roof, Mike sat down hard on her butt. She was sweating, her muscles burned. Nicholas looked to be in one piece, but she'd bet the wound in his side was bleeding again.

"Gareth, there's a first-aid kit in my bag. Your hands are a wreck. Nicholas, do you know your face is black?" Where was her brain? "And how is your side?"

"My side is maybe bleeding a bit, but I'm all right. The pilots?"

Gareth shook his head. "The missile took out the cockpit. The chopper flipped over in midair before it went over. They were gone before it hit the ground."

Mike closed her eyes against the pain of it. Between curses, Nicholas got on his radio and relayed their situation. Adam had heard the whole thing, but the chopper's comms were down so he couldn't speak to them.

"Adam, you probably can't hear me, but we must abort the mission. I hope the Zodiacs are waiting."

Gareth got painfully to his feet. "We'll shimmy down the side of the house and get to the boats, if they're there."

Mike said, furious, "Stop it, both of you! We are not aborting this mission. There haven't been any more attacks. We can't let the pilots' lives be wasted by giving up now. Nicholas, give me the shaped charge. We're going in."

Gareth eyed her like he would a wild animal.

"Mike, listen. Someone in that house shot a missile at us and took out the chopper. There may be more missiles at the ready, you know that. The only reason there haven't been more attacks is they think we're dead."

"They'll kill Isabella if we don't get to her, if they haven't already. Give me that frigging shaped charge now."

Nicholas handed it to her. "Gareth, whoever told you this job was a walk in the park?"

Gareth laughed, got his hands bandaged and taped.

Mike nodded, walked over to the glass skylight, and pressed the shaped charge into place. She stepped back and activated the trigger. The explosion was hard and fast. The glass skylight shattered inward perfectly, as it was supposed to, and Mike tossed them the rope.

"Gareth, can you climb down that rope with your hands?"

"I'd like to say I rappel as well as you two maniacs, but the fact is"—he waved his bandaged hands—"I'll be slower, but I'll follow you down as best I can. Go."

Nicholas took the rope out of her hand. "Mike, back off, I'm going in first. I was the one hanging off a roof, not you. I deserve a reward."

She couldn't help it, she grinned at him. He looked dangerous and pissed off. He flashed a light into the darkness below them. All was quiet. "If

Adam's plans are correct, below the skylight is a library."

He pulled his weapon into place across his chest and went down the rope, hand over hand. Mike did the same, and Gareth came last. Mike heard his sharp intake of breath, knew his hands had to hurt. She thought of the bleeding wound in Nicholas's side. She kept quiet and rappelled.

They landed lightly on a hardwood floor. Nicholas flashed his light on the walls. They were in a massive room, every wall covered with floor-to-ceiling shelves filled with books, thousands of them.

Once they'd crept out of the library, the house looked different. Nicholas whispered, "They must have had work done since Adam's blueprints."

"Yes, but the aviary still has to be to the west, stairs to the lab to the east, down one floor."

Gareth said, "Wait, do you hear something?"

They heard a low shriek. "The aviary," Mike said, "there must still be birds in there."

Gareth said, "They're safe enough. The fire is outside. They must be scared. The stairs are ahead. I wish there was a separate set, I hate to go down the main staircase like this."

"No choice," Nicholas said, "so let's do it."

They stuck to the walls, inching down the stairs, one step at a time, guns held at the ready across their chests. They heard another cry, getting louder.

"That's not a bird," Nicholas said. "That's a person. It sounds like someone's keening."

Gareth put a hand on Nicholas's shoulder. "Shh. Listen."

There were words now, but they couldn't understand them.

"What language is that?"

Mike said, "I don't know. Ardelean is Romanian."

Nicholas was shaking his head. "It's not Romanian. It's not like any language I've ever heard before."

Faintly, in the background, they heard an all-too-familiar sound—the unmistakable metal snick of a magazine being slammed into a gun.

Before anyone could react, bullets sprayed the staircase.

CHAPTER SIXTY-SEVEN

They ducked. It seemed like forever before silence came again. "There," Nicholas said, "that's the final spray, that's the whole magazine. Go!"

They charged down the stairs, Nicholas in the lead, spraying three-round bursts. At the bottom of the stairs they took cover behind statues, all in marble and bronze. The hall fell eerily silent again. The gunman was biding his time.

Mike said quietly into her comms, "Ben, are you scanning the house? What's thermal saying?"

"Having a hard time. If I didn't know better I'd say the place is lined in lead. We're barely getting readings, but it looks like three bodies to your east. Other side of the wall from where you are."

She heard Nicholas say, "Hold on," and then a clatter. Immediately, gunfire opened up again, spraying the room. This time, Mike could see where the shots originated.

"The wall in the corner—there's a freaking weapon hanging from the ceiling."

Nicholas said, "And it's automated, on a motion sensor. I'll throw another canister. When I do, you two bolt for the hallway."

"What's to say there won't be another gun?"

"Probably is, we'll have to take each room as we go. Three, two, one, break."

There was a clatter, and the weapon went off in a flash of light. Mike ran, hard, toward the darkness, pulling up short just inside the hallway. No new guns went off.

She said, "We might be in luck. I see light at the end of the hallway."

"Anyone with ears knows we're here," Gareth said. "Whatever, or whoever, is behind that door is going to be pretty angry when we blow through."

Mike gave him a mad grin. "Let's go."

Carefully, they duck-walked down the hallway, silent as they could be, all geared up. Mike could smell blood, knew it was Nicholas and Gareth, and worried. But then they were at the door, and Gareth placed two explosives on the hinges.

"Biometric locks. Hopefully, this door isn't all steel."

Nicholas said, "Only one way to find out. Behind me, both of you. Go, go, go." They ducked and covered their ears, and he hit the trigger on the charge.

The door blew inward. It took Mike's eyes a moment to adjust before her ears registered the screaming.

The man charged them out of nowhere, an automatic weapon in his hands, spraying bullets. He passed through their sight so fast Mike didn't shoot back, afraid she might hit Isabella.

Nicholas continued firing through the open doorway, Mike crouched behind him. She heard a cry. "Gareth, you're hit?"

He was crawling to the safety of the hallway just outside the blown door. "Grazed my leg. Go on, I'll be right behind you."

Mike stepped to the side of the doorway, went down on her knees to cover Nicholas. She saw the man who'd charged at them crouched to the left of the door, ready to shoot again the moment Nicholas cleared the doorway and came into the room. His hair was white blond, and his teeth were bared in fury. He saw Nicholas and lurched up and into the open, his weapon high, too high, and Nicholas shot him in the chest. He staggered back, but didn't fall.

"Nicholas, he's in Kevlar!" and she shot at his legs.

He was down, groaning, on his side on the floor, grabbing his left leg. Nicholas shouted, "FBI, put down your weapon," but the man groaned once and went limp. A huge pool of blood spread across the perfect white floor.

"Artery shot, Mike."

They heard a woman's voice shout, "Careful. It's rigged, they rigged—" before she was cut off.

They froze. "What's rigged?"

They heard her garbled voice. Someone had his hand over her mouth. They studied the room that looked like a large hospital suite but didn't see anything that could kill them.

"Isabella," Mike called. "Is that you? Are you all right?"

There was scuffling and more muffled yells. Nicholas took one step forward, heard something metallic grinding and ducked just before a sharp edge of metal swung right at his head. Mike ran forward, went down on her knees, and skidded. They collided.

Nicholas grabbed her arms to hold her steady. "What the bloody hell was that?"

"I don't know, but it nearly took off your head. She was right, the place is rigged."

Mike leaned up, whispered against his ear, "The defenses must be on motion sensors. Maybe if we stay low, we can get them to go off without killing us."

They crawled. After ten feet, they saw Isabella, wearing a hospital gown, her legs webbed to the bed. But she wasn't alone.

She was sitting up, and a man was holding her

in front of him. They were tethered together, connected by a long tube running from her arm to his. It was dark red. What was going on here? A blood transfusion? This man was taking Isabella's blood?

Was this Roman Ardelean's brother? Tall, pale as death, and he looked like he wanted to vomit. He'd flattened one hand over Isabella's mouth and the other hand held a scalpel to her neck.

What was his name? Radu. Yes, Radu Ardelean, and he was ill, Barstow had said. Mike whispered his name to Nicholas, but he already knew. They knew Radu had seen them, but he wasn't looking at them. No, he was looking over to where the older man lay on the floor behind them, an ever-spreading pool of blood snaking toward them. There were tears in his eyes.

He spoke to them in a language they didn't understand. Then he shook his head and said in stilted English, "Don't come any closer. I don't want to kill her. She is my life, but I will if you make me."

Isabella bit his hand, and he flinched. He stuck the scalpel into her neck, drawing a drop of blood.

Mike sat back on her heels, her mind racing, but when she spoke, her voice was calm and soothing. "You are his brother, aren't you? You're Radu Ardelean."

"Yes, but it doesn't matter. If you leave us, we will be fine. We belong together. She is my blood sister. She'd tell you that, but she's scared."

"Why don't you let your blood sister speak to us?" Mike crawled a few more feet, then a few more, and sat back on her heels again. Nicholas stopped behind her. She felt his hand on her leg.

Slowly, Radu took his hand from Isabella's mouth, but the scalpel remained against her throat. They saw another drop of blood. Mike would swear his nostrils flared, as if he was breathing in that blood on her neck, as he whispered, "Tell them, sister, tell them we belong together, that I will die without you."

Isabella couldn't get any spit into her mouth. She was still weak and light-headed from the loss of blood, but she had to get it together, had to. She swallowed and swallowed again, aware Radu was behind her, breathing hard, nearly over the edge he was so frightened, so desperate. She wasn't about to try to shove him off. She said quietly, her voice infinitely calm, "Yes, Radu isn't only Roman Ardelean's brother, he's his twin. He has an untreatable hemophilia that runs through our familial line. He's right. With the recipe from the Voynich and my blood, he could be cured." The scalpel eased out of her neck, and she swallowed again.

He whispered against her neck, "Tell them you belong with me. Always."

Nicholas heard him, of course, and said, "Radu, we can't leave her with you. You have to let her go." He continued to crawl forward until he was next to Mike.

Radu's face hardened, then he looked again toward the older man's body, and suddenly, he seemed to fold in on himself. He whispered, "No, no," and his voice was filled with soul-deep grief. Yet again, he pricked her skin with the scalpel. She flinched but didn't make a sound. Blood trailed down to stain her white hospital gown.

Mike raised her hand. "Stop, don't hurt her. She's innocent in this, and from what we see, what she's said, we know you are, too."

Nicholas said, "Radu, please, put down the scalpel, and we can talk about this, civilly." He rose slowly to his feet.

"You killed Iago."

"We didn't want to, but we had no choice. He was trying to kill us."

"He was protecting me. Iago always protected me, since I was a little boy. Don't come another step closer."

Mike stood as well, moved to stand beside Nicholas.

Radu said, "I'm telling you, you want to stop walking, right now. You really should pay attention."

Nicholas stopped, but Mike took another step, and another. She saw Radu reach out his hand and touch something at the side of a counter, and the whole world disappeared.

CHAPTER SIXTY-EIGHT

She was falling, a black maw below her. She couldn't think, couldn't begin to understand. She heard Nicholas shout her name, but she couldn't stop, she was falling, falling—something was choking her—

Nicholas, Nicholas, I'm so sorry— Her neck slapped to the side, hard, and she was jerked to a stop, like a bungee cord, only she wasn't dangling in space. She banged into a hard wall, the breath knocked out of her. She realized she was choking and pulled hard at the gun strap now twisted tight around her neck. She couldn't loosen it, it was cutting off her air. She heard Nicholas yell, "I have you!"

She dangled in the darkness, Nicholas's hand holding the gun strap, and she was tearing at it, trying desperately to loosen it. She realized the strap was pressing against her jugular. She couldn't breathe, spots started to dance in front of her eyes. She struggled, but nothing worked.

"You're okay, Mike," he called down to her. "Breathe, your wind's been knocked out, little sips of air, I have you. You aren't going to fall."

He quickly pulled her up through the darkness, back into the white room. Her gun clattered against the metal edge of the hole, ripped free of her body. It was a long time before it hit bottom.

She landed on the floor, arms and legs splayed out, wheezing for breath. Nicholas saw what was happening and grabbed the strap he'd caught and pulled it away from her neck. "Breathe! Breathe!" She did, a great shuddering breath went through her, and she rolled up, pulled her knees to her chest, rocking, rocking. He was rubbing her back, her sternum. She wheezed out, "That's better. I can nearly breathe again. Did I break my neck?"

Nicholas quickly looked back to see Radu hadn't moved. He still pressed the scalpel to Isabella's throat. He was watching them, a strange expression on his face. As for Isabella, she looked frozen, probably too terrified to move.

"No, your neck's fine. Sorry, I didn't see I was choking you." Instead of saving her he could have killed her. He brought her close, continued to rub her shoulders, her neck. When she was breathing easily once again, she looked over at Radu Ardelean, but he wasn't looking at them. He was looking at the empty expanse between them.

She looked down. There wasn't a floor between them. It was gone. It had opened, and she'd fallen through.

Radu said, nodding, "Oubliette. It goes down a good thirty feet to a stone floor. Remember, I did tell you to stop."

She stared into that huge black hole, at least ten feet by ten feet. Thirty feet to the bottom? If Nicholas hadn't caught her by the gun strap, she would have died or her body would have been so broken— She swallowed. A gift, a miracle. She felt Nicholas's hands now resting lightly on her shoulders. She was alive. She drew in a deep breath and lifted her hand to squeeze his.

Nicholas said slowly to Radu, "An oubliette, built into this house. It's not on the architectural plans."

"I wouldn't know about that. Roman told me about it, said he couldn't imagine it would ever be used but showed me what button to press—" Radu pointed to a small black spot on the edge of a counter close to him. "Roman said it was like an oubliette our ancestors used, like the one in their castle, a surprise defense."

"What ancestors, Radu?"

"Tell them, Isabella."

She felt the scalpel ease back, swallowed.

"Their most infamous ancestor, and mine, too, perhaps, is Vlad Dracul III, but—"

"No, that's enough," Radu said against her cheek, and it looked to Mike like he breathed in the blood on her neck. He raised his head. "I assume your helicopter is what's burning outside the windows? I heard it coming. Iago set off the missile. It would have crashed through the window, but Roman put in special glass. But you made it to the roof first. And you made it past the guns in the gallery, and the gauntlet." He looked at Mike. "You were lucky this man caught you, or your body would be broken on the stone floor at the bottom of the oubliette. Iago says that luck is sometimes the conqueror's best friend. If Vlad Dracul were here, though, he'd kill you both and stick your heads on a pike."

Nicholas said, "It's time to put a stop to this, Radu. We have your brother in custody."

"No, that's a lie. My brother called me, he was about to blow up a theater, I believe."

Nicholas felt the blood drain from his head. He called over his shoulder, "Gareth, you and Mike cover him." And unspoken was *If he tries to kill her, shoot him dead.*

Gareth was sitting on the other side of the oubliette, one of his socks tied around his wounded leg. He raised his gun to point at Radu. "I'm okay."

Nicholas turned away, tapped his comms. "Is anyone there?"

There was silence.

He pulled his mobile out of his zippered thigh pocket and dialed his father's number. It went to voice mail.

He called Adam, who answered on the first ring.

"Nicholas, are you and Mike alive?"

"Yes, but it's very complicated. My father?"

"We lost comms with your dad. Nicholas, there's been a bombing at the Prince Edward Theatre. We don't have any information yet, but I'll call the moment I get anything. Keep your phone close, okay? Your dad, I'm sure he's okay."

Nicholas pushed down the rage and the fear, pushed away the sight of his father's body, dead, burned. His mother's face—he felt the fear clog his throat, then, "You call me the moment you know something. We're talking to Radu Ardelean, Roman's twin brother. Do you know where Ardelean is?"

"No, we don't. The whole operation went sideways. There are several teams heading your way, with medical services. You're bringing out both the brother and Dr. Marin?"

"To be determined." Nicholas turned back to Radu. He said, his voice so rough with rage Mike flinched. What had he been told? Nicholas enunciated every word. "Where. Is. Your. Brother?"

Radu shrugged. "So he's escaped you. I never doubted he'd beat you. Killed your team, did he?"

"He murdered my father!" Nicholas raised his Glock, but he couldn't get a clear shot. He couldn't run at him, the oubliette was in his path.

But Isabella saw her chance. She drove her elbow into Radu's belly, and he went flailing backward. The tubing in both their arms tore free.

There was a moment of silence, then Radu cried out. He was looking at his arm, watching blood begin to well at the site of the needle. He pressed down so hard his knuckles whitened with the pressure, but it didn't stop the blood. He had to compress the vein so no more blood could get through. It was physically impossible—only it wasn't. Radu said, his voice strangely calm, remote, "There is hemostatic gauze in the drawer. I need it."

Mike said, "We can't get to you. The oubliette is in the way."

"On the wall, to your left. There's an override switch. Please, hurry."

Gareth slapped at the button, and the floor closed. Nicholas rushed to Radu, rolled him onto the hospital bed. Radu cried out in pain and curled into a ball, moaning. "No, don't touch me, I can't stand it."

Mike came up to his side. "All right, it's all right. We won't touch you."

Radu whispered, "The gauze. Please."

Mike didn't hesitate. She reached out her hand. Nicholas said, "Don't, Mike," and she stopped short. She looked at Radu.

"I swear to you it's not a trick. It's not a trick. The drawer won't explode. If you don't get it on the wound, I'm going to bleed to death."

They saw blood dripping from between his fingers now, saw the stark fear on his face. She pulled open the drawer, saw a stack of military-grade hemostatic gauze packages with the brand name QuikClot on them.

She opened one and slapped it on his arm. "You won't bleed to death, you'll see, the pressure will cut off the vein."

Nicholas quickly released Isabella from the webbing. She ran to stand over Radu, the tubing dangling from the needle in her arm. "What he has, it's a different kind of illness."

Radu answered, his voice remote as he stared down at his arm. "Most hemophiliacs can't simply bleed to death. It's true, I have a disorder that isn't treatable. My blood simply won't clot. Even with the vein compressed, it doesn't matter."

Mike said, "What else can we do?"

"Pressure, and the medicine on the counter. The green self-injectable tube. It's still in development, experimental, but it's my only chance."

She had the tube in her hand when she saw the edges of the hemostatic gauze were already red and pooling.

"Inject that into my neck, please. Just here. Please do not touch me with your skin while you do so. I don't like being touched. Except Isabella.

She's my sister." He pointed at the artery. He bent his head, and she jammed the auto-injector pen against his neck and depressed the button. He winced but didn't make a sound.

"This is experimental, how, exactly?" she asked.

"As in I've never tried it before. I haven't had a bleed in years."

He lifted the edge of the now-soaked gauze. Even Mike knew this was bad—the QuikClots were designed to stop bleeding, to save lives on the battlefield, but for Radu, it wasn't enough to stop a simple IV needle removal. And he believed Isabella's blood would cure him? She pressed down against the site with all her strength, but it didn't help, blood still poured out of the wound in his arm. Her hands were red with his blood. But how could that be? Was he bleeding internally?

Mike said, "Your neck is bruising, Radu. It's almost black." And she slapped a fresh gauze pack in place, applied more pressure.

Isabella touched his uninjured arm. "We need to get you to a hospital, Radu. Surely they'll be able to do something."

Radu said, his voice still remote, almost disinterested, "It won't matter. The bruising on my neck wasn't supposed to happen. It means the medicine didn't work. At the rate I'm bleeding, I'll be dead soon now." He raised glazed eyes to their faces. "Roman researched a dozen people, so many that could possibly be of our line, tracked them down, and exsanguinated them to give me their blood. None worked until Isabella." He gave a laugh so thin and insubstantial it was like smoke. "And now I'm self-exsanguinating."

The blood was pooling beneath him now, dripping onto the floor.

"We've designed a whole life around making sure I didn't have a bleed. Isabella, you are my only hope." He spoke to her in that strange, guttural language. She whispered back in the same language, then turned to them. "I'm going to try to hook us back up. My blood—it might help."

Nicholas said, "I'm sorry, we don't have the training for that. Listen, the medics will be here soon—"

Radu lifted the gauze from his arm and stared at the pulsing blood. He whispered, "Roman is going to be furious with you. He has tried so hard." And he slid over onto his side, his eyes closed, his hand pressed against the gauze in the crook of his elbow, now red with his blood. He called, "Isabella? You're all I have."

She grabbed the needle adhesive still sticking to his arm and shoved the needle back in, hoping she'd hit the vein. She straightened the tubing on her own arm and lay down beside him. She took his hand in hers. "Lie still and feel my blood come into you, Radu. You will live, do you hear me? My blood will make you live."

She felt him sigh. Felt him squeeze her hand.

He was so cold, shivering now, though it was very warm in the lab. "I'm here, Radu."

He whispered in Voynichese, "Tell Roman, tell him your blood is the key. Your blood. The potion isn't important, not the book, not the pages. You are the cure, for me. Make sure he knows. I don't want him to blame you, kill you." His voice faded until his last words were a faint whisper.

His eyes closed.

"I'll tell him, Radu. You must hold on. My blood is flowing into you. You must hold on."

Nicholas and Mike watched the blood, Isabella's blood now, flowing out of his arm, pooling on the floor.

Gareth limped up to stand beside them. Isabella pulled the needle out of her arm, applied pressure. They all stood in silence, helpless, and watched Radu Ardelean die.

CHAPTER SIXTY-NINE

If you stand on the pavement outside the Royal Hotel on Whitby's West Cliff and look out across the harbour town as the sun goes down, you can pretty much see, in their entirety, the early chapters of Bram Stoker's *Dracula*. Across the bay, in the shadow of the half-ruined abbey, sits St. Mary's Churchyard, where Lucy Westenra was attacked by the vampiric count. Below is Tate Hill Sands, where the ship carrying Dracula ran aground, its crew missing, its dead skipper lashed to the wheel. The 199 steps, known locally as the Church Stairs, rise to the East Cliff, up which Dracula, in the guise of a black hound, ran after arriving in Whitby.

—*The Guardian*

Whitby, England, the Southern Coast
July 1890

The sea looked glorious and smooth as glass. The storm had passed, and the air felt light, as if anything was possible.

He sat on the bench and relaxed. He deserved this holiday, needed to rest and rejuvenate before his family arrived in a fortnight. He'd been exhausted by the work on his latest play.

After he'd moved into his rooms at Mrs. Veazey's guesthouse at 6 Royal Crescent, he'd gone out to ramble through the town, climbed the 199 steps to the ancient, crumbling abbey. He even wandered through the boneyard, touched by the graves—some of which had no occupants, the stones markers for those lost at sea—writing names in the notebook he always carried in his breast pocket. Finally, pleased, he took a seat on a bench and watched the ships at sail.

Something about this place intoxicated him. Perhaps he felt a certain oppression, a Gothic sort of darkness despite the cheery red roofs and the calls of the gulls over the water. It spoke to his creative mind, his heart. A fog bank rolled in, and he delighted in the sudden coolness, the droplets of moisture gathering on his mustache. He closed his eyes, content.

"Hello. May I?" He opened his eyes to see a stranger standing before him, a great white-and-gray falcon on the man's fist. Would she get lost in the thick fog if her jesses were removed? "Certainly," he said, and made room. "What a magnificent falcon."

"Her name is Mina. She is a peregrine."

He saw the stranger wore a leather gauntlet,

and when he said the bird's name, he put a chunk of raw meat on the glove. The bird gobbled it down. He asked, "Have you toured Whitby before?"

"Oh, I live here. Over there." The stranger waved a negligent hand toward the cliffs. "I am called Reuben Stow."

"I am Bram Stoker. It's a pleasure."

Stow asked, "You're up from London?"

"I am. I'm a writer. Well, and a producer, a financier."

Stow's eyes seemed to glow. He leaned toward Stoker. "You are?"

"I am. I wanted to spend some time alone, to relax, to let errant ideas slip into my brain, until my family arrives." He grinned at what he'd said, shrugged. "A writer is always on the lookout for ideas, for inspiration, I suppose."

Stow threw his arm forward, and the bird launched into the sky. She pirouetted in the air above them, the long stokes of her wings taking her out of the sea. They watched her dance in and out of the clouds.

Stow said, "Mr. Bram Stoker, writer, for your inspiration, I suggest you look in the Whitby library, at the end of the street below. There you will find a book written by a fellow countryman of yours, Wilkerson, and his travels will give you what you seek. It will spark your imagination, and the rest of the story will come to you then."

"What I seek? No, you misunderstand me. I'm not looking for anything."

"Yes, you are. A writer is always seeking. My beautiful Mina is a wonderful example. She seeks the hunt, fresh meat, the ability to fly and to sleep safely. I provide her with all of these, and so she stays with me. You, my new friend, are very much like the falcon. You seek a story, a story to make you famous. A story to both delight and terrorize. A story to make your friend Irving happy, yes?"

Stoker was unnerved. How did this stranger know this? He felt vaguely alarmed, not a little afraid.

"I suppose I am always looking for a good story," he said stiffly, and he rose. "Perhaps it's time for me to be off."

"I know a good story."

Stoker stopped, couldn't help himself. "You do?"

"Oh, yes. It is the story of brothers bound by blood. They walk the earth together, never at rest."

"Oh, I see. They're ghosts."

"No, no, not ghosts. They are something very different indeed. Something very old. It is the blood, you see. They have pages from a long-lost book that gave them the knowledge they needed to use blood as food. It's quite a gruesome tale. I can tell it to you if you like."

Stoker relaxed. He knew this sort of fellow. He would wait for his prey in the boneyard of the abbey, scare the tourists with a ridiculous tale, then demand coin. He was a modern-day bard.

Still, there was something about this man that made him uneasy, ran little skitters of alarm up his arms. Stoker stood. "I imagine it is quite a story. Sadly, it's getting late, and I must be off."

Stow looked away from him, out to the sea. He whistled once, sharp and low, held out his arm. "Good day to you, Mr. Stoker. Do not forget to visit the library. It is really critical to you and your career."

The bird landed hard on the man's fist. He gave her a treat and bowed his head toward Stoker, then stood and turned away.

Stoker shook his head, rubbed his eyes. Impossible. Impossible. It seemed from one moment to the next, the man and falcon were simply gone, disappeared.

He was tired from the journey, exhausted from managing Irving. He was hungry and thirsty, and now he was seeing things.

Yes, he needed a rest.

He took a last look around the abbey and started toward the stairs. Supper and sleep, and he'd explore the rest of the town in the morning.

He felt eyes on him, and he whirled back to look at the bench, at the grounds of the abbey, at the cliff, but no one was there. He saw a mist move through the boneyard, obscuring the gravestones. It moved toward him, closer and closer. He was frozen until the mist began to curl around his feet. As if released from a trance, he ran down the stairs, not looking back.

Later that evening, as he made plans to visit the town's library, he was compelled to record a name in his notebook—why, he didn't know.

Mina. And I will name my heroine Mina.

THE FIFTH DAY

SATURDAY

Dracula, a 1897 Gothic horror novel by Irish author Bram Stoker, introduced Count Dracula and established many conventions of subsequent vampire fantasy. The novel tells the story of Dracula's attempt to move from Transylvania to England so that he may find new blood and spread the undead curse, and of the battle between Dracula and a small group of men and a woman [Wilhelmina "Mina" Murray Harker—Jonathan Harker's wife] led by Professor Abraham Van Helsing. . . .

After Dracula learns of the group's plot against him, he attacks Mina on three occasions, and feeds Mina his own blood to control her. This curses Mina with vampirism and changes her but does not completely turn her into a vampire.

—Wikipedia

CHAPTER SEVENTY

We're coming to you live with breaking news. There was a bombing last evening outside the Prince Edward Theatre, resulting in the death of Corinthian Jones, Lord Barstow, prominent consultant to MI6.

"Also, a military helicopter was downed on the grounds of the home in Twickenham of the genius scientist and founder of Radulov Industries, Roman Ardelean. Mr. Ardelean is being sought by police to answer questions for a variety of charges, including the assassination of Lord Barstow last night. We start the news now."

CHAPTER SEVENTY-ONE

A feather-perfect hawk, sitting on a clean perch, with well-greased jesses and a clean leash, in proper accommodation, is a pleasure to behold. Hawks wearing poor and ill-kept furniture, sitting on filthy blocks and perches and in no proper accommodation are a disgrace to the falconer and, indeed, to the sport.
—Emma Ford, *Falconry: Art and Practice*

The Savoy Hotel
Strand, London

Roman Ardelean called Radu's personal line. There was no answer. He called Iago's phone. No answer. What had happened? Had he taken all of Marin's blood in his greed to be cured immediately? He called one of the house lines, but it appeared to be dead. He felt fear begin to thrum deep. And then he turned on the television to see his face plastered at the bottom on the newscaster's desk. And he heard about the helicopter crash at the Old Garden.

They'd found him. They'd found Radu. Where was his brother? Had they taken him into custody? How to find out?

Roman had killed Barstow, the sodding bastard, so that was something, but now he didn't care. Where was Radu?

Would they find him here at the Savoy? He'd used the Laurence Bruce disguise and a fake name. But they'd found out everything else. He listened to the news talk about the man with Lord Barstow, who had escaped serious injury—Harold Drummond, consultant to MI5.

He kept dialing both Iago's and Radu's private phones. Still no answer. He was worried, too, about his cast. He had instructed the cast to fly north to the estate, but Arlington refused to be parted from him. She'd flown to him last night without his calling her, her talons digging into his arm, drawing blood, and he'd had to smuggle her into the hotel under his coat. What did she know that he didn't? Did she have some sort of extra-sensory ability to sense danger to him?

She sat now on the back of a chair, her talons gripping the silk, watching the television, as he was. He'd ordered room service for them both, asked for pheasant, raw, and a juicy steak, rare. The hotel, circumspect as always, delivered both without comment. He was grateful for Arlington's steadying presence. He stroked her feathers, and she rubbed her face against his hand. He thumbed another dose of LSD onto his tongue.

He wondered if Barstow had confessed all to Drummond, if he'd admitted to his role in screwing over Radulov using Temora, and if Roman had met him at the Prince Edward Theatre, he knew he would be dead or in custody now. He had to assume that Drummond, that his son, Nicholas, that all of them, knew everything. He couldn't afford not to assume that. Where was Temora? Could he find him? Find out if he'd tried to warn him by sending the video, or taunt him? He didn't know. It didn't matter. In the end, Temora was the tool Barstow had used to destroy Roman.

He thumbed another microdose onto his tongue, then another. A strong, hard voice filled his head, *his* voice. *Screw Temora, he was always jealous of you, he was taunting you, not trying to save you. No, you have to save yourself. You have to save Radu.*

His company was in ruins, the stock price plummeting, his drone army was unpaid for, his brother deathly ill—ah, but they had Isabella and the pages. She would cure Radu. But it was time to flee. They'd take her with them, and she'd be his permanent blood bank. All would work out.

He thought of the billon pounds he'd never get now. Where had Barstow stashed the money? In foreign accounts, of course. He'd never find them.

Still, none of that mattered anymore. They were hunting him now. Why wasn't Radu or Iago answering their phones at the Old Garden?

Finally he tapped into the house server, on his mobile, only to find someone had locked him out. Of his own server. His own house.

What was happening?

He patched in through a coded back door they wouldn't be able to follow. From what he could piece together, Drummond, Caine, and a DI from Scotland Yard had dropped onto the house from a helicopter, and Roman's elaborate defense system had worked perfectly. The antiaircraft missile hidden in the chimney had shot down the helicopter. The guns, gauntlet, and oubliette had all been triggered. All his defenses had worked as they should. But what had happened? Had Drummond stopped Isabella from giving her blood to Radu? Worry clawed and dug deep. He thumbed another microdose to slow his heart rate, to allow him to think clearly.

The internal cameras mounted inside the walls of the house had never been used before, and he'd forgotten all about them, until now. Radu hated the lack of privacy, but Roman had insisted there be a way to check on him when he wasn't there, when he was traveling, or when he was hunting with the cast. In case something happened. In case he had a bleed and they couldn't control it. In case Radu felt the pressure of his loneliness and opened a vein.

In case.

What he saw he couldn't comprehend, couldn't accept, but it was true—the lab was in shambles. People—strangers—shifted through the room, in and out of the view of the cameras. Tyvek-clad, they seemed to dip and glide around the space, their dance making it look more like a Level IV biohazard lab, one that dealt with research on hemorrhagic fevers and other extreme-risk biological hazards. They moved as if in outer space, slowly, carefully.

At that moment, he knew he couldn't handle what he was about to see and slid two more tabs of LSD in his mouth to keep him calm, to keep him centered. To keep him distanced from this horror he was viewing.

He shut his eyes and allowed the drugs to take effect. When he felt his heart slow, and his breathing deepen, he reopened his eyes. Arlington watched him with great curiosity, love in her yellow eyes. As if she knew he needed her strength, she flew to the back of his chair. Her jesses trailed on his shoulder. She stood carefully, not allowing her talons to hurt her master.

Roman swallowed once more and looked.

His brother was small in death, curled on his side, his legs drawn up, like he had slept when they were children. They'd slept that way together each night, with legs drawn up to their stomachs, like two small commas back to back.

Radu was dead, Drummond had murdered him. Where was Isabella? Roman grew light-headed and so cold his teeth began to chatter as if it were he who'd lost his blood, not his brother.

He realized he was keening, like Radu when he was so upset he was beyond control, Arlington beside him, cheeping through her nose. Radu—losing him was something he'd fought against for their whole lives. He'd protected his brother, created a safe space for him, studied everything he could. Harassed, stolen, murdered—no life had been as sacred as Radu's.

Arlington cheeped again. He swung out his arm, and she went straight to the fist. He pulled her to his chest. His arm was a mass of scars from years of falconry—Roman didn't like the gauntlet, loved to feel the talons of his birds against his bare skin. But Arlington was gentle. She nestled her beak under his neck, and they stayed together for a very long time, the man lost in misery, the bird his comfort.

In the end, he stood, shut off the cameras so he wouldn't see them touching his dead twin.

He set Arlington gently back onto the chair and started to plan.

Run?

By himself? But for what? To save and rebuild his company? To grow old alone with only his cast?

Everything he cared about was gone. He was wanted now—he was the hunted.

He'd heard a legend that the lost pages of the Voynich were cursed, and that's why they were torn out. Did he believe the legend now? He thought again of all the people sacrificed in his search to find a blood match for Radu, all his intellect and enthusiasm he'd brought to bear on building Barstow's drone army. And now there was nothing left. Nothing at all.

Barstow, so high in the British government, one of their favored sons, had proved himself a self-serving greedy monster. Roman saw all of those arrogant cabinet members gathering together, scheming how to use him, to steal from him. They'd stolen everything from him.

He would not let them win.

Roman stood tall, brought the bird to his fist, looked deep in her yellow eyes. He walked to the window, drew back the blinds. The city sprawled below him.

"Are you ready, Arlington? We are going to burn London to the ground and dance in the ashes."

Arlington nuzzled his neck and cheeped.

CHAPTER SEVENTY-TWO

The Old Garden
Twickenham
Richmond upon Thames, London

Nicholas absently rubbed the wound on his side as he watched the team work. Mike had patched him up again, disinfected and rebandaged him. The first paramedics to come had taken Gareth to the hospital. They'd recommended Nicholas come as well, but he'd only shaken his head.

Isabella hadn't said much since Radu died. She'd been silent when the paramedics had removed the tubing from her arm, and applied a pressure bandage. She continued silent as they tended to Radu.

Nicholas knew she was in shock, but he wasn't concerned until she began shaking uncontrollably. He lightly laid his hand on her shoulder, looked up to see the second responding paramedic watching them. "Go with him to the hospital. They'll take care of you. We'll speak later, when you're ready."

He and Mike watched her be carried out in the arms of the medic, her head on his shoulder. She was accompanied by two Metropolitan Police officers to stand guard, just in case. Knowing Roman's resources, Nicholas didn't doubt he now knew his twin had died. And he would blame them. What would he do?

Nicholas immediately called his father's mobile, and to his profound relief, Harry answered immediately. "I'm all right, Nicholas, only a bit fried at the edges. You probably know what happened: a drone dropped a bomb on the Range Rover, nearly in front of the Prince Edward Theatre. Barstow is dead, and my driver, Higgins, as well. Before you ask, no, we haven't yet found Roman Ardelean. Tell me what happened at his house."

After Nicholas was done, his father was silent for a long time. Finally he said, "A tragic conclusion. But Isabella is safe and on her way to hospital. Now, Barstow told me a great deal more before the bomb. He confessed everything, but only because, I think, he knew Ardelean was going to kill him. I'll tell you the whole of it later, after you finish going through Ardelean's house."

"Father, wait. Why did Ardelean kill Barstow before he'd gotten the money?"

"Ardelean isn't stupid, he knew it was a trap.

But the biggest reason? He had to have found out it was Barstow who ruined Radulov."

"Others are working, Father. Tell me the rest of it. What did Barstow tell you?"

"He said he used a young man named Caleb Temora. You asked for the list of Radulov's terminated employees? Well, this man was on the list. He and Ardelean had a falling-out—he was recruited to ISIS. Barstow's people pulled him out a year ago. Barstow forced him to build the hack that spread the ransomware through MATRIX. I tried talking to Temora, but he isn't willing to play ball, as your mother likes to say. When you're free, I want you to question him."

"Where are you holding him?"

"He's jailed in a black-ops site in Mayfair. Listen, Nicholas, after all that's happened, and given Ardelean's increase in drug use, I can't imagine he's all that rational at this point. Revenge was more important to him. Wait." A moment later, his father said, "That was Adam. Evidently Ardelean stayed overnight at the Savoy. He must have conducted the attack on the theater from there. Ian and a team went to the hotel, spoke to the desk, and facial recognition confirmed. Ardelean was wearing a disguise and used a false name. Ian was told he was already gone. They searched his room, but all the team found were a few feathers—so one or more of his birds was there with him. Unfortunately, he's disappeared again. We have operatives at every known address, but nothing. He's gone to ground. Nicholas, I think events are moving too fast. Come now, speak to this hacker Temora."

"Give me an hour, Father. I'm stripping the computers to take to Adam to analyze, then we need to stop by Thames House. Get me the address, and we'll meet you there. And, Father?"

"Yes?"

He swallowed, cleared his throat. "I am very glad you're all right. Mum would have killed me if something happened to you."

"She very likely might have. Now you know how I felt when Barstow shot you." Harry laughed and rang off.

When Nicholas finished ripping apart the last computer, he joined Mike in the lab suite. "I see a lot of jars and bottles and test tubes. Any idea what it's all for?"

"This section is for synthetic LSD, I believe. They were manufacturing their own. There are large quantities of ergotamine and lysergic acid."

Nicholas read some of the labels. "Hydrazine, hydrochloric acid, sodium nitrate—yes, they were manufacturing LSD. All of the components necessary for the epibatidine are here, too."

"It's going to take hours to catalog all of this." She put a hand against his cheek. His face was still smudged with smoke, and his hair had dust and bits of debris in it from the roof. She leaned up and wiped her finger across his nose. "Ah, that's better. I've really smeared it now. Your dad's truly okay?"

"Yes. Adam found out Ardelean stayed overnight at the Savoy, but he's gone to ground. You'll like this—Barstow was apparently using a hacker who worked for Ardelean before they had a falling-out. Barstow used him to try and dismantle Radu-lov. We're going to go talk to him—name's Caleb Temora—as soon as you're finished."

"Oh, I'm done. Nothing more I can do here. Just curious why LSD, of all things." She cocked her head. "The two drugs we know they were making do have something common—they were both tested for mood stabilization and pain relief in the sixties. And microdosing is popular again, small doses stabilize your mood."

Nicholas said, "Evidently Ardelean was using more and more."

"From what I've read, too much and he'd go off the rails, lose objectivity, lose sight of what was real and what wasn't. And paranoia, to list only a few things that could happen."

"Isn't that all we need? A genius who's gone crazy." He waved the hard drives at her. "If you're done here, let me show you something else interesting—a pilot's nest for the drone system. Then we'll go talk to this Caleb Temora."

Ardelean's homemade air traffic control center was a room at the end of the long hallway. Nicholas pressed some keys, and huge screens whirred to life—aerial maps, weather forecasts, the flight paths of all of London, lit up in reds and greens. There was a cockpit, as well, facing the screens, with a huge gearshift. He said, "This is how they were flying the drones. Remote access—they can fly one from the other side of the world with this setup. It's military-grade, like our folks have. At least we know where the drones were being piloted from, and how."

Mike could only marvel. "To think this was in the hands of a civilian, practically in the middle of London. At least we can feel safe that the drones are grounded."

Nicholas said, "We can't know that Ardelean doesn't have another flight command." He studied the keyboard, said, "I think their pilot was Radu, and he's lying dead in the other room. See, all the software is coded to him. Unless Roman pilots them himself, which is obviously possible—" He shrugged. "At least we've shut down one level of his operation. Now, let's get these hard drives to Adam. I'd like a shower and some food. Then we need to go talk to this mystery hacker my father is guarding."

She followed him. "I want the MI5 physician to check your wound again."

He shook his head. "Not necessary, don't you remember? A medic went over me, pronounced me good to go."

"He did no such thing. He stared at you and shook his head."

"You know what I really want? A big, juicy American hamburger, maybe with cheddar on top, lots of onions—"

"Oh, be quiet. I know you, you won't eat or sleep as long as we have a drug-addled genius with a drone army on the loose."

"Sadly, you're right."

CHAPTER SEVENTY-THREE

The Federal Aviation Administration projects that by 2020 there will be 7 million small drones occupying U.S. airspace.

—*GCN*

MI5 Headquarters, Home Office
Thames House
12 Millbank
Westminster, London

Adam bounced up from his seat like a cork when they came into the room. "You guys look like you've been in a war. You okay?"

Mike patted his arm. "We're okay. We promise."

"Good, because that wasn't cool. Do you want to see the video of what happened?"

Nicholas nodded. "We missed something rather major on the satellite pass. I'd like to see where the missile battery was hidden."

Adam had the video queued up. He didn't tell

them he'd already watched it fifty times, heart in his throat every time.

He hit play. "Here's your chopper, comes in quiet, perfect, hovers. Mike goes down, and, as she does, look here. The surface-to-air missile came out of the chimney. It was disguised to look like a piece of brick. The whole section slides free, and it launches, a direct hit on the windshield of the chopper. We think it was on a motion sensor."

"Bloody hell."

"Exactly. Nicholas, there you go. Your jump coincides with the missile launch, and, as you can see, the helicopter goes ass over teakettle, barely misses Mike's head with the rotors, and flings you into the air as it flips, catapults Gareth to the edge of the roof, where he falls and you catch him, and goes down the building. Serious acrobatics ensue, and then Mike saves you and Gareth.

"I'm so sorry about the pilots. They didn't know what hit them, literally didn't change their speech patterns. It was so quick." His voice cracked, and Nicholas put a hand on Adam's shoulder.

"It felt like a thousand years up there. Thank you for this. Now." He dropped a waxed canvas bag in Adam's lap. "Here are all the hard drives from Ardelean's house and laboratory."

"Yeah, what was the laboratory about?"

"Manufacturing drugs. Epibatidine and LSD, for starters. But I'm sure there's more—there was an entire genetics laboratory there, high-end stuff. You let us know what you find, okay?"

"Copy that. You're heading to meet your dad? Here's the address. That's where they're holding the hacker Temora. And, guys? You've just aged me nearly a year, and I don't want to be twenty-one yet, too adult for me. So be careful, okay? Ardelean has to be royally pissed. I'll bet he plans to give a new meaning to being on the warpath."

Once Adam was alone again, he set up a pipe directly to Gray in New York, and the two of them began communicating through a separate, secure video feed. "How are the bosses?"

"They've been better. It was a long night. But they're both alive and in one piece, so that's an upside. Nicholas brought me all the hard drives."

"Good," Gray said. "How about we divide and conquer. You take half the terminals. I'll take the other half. See what we can find."

"Sounds good." Adam spent twenty minutes setting up all of the hard drives on their dedicated terminals before he started pulling data out of them as fast as he could. Gray, remotely accessing his half of the terminals, whistled quietly to himself.

"What are you seeing?"

"There's a lot here, Adam. Most of it is encoded—it's going to take ages to sift through it all. Definitely experiments, years of data. The chemistry is astounding. If they'd been doing this in a government or university lab, they'd be Nobel contenders. I count three separate genome-related medications that they've developed. Two didn't work in human trials, but the third showed promise. I assume that's what Radu had Mike inject into him."

"So when you say human trials—"

"Radu was the guinea pig. My God, he could have killed himself ten times over if any of this went wrong."

"This server is all artificial intelligence generating information on the Voynich manuscript. We're talking years of data and papers and footnotes. But the language itself—this is artificial intelligence at a whole new level. They were even starting to experiment with drones flown by AI instead of pilots. Now that's a dangerous thought. These guys are geniuses."

"Yes, they are. Imagine if they'd shared with the class. Here's yet another new programming language, but I've never seen anything like it. I can't make heads or tails."

Adam said, "That one I've seen. It's based on the Voynich. They used it to build a completely new system that would allow them to infiltrate every computer that houses MATRIX."

Gray whistled. "You know how dangerous that is? MATRIX is also on the servers at NORAD. And many other sites I wouldn't want to allow control of to a couple of whack jobs who've built a new world no one can understand. They can highjack anything, everything, at any time. Very dangerous."

"Radu is dead, Roman's in the wind, and we're responsible for figuring out what he might be up to. So instead of worrying, let's keep pushing."

Gray grinned. "Oh, how soon they grow up. I remember the days not long past when you would get yourself lost in the minutiae for fun."

"Yeah, well, you guys made me a white hat for real, so now I have no choice but to be serious about it." He went silent for a moment. "This scares me, Gray. I've never seen anything like it, and I've seen a lot. If they've shared any of this with their people at Radulov Industries, and there are people out there capable of hacking these systems, we have no control anymore. I mean, we have to put out an advisory that all government computers cease using MATRIX at once, do you agree?"

Gray nodded. "Yes, we do. It's a good lesson. We've never truly had control, my lad. We never have, and we never will. Wait, what's this?"

He pulled a folder onto the screen, double-clicked it. A series of schematic drawings appeared, layering one on the other. "This is exactly what I didn't want to find."

"What is it?"

"The blueprints of Thames House, River House, Buckingham Palace, Westminster Abbey, and Parliament, according to the labels. Detailed, thorough, and current. You better get Nicholas on the phone."

"Dialing him now. What do you think it means?"

Gray said, "Here's a lesson for you—always anticipate the worst. "

CHAPTER SEVENTY-FOUR

MI6 Safe House
Farm Street
Mayfair, London

On their drive to Mayfair, Mike chowed down on a bag of bacon-flavored crisps, well, really, chips, they'd gotten out of a gas station a block from MI5. She had a banana ready to wash it down. Nicholas drank coffee and ate a bag of vinegar-and-salt.

Mike upended the bag into her mouth to catch the last of the crumbs, then crumpled it and started peeling her banana. "Why can't we have these in the U.S.? It's not fair, Nicholas, really it's not. I mean the chips, not the banana. I've never seen so many flavors, but seriously, these crisps—chips—are incredible. Wish I'd grabbed two bags."

"I'll get you a whole case for Christmas, how's that sound?"

"Perfect." She scooted across the seat and put her head on his shoulder. "Please tell me we're going to catch Ardelean today. I don't know if I'm up for any more bombs or fires or guns."

"I have a good feeling about this meeting with Temora. Maybe he'll know how to get him or where he is."

Nicholas parked a block away, in front of a dark Jesuit church, and they went in on foot. The town house was a four-story tan brick with large-paned windows and wrought-iron Juliet balconies. The street was charming. Mike could only imagine how festive it would look at the holidays. Did Brits, she wondered, decorate for Christmas as elaborately as Americans?

She said, "Seriously nice place for a safe house." Nicholas nodded.

"Hide in plain sight. Always better."

They knocked, and the door opened. A stranger waved them inside. When the door shut behind them, Mike smelled chlorine, curry, and wood smoke. She saw a huge circular stairwell in front of them, very modern decor—minimalist and sleek.

Harry was waiting for them by the stairs. Father and son hugged each other, hard, then stepped back. They were men of few words, Mike knew, so she wasn't surprised when Nicholas went right to business.

"Where is Temora?"

"In the basement. This house is equipped for four prisoners at once, or a team of operatives. Right now, there's only Temora. There's a pool, a gym, a server farm, and a bomb shelter, too. MI6 does it up right."

"I'd like to speak to Temora alone."

Harry started to protest, and Mike shook her head, but Nicholas held up a hand.

"Trust me. This guy is a hacker. If we all go in together, he'll talk in circles just to piss the two of you off. I'll go in alone, hacker to hacker, see if I can get the real story from him."

Harry said, "Understand he's angry, Nicholas. Don't trust anything he says—don't take it at face value. From all I've found in Barstow's files, he plays games. We haven't yet figured out what he wants."

"Understood."

Harry walked them to the back of the house, where the glorious center stairwell gave way to a set of metal stairs with rails that reminded Mike of a submarine. They went down carefully and through a door into a metal hallway, where the claustrophobic sense of being underwater continued. The basement was unlike the upper floors—it was utilitarian, cement walls, and reddish lantern lights.

The interior of the prison was cool and felt empty. The cells were quiet. Nicholas had no idea who had been kept behind the thick steel doors, nor did he want to know. He'd left this world behind years ago, and it made his skin crawl to have to work his way back in, even for a short time.

Harry stopped in front of a steel door on the right of the hallway.

"We're right here if you need us. The mic is on in his cell. We'll be in the central room at the end of the hall, just there. Call out if there's trouble."

"Thanks. I'll be fine." Nicholas stepped through the thick gray door. He wasn't a fan of tight spaces and was relieved to see the basement prison was roomier than he'd expected.

A guard waited silently halfway down the hall. When Nicholas nodded, the guard opened another thick door, and Nicholas slipped inside, ignoring the crawling sensation of being locked inside a steel cage.

The man sitting on the bench was thin, pale, and his head hung low. His long, lank hair hung around his face. He raised his head, and Nicholas saw the fierce, burning intelligence in his eyes.

Temora wasn't more than twenty-five. He was studying Nicholas closely. Nicholas didn't move, didn't speak. Finally Temora said, "You're Nicholas Drummond." He sat back, crossed his arms, and said with a sneer, "So the big man's come to gloat."

"If you know my name, then you know me better than that. How did you end up here? Held by Security Services? Tried to go to the dark side, did you?"

"I did no such thing, and those bastards upstairs know it. I'm innocent."

Nicholas sat down across from him. "Come now, Caleb, a private messaging system built expressly for ISIS operatives says differently. If you'd warned our government about the latest attacks, perhaps they'd believe you weren't working for the other side."

Temora shook his head, his long hair swinging back and forth. He muttered a curse, then said, "Do you have any idea how hard it is to serve two masters?"

"No. Because I've never thought there were two masters to serve, only one. Our government."

Temora looked away, licked his cracked lips.

"Water?"

After a moment, Temora gave a tiny nod. Nicholas looked up at the camera in a silent demand. A minute later, there was a knock at the door, and a bottle of water was handed in. Nicholas cracked the top and gave the bottle to Temora, who drank it down in a few gulps.

"Thank you."

"You're welcome."

"Care to tell me why the bloody hell you're here, Drummond?"

"I'd like to talk about an old friend of yours. Roman Ardelean."

Nicholas could have sworn Temora sneered.

"I figured."

"I need to know how to stop him, Caleb. He's killed four important people here in England, not to mention a couple of dozen innocent people across Europe. He's planning something. An attack of some kind. We need to know what it is."

"I haven't talked to that egomaniac in years. I have nothing for you."

"You know him better than we do. You worked for him, earned his trust—he respected you. Barstow forced you to hack into his company's computer systems. You're our best chance at stopping him right now, before he burns down the city. You help us, and I'll get you out of here."

"Talk to his freak of a brother. He knows him better than I do."

"His brother is dead."

Temora's eyes narrowed. "You say Radu Ardelean is dead?"

"Yes."

"Did you kill him?"

"In a way, I suppose. I was part of a raid on Ardelean's house to save a woman he'd kidnapped, a twin like himself, who could read and speak Voynichese. Unfortunately, there were complications. He bled to death."

"Well, it's a bloody miracle he made it this long. It's taken serious cash to keep that man alive. His hemophilia was off-the-charts bizarre, nothing in modern medicine touched it. Imagine not being able to close off a vein, unheard of. I thought it really wasn't hemophilia at all. Something else—"

"How about something in not-so-modern medicine?"

"You mean Roman's ridiculous idea that the Voynich held the key to curing all of Radu's ailments? Yes, I know all about their attempts to find the missing quires.

"If Roman and Radu could truly read the Voynich, then they must be the only two on the face of the world. I couldn't read it, and I can read any code."

"It's not a code, it's a language. Only certain twins can read it."

"Yeah, yeah, so you said. Do you know I even saw the original manuscript? Barstow had it stolen from Yale. Ah, I see you didn't know that. Here's another freebie. The original Voynich is at his house, in his safe. He bragged about it."

"Thank you. Whatever else the Ardeleans believed, they trusted the instructions in the manuscript to cure Radu, that and the right blood."

"I don't suppose you know they also used it as the basis for their encryption, believing they were the only ones who knew the language and so no one could ever crack their systems?"

"I do, actually. Tell me, you can't read the Voynich, yet you cracked their systems?"

"I had a leg up. Being on the inside of the company was a help for Barstow's mission, wasn't it? They may have been crazy, but Radu and Roman knew how to design bulletproof code."

"How'd you get in, then? If it's bulletproof?"

"Drummond, you of all people know all code is designed with a back door. I simply opened the one I'd left behind and walked in. Made their lives a living hell for a bit."

"Does Ardelean know you went into ISIS as an operative?"

"Of course, he always could find just about anything he wanted to know. But he couldn't catch me." He shrugged. "Sure, I helped them out for a while, but I didn't like it, too strict for me, the violence too senseless. I'm an anarchist, not a zealot."

"How did you manage to send me the video of you and Barstow? And why?"

"Barstow had planted a camera in here—look over your shoulder." Nicholas looked up, saw the red eye beaming down on them. The exact view in the video. "When I agreed to screw around with Ardelean's code, Barstow gave me a computer. Piece of cake to send out a video, telling all. It was time to out the old bastard."

"It helped, thank you." Nicholas said nothing else, waited, waited, and Temora started up again.

"Look, I have no idea what Roman's planning. I can't help you."

"I think you can, Caleb. You said it yourself. He has a bone to pick with you. The moment he finds out you're involved, he's going to come for you, and he's going to make you wish you'd died in one of those coded hellholes you crawled out of. He is bent on vengeance against everyone he feels is responsible for ruining him and killing his brother. He has the tools to accomplish this, too."

"Yes, he does. His software resides on ninety percent of the computers in the free world. A few keystrokes and he could shut it all down: power grids, air traffic control systems, satellites. Without phones and power, money or food, the world would descend into chaos. He could close the doors of the grocery stores and open the doors of the prisons. He is omnipotent."

"So he controls the computers. What else does he have?"

"What else does he need?"

With a brief glance at the camera and a raised eyebrow, Nicholas said, "He has a weaponized drone army."

Temora started to laugh, shaking his head. "Amazing, absolutely amazing, but I'm not surprised, not really. Roman has this strange patriotic streak in him, wants to wipe out terrorism, arm poorer countries. So he did it. I wonder why Barstow never told me."

Nicholas shook his head. "I'm asking you nicely to tell me what you think Roman's going to do next. He's already killed Barstow. Is he going to run? Hide? Or attack?"

Temora's eyes lit up. "He killed Barstow? Good

for him. I wish I could have killed the old monster, but I couldn't." Temora paused, then said, "I'd say Barstow was pretty close to being crazy, crazy evil. You want to know what's sad? The old bugger believed all the lies he spewed."

"Where is Ardelean, Caleb? What does he plan to do for revenge?"

"Sorry, I swear I don't know what his end game might be. But whatever it is, it will be big. Huge. Since you people killed his brother, he's not going to run. He's going to come after all of you with everything he's got. It's always personal to him. Very, very personal."

CHAPTER SEVENTY-FIVE

Upstairs, Nicholas put a frozen pizza in the oven while Mike pulled together a quick salad. Then he, Harry, and Mike sat at the table and ate, discussing their next moves.

Nicholas said, "There's one thing I believe Temora about. Ardelean is going to come after us. He already has twice, no reason he won't try a third time. If he blames us for his brother's death, then we're in twice as much danger. We have to find him."

Mike swallowed a bit of pizza. "Let me call Adam, see if he's found anything yet."

She put her cell on speaker when Adam answered. "Gray and I were about to call you. Sorry, guys, we don't have good news. The blueprints for several major London landmarks were on

Ardelean's hard drives. Maps, detailed information, insider stuff, things not available to the public. Seems he used his connections to the servers to lift all the information he could possibly want."

Nicholas asked, "So how many possible targets?"

"There are eight different spots around London that he's done epic amounts of research on. I'm talking all the major tourist destinations and government buildings. It's going to take us a while to find out if there's one he's favored over another. He still may try to kill you guys off one at a time, or he may focus on a single huge attack. We don't know yet. He's up to something, regardless."

"Get back to it, Adam. Find everything you can and send it our way."

Nicholas patted his mouth with a napkin, stood up. "Come on, Mike, let's go talk to Isabella. She might have heard something, seen something to help us figure out what he plans next."

Harry said, "I'll keep talking to Temora, see if I can't sweeten the deal. If he gives me anything, I'll let you know."

When the door shut behind them, Nicholas realized the sun was dropping behind the mews. They stood in ready silence on the stoop for a moment, listening—no drones above them.

Nicholas pulled on his leather jacket, and

they started down the street, back toward the church.

Mike saw a garden along the way, chestnut and limes lining the sidewalks, the leaves full and deep. White flowers sprinkled the beds like dropped pieces of cotton. The evening felt calm, and still. There was no one around, only the distant sounds of traffic.

Nicholas glanced at the pink sky. "I didn't realize it was so late. The car will be waiting on the other side of the church. Let's cut through to the hospital."

A man's deep voice said from the shadows to the left, "And ask that lying bitch why she let my brother die?"

Mike's hand went immediately to her weapon. Roman Ardelean said very quietly, "Don't even think about it." But she didn't pause and she was fast, her Glock out in instant. Even as she opened her mouth to tell him it was over, he said in that same quiet voice, "Tsk," followed by a strange word that sounded like *Obține*.

Mike felt a flash of air and a sharp sting in her hand. Her Glock clattered to the ground, and the tail of a falcon disappeared into the tree-lined street. She started to duck toward the weapon, but the bird took the corner at speed, turned in her wings, and shot between her and her Glock like a missile.

The voice from the shadows called out,

"Stop. Arlington does not approve of weapons. She's been trained to take down drones, but she sometimes acts on her own where handguns are concerned." He turned to Nicholas. "Wise of you to stay still, Drummond. I believe she would go for your eyes."

Nicholas said nothing, stepped quickly to Mike to see her hand was bleeding. He said to Ardelean, "A handkerchief to staunch the bleeding," and he slowly pulled one from his breast pocket. As he did, his other hand reached for the gun under his arm.

"Now, Drummond, do be careful where you put your hands."

Nicholas didn't move. "Are you too afraid of us to show yourself? All you have going for you is a killer bird?"

Ardelean stepped from the shadow. He was wearing dark jeans, a black T-shirt, and leather jacket, and on his wrist sat a falcon. He held no weapons, only the bird. Nicholas knew he could pull his Glock and kill the bird in a heartbeat.

Ardelean said, "You invaded my home and you killed my brother. However, you have given me what I wanted, so treat this as a warning. Stop. Go home."

Mike said, as she pressed Nicholas's handkerchief to her hand, "If we stop, will you stop? Murdering people for their blood, killing Dr. Marin's fiancé for no reason at all, killing Alexander and Vittorini, Hemmler and Donovan, not to mention sending your drone after us and the train?" Her hand throbbed and burned. The talons had dug deep.

Ardelean said, "Your brains are so . . . limited. You see and understand so very little. Yet again, I have found that true of so many of my fellow human beings. Then there are the corrupt greedy ones, like Barstow. You may leave now, talk to Isabella, ask her why she failed to save my brother.

"Drummond, if you take one more step, Arlington will tear out your eyes and then your throat. She's hungry. We took down a rabbit earlier, but she's at her flying weight and fast, and I need to feed her more." He paused, looking back and forth between Nicholas and Mike. "Will you never learn—"

Nicholas sprang. Ardelean tossed the bird forward, right at Nicholas, but the falcon didn't go for Nicholas's face, it veered off.

Ardelean was ready. He slammed Nicholas's leg with a roundhouse kick, smooth, fast, deadly.

So he was trained in martial arts. But Nicholas was, as well.

Could Mike get her Glock before the falcon attacked her again? She had to try. She grabbed it off a patch of flowers and turned to shoot, but Nicholas had already fought him back into the trees, his hands a blur, his fists hitting Ardelean's forearm, his leg striking down toward the man's thigh with such force he almost lost his balance when Ardelean managed to jerk out of his way. He punched Ardelean in the breastbone with his palm, making the man stagger backward, but he was on Nicholas again, his fist in his kidney.

They were well matched. Mike was afraid to move closer—the bird was perched on a limb right above her head. They were too close: she couldn't take a chance shooting Nicholas.

Mike suddenly had a clear shot. She brought up the Glock, and the bird, screaming, hit her arm as she fired. The shot went low, splitting a branch from the tree. The bird turned on Nicholas.

Ardelean disappeared into the trees. The bird screeched and flew after him.

"There, there!" Mike called to Nicholas, pointing.

Ardelean was in a full-out sprint, heading west, through the gardens, past iron benches, the bird circling back to cover his retreat. They gained on him. Ardelean suddenly turned and shouted out that strange word again—*obține*. The falcon whirled into motion in front of them, wings out, attacking with a shriek.

Mike threw up her arms to protect her face and lost sight of Ardelean as she fought off the bird. Nicholas grabbed it by a tail feather, going for its jesses, but its sharp feet were no match for his flesh. The bird dug in, launching herself into the air off Nicholas's battered hands, wings beating hard as she flew away.

They were suddenly surrounded by silence, the city around them holding its breath. "I don't know which way he went," Nicholas said, turning in a full circle, then stopping and listening. Nothing.

Mike was bending over, panting. "I should have shot it, but I just couldn't make myself do it. I'm an idiot."

A heartbeat later, a motorcycle roared to life.

"There, he's on a bike. Go, go."

She started to run, but Nicholas grabbed her arm. "No, Mike, we can't get him now." She looked up to see his nose was bleeding, and he had a small cut above his right eye. Mike's hands were bloody, her arms cut from tree branches and the bird's talons.

"I should have shot that wretched bird, I should have—"

He lightly touched his finger over her mouth. "It's all right. Ardelean's already too far away. We'll never catch him."

"Nicholas, what did he mean that this was just a warning because we gave him what he wanted?"

Nicholas felt fear ice his belly. "Listen."

The unmistakable whir of a drone's rotors.

Nicholas yelled, "The safe house. He's going to attack the safe house. He must know about Temora!"

As Roman sped away, his bruised ribs began to throb. He looked up to see Arlington, flying overhead, always watching him.

"All is well"—and he laughed. He used his headphone to make a call.

"Do it," he said.

CHAPTER SEVENTY-SIX

They hurried back to the safe house, eyes to the sky.

Harry opened the door, stared at them in shock. "What happened? Are you all right?"

"*Father, Ardelean wants to kill Temora. He's going to send a drone to bomb the house. We have to get him out now,*" and Nicholas bolted for the basement door. Harry sounded a silent alarm that Mike saw start to flash on the wall, a blinking red light. She could feel the house come to life under her, heard shouts as Nicholas reached the cells.

And then she heard the unmistakable sound of a drone and a loud whoosh.

She threw herself toward the basement stairs, pulling Harry with her, the two of them tumbled down the metal staircase, just as the missile burst through the ballistic glass window and exploded in the sitting room.

The concussion made her eardrums pop. She cried out, felt blood start to trickle from an ear. She realized she and Harry were tangled together at the base of the metal stairs. The flashing red light strobed over Harry's face. His eyes were closed, blood snaked down his face. "Oh no, Harry!" Vaguely, as if she were underwater, she heard Nicholas shouting for her. "I'm okay! I have your dad. He's hurt."

He was there in a heartbeat, first gave her a quick once-over, then touched the blood on his father's head, over his right ear. "Dad, can you please wake up?"

Harry's eyelids fluttered, and Nicholas let out a shaky breath. "Tell me you know who I am."

Amazingly, Harry smiled, not much of one, but it meant everything to Nicholas. "Ah, are you the prime minister? Come, Nicholas, I'll live to fight another day."

Nicholas gave a laugh. "Good, but we need to get you out of here. I smell smoke coming from upstairs. There's a back door. Dad, can you stand?"

Harry managed a nod. "There's a back door." He was weaving as Nicholas pulled him up. Mike felt wobbly herself. Her ears hurt, and she had the oddest sensation of vertigo every time she looked to the side. It was odd, but her hands didn't hurt anymore.

"Nicholas, look."

They saw flames licking the opening to the basement. "Let's collect everyone and get out of here."

Temora was in the hallway between the two guards she'd seen earlier, eyes wide, scared to death.

"What do you want us to do with him, sir?"

Harry managed to say, "We're all going out the back door, Connor. Bring him along. And take care."

Temora said more to himself than to them, "Why is Roman attacking me, trying to kill me? I helped him. I let him know Barstow was using him. I sent him the bloody video, showed him what Barstow was really like, that old monster. He should be thanking me, not trying to kill me."

Nicholas paused only a moment. "You said it yourself, Caleb. With Roman, it's always personal. You betrayed him, and he never forgot it."

Nicholas led, holding up his father, the guards followed with Temora, and Mike took up the rear, ears ringing, keeping her weapon up. At the end of the hall was a steel door, and, farther down, another. They secured the doors behind them as they went, and within five minutes, they were stepping up a flight of metal stairs into the garden off Farm Street.

Nicholas said, "Connor, take Temora to Thames House, to MI5. Keep him safe. We'll take Harry to hospital."

Mike watched the skies for birds or drones, but it was quiet, business as usual, trees ruffling in the night breeze and pigeons cooing.

The car that had brought Harry was back on the corner, waiting. The driver, a seasoned MI5 agent, didn't miss a beat as they bundled Harry into the back seat. He said, "Let me tell you it's good to see you all alive. The house is burning, coppers are all over the scene. Mike, you're bleeding, too, there's a kit in the back of the seat. We're going to get blasted in the news for this one. Where to, Mr. Drummond?"

Harry said, "Take us to Chelsea and Westminster Hospital."

Mike closed her eyes. Everything hurt, even her eyebrows. She heard Nicholas speaking to his father, assuring himself that he was all right. Then she felt Harry take her hand.

"Thank you, Michaela, for saving my life."

CHAPTER SEVENTY-SEVEN

Isabella was drifting off to sleep when a knock sounded on the door.

"No more needles," she called out.

"How are you, Dr. Marin?"

She opened her eyes to see the female FBI agent who'd come to save her. Her blond hair was in a ratty ponytail, and she wore black-framed glasses. From twelve feet away, Isabella could see dark bruises on her wrists and arms, see how pale she was, the thick white bandage wrapped around her hand.

"What happened?"

Mike knew her voice was too loud because of her eardrums, but who cared? "Well, let's see. Since I saw you last, a crazy falcon attacked me, Ardelean shot a missile into a house I was in, and I fell down a flight of stairs." She came forward. "My name's Michaela Caine, special agent, FBI. But none of this compares to what you've been through—may I call you Isabella?"

"Yes, please."

"I'm Mike. Now, tell me the truth, how are you feeling?"

"I guess I'm okay, really. I keep telling them I'm fine, but they won't leave me alone. A missile? Like the one they used to shoot down the helicopter?"

"Yes. Don't worry. No one else was hurt."

Isabella licked her tongue over her dry lips. "It seems like a nightmare now, like something so horrendous it really couldn't have happened. But I know Gil is dead—at least in my head—but not here yet." She touched her heart. "I know Radu is dead, too." She swallowed tears. "Does Radu's brother know he's dead?"

"Yes, he does. And unfortunately, we can't find him. But we do know he's a very angry, out-of-control man at what he now sees as absolute betrayal. It doesn't help he's probably over the edge on all the LSD he was taking. He's out for revenge. He blames those in power because they sent a team in a helicopter, namely us, to his home to save you, and Radu died. He blames all of us, really."

Mike saw Isabella was trembling. She stepped to the hospital bed and touched her shoulder. "All you went through, it was horrible, all of it. I don't know everything Ardelean did to you, but still, Isabella, you tried to save Radu. No, no, his death wasn't your fault. You were heroic. But what about the Voynich?"

"It was about a recipe in the Voynich, part of it in the missing pages that I had. And it was about blood and how to combine them. What do you know about the Voynich manuscript?"

"One of my teammates was in art crimes, Agent Ben Houston. He worked the case when the Voynich was stolen from Yale. You met him, I believe. With Melinda St. Germaine?"

"Oh, yes. Was that only a couple of days ago?" She shook her head in wonder. "It seems like a decade. Agent Houston was kind and knowledgeable."

"I know no one has ever been able to translate it or decode it—so tell me."

Isabella nodded. "The Voynich tells the story of the illegitimate line that started with Vlad Dracul's half brothers. I've pieced together what I can and I think one of the twins was ill, an affliction of the blood. They tried to cure him—with herbs, with baths, but they didn't know how blood worked. And so, when the brother Andrei bled uncontrollably and weakened, they came up with the idea to replace the blood. So Alexandru, the stronger of the two, found him blood to drink. This wasn't quite that clear in the manuscript, but I believe it's close enough.

"The Voynich manuscript is a record of their conversations about how the experiments were going. Roman and Radu both read and speak Voynichese. They've brought those two long-ago brothers into the present. Radu is—was—a brilliant scientist. Very strange, because of the limitations of his illness, but brilliant. The experiments he was doing were completely out of the box. The equipment—sorry, you already know this. Did Radu want me to give him all my blood? He wanted so much to live, as did Roman. Perhaps I would have survived for a while, depending on how long they would allow me to replenish my blood. Was I the match they'd been searching for? Yes, I believe so. Roman killed so many people, primarily Romanians, searching for a match. I think Roman made Radu into a monster."

Mike shook her head. "No, he valued himself, his own life, over anyone else's, including yours. He called you his blood sister, yet, if it came down to it, do you think he would have hesitated to exsanguinate you rather than accept his own death? None of it was right, Isabella. All of it was centuries-old madness.

"Your physician told me they'd drugged you, there were still traces in your blood."

"Oh yes. After all the initial terror, whatever the drug Roman gave me made me feel wonderful. I wasn't afraid any longer, even when they wheeled me in and hooked me up. I wasn't even afraid when I saw my blood flowing through the tube into Radu's arm."

Mike said, "Did either of them mention where Roman lived when he wasn't at the house with Radu?"

"They have some estate up north, where Roman takes his birds." She shuddered. "He let one of them feed on my stomach. I will have the scars forever."

Mike couldn't imagine. "I'm sorry."

"I'm alive," Isabella said. "Without you, I'd be dead."

Mike merely nodded. "Tell me about the missing Voynich pages you found in the British Museum. Isn't that why Ardelean kidnapped you in the first place? To get those pages, to complete his recipe for Radu?"

Isabella stared at her, then shrugged. "You're going to think I'm crazy."

"Try me."

"Okay. Maybe back as far as the time of Vlad Dracul, pages were ripped out of the manuscript. At some point, the pages were separated from the main manuscript, and moved from place to place. Where, I don't know, until a young girl saw a man bury the pages under a rowan tree in Eastern Poland, back in 1912, I think. She was part of a large Romany tribe camped close by. She dug the pages up and took them back to the camp and showed them to my great-great-grandmother, Kezia. She was also known as the Old Princess. She could read the pages and prophesied twins of her line would come and they would read them and re-unite them with the great manuscript, as she called the Voynich.

"Their stories were passed down to me. My sister and I were the first twins in nearly a hundred years. But my sister died when we were four years old. It was then I told my mother I heard the pages weeping.

"She and my father believed the pages would drive me mad, so they buried them in a lead box so I couldn't ever hear them again. There's more, of course, but eventually, after my mother's death, in her will, she told me where to find the pages."

Isabella studied Mike's face. "You might be-lieve me mad, but it's the truth—even before I unwrapped the pages, I heard them singing to me, talking to me, and yes, crying. And I knew I had to reunite them with the great manuscript.

"But someone had stolen the Voynich from the Beinecke at Yale the year before. If I'd known in time, I would have stolen it myself. Instead, I came up with a plan. I pretended to find the pages and made a big announcement, praying the person who'd stolen the Voynich would come after the pages. I wanted him to come.

"I had a gun. I was ready." She shuddered. "But it all happened so fast. I accepted Gil's mar-riage proposal and this Dr. Laurence Bruce, really

Roman Ardelean, showed up at the front door." She swallowed. "Only he wasn't the one who stole the Voynich."

"No," Mike said, "he wasn't. Actually, it was a very bad man named Corinthian Jones who stole it, as leverage, to use on Ardelean. We even know where it is—in his safe."

Isabella's eyes flashed. "Do you know where the loose pages are too? I know Roman had them that night."

"I don't know, but I will alert everyone still at the house to look for them."

"Are you going to put me in a straitjacket?"

Mike flashed back to the Koh-i-Noor diamond, its magic, its prophecy, and slowly shook her head. "I've seen and heard so many strange things this past year—well, let me say if we're talking straitjackets, they'll have to get two, one for each of us." She leaned down, smoothed a hand across Isabella's forehead. "Before the Voynich is returned to Yale, you can reunite the pages—yes, I know we'll find them—with the great manuscript." She paused, then said, "The Old Princess, that's a lovely name.

"Now, can you think of anything to help us figure out what Ardelean might do?"

Isabella shook her head, said instead, "Thank you for saving me."

Mike nodded and walked to the door. Isabella's voice stopped her.

"Wait—I remember he did say he had plans, big plans. Something to do with a shipment and a man named Barstow. I only heard bits and pieces of the conversation, and something about it was time for this program to come to light. He was going to give the world a show. I don't know what program he meant."

Mike said, "I do. Thank you, Isabella."

CHAPTER SEVENTY-EIGHT

Mike found Nicholas and Harry in a treatment room inside the A&E—accident and emergency—wing. Harry sported a butterfly bandage on his temple and was in a full-blown argument with the doctor, who wanted to admit him for observation overnight.

"No, absolutely not. I passed the concussion protocol, and I have things to do."

Nicholas said to the harassed doctor, "You aren't going to change his mind, I'm afraid. I'll make sure he doesn't exert himself."

The doctor handed them the discharge papers, and Mike heard him calling them mother hens as he walked out past her. She waited until the three of them were alone to say, "Isabella confirmed Roman's been killing and exsanguinating men and women, primarily Romanian, all over Europe, hoping they might be a match to Radu, for a cure. He's the Vampire Killer. She told me some other things, too, about the pages and the Voynich, how it came down to her. It's all very strange."

Nicholas said, "You and I, Mike, strange always seems to find its way to us. Now, one mystery solved. You'll get that news to Penderley so he can start the proceedings with Interpol?"

"Already texted him."

Harry, shrugging on his smoky, dirty jacket, asked, "No ideas from her where Ardelean might be or what he might be up to?"

"She says no, outside of overhearing him tell his brother a shipment had arrived and he was going to bring the program to light."

"The drones," Nicholas said.

"Probably. But how, and when? She didn't know anything else, and I believe her. To make her cooperate, he threw food on her stomach and sent a falcon for it." She told them the rest, Harry asking questions, many of which she couldn't answer.

Harry said, "We all need food and sleep, and no more drone or falcon attacks. Ideas?"

Nicholas said, "The Connaught?"

Harry nodded. "Why not? Ardelean can't be scoping out all the hotels in London, can he? I'll get us a large suite, have Adam and Ben meet us there. I'll put it under the name Oliver Kittredge." He chuckled. "They'll know what to do."

Mike yawned, and her ear cracked. Her head cleared. "Finally."

"What happened? You okay?"

"Yes, it was my ear. It's been hurting since the safe house exploded. I'm fine. Sort of tired, that's all. Let's get ourselves to the Connaught. Is it a fancy place as befits the two of you?"

The three-bedroom suite at the Connaught was beautifully appointed, with a marble fireplace, exquisite blue velvet sofas, and floor-to-ceiling living room windows looking over the sleeping occupants of Mayfair. They set up the computers on the dining room table and ordered fancy pizzas, club sandwiches, warm tomato basil soup, a whole cheesecake, and a separate order of fish and chips for Adam, who swore he wasn't going to eat anything else for the rest of his life.

Melinda joined Ben and brought news from Downing Street. "The U.S. president's trip is not going to be canceled. He'll be showing up tomorrow as scheduled. First stop, Downing Street, then a press conference at Lancaster House. Then he'll do Buckingham Palace, then he speaks to Parliament. A private dinner is last on the agenda, at Winfield. I'm telling you, every stop is a target. We've warned them it's not safe, but he's stubborn."

Nicholas laughed. "You don't know the half of

it, Melinda. Mike and I learned that the hard way at Camp David."

"Problem is," Adam said, chewing a fry drowned in vinegar, "every single place except the dinner is on the list of blueprints we found on Ardelean's hard drives. So Ardelean could be planning an attack on any of them."

Nicholas said, "Or none of them. Bringing the 'program to light,' and what else did Isabella say, Mike?"

"Give the world a show." She took a sip of soda, continued. "Look, he's lost the one thing that mattered to him, his brother. And he believes everyone in the government is responsible, and that includes the prime minister. He could fly a drone up to 10 Downing Street and shoot off a missile right through the windows like he did at the safe house, and no one could stop him."

Harry said, "He wants to give the world a show—and to me that means he wants to make a big splash, make a definitive statement, kill as many people as he can. And the sites with the extensive blueprints are the most likely targets."

Ben asked, "So then, what do you think would bring him the biggest bang for the buck? Buckingham Palace or Parliament?"

Melinda said, "I forgot—they're going to be having a barbecue at Buckingham Palace, like they did with President Obama. It will be outdoors. The PM and the president, manning the grill."

Nicholas jumped up from his seat. "That's it. Adam, bring up the plans for Buckingham Palace. What better way to show off his army than attacking the president and the prime minister, and blowing up the Queen's house?"

CHAPTER SEVENTY-NINE

Sky News
London

There are now more allegations against Corinthian Jones, Lord Barstow, who died last night in a bombing near the Prince Edward Theatre. We've received information that detail an array of allegations, from money laundering to sexual harassment to coercion and entrapment. The list of names involved is long. Many of them are dead after being attacked over the past few days, and we are endeavoring to separate allegation from fact.

"As you already know, we at Sky News are not going to release charges until we're able to confirm the leaks to us are real, and these we will report as we get them.

"Meanwhile, a home in Mayfair was destroyed today, where witnesses say the residence exploded. A gas leak is given as the official cause. No one was injured in the blast, and the fire has now been put out. The owners were on vacation in the Seychelles and say the house has been empty for the past few months.

"In other news, the U.S. president comes for his first state visit tomorrow. With a long and busy day, Londoners can expect road closures and other annoyances—"

CHAPTER EIGHTY

A 2012 study, published in the journal *Cell Biology*, analyzed genomic data from 13 Romani communities across Europe. The researchers concluded that the Roma people left northern India about 1,500 years ago; those Roma now in Europe migrated through the Balkans starting about 900 years ago. These data confirm written reports of Roma groups arriving in medieval Europe in the 1100s.

—*Live Science*

Florida
One Year Ago

Nadia lay in a dream sleep. She heard people moving around, speaking in quiet voices, occasionally touching her, but when they bothered her, she simply willed herself to sink deeper in this luminous place where anything seemed possible. She let the years and the decades sweep her back like a slow, gentle tide. She saw faces, some making her happy, others not. She smiled when she recognized her great-grandmother, so old, her face so seamed by the sun, she looked like lovely old leather. She loved to tell Nadia the favored story back in the olden days when Elena, a young girl in their tribe, had come upon a man burying something beneath a rowan tree. It was in Poland, yes, before the tribe moved back to Walachia. Elena's parents had come to Kezia, who was called the Old Princess, with the pages, and she gave thanks when she saw them. She'd formed the strange words in her mind, then spoken them aloud to all, and showed them strange red and green pictures, had taken a stick and used it to scratch more of the strange plants and figures in the sand next to the fire pit. No one understood the words or the strange drawings, but all marveled at her gift, for she was above and beyond them. She told them the pages were from a great manuscript.

Nadia knew the story so well, passed down from mother to daughter for two generations. The Old Princess had prophesied that one day, special twins would be born into the family, twins who would read the strange words and understand the strange drawings. But Nadia's mother hadn't given birth to twins, only to her, Nadia. And the Old Princess had died at nearly ninety years old. Before she breathed her last, she'd whispered again to Nadia's mother, "Wait, wait."

She floated through the years, her memories, watched her mother grow ill and die, saw herself young, limber, very talented, a gymnast for the Romanian Olympic team, and she was very good at it, winning, always winning. But then she'd wanted to leave Romania, to be free, and managed to be granted asylum in the United States. She moved to Florida, a flat land of endless sun and water, but she missed the mountains of her birth.

Years, decades, floated like clouds, showing her mother's memories, maybe others' memories too, and she'd catch one and linger and savor. She saw Jackson's hard face, a man of few words who'd loved her deeply, but she saw he was sad because Isabella's small twin sister, Kristiana, had died. He and Nadia had wept together, though he'd said little. Time rolled forward, still slow and easy, but she was aware of its passing, aware of herself in the passage of time. She saw herself sitting on a sandy beach one lonely day, half-watching Isabella play in the warm ocean. She saw the Old Princess, heard her say clearly, as if she were but a foot away, "I told your mother there would be twins, but there weren't twins for her. But it was you, Nadia, it's you who birthed twins, and they will listen and hear the pages speak and sing and cry to be reunited to the great manuscript."

But Kristiana was dead. Nadia, the floating

Nadia, didn't say anything. Isabella was still a twin even though she was now alone. And then she knew what she had to do. She saw herself young, still supple and vigorous, pawing through an ancient trunk in the attic of that small house in Florida, finding the box that still held the linen-wrapped pages, all of them torn on the edges, all save one that someone had cut from the great manuscript.

She'd shown Isabella the pages and soon regretted it. Her daughter read them easily, as the Old Princess had, and she'd made drawings like those on the pages, only the colors weren't ever right, no matter which ones Nadia bought. Isabella said they were about plants and medical sorts of things she didn't understand. She said the pages spoke to her, they sang to her, and they cried for what they'd lost. And her daughter continued to read the strange words, deep into the night, the pages becoming an obsession.

And Nadia, that anxious young mother, feared for Isabella's sanity, for the little girl grew withdrawn. That long-ago Nadia had grown frantic, as had Jackson. He'd wanted to burn the pages, but Nadia could not—they'd been passed down from the Old Princess, generation after generation. To her. To Isabella, a twin.

She saw herself, unable to destroy the pages, and she looked down from where she glided above and watched herself as a young mother bury them in a lead box so Isabella couldn't hear them calling to her, crying to her.

Then, coming through a seam in time was the Old Princess Kezia, and Nadia saw herself trying to explain, telling her over and over she wanted to protect Isabella, that her precious child was going mad and it was because of the pages. She saw the Old Princess, heard her speak, her voice hollow and so very old, even in that lovely dream sleep, and she saw a soft breeze that surely wasn't really there softly ruffle her snow-white hair around her face.

Nadia said to the Old Princess, "Isabella is a young girl, not of the same ancient superstitious world as you. In this modern world, there are no ties to magic or mysterious words or languages or unknown drawings."

Where had the Old Princess gone? She drifted, seeing things and people from a great distance or up close, it didn't seem to matter. Some of them were deep inside her, locked away forever, her memories of them soft as long-ago sunlight on her face.

When had Isabella become enamored with the Voynich manuscript? Then there came the day, that single day, so clear she wondered if the Old Princess had sent it to her now, in this soft, wonderful place where nothing bothered her, where nothing could really touch her, the day she'd told Isabella, "The pages, they're lost, gone forever. You must forget. Forget."

She lay there, as if cushioned on soft white clouds, saw herself begging Isabella to swear she would never tell anyone she could read the great manuscript, the Voynich, promise, promise, because Nadia knew it would lead to tragedy, and Isabella had agreed.

Nadia saw the Old Princess hovering beyond her, and she turned and saw her old wrinkled face had smoothed out. She nodded and whispered to Nadia, "Do not be afraid, my beautiful one, soon you will be with me. Soon, but first you must tell Isabella where you buried the pages. She is the only one to reunite them to the great manuscript. You cannot fail, my beloved, you cannot."

And for some reason no one at the hospital could explain, Nadia Gabor Marin came out of her morphine-induced coma and asked to write another single line to her will. And she wrote in a surprisingly strong hand to Isabella where she'd buried the loose pages and page 74.

THE SIXTH DAY

SUNDAY

Westminster Bridge is 252m long and 26m wide. It's an arch bridge with seven iron-ribbed elliptical spans; the most spans of any of the Thames bridges. Westminster Bridge was painted green in 1970 to match the seats in the House of Commons, the part of the Palace of Westminster closest to the bridge. Lambeth Bridge, further upstream, is painted red to match the colour scheme in the House of Lords.

The first Westminster Bridge featured semioctagonal turrets at intervals along the crossing to provide shelter for pedestrians. But these cloistered cubby holes soon became haunts for vagabonds, muggers and prostitutes. In the end, 12 night watchmen had to be hired to guard travelers as they crossed the river.

—LONDONIST.COM

CHAPTER EIGHTY-ONE

Air Force pilots near Las Vegas can fly drones 7,500 miles away in Afghanistan. The Air Force has 65,000–70,000 people working to process all the data and footage it's currently collecting from drones.

—*Forbes* Magazine

Drone Flight Facility
Warehouse on Thames
North London

The room was pitch-black, the screens lit with tracers of red and green, like a demented Christmas decoration, overlaying on a topographical map of central London. There were five pilots at the ready, hands on controls, and the drones were amassed on the makeshift runway, the camouflage canopy stretching for hundreds of feet above them, sheltering the fleet from prying eyes. Roman needed to get them in the air and keep them low, away from the radar so they wouldn't be seen before he was ready, before it was too late.

Cyrus Wendell, captaining the fleet, said quietly, "You were right, sir. The threat worked. They changed their plans, no more ridiculous barbecue at Buckingham. They'll all be in Parliament, as you wished. Where will you be, sir? We wouldn't want a mistake."

"No, we wouldn't, Cyrus. I'll be on the boat, with the cast. It will be their first major exposure to the full army in a city environment. I want to be able to guide them until we arrive."

To the pilots, Roman gave a different speech.

"Gentlemen, this is a watershed moment for our company. We've been tasked with building the biggest threat detection system in the history of Britain. Our drones will protect the skies of this city, will be used to stop attacks on our homeland by the people who hate us, who wish us dead. You are the front line of defense for your country. Be proud."

There were cheers and applause. They were patriots, they were thrilled to be a part of this program.

Ardelean continued, "The plans are set, the flight paths programmed, all you need to do is get them in the air and the program will take over and fly them on instruments. You will only be needed if the drones go off course, or if it looks like one might be taken. Then, and only then, will you be allowed to take them over manually."

"Copy that, sir. We're ready for the final test run. All circuits are go."

"Then let's fly."

He patted Cyrus on the arm, Cyrus, his one trusted employee, the one who knew he'd lied to the pilots, who knew very well this wasn't a test, that there was no way to take the drones off their course once it was set, that Roman alone had control of their flight paths.

Roman headed for the dock. His fifty-one-foot Bladerunner speedboat awaited, and the cast was aboard, hooded, sitting on their cages, their flying jesses already on. Arlington stamped her feet; she was ready to get in the air.

He started the engine and heard the drones spark to life as well. He set the telemetry in his ear so he could keep track of the cast.

This is for you, Brother. We come from the skies; we come from the water; we come to hit them in their most vulnerable place. We will kill them, as they killed you.

Roman unhooded his falcons. They were hungry; they were ready. He stroked a wing here, a head there, making sure they all felt his touch. Arlington cheeped happily. She was excited, ready, and the rest of the cabal wagged their tail feathers in response.

Roman smiled at them, his beloved children. "It is time, my lovelies. Conserve energy. It will be a long flight. Now, fly."

CHAPTER EIGHTY-TWO

The Connaught Hotel
Carlos Place
Mayfair, London

Nicholas woke with a sense of unease he couldn't shake. Something was wrong, but what? The sun was up. Mike lay next to him on her back, one arm flung over her head, her beautiful hair spread across the pillow. He lay still, thinking, reassessing everything they'd done.

Mike sighed, rolled over, and saw he was awake. She raised her hand, touched his shoulder. "You okay?"

"Something's worrying me, and I can't figure out what it is."

"We spent half the night warning people and planning for every contingency."

"We're missing something, I know it."

She leaned up to kiss his whiskered cheek. "Every law enforcement official in London will be on high alert today, Nicholas, all eyes focused on the president and the prime minister. Everyone is ready if there's an assassination attempt."

"No, no, there's something we're missing."

"We'll be at Buckingham Palace for the barbecue. They have fighters ready and sharpshooters on the roof to take down any drone that tries to dive-bomb us. Secret Service will be all over the president and the prime minister. We're only backup today. Now, do you want some breakfast? I saw some waffles on the menu and you know, I'd kill for waffles. Maybe with some strawberries on top." She touched her fingers to his shoulder. "Nicholas, we do the best we can." He said nothing. Mike looked around, saw her nightgown draped over the bedpost and pulled it over her head. Still, he looked preoccupied, worried, rather than looking at her, very unlike himself.

"Come on, Nicholas, maybe they can make you a frittata as good as Cook Crumbe's at Old Farrow Hall. Who knows when we'll be able to eat again."

"I don't want the president at risk at all. I want to find Ardelean before he has a chance to send a drone or one of his falcons." He shook his head at himself, lifted the phone, and placed a breakfast order, with lots of strong coffee.

When he hung up, Mike had slipped from the bed and was headed to the shower. He watched for a moment, smiled at the incredible wild hair around her head and the rest of her, then got up and walked to the window to stare out at the city. Roman Ardelean was out there somewhere. He'd told them they would die if they didn't go home.

Nicholas joined Mike in the shower.

They drove to Buckingham Palace in three separate black Range Rovers. Today Mike saw nothing but bright blue and an incredible shining sun overhead, the cold rain long gone. A perfect day for a barbecue.

She felt a shiver, leaned close. "You were worried this morning we'd missed something. Well, now you've got company, I feel it, too. Something isn't right."

"I don't suppose you know what it is?"

Nicholas's mobile rang. "Melinda, is something wrong?"

"No, no, the schedule changed. No announcement. We'll be going to Parliament instead of doing the barbecue at Buckingham Palace. The Queen will be there, too. She'll be speaking to the House of Commons, about Brexit, as well as the president and the PM."

"When did the schedule change, Melinda?"

"This morning sometime. We were just called to session. I don't know the details. I'm assuming they finally listened to us, decided to keep everyone indoors instead of parading them out under the clear blue sky for target practice. Or they got a threat, and that caused the change of venue. I don't know."

Nicholas looked at Mike. "It's a right relief. Good for you. We're on our way."

The cars did a turn and drove back toward the Thames.

Mike said, "You know what? It would take serious armament to get into Parliament."

Nicholas said slowly, "True, but I wouldn't put anything past Ardelean."

The Carriage Gates, where another attack had taken place, was smothered in security. They weren't subtle about it, either—no less than twenty SWAT-geared officers, along with a bevy of armed officers and regular Metropolitan Police. Tourists were forming a line across St. Margaret Street, in Parliament Square. Nicholas remembered his first visit to Parliament with his grandfather when he was three years old. He'd been overwhelmed by the incredible rooms, one after the other, the sheer opulence, the huge golden building, glistening under a bright sun, just like today. *The seat of all that was right and just*, his grandfather had told him, and he'd never forgotten. *In theory*, his grandfather had added. Nicholas hadn't forgotten that, either.

Nicholas studied the crowd. "Visitors to this city always do have a keen sense of something about to happen."

"Nowadays everyone is so hypervigilant when

they see a bunch of law enforcement, they assume something's happened or is being prevented from happening."

"It looks secure. Where do you want to set up? Inside?"

She shook her head. "Honestly, I am much more worried about security outside than in. Ben can go inside with Melinda and your dad. Let's stay out here. I'm sure Penderley's people will be happy to have you around."

"Maybe. I agree about our staying outside—we can keep watch."

They were expected. The Range Rovers were ushered through the gate into the courtyard, then thoroughly examined. When all was clear and they were out of the cars, Nicholas and Mike looked immediately at the sky. They saw nothing of concern. Ben trotted up.

"Ben, Mike and I are going to stay out here. You're our extra layer of security inside. If anything feels off, don't question, yell out."

Ben nodded, passed out comms. "Adam is monitoring everything. If there's trouble, you'll know." Mike put hers in, tested, heard Nicholas and Ben loud and clear.

Adam said, "Good morning, lady and gentlemen, the temperature is twenty degrees Celsius and the skies are blue—a magical surprise. All is nominal on the field. Play ball."

They all laughed and split up to their stations. Mike and Nicholas watched Ben and the rest of the team head inside the massive Parliament building. Nicholas saw his father pointing them out to the guards at the doors, knew he was letting the men know they were to be allowed inside, without interference, should the need arise.

Mike asked, "If something happens in there, do you know how to get to them?"

"Oh yes. My grandfather has spoken in the House of Lords a number of times. I used to be allowed days off school to come watch." And again, he remembered his first visit.

"I sometimes forget one day you'll be Baron De Vesci, a peer of the realm, and wear a wig and talk on the floor."

"Let's all pray by the time that happens, they will have done away with the wigs. Come with me, I want to show you something."

They listened to their comms as the updates from Ben came in.

"The Queen has arrived."

"The PM and the president are here."

"The session is starting."

"All is well, they're speaking."

"Estimate we'll be done in fifteen minutes and on our way out to the terrace for the reception."

Mike followed Nicholas out of the courtyard,

to the Thames and Westminster Bridge. They were
under the shadow of Big Ben for a moment, then
they were walking out onto the bridge.

Nicholas pointed to the canopied terrace of
Westminster. She saw guards patrolling.

"Last year, a security assessment found terrorists could get from the river into the Commons
Chamber in less than five minutes. A resilience
test. It was a massive failure, or a massive success,
whichever side of the fence you're on."

"You'd think they'd secure this area first. I see
only a dozen guards. Anyone could come up with
a boat—"

"—or a drone." He shrugged. "I know I'm
being paranoid, but for some reason, it still doesn't
feel secure, it's—"

"Nicholas, look! There, at ten o'clock."

They saw a dense cloud moving toward them,
impenetrable, like a thick fog bank spilling down
the river. Only it wasn't a cloud. Nicholas tapped
his comms, shouted, "Alert one, alert one! A sky
full of drones. Ardelean is coming!"

She vaguely heard the responses and calls
begin, everyone going on alert. Mike watched the
mass grow closer, heard the massive whine of thousands of rotors.

"Go! Go!" Nicholas pulled her from the rail,
but she couldn't help it, she looked back as they
raced across the bridge toward the Parliament
courtyard.

They saw a nightmare. The cloud was becoming more detailed as it drew closer. Soon they saw the birds, then the drones of every size, rotors whirring, flying in lines ten drones wide. They were being led down the Thames by Ardelean's falcons, flying in a V, and Mike would swear the lead bird was the bitch who'd attacked them yesterday.

She heard shouts and looked west, more drones, coming in fast, and from the east and south, even more.

She saw the water churning beneath the northernmost cloud of drones. She pointed, pulled her weapon.

"Look, Nicholas, the speed boat. It's Ardelean! He's leading his army."

Mike started shooting at the boat, emptied her first magazine before Ardelean got within range.

"We're bloody surrounded!"

Her heart sank. There was no way to win this fight, and she knew it. It didn't matter, she slapped a fresh magazine in place, yelled in her comms, "We need as much air power as we can get out here. Every weapon needs to be trained on the skies. The drones are coming in too fast for us. We need real armament."

She heard voices, shouts, orders. She shut her eyes, praying, then started firing into the sky.

CHAPTER EIGHTY-THREE

Hot metal rained down as bullets hit drones. Mike, Nicholas, SWAT teams, armed police, everyone was shooting into the sky.

Nicholas slapped an M4 into Mike's hands, and she went down on one knee beside him.

"Nicholas, the terrace, look! They're wiping out the security there." They ran toward the center of the bridge, dodging the barrage of bullets, the grenades. Her ears rang with the incredible battle sounds, the screams, and her eyes watered at the acrid smell of smoke. She jerked at his arm. "Nicholas, how do we stop them?"

He yelled into his comms, "Alert one, be advised Ardelean is coming in from the river, through the Terrace Pavilion entrance!"

Harry shouted, "That leads to Westminster

Hall! We are barricading in the Commons. They've activated the security protocols, everything's being shut down. There's no way he can get in here. What's happening out there?"

"The drone army is killing everyone in sight. Ardelean is controlling them."

"Nicholas, look. The birds."

Ardelean's cast of falcons was flying the length of the terrace, swooping, diving in and out like bats after mosquitos, and several smaller drones joined them, patrolling. Mike could see the bodies of the guards now, their blood spilling into the Thames. She yelled into her comms, "Terrace, all guards down! All guards down!"

Nicholas said into his comms, "Father, we can't come from outside. Those drones will tear us apart before we get anywhere near them. We're going to have to get to him from inside. How do we do it?"

"Nicholas. Do you remember the tunnel? I showed it to you a long time ago."

"Yes, yes, I remember."

"We'll be bringing the president and the PM out that way, but be careful. No one's used the tunnel in almost a century."

They took off toward Big Ben. The sky was dark with smoke, fires raged along the edges of the building. There were bodies strewn on the ground amid smoking chunks of drone. First responders were racing into the nightmare scene, police firing into the sky. They saw a double-decker bus on its side, people crawling out through broken windows, heard screams, crying, and bullets, so many, deafening. They were in the middle of a war zone.

Finally, they heard the throaty whine of a Typhoon jet. Nicholas yelled, "Military is here, thank all that's holy."

They raced past Cromwell Green and the Old Palace Yard, down St. Margaret Street, running hard, to the corner, to Millbank House.

They dashed inside, badges out so the security wouldn't toss them to the ground, ignoring shouts and cries of "What's happening?" They pushed through the crowd of people who'd taken shelter inside the stairwell.

Nicholas pulled open the door, and they went down, and down, and down again.

"Nicholas, where are we going? What's this tunnel?"

"There's a tunnel between the two buildings, in case of emergency. It's ancient, shut down after World War II. Part of it collapsed. It wasn't deemed safe."

Mike said with absolute conviction, "It'll be safe enough."

He sent her a mad grin, led her through the basement to a dark, cobwebbed corner to an old, wooden door with a gleaming lock and a NO TRESPASSING sign.

"Step back." Nicholas shot off the lock. He

kicked open the door, and a great gust of dust hit them in the face.

Nicholas coughed, choked out, "If the tunnel's not blocked, we'll be able to pass under the Chancellor's Court, just off the Peer's entrance. The terrace pavilion is on the opposite side of the building. You ready?"

"Let's go."

He took a small Maglite off his vest and shined it into the darkness. "Careful. There's still rubble and who knows what else in here. Watch your step."

She nearly stumbled on a pile of rocks, righted, and jumped over a huge chunk of timber. The air was dank, smelled of long-ago dirt and long-ago death, entombed and left to rot.

They dodged and ran. Nicholas swiped a spiderweb from in front of his face.

He grabbed her as she stepped down on a chunk of wood and her foot rolled. She knew immediately she'd hurt her ankle, but it didn't matter. She took a step and another. "I'm okay, keep going."

Adrenaline masked the pain enough so she could continue on. It hurt, it hurt a lot, but no choice. She moved with him forward, ever forward, into the darkness.

"Here, at last," he said, and started up a decrepit metal flight of stairs. They were three stories down, she counted over one hundred stairs, aware of pain tearing through her ankle, and then the door was in front of them.

It was locked. Nicholas banged the door, shouted, "Father? If you're there, a little help, please."

With a massive creak, the door opened. There stood Harry Drummond, backlit by the interior of Westminster Palace. "Took you long enough."

Nicholas grinned and stepped through, pulling Mike with him.

They scarcely heard the battle rage outside— the walls were so thick. The room wasn't large, but it was clean, neat, and, at the moment, full of a dozen very serious men and women bristling with weapons. Coming toward them, surrounded by guards, came the Queen. They hustled her into the dark tunnel without a word. The president went next, cocooned by Secret Service. He stopped when he saw Nicholas and Mike.

Nicholas said, "Sir. It is good to see you again, though I apologize for the circumstances."

"Nicholas, Mike. I always wondered about an escape hatch from Parliament." And he shook both their hands. "You two will take care of this, won't you?"

"We will, sir," Mike said.

A Secret Service agent nudged the president. "We must go now, sir."

The president gave them a salute and disappeared after the Queen into the darkness.

The prime minister was right behind the president, his security detail herding him toward the tunnel. He stopped, though, said, "Good luck," before they hustled him into the dark.

Harry slammed closed the door behind them, barred it. Nicholas helped him move the tapestry and furniture back into place. "Everyone's together in the Commons Chamber, including Ben and Melinda. We assume Ardelean is in the building, but we don't know where."

Nicholas said, "By the looks of the firepower he had, I'm betting he came in through the Terrace Pavilion. He must expect them to take the Queen, the president, and the PM out that way. He probably knows exactly what sort of security protocol would lead to that scenario and created it. He wouldn't know about the tunnel, though. No way. It's not on any blueprint."

Harry gave them fresh magazines for their weapons. "Then let's go get him."

Mike looked behind her as they left the small, beautifully furnished room. No one could tell that the still-vibrant Flemish tapestry of a medieval hunting scene covered the entrance to freedom.

CHAPTER EIGHTY-FOUR

The Palace of Westminster—Parliament—
was built on the site of William the Conqueror's first palace. Rebuilt in Victorian
times as a Gothic fantasy palace, it is an
eight-acre jumble of buildings, courtyards,
passageways, and corridors. There are 100
staircases, more than 1,000 rooms, and three
miles of passages.

—BBC.com

Parliament
London

Roman knew all doors to the building would be
heavily guarded, knew the biometrics would
shut them all, making those inside feel they were
safe. He also knew his Night Hawks would be the
hardest weapons to defend against once they were
inside, and he had a computer program installed
that would open all the locks and let him move

anywhere in Westminster Palace he wanted. He'd shut down their cameras, shut down their fire suppression systems.

He owned Parliament now.

The drones had worked perfectly, taking out all the exterior river guards. He thumbed a microdose onto his tongue, waited a moment, felt the punch of it, thumbed another. Barstow was dead and that gave him a shot of pleasure. But Barstow was only one of the dissolute powermongering monsters who believed they could do anything, betray anyone, and get away with it. They believed themselves immune from justice, above any laws they themselves had made. They—his own government—had killed Radu, and now they wanted to destroy him, and after all the technological advantages he'd provided them, the drone army he'd gladly built to help shut down terrorism. All a lie, a joke. Betrayal rang in his head, gnawed in his belly, and he fought back a scream of rage. No, no, another microdose to steady him.

His heart was pumping hard, his brain sparking with power, tunneling the world, making it narrow to a pulsing red point. It was time, time to prove who and what he was. It was time for payback.

He held out a fist, and Arlington came to land. He nuzzled her head, and she cheeped at him.

"Tired, my love?"

She cheeped again, agreeing with him, he

knew. "I am, as well. We're almost there." He gave her a grouse neck from his jacket, and went inside Westminster Hall, the drones and birds buzzing all around him.

It was almost quiet, if you could call the panic of hundreds of people silence. He knew everyone was looking out at his birds doing their mad dance before they dive-bombed the windows, scaring the people inside to death. It was a deception he'd learned from them. They loved to distract, to get their prey ready to move in the wrong direction. A game his falcons played when they were hunting on the estate.

Enough fuss outside, and he would be able to slip in the back.

He could smell smoke, feel the concussions of the missiles outside. He couldn't keep up the onslaught forever; he would eventually run out of ammunition. Once it was all gone, the drones were programmed to divert back to base—if they survived the attack, of course. And these degenerates, these self-serving criminals, he would punish them, kill them all. What made him so confident was the fact they didn't know his limitations.

He knew in the event of an emergency, Parliament had procedures in place for everything—fire, bomb threats, biological attack, suspicious packages—you name it, they had procedures, procedures, procedures, endless lists of procedures.

He knew exactly what security was doing inside Parliament. They needed to get the PM out of the building, but since there was a war raging outside, the normal procedures couldn't be followed. They'd try to get him out another way or secure him inside a designated room. Roman knew they'd conclude the PM—and hoorah!—the bloody president of the United States, and the Queen—well, he did feel a bit of remorse about killing her—would all be safer inside. And he knew exactly where they'd be taken. He also realized getting through security would be hard, even with his drones and Arlington.

So, he'd make them come to him.

He pressed his comms and said to Cyrus, "Now!"

One of the drones flew into the hallway and disappeared. Moments later, a huge explosion rang out, so close and loud the birds shrieked. Roman laughed.

He didn't want to kill them with the bomb, no, but he knew they'd make a break for it the moment the room filled with smoke and they'd have to leave, and they'd come right to him. He wanted to look at the prime minister, the head of the monster, the one ultimately responsible for the mission to kill his brother. He wanted to kill him, face-to-face, like a man. He stood in Westminster Hall, a vast empty space, once the center of British justice. It made him laugh at the irony. This time he would mete out justice. He was prepared, the drones hovering and ready.

He waited, listened, stroking Arlington's head. Normally he would hood her, but he wanted her ready, needed her keen senses to alert him.

It didn't take long. He heard them coming, heard the voices, the calls, and readied himself. He'd blocked all other egress points from outside with drones. They had no choice but to come to him, from the Commons Chamber where they huddled to the small waiting room for guests that connected to the library and into the great hall.

He slowed his breathing, calmed his pounding heart. Once he killed the PM, his prime target, he wanted to kill Nicholas Drummond. He'd led the team that killed Radu.

They were coming closer, the voices louder now. He pulled two Night Hawks from his vest, set them on the floor, set the needles in place, and started their engines. They whirred into life, rose into the air. He used his wrist to position them, one above him, one on the opposite side of the entrance.

This was almost too easy.

CHAPTER EIGHTY-FIVE

That was a bomb! What's Ardelean doing?"

Nicholas said to his father, "He's driving them. He thinks security is following protocol and taking the president, the Queen, and the PM to the river."

Harry said, "So if he came in the Terrace Pavilion, he might still be there. Let's go. I'll follow you."

Nicholas hit his comms. "Ben, you have Melinda safe?"

"I do. Go ahead. We're fine here. The drones are still attacking, but the worst is over. There are some inside buzzing around, but we've been shooting them down. It's like the Wild West in here. Sounds like the response outside is knocking those back, too."

"Copy. Adam?"

"I'm watching the terrace, but I don't see him. Parliament's internal security system isn't working—he's jammed the cameras. Oh yeah, Ardelean punched in a program that's halted the subway cars in their tracks. The entire tube system grid is offline."

Nicholas closed his eyes at that news, imagined the chaos underground. Nothing he could do about it. "Okay, Ardelean's here, I can feel him."

They started off at a jog. Mike was limping, couldn't help it, and Nicholas pulled up short.

She said, "Let's go, it's nothing. I twisted it back in the tunnel. Go, Nicholas, we don't have time to waste."

His warrior. They set off again, Mike on his heels, gritting her teeth against the pain.

The terrace pavilion was on the opposite side of the building. Security was thick, but, with Harry, they quickly passed through every checkpoint. It took ten minutes to get to the terrace, with its stunning view of the river. They saw falcons and drones still swooping and diving, but not attacking.

"You're right. He's here. The birds are waiting for him."

Nicholas took them to a door tucked away in the corner of the Commons Library. "If I'm right, he's going to be on the other side of this door."

Harry said, "He'll have those small drones with him."

They heard the loud voices of people coming. Nicholas quickly called Ben. "Keep everyone back. Stay in the Commons Chamber."

"Too much smoke, people are freaking out. We need to get them out."

"Then don't come toward the river. Lead people south, toward the House of Lords. And watch out for drones."

"Copy that."

"Okay. Now, we need a diversion."

Mike pulled a thick book from the nearest shelf. "Sir, is this one really important?"

Harry shrugged. "They're all important, but it's better than sticking our heads in."

The terrace river entrance was on the bottom floor. They crept down the library stairs, into a kitchen that fed onto the terrace, Mike with the book in her hand. At the door to the terrace, Nicholas raised his hand. He took the book from Mike, waited for her to get into position with her Glock, her back against the wall. An M4 would be better, but it would be too unwieldy in the tight space. He motioned his father to stay back.

Nicholas put a hand on the door handle, signaled with his fingers *three, two, one*, then threw the door open and tossed the book into the dark space beyond.

Mike came through right after him, her gun up.

It was dark, too dark, but she heard the faint whir of a drone. She shot toward the sound, into the dark, and the whirring stopped.

One down.

She heard the flap of wings and was ready when the falcon slammed into her. She struck it in the chest with her fist. The bird wheeled back, not hurt, but surprised. Suddenly there was light in the room, the switch turned on by Harry, and they saw Ardelean wasn't there.

And then Nicholas realized where he was. "Westminster Hall, he's in the hall! He's got a whole army of drones with him. He was trying to herd everyone there. Up the stairs, up the stairs!" Nicholas took off, straight up the stairs into Westminster Hall.

Ardelean was standing with his back to them, arms spread wide.

Above him, motionless, were hundreds of drones.

His falcon saw them, though, and shrieked a warning. Ardelean turned slowly, stared at Nicholas.

He said, "Drummond, how nice of you to come before all those rapacious grasping criminals come flooding in here, believing they'll be safe from me. It saves me the trouble of tracking you down. Do you know, I believe it's time for you to die. Like my brother."

The small drone moved into position by

Ardelean's shoulder, but before it could fire, Nicholas shouted a command at the falcon, a word he'd overheard Ardelean scream to his falcon that made it attack Mike.

"Obține! Obține!"

The falcon wheeled in midair and went after the small drone, shrieking, talons out. She whipped the drone to the floor, then flew after another, then another, before dropping to the stone floor, exhausted wings spread. She looked to her master for a reward, confused when there was no fresh meat coming.

Instead, Ardelean screamed in rage. "No!" He yelled for the falcon to attack, but the bird faltered, confused by two masters yelling at her.

Ardelean pulled a stiletto and hurled it at Nicholas, but Mike shoved Nicholas hard. The knife struck deep into the wall an inch from his head.

"No!" Roman screamed again, a death cry, and came at them.

"Stop!" Mike yelled at him.

But he didn't. He was no longer thinking, he was a missile set on his course.

Nicholas fired, catching Roman in the throat. He spun in place, then crumpled to the ground almost at Nicholas's feet.

Nicholas yanked the wrist communicator off Roman's arm and smashed it to the ground, stomping on it for good measure.

The drone army dropped to the floor.

"Arlington," Roman whispered, the name slurred in blood frothing from his mouth. The bird flew to his side, cheeping, hovering over him. His arm lifted, and Arlington stepped onto her master's fist for the last time. He stroked the bird once, then his hand fell to his side. His head fell backward, his sightless eyes staring at the ceiling.

No one moved as the bird began to keen, a sound that made the hair on their necks stand up. They watched silently as the bird hopped on her master's body, paced up and down, nudged his head, his arm, flapping her great wings, as if to protect him. She looked back at Nicholas for a moment, and he would swear he saw something primal and vicious in her eyes before she hopped forward, and her sharp talons ripped a chunk out of Ardelean's throat.

EPILOGUE

One Week Later

Mike suffered the boot, no choice. Her ankle was fractured, not badly, they said, only a hairline crack. But it still hurt like blue blazes to walk on, so they gave her a pair of crutches. How long for her ankle to heal? Not all that long, they said, and after telling her to keep weight off it, sent her on her way—released her into the wild, Nigel said, when he saw the ridiculous boot that marched up nearly to her knee.

It hurt to look at herself in the full-length mirror in Nicholas's bedroom because all she could see was the boot, black as her dress, so that was something, certainly better than candy pink. No, she wasn't a pretty sight.

Nicholas and Nigel came into the room. Nigel stopped in his tracks. "Ah, you look fetching, Mike."

Fetching? She'd like to smack him, but, with

the boot, she couldn't move fast enough. "I look like an idiot. Come on, Nicholas, you need to man up and tell the truth."

Nicholas said simply, "You look like a hero."

"That's correct, Mike, your badge of honor," Nigel said as he handed Nicholas his jacket.

No, not a jacket, a morning coat. Nigel patted down his shoulders, stepped back. "Very nice indeed."

Nicholas gave him an incredulous look, shot his cuffs, and walked to stand beside her. Together they studied their fading bruises.

"It's the Arnica balm," Nigel said. "The bruises are nearly gone."

True enough, but the bruises were the least of it. It was the lingering nightmares, Mike knew, filled with mechanical birds shrieking, their razor talons ready to strip off her face.

At least the real falcons had been sent from both of Roman's estates and given to a falconer in the Lake District, who was reprogramming them. They were far, far away. Even so, she shuddered. "I'm going to have bird phobia for a while."

"It will pass." Nicholas kissed her temple. "As for myself, I can't seem to step outside without studying the sky for drones. Still in all, we survived. We're quite the team, don't you think?"

"Yes," she said. She eyed him up and down. "I'm thinking you could introduce your morning coat to the New York field office, set a new style."

"My Glock wouldn't fit well under it, alas. Now, Agent Caine, I lie not. You do look lovely."

She licked her lips, stopped, she didn't want to ruin her lipstick. "Well, okay, I'll admit it, I'm nervous."

He kissed the tip of her nose. "The Queen already loves you for saving her life, and the PM, and the president, not to mention Parliament. It's a great honor, Mike. And it's important for the country for us to be acknowledged. My father has been informed by Her Majesty's secretary that she is very pleased to knight me and dame you. He said the investiture had already been set up, but Her Majesty insisted we be added."

"Do I have to be a dame? What does that even mean?"

"You'll make a great dame."

She punched him in the belly, and he obligingly grunted. He saw her color rise. Excellent, she'd forget her nerves soon enough.

He swept her up into his arms and carried her down the stairs, Nigel following with her crutches.

No nerves now, she was poking his shoulder and laughing, and so was he.

The car was waiting, the baron, Harry, and Mitzie inside. Harry was also dressed in a morning coat, Mitzie in a lovely embroidered white jacket over a sheath dress. She held a huge silk-and-felt hat in her lap.

Mike stared at her. "Oh, my, you look gorgeous. And imagine, your shoes match."

Mitzie laughed and said exactly what Nigel had said. "You look fetching, Michaela. Now, let's get you settled, then we must be off or we'll be late."

Once inside Buckingham Palace, Mike tried very hard not to gawk. Now, this place had glamor. Imagine, Queen Victoria had walked through these incredible rooms with all their huge gold paintings, down these wide hallways, up and down the imposing staircases.

Harry steered them to a small staircase, a white sign on an easel in front of it: Recipients. Once again Nicholas carried Mike up the stairs, followed by Harry with her crutches. Mitzie and the baron took a seat in the gallery.

I have to remember everything to tell my grandkids. The Queen, there she is, the Queen of England, and I'm going to be a dame. But what's a dame? Does it mean free Starbucks?

Mike's brain continued to squirrel around even when Nicholas took her hand, squeezed it, and the ceremony started with nearly fifty people to be knighted and "damed." Everyone sang "God Save the Queen," then they were smoothly settled into place in the line to be presented to Her Majesty.

After Harry went forward to kneel before the Queen and accept his cross and her tap on his shoulder, Nicholas followed, tall, straight, so gorgeous she wanted to leap on him, but that wouldn't do, not here, not that she could with the cursed boot. He was knighted, he and the Queen spoke, and Mike heard him laugh.

Mike knew she was going to throw up on her boot. Or she'd slip on the crutches, her hands were sweating so badly. Nicholas waited for her down the hall, looking somber as a judge, but then the grand voice called out, "Dame Michaela Caine, for services to the security of the country." She smiled widely at him and walked forward, didn't even fall off her crutches. And then she was in front of the grand dame herself.

The Queen pinned the medal to Mike's left breast and the commander insignia to her waist.

Elizabeth said, "You acted admirably, madam. You saved many lives. We are most grateful for your service to our country."

"Thank you, Your Majesty." Was that her voice, all quavery and insubstantial? Oh dear, yes, it was.

The Queen took a long look at the boot, then shook her hand, and looked to where Nicholas stood beside his father, watching. "Take care of our young Brit. His grandfather will have my head if something untoward happens to him."

This time Mike's voice was full-bodied American, reaching the entire gallery. "I will be his St. George, Your Majesty."

She would keep him safe, her Sir Nicholas.

———

Melinda, Ben, Adam, and Dr. Marin joined their small party back at Drummond House in Westminster. Nicholas saw Adam had moved away from the group, trying, he knew, to protect the fresh, hot chips Cook had made especially for him.

Nicholas nudged him with his shoulder, nodded toward Ben and Melinda. "Hey, you're getting to be an old man, already twenty. Ready for a girl of your own, Adam?"

"I sort of like that one with Ben."

"She might be a whisker too old for you. No, better to let my mother find someone your age. What do you think?"

Adam appeared to give that some thought, but he said, "Oh yeah, Nicholas, I forgot to tell you, they got Ardelean's right hand, a man named Cyrus Wendell, and he evidently won't say a single word. So Ardelean did have someone loyal to him. The coppers also arrested Ardelean's manager at his main installation in North Berwick, Scotland, Raphael Marquez. Unlike Wendell, he couldn't wait to tell everything he knew, which is plenty. Now, about your mom on the hunt for me? Okay, maybe."

Dr. Marin stood nearby, listening and nursing a vodka tonic. Mike said to her, "Do you think Adam will let Mrs. Drummond set him up?"

Isabella smiled. "He did say maybe, and if he's smart, he'll at least consider it." And then her smile fell away, and Mike knew she was thinking about her fiancé and the subsequent nightmare she'd survived.

"When do you plan to go back to work?"

"Next week, I think. There's so much to do, and glory of glories, Persy didn't fire me." She smiled again, and this one wasn't forced. "Imagine, you found the loose pages beneath the mattress of Radu's bed. And now we've restored the Voynich to the Beinecke. Since I'm the one who made the 'discovery,' they've asked me to come to Yale and personally inset the pages. They're talking a big ceremony. They want me to read from the Voynich," she said, more to herself than to Mike. "The pages will like that. After so many hundreds of years, they'll finally be together again, back where they belong."

Mike didn't want to go there, so she said, "That will sure put the Beinecke on the map. Are you ready to be a world-recognized celebrity? The only scholar ever to decipher the Voynich?"

Isabella shrugged. "Here's the question. Do I tell them the truth? The whole story going back to Vlad Dracul?"

Mike said, "That's up to you, but perhaps it's time. And perhaps there'll be other special twins of your line to read the Voynich."

"I do wonder about that. But if I did tell the whole story, they might lock me up in an institution." And she laughed, a small laugh, but it was a start. "Oh yes, I've got something to show you." Isabella reached into her black handbag and pulled out a piece of newspaper, handed it to Mike.

Mike read, then raised amazed eyes to Isabella's face. "They've found Dracula's tomb, in Italy, near Naples, of all places? Why in heaven's name would Dracula visit Naples, much less die there? Not Transylvania? And how did he even die?"

"We'll see. It's still more supposition than fact." She paused a moment. "I wonder what Roman and Radu would think of it?"

Nicholas came up to Mike, took her elbow to take some of her weight off her foot. "How's the boot?"

"Getting heavier and heavier."

"Hang in there, as you Yanks say. Not much longer." He spoke to Isabella, then guided Mike away.

She fingered the medal over her breast. "I sent photos of the medal to my parents. My dad texted to congratulate me and I know he was bursting at the seams. My mom now, I bet she was already out the door showing it to the neighborhood. Hmm, so now I'm to call you Sir Nicholas? Not, say, Sir Lamebrain?"

He smiled down at her. "Both have a ring to them. I was thinking we need to run away from home for a while."

What was this all about? "As in no bombings, no guns, no birds, no drones for a week or two?"

"Not a one."

"Yes, Nicholas, that would be grand."

He reached into his jacket pocket and pulled out an envelope, waved it in her face. "I spoke to Savich and Zachery, and they've given papal dispensation for all of us to take some time off. I've already booked us a flight. Since you have to stay off that foot for a while longer, I thought maybe floating around some islands on a yacht for a few days, something calm and sedate. Near Santorini."

"Santorini. Oh yes, Nicholas—ah, Sir Nicholas."

There was a flash from the window, and Mike started, her heart going into overdrive. "What was that?"

He lightly ran his fingers over her cheek. "Only a swallow from the tree outside. Only a swallow."

AUTHORS' NOTE

No one knows what strange byways the missing Voynich quires have traveled over the centuries, how many eyes have puzzled over the pages, how many hands have touched them, felt the magic in them. Did the pages meet Napoléon? Bram Stoker? Rasputin?

We know the manuscript itself went to England and was studied in the sixteenth century by John Dee of Queen Elizabeth's court. Many have suggested possible authors of the strange book, but none have ever been proven. So even today, no one knows who wrote it, where it was written, or what its coded language means. The Voynich continues to confound scholars as one of the few remaining unbroken ciphers in the world.

So maybe, just maybe, this incredible journey is exactly what did happen.

Catherine Coulter
J.T. Ellison

KEEP READING FOR AN EXCLUSIVE
SNEAK PEEK AT CATHERINE
COULTER'S NEXT THRILLER IN THE
FBI SERIES

THE
LAST
SECOND

AVAILABLE MARCH 2019
FROM GALLERY BOOKS

BY CATHERINE COULTER
J.T. ELLISON

PROLOGUE

There was a large mirror on the wall of the white room. Dr. Nevaeh Patel sat in a hard plastic chair, leads from a lie detector machine hooked to her left hand, a thick cord wound around her chest.

She was the one who'd insisted on the lie detector. After the embarrassment of having her mission cut short, being replaced by another astronaut and brought back to Earth, two weeks on the ground of tests, physicals, conversations, polite glances, and outright stares, she'd gotten tired of their disbelief and insisted on being tested.

Still, this final indignity was almost too much for her to bear. All she'd done was tell the flight director and flight doctor the truth about what she'd seen during her EVA—extravehicular activity—outside the International Space Station, what she'd heard. It had been real, they had been real, and the powers that be didn't believe her. On board the space station, they'd subjected her to batteries of tests, extensive psychological profiling, and concluded she had been suffering from zero-gravity-induced hallucinations. They rotated her off the ship and grounded her in Houston so they could do it all again.

Which was an affront to everything they claimed to want from their mission—NASA's ultimate goal was to find planetary life, for heaven's sake. Which she'd done.

The flight director himself, Dr. Franklin Norgate, now sat across from her, a clipboard in his hand. He wore a gray plaid short-sleeved button-down and a skinny black tie, his normally kind eyes guarded. He was as smart as she was, maybe more so. She'd always respected him, seen him as quietly intimidating.

To his right was the examiner, a blank-faced man introduced only as Jim, in his fifties, bald as an egg, a mustard stain on his black tie, like a Rorschach blot. There had been Rorschach tests, too, earlier today and during the innumerable conversations with NASA's psychiatric team over the past two weeks.

What was wrong with them? They were being idiots. Nevaeh had successfully made contact with an alien species. The Numen, they were called, gentle, kind, fascinating beings. And NASA was treating her like she was insane.

She shivered.

Franklin asked, "Are you cold?"

"It's chilly in here, yes."

"I'll see if they can make it more comfortable for you." He stared at the mirror, and a moment later, she felt the air-conditioning kick off. She nodded her thanks.

The examiner gave her the same strangely blank, polite smile all the other experts had been giving her.

"Ready to begin?"

"Yes."

"Good. As I mentioned earlier, only yes or no answers. Are you comfortable?"

"Yes."

"All right then. I'm going to ask you some control questions in order to develop a baseline. Is your name Dr. Nevaeh Patel?"

"Yes."

"Is your first name—Nevaeh—'heaven' spelled backward?"

"Yes."

Silence, scribbling, then, "Did you attend Stanford University?"

"Yes."

"Did you study physics and astronomy?"

"Yes."

"You received your Ph.D. in astrophysics from MIT?"

"Yes."

"Are you an astronaut?"

"Yes."

"Do you live in Michigan?"

"No."

"Do you live in Texas?"

"Yes."

"Are you being truthful with me?"

"Yes."

"Did you speak with an extraterrestrial being on the International Space Station on your last mission?"

"Yes."

A pause. The men shared a glance.

"And did this extraterrestrial being tell you to harm anyone on Earth?"

"No. No, of course not."

"Dr. Patel, I must remind you, yes or no answers only."

"No."

"Were you paid by a foreign government in the past two years for any services?"

"What? No!"

"Yes or no only, ma'am. Were you paid—"

She was starting to sweat now, why, she didn't know. She regretted asking them to turn off the air. "No."

"Did the alien being you spoke with have a foreign accent?"

She had to think for a moment. Were their words accented? Or did they sound very much like her own voice, an echo of something kind and gentle, but in chorus, as if there were hundreds and one, all at the same time? "No."

"Were you stationed on the International Space Station for almost six months, beginning in October 2010?"

"Yes."

"Were you the chief science officer on the mission?"

"Yes."

"Did you lose your tether on an EVA outside the ISS?"

"Yes." Her heartbeat spiked, she couldn't help it. She was hurled back to the moment when she knew her life was ended. She clearly saw the tethers breaking, her gloved hand missing the handhold, felt her body flood with adrenaline. She was in space, floating away from the space station. Her jet pack didn't respond. She was so royally screwed, she was dead.

Then the strong, gentle hand caught her, and a hundred melodic voices spoke as one in her mind. *You are not going to die today. But you must tell them we're here.*

She shook her head, refocused on the room. It happened so often, her drifting back to the moment the Numen had saved her.

The examiner was watching her closely. "Did you encounter an extraterrestrial being on this EVA?"

"Yes."

"Did you speak with this alien?"

"Yes."

"Did the alien tell you to come back to Earth and tell us of its existence?"

"Yes."

"And the alien then lead you back to your port so you could rejoin the crew."

"Yes."

"Are you forty-nine years of age?"

"Yes."

"Do you have blond hair?"

"No."

"Do you believe extraterrestrials are trying to communicate with us?"

"Yes."

Silence. More scratching, then the man nodded and the machine's lights went off.

"Thank you. We'll unhook you now."

Norgate said, not unkindly, "You can wait in the hall."

She started to speak, then shook her head and left the room. They thought she was crazy, she'd gone off the deep end and couldn't be trusted. Space madness. Hallucinations in a stressful moment. They weren't going to believe her, no matter what she said, no matter what the machine indicated. She could see it in their eyes.

She went to the hallway as instructed. She was good at following orders, it was one of the reasons

NASA recruited her in the first place. Brilliant, compliant Nevaeh. So respected for her leadership, so adored by her peers.

She knew everything was about to change.

Norgate said, "So? Did she pass?"

Jim Carstairs, the examiner, said, "Yes. Yes, she did."

"Let me see it."

Norgate took the sheets of paper, saw the spikes and flat lines, so much like the EKG he'd had at his last physical.

"I don't understand. She really passed?"

Jim said, "With flying colors. Either she's telling the truth, or she's convinced herself what she saw, what she heard, was truly an alien species. I'll write it all up for you, but she wasn't lying to us. Whether she's relating what really happened is a whole different matter."

Franklin Norgate raked his fingers through his hair. "The press is going to have a field day with this."

The door to the exam room opened and Dr. Rebecca Holloway entered. Tall and thin from an extreme running regimen, Holloway was the lead psychiatrist for this NASA facility. In the end, she was responsible for deciding whether Dr. Patel could go back to space or was finished as an astronaut. Norgate was relieved he didn't have to make the call. He knew he was a coward, but he was grateful it wouldn't be on his head.

"You saw?"

"I did. Dr. Patel absolutely believes she communicated with aliens."

Norgate said, "I would hate to lose her, Rebecca. She's brilliant. Capable. One of the best astronauts we have in the program."

"She also seems to be suffering from serious delusions, Franklin. You know we've seen this happen before. Not to this extent, of course, but we've had astronauts toppled over into madness. It's why we screen them so carefully to start with. I can't believe she made it this long without showing her mental issues. She is brilliant, which is probably why she's been able to control the visions. Until now, at least. The stress of the incident has made it impossible to hide her problems any longer. I'd say it broke her, irrevocably. Maybe it was inevitable, given who and what she was."

Norgate rubbed his chin. Given who and what she was? What did Rebecca mean? "You're being awfully harsh, Rebecca. I don't know if we should give up on her so soon. Maybe some therapy, some time off—"

Holloway shook her head. "Sorry, Franklin, but there's no way I'm clearing her for flight. I suppose she did show some skill during the incident. It appears she kept her head about her, managed to get reattached to the ISS against all odds. But she shouldn't have been in that position in the first place. In my professional opinion, I believe the stress of the incident has manifested into something bigger and deeper. The delusions she's having about these aliens— it's entirely possible she's had a psychotic break and is going to present with a severe mental illness after more testing. She's sick, Franklin, and I'm grounding her."

He sighed. "All right, I'll tell her. Can we at least keep her attached to the next mission, for publicity's sake?"

"I don't think you'd be doing her any favors. Think this through, Franklin. What it looks like is she tried to commit suicide. She unhooked her tether—"

"A mischaracterization, you saw the tapes. Her tether got tangled with her fellow astronaut James Verlander's and they were trying to get themselves straight."

"That's what you think you saw, what she claims, too, but what I saw, what others saw as well, was an astronaut unhook herself and kick off into space, Franklin. It was a miracle she was able to turn around and reattach. Now she's back on Earth talking about meeting aliens. I know you believe in her, always have, but I don't. Not now. She's not stable. I can try some new therapies and reassess in six months, but I can't guarantee you she won't be worse. Psychopathy like this, she could very well be more embedded in her delusions."

Dr. Holloway exited the room, the door closing behind her. The click rang of finality. Norgate stared at the closed door. Holloway hadn't ever liked Dr. Nevaeh Patel, he'd known it immediately. Jealousy? Had Nevaeh known the extent of Dr. Holloway's dislike? He doubted it. Before this fiasco, Nevaeh had been totally focused on being an astronaut, readying herself to go to the space station. She probably hadn't even noticed Holloway. But now, of course, her entire future had been decided by one person. Not that it mattered now. Rebecca Holloway's word was final and he'd lost his best astronaut.

Now he had to break it to Nevaeh that she was grounded.

In the hall, Nevaeh stood erect, hands behind her back, legs shoulder-width apart. She looked—resigned. When she met his eyes, he shook his head slightly, and she bit her lip.

Norgate said, "It's only six months."

Nevaeh gave an ugly laugh. "We both know I'm finished here. What I don't understand, Franklin, is this: I've given you the information NASA's been searching for since its inception, and instead of doing everything you can to confirm what I'm saying, you're kicking me out."

"It's just six months, Nevaeh—"

It was Rebecca Holloway, she knew it. "I quit."

And with that, she walked away, shoulders back, heart breaking in two. And the Numen, silent until now, said in a soft, sibilant, and single voice, *It will be all right, Nevaeh. We chose you. You will find us again. We will help you.*